The Arkis Tales
Volume I

# Things As They Were

### Renée Tamsin

To all the greats,
May your stories live on

# CONTENTS

## Part One

1    NOT ALL STORIES HAVE TO END     4

2    A MERCIFUL END     10

3    FUNERALS ARE FOR THE LIVING     22

4    THE LADY OF CAVERLY MANOR     30

5    A SECRET AFFAIR     39

6    SILLY COUSIN STELLA     46

7    THROUGH THE PAGES     56

8    THE CLEVER BEAUTY     73

9    THERAPEUTIC TRAGEDY     82

10    ANNE'S BEEF WELLINGTON     92

## Part Two

11    A KEEPER OF HAPPILY EVER AFTERS     114

12    FIX THE STORY     128

13    FLEETING WORDS     141

14    THE LEGEND OF THE AEREST     152

15    A WORTHY OPPONENT     163

16    THE MAY DAY RIDE     172

17    THE OTHER SIDE     185

18    THE FOOL'S NOBLE ERRAND     198

19    THE DESIRED EFFECT     217

| 20 | THE TALE OF THE AUTHORS | 224 |
| 21 | A HERO'S JOURNEY | 237 |

# Part Three

| 22 | THEIR SOLEMN RETURN | 246 |
| 23 | THE BELATED BEN CAVERLY | 250 |
| 24 | A QUEST FOR THE SCABBARD | 268 |
| 25 | THE LADY OF THE LAKE | 275 |
| 26 | A HERO'S WELCOME | 290 |
| 27 | FROM THE SHADOWS | 299 |
| 28 | THE MORE REFINED STRATEGY | 307 |
| 29 | THE SORCERESS OF AVALON | 312 |
| 30 | A NEW ERA OF REGENTS | 317 |
| 31 | DECISIONS MAKETH DESTINY | 325 |
| 32 | A CAUSE WORTH DYING FOR | 336 |
| 33 | THE AID OF AVALON | 343 |
| 34 | THEY ALL FALL IN | 351 |
| 35 | BROTHER TO BROTHER | 357 |
| 36 | ROUND TABLE UNBROKEN | 367 |
| 37 | THE BEGINNING OF THE END | 370 |
| 38 | THE DEVIL'S DEN | 376 |
|  | EPILOGUE | 381 |
|  | APPENDIX | 391 |
|  | ABOUT THE AUTHOR | 411 |

# Acknowledgements

As expected, I feel the need to acknowledge my family members and dear friends, but particularly for inspiring the characters and concepts that piece together the essential colors of this story which needed to be told. You know who you are. And given time, and seemingly endless sequels (and prequels), you'll all no doubt be mentioned by name. Bless your lovely souls.

"IT IS ONE THING TO WRITE AS A POET AND ANOTHER TO WRITE AS A HISTORIAN: THE POET CAN RECOUNT OR SING ABOUT THINGS NOT AS THEY WERE, BUT AS THEY SHOULD HAVE BEEN, AND THE HISTORIAN MUST WRITE ABOUT THEM NOT AS THEY SHOULD HAVE BEEN, BUT AS THEY WERE, WITHOUT ADDING OR SUBTRACTING ANYTHING FROM THE TRUTH."

~MIGUEL CERVANTES~

# Prologue

Every story must be told. Looking around, I have come to deeply appreciate those already chronicled and sorted amongst past legends; shelved volumes, grouped according to era, with their ancient leather bindings cast an intimidating shadow over what I am about to begin.

While I am not uneducated, the Herculean task of giving this legend the proper documentation is entirely formidable. However, I am honored. After all, words have a depth and power that must be harnessed and shared. Every experience deserves to be immortalized by the magic of words.

As I sit here at my desk, a Looking Glass propped directly to my right, quill in hand, I have the sudden realization that this could be the most important epoch that will ever grace the shelves of this library. All that's gone before has been merely preparation for all that is to now come. And so I take a breath, smooth the parchment, exhale, watch, and record the first words of the final age of the War of the Galdere.

# Part One

## Guiding Fortunes

# 1

## NOT ALL STORIES HAVE TO END

The proper place to start is always the beginning. But that's not completely necessary. I think that the best place for me to begin is my favorite part...

During this time, the human race was at odds with itself. By now, the second Great World War had barely ended earlier in the year. Britain was beginning its recovery, as was the rest of the world. Soldiers had returned home to what was left of their civilian lives, seeking mental and emotional refuge with their families. Sadly, not all found such refuge, as is the case after any war. War does that to people: it weakens and, somehow, strengthens them.

One fortunate father found strength upon his return swimming in the big, blue, sky eyes of his beloved daughter. He referred to her eyes as such, not only for their stormy blue hue but also for their vast, unending depth. At the age of five, his little blond, blue-eyed beauty had the innocent curiosity and imagination to melt your heart and cause you to question your own quick judgment. This father also saw what you will soon see:

how these eyes had the unquestionable potential to look beyond what anyone else could ever dream. Beyond even what the sky itself pretended to limit.

The night this father returned to his scholarly home in Oxford, he wrapped his daughter in his arms, sat in the oversized armchair in his library, and read his little darling a story. It was a classic, as was his way. He only exposed her to the best. Being a classicist, and a very well-read one at that, he was prone to being particular.

This particular story, however, always struck him more personally than the others, even to the point of reverent silence. Each previous time the young girl picked the book from its shelf, he stalled or distracted her until she chose a less painful alternative. But, today, her curiosity was not to be deterred.

"Daddy..." The child prodded her father's chest. "What happens next?" She was growing impatient, anxiously nestled in her father's lap and urged him to continue.

The father sighed. He knew he could never get past this part. Of all the hundreds of stories surrounding him, tucked away on his library shelves, this one he just couldn't finish. He knew how it should have ended, but he couldn't bring himself to say the words. The untrue closure was something he couldn't inflict on his daughter. He sighed again and shook his head.

"What do you think happens?" he asked her. He watched the creative juices brighten her eyes enthusiastically. Her cheek dimpled as she made her thinking face, crinkling her mouth to one side.

"Why couldn't the king find another gold dish so that other fairy could be invited? Isn't the king quite rich?" she asked after a moment of pondering.

"Hm...yes, I suppose you're right. He could have just purchased another golden dish for the thirteenth fairy. But he didn't. The story is already set, my love."

"I want to change it." She sat with her arms crossed.

"What's happened has happened, my dear. You can only change what happens next. Princess Briar Rose is about to touch the spinning wheel and fall asleep for one hundred years. What can be done?"

"Okay," she calculated, straightening her back. "The princess doesn't sleep for a hundred years."

"Oh, she doesn't, does she?"

"No, she doesn't. Because the curse gets broken early."

"Is that right?"

"The good fairies help because they're magic. They all go to the evil fairy's house and fight with her. And then the good fairies win—because good always wins. And when the evil fairy is all gone, so is her evil magic. And then the princess wakes up, and everyone has a party—with wonderful sweet treats and every good thing. The king and queen invite other kings and queens, and one prince meets the princess, and they fall in love..."

"And it's a happy ending for all, eh?"

"No. It isn't."

Taken by surprise, the father glanced down at his daughter, looking for an explanation. "What sort of an ending is it then?"

"Not all stories have to end, Daddy." He chuckled. Her tone was so honest and matter-of-fact as if it were as true and resolute as her name.

"Of course," he cheerfully agreed.

"They don't end. They just have to stay happy."

He kissed the top of her head affectionately and nodded. "Hm, happily ever afters are very important."

"Everybody knows that, Daddy."

"Yes," he chuckled. "But, not everyone thinks that way, unfortunately."

"Why not?"

"Well...there are bad people out there, my love, who want to destroy happily ever afters."

"What?" The child spun around to face her father, balancing her knees on his and holding on to his steady shoulders. "That's not fair!" she exclaimed. "Somebody needs to stop them!"

"Oh, don't worry, dear. Some people do. Special people."

"Really?"

"Well, yes. Let me tell you a different story, all right?"

"Okay." She settled back down in her father's lap and buried the back of her curly blond head against his shoulder.

"Once upon a time..." he began, "there was an older man, a mysterious trader, who came upon a young man who was taking his cow to the market because it had stopped giving milk. The trader offered him a handful of so-called 'magic beans,' in exchange for his cow—"

"Daddy, this is Jack and the Beanstalk. I already know this story."

"No, you don't. Now be quiet." She was silenced, and he then continued, "After the trader left the young man and was on his way home, he came upon a wrinkled, ancient sorcerer with a crooked cane and a bad limp. Now, the trader was quite rude, and he mocked the crippled, old sorcerer. So the sorcerer tapped his crooked cane against the stone road and magically struck the trader down, which caused him to fall to the ground.

"The sorcerer then enchanted the dried up cow—turning it into a pile of leather, forming a very long, very special cloak. Enraged, but unable to speak, the trader laid there and listened to the sorcerer. The sorcerer told him that, despite his apparent rudeness and stupidity, he saw great potential in him. He then told him that from then on, he would redeem himself by spending his life fighting the forces of an evil sorcerer who means to do far worse things than turning cows into leather—"

"Like destroying happily ever afters?"

"Quiet, love," he warned. She was silenced once more, biting her lip in anticipation. "The old sorcerer instructed the trader to save other realms from evil until his calling was fulfilled..."

"And?" the little girl squealed softly, barely containing her excitement.

"And, the trader had a change of heart that day. He thenceforth dedicated himself to saving happily ever afters."

"How does he do it all by himself?"

"Oh, he has helpers, of course. Some people with the special magic like the sorcerer gave to him, and some regular people too. There are always good people around," he smiled.

"Does he do it forever and ever?"

"Well, no. Not exactly. He sort of...passes it on and on. To someone, new...whenever change is needed."

"Is it still happening right now?"

He chuckled. "Well, my love, it's just like you said. Not all stories have to end."

# 2

## A Merciful End

I have always thought the weather was a curious thing. Either the melancholy weather causes one to be depressed, or one's pure state of depression causes the weather to be melancholy. Whichever the case, on a date approximately eighteen years after our story began, either the gloomy showers of Boston caused Ben Caverly's depression, or Ben Caverly's depression caused the gloomy showers of Boston. As dreary as it seemed, this didn't disconcert him. His own English homeland regularly promoted this sort of damp melancholia, so the weather, however much it mirrored his disposition in the sky, had no actual effect on him.

His cab pulled in front of the local hospital, splashing a muddy puddle along the pathway to the door. Ben's gut began to wrench again, as it had in increasing intervals since he received the phone call a few days prior. His hair was already darkened by the rain and his reflective eyes betrayed what the cab driver had suspected the moment the man slid into his cab.

He didn't particularly want to be here.

There are many reasons for one's reluctance. Some are reluctant because of complete disinterest. Others, like some of those we have yet to meet, are reluctant because of their struggle to accept reality. And others, like our friend Ben Caverly, are reluctant because of expectant dread. Every step he took to those hospital doors, the more he wanted to turn away.

But he couldn't. He couldn't do that to Albert. The pain of losing his own father was painfully re-lived as he walked through the hospital halls, imagining his old mentor lying on his deathbed.

At the end of the hall, right outside of Albert's room, he saw a familiar, robust, man with lightly salt-and-peppered hair and a thick goatee. Frank Marcus waited for him, solemnly leaning against the wall. As Albert's longtime friend and colleague, as well as his legal consultant, Marcus had been with him for as long as Ben had known him. The two middle-aged men had met when their respective nations served together in the Second World War and had been intimately connected ever since. War, with its onslaught of trauma and adrenaline, tends to create an unbreakable bond between its victims. Marcus was the first to contact Ben the moment Albert had become mysteriously ill.

"Mr. Caverly," he acknowledged in his thick Boston accent. The two men shook hands and exchanged solemn looks of understanding. Ben didn't have to ask how Albert was doing; the expression on Marcus' face said more than any combination of words could have. "He's still awake. He's been asking for you for the last two days."

"Hm," was all Ben could say.

Marcus chuckled softly. "Well, you haven't changed at all, son. Still gotta lot to say, huh? You're looking good, though. Healthy, I mean. How was your flight from Oxford?"

"Erm, long," he answered. "When did all this happen?"

Marcus sighed, shaking his head. "His last business trip. I think he went to give a lecture at some university I've never heard of in Croatia or something. Anyway, he came back a week ago and two days later, he was bedridden. Doc says it's got to be some sort of virus. His body is deteriorating faster than anything they've ever seen here, and they have no idea what's causing it."

"Well...it must be something..."

"They can't explain it. What's worse is he's talkin' nonsense, telling outlandish war stories."

"How is that nonsense?"

Marcus lowered his voice. "It's not the World War I saw, that's for sure. He's saying he met a sorcerer while he was out looking for his brother overseas. A sorcerer. His doctor says he's unfit. Carol has power of attorney–which I coulda swore would devastate him, but he doesn't seem to care. Just cares about talking to you and Stella."

Ben's brows were furrowed curiously, but they smoothed and lifted at the mention of Stella's name. He hadn't heard her name in over a year, and hadn't seen her even longer. He swallowed hard. "How is she?"

"Your guess is as good as mine," Marcus shrugged. "She seemed to handle the news like when Mrs. Kennedy heard about that blonde bombshell bombin' her husband. Stone cold decorum. Did ya hear about...? Nah, ya probably didn't, across the pond. Anyway, who really knows? Stella could break any minute now without warning. She's down in the cafeteria with Carol right now. He wanted to see you first."

"Hm." Ben inhaled deeply, nervously adjusting his tie.

The two of them, teacher and student, hadn't seen one another face-to-face in over a year. For the first time since he met Albert in that dusty Oxford lecture hall, Ben didn't know what to say to the man. His words were frequently few, but always purposeful and precise. Marcus gave him an encouraging pat on the shoulder before he braced himself and entered Albert's room.

Death often leaves its foreboding mark before actually claiming its victim. Albert Towson, for example, the once vivacious and energetic man, now lay in the hospital bed, looking small, helpless, and fighting consciousness. His pale face had quickly aged. One of death's varying signatures. The poor man was no more than fifty years of age, yet he seemed nearly eighty. The spreading illness had eaten away so much of his body weight that his cheekbones protruded alarmingly against his sagging skin, and his once light eyes were now sallow and sunken. However, despite the appearance of death's impending triumph, there was a smile on the man's face that displayed a strange sort of victory.

While I must empathize with the notion that death takes its toll on the previously strong, I have also noticed that the truly strong show the most strength within the short time before death claims them. When Albert saw Ben Caverly enter the room, he tried to sit up in excitement but lacked the energy. Instead, he laid back down and weakly waved his right hand, gesturing for Ben to come closer.

"You came," he said softly.

Ben simply nodded. "I did."

Albert's weakened hand touched the end of Ben's coat sleeve as he stood beside the bed awkwardly. "Thank you for not asking how I'm feeling," Albert feebly joked. It's a generally agreed opinion that inquiring after a dying man's state of being can be quite tedious; ask any dying man.

Ben smiled a little. His friend's once thick English accent was beginning to fade. He had been in America for too long. "I considered, but decided against it."

"It's not so bad, you know. In case you were wondering."

"Is it not?"

"No. I only feel weak. No pain, really. Much more merciful than I expected."

Ben frowned. "You expected an illness to be capable of mercy?"

Albert chuckled. "Oh, bless your mind, Benjamin. Sit down, son," his voice hesitated, "I have something I need you to do for me."

Ben grabbed the nearest chair and pulled it closer to the bed. "Of course. Anything."

With his hands in reach, Albert grabbed one of them, placing it on the bed beside him. "Had I ever had my own son, he couldn't...have compared...to you."

Albert's speech was slowing, but it was difficult to discern whether it was due to exhaustion and weakness or careful deliberation as to his following words. Dying is quite exhausting, you know. "Your mind...and your heart...Ben, you are the greatest man...I have ever known."

"Albert..."

"Let me...finish, my boy."

Ben's humble protests fell silent.

Albert cleared his throat and inhaled deeply before continuing. "I'm ready to go, Ben. It's...my time. I don't regret...anything...and I know life will...push on as it did before. I know that everyone says that, but I'm not worried about a thing...honest." He paused. "Except for the one thing I value the most in this world. Ben...you are the one and only man I trust to care for...her."

"Her."

"Stella will receive a very substantial inheritance once I am gone...but there is a bit of a catch. When I...wrote my will, I intended for Carol to have control over my finances until Stella became...eligible. Carol is not the sibling I would have preferred to inherit....but Gabriel....Carol has reverted back to her wasteful ways over the last couple of years. I don't trust her as I once did. I'm afraid she'd only squander the inheritance before Stella..." He paused to breathe slowly.

"Reaches a certain age?" Ben suggested.

Many wealthy families have written requirements into wills, ensuring their heirs reached a certain age of maturity before receiving their inheritance. Stella, however, was twenty-three years old—a bit older than the usual age of acquisition.

The corner of Albert's mouth tugged upward, almost in a smile, but a complex one. "Though both would disagree...Stella can be as reckless as my sister. My anxieties of her wellbeing may have heavily influenced the original clauses of my will. Dear Stella...must be married to inherit."

"Albert..." Ben started again.

"I'm sure Marcus informed you that my hands have been somewhat tied...I don't particularly understand why...Ben, I don't want to die knowing my daughter will fall into destitution. I never anticipated....it's only since I've come home that I've considered Carol would abuse the inheritance before Stella could receive...it naturally. She's always required a special touch. I know that she has her...difficulties..." Albert closed his eyes for a moment, his voice weakening. "And I know I have no right to ask this of you, Ben..."

"You do," Ben said quietly, closing his eyes as he said the words.

"Hm?"

He sighed, opening his eyes to meet Albert's, and spoke slowly. "I will do whatever you ask of me."

Albert stared at him for a moment. He had expected a very different answer–a series of further questions or suggested alternatives, perhaps.

"I would never require this of you, Ben. Marriage is not something to enter into lightly..." He cleared his throat again and glanced at Ben only from the corner of his eye as he spoke. "However, Marcus assures me that only six months would be necessary...and, provided it is not consummated, you may file for the annulment...the moment she receives her inheritance. It need not be long-term."

"I understand."

"I don't want this to be an unhappy arrangement, Ben. You've...you've been through enough. I don't want you to...agree to something purely out of obligation. You owe me nothing. You can't imagine just how important she is, Ben...and how important it is for her to be looked after."

Ben placed his other hand over Albert's and leaned in, looking into the old man's eyes. "She will be taken care of, Albert. I swear to you."

Albert stared at him once more, his eyes studying the young face. He had seen Ben grow up before his eyes since he was a young student. He had taught and nurtured the young man and his impressive intellect for many years—even distant teaching position at Harvard could not separate the teacher from the student. Albert sent a constant stream of letters and phone calls back to Oxford, never losing touch with him. Ben was a son to him, a man he would trust with his life and, evidently, his daughter.

But, knowing what such a request entailed—binding himself to a woman, for however long, not of his own choice— Albert anticipated rejection. With Stella's nature being so intense and rebellious, Albert knew what a challenge it would be for any man to take on. But looking into Ben's eyes, he could sense the earnest sincerity of his promise.

*She will be taken care of, Albert. I swear to you.* They were the only words Albert cared to hear before death claimed him.

As Ben shut the door behind him, he began to ponder over the implications of his promise. He would do anything for Albert, beyond doubt, but when he saw Stella and her horrid aunt approaching, he very briefly questioned his dedication to his dying mentor.

Stella had always been an incredibly attractive young lady, about ten years his junior. Ben assumed her mother had been a great beauty with thick, blond hair, stunning blue eyes, and petite, round features—for that was the only explanation as to how Stella came to inherit her adorable countenance. And he would be right to assume so. For indeed, the late Mrs. Towson was graceful and striking. Even without being privileged to know Stella's mother, anyone could see her father was not one to pass along physical appeal. While Albert was not an ugly man, in any way, his sister was a stark contrast to her niece.

Carol Towson was a woman who had never married. She lost a chance in her youth and never cared to seek another, and it was no wonder why. She had not aged gracefully, by any means. Her face was permanently scrunched, her wrinkles having formed around her signature scowl, and her once-rich, auburn hair was heavily dusted with grey. She never smiled, on principle, and she walked with a haughty strut. Her stride was shorter and more deliberate than that of her niece, which caused her to lag behind as they neared the two gentlemen.

Stella noticed Marcus fighting to keep his eyes open, and she smirked.

"Frank, you should have yourself a little cat nap while you wait," she suggested. Her native English accent had transformed over the years into a more transatlantic variety, to which she had grown more accustomed. "You haven't slept for days."

"I would have, but your father needed me," Marcus drowsily replied. "And couldn't I say the same about you, young lady?"

"He would have been fine, whether you had been there or not. And, no, you couldn't."

Marcus cleared his throat diplomatically. "I think 'fine' is a relative word. Besides, I wanted to see ya pretty face, Stella."

"You could have done without that, I am sure," Carol's shrill, haughty English voice chimed in as she caught up.

"Oh, ignore her. She's a little bent," Stella gestured behind her as her aunt's heels clicked too loudly when she neared. "Nothing new, though. I think she's got something stuck up her—"

"That was inappropriate, Stella. Acknowledging the man's dark circles and bloodshot eyes. Positively ill-mannered." Marcus and Ben exhaled in relief that Carol had not heard Stella's crude remark. "Americans may speak that way, dear," Carol continued, "but that doesn't mean you have to. Now, try again, this time by politely saying 'How are you, Mr. Marcus'? And then allow him to respond."

Without repeating the question, she looked at Marcus expectantly, waiting for an answer.

"Oh, well...as good as I can be, ma'am, considering everything. He's talked to Ben already, so I believe that makes it your turn, little miss." Marcus nudged Stella's elbow gently, leading her toward the door.

However, she was ignoring both Marcus and her abhorrent aunt, looking instead at Ben. It was as if she hadn't noticed his presence until Marcus addressed it. She probably hadn't recognized him, not that he expected her to. It had been several years since they last saw one another, and he was genuinely surprised at himself for recognizing her.

They had been no more than acquaintances, introduced through Albert. But, now that they were to become much, much more, Ben thought it appropriate to acknowledge her, at the very least.

"Miss Towson," he nodded. "How are you?"

"Still standing, thank you," she replied slowly.

Her expression confused him. It went beyond lack of recognition. It had turned into an expression of confusion, and even suspicion. Her lips were scrunched delicately to the side of her face in contemplation. She didn't understand why he was there, or rather, why her father needed to speak with him in particular.

*Albert hasn't told her*, Ben thought. He should have assumed Stella would have been the last to be spoken to. If history was any indication, Stella's consent would make or break the planned arrangement. Marcus gingerly closed the door behind Stella and stepped back to watch her interaction through the beige blinds of the room's interior window.

"I take it you agreed," Marcus mumbled under his breath, loud enough for only Ben to hear.

Carol found a bench in the hallway to sit on and rest while she waited for her niece, so she was relatively out of earshot.

"I did," Ben replied, matching his low tone.

"I'm glad. She's a good kid. Strange as the parameters of the will seemed, even for traditionalists like the Towson's, I think Albert knew exactly what he was doing. She's smart, but I think she has a lotta growing up to do. Not that six months' worth of growin' up will be enough for her to handle the estate, but hey—like I said, Albert knows what he's doing." Marcus inhaled as he spoke the words and then cleared his throat. "I hope. It'll be good for her, I think...if she agrees to it."

"Do you think she will?"

"I think if she knows what's good for her, she will. She's had such a cushy life. The thought of bein' broke is gonna scare the daylights outta her."

"Hm." Ben watched Stella sit on the side of her father's bed and hold his hand dearly. The defiant disposition she had walked in with dissipated merely by her father's touch. He saw Albert speak to her with a very gentle look in his eye, a look that tamed her. Tears were welling in her eyes at hearing his loving words.

After a few moments, she wasn't able to look at Albert without crying, so her gaze fell down to his hand intertwined with hers. Something, however, made her head snap back up. Ben assumed Albert had proposed his arrangement. After a few more soft words, Albert calmed her once more. Nothing quite calms a girl's wild heart like her father's voice.

"Hey," Marcus nudged him. "I'm just as curious as you are, Ben. Let's take our minds off it? Why don't you and I get something to eat? Give them a little privacy, yes?"

Ben sighed and nodded. "Yes, of course."

# 3

## FUNERALS ARE FOR THE LIVING

In keeping with the dying man's wishes, the uncomfortable couple was married in a small, private ceremony in the hospital's humble chapel, surrounded by the appropriate witnesses. Albert was wheeled in by Frank Marcus and positioned contently in the front row. It may not have been ideal, but at the very least, Albert was able to give his daughter away before he passed.

Curiously, the sick man was the only one in the chapel smiling. Even the reverend bore an expression of disapproval—most likely the result of learning the shallow circumstances surrounding this holy act of matrimony. All were solemn, but good old Albert was ecstatic.

Stella hadn't even bothered dressing up. Her casual, dark blue cotton dress and a pair of short, brown Mary Jane pumps were good enough for her. Her efforts and expressions were vacant but it was clear to see that her mind was spinning.

Ben made a small attempt with his pressed Oxford shirt and suit, but the couple still seemed quite odd from afar. Actually, they seemed quite odd from up close. Neither feigned any sort of emotion in their basic vows. They couldn't even look one another in the eye. They stood across from each other, mumbled their "I dos", half-heartedly exchanged their plain wedding bands, and held their breath as the reverend said, "Man and Wife."

And then there was Albert, hunched awkwardly in his wheelchair. He watched and smiled as if there were more to the wedding than its financial saving grace. The smile was all his failing energy would allow, but it displayed intensely understated enthusiasm. He had lived to see his only daughter wed to a man he trusted would care for her. Take my word for it. That is all a father needs before taking his final breath.

The joy engulfed him thoroughly, in turn taking its toll on his mortal frame. His voice faded even further as the day went on, resulting in a comatose state that lasted one blissful hour before he passed. Blissful for him at least, because it was the most peaceful, transitional feeling. Albert knew exactly where he had been, and he knew exactly where he was going. The serenity and excitement of it all are quite enviable. The sound of his daughter's voice, reading him the stories from her childhood, soothed him toward his final journey.

And then he went.

The funeral was as simplistic as the wedding. Most of those in attendance were those who were with Albert when he died. Frank Marcus had invited some other colleagues from Harvard and Carol invited both of her friends, as well.

Marcus wore his old military uniform and was accompanied by fellow soldiers and veterans who respectfully attended for the twenty-one gun salute and flag ceremony. Albert fought as a British soldier in the war, but given the circumstances, Marcus was able to arrange his own military contacts to give the man the proper military funeral he deserved. As such strong allies in the war, the American soldiers were very happy to comply.

The reverend from the hospital, Reverend Jamison, conducted the service, which was held at the small church and cemetery down the street from the hospital itself.

After the salute shots were fired, two soldiers carefully folded a British flag and placed it gently in Stella's unsteady hands. Her eyes were dry, her expression stoic, as she wrapped her arms around the flag, holding it close to her chest. Marcus presented the eulogy—quite touching, it was—and then he asked Stella to say a few words about her father.

"No." She stood, defiantly tightening her grip around the flag and staring intently at the closed casket which laid beside the deep grave.

Avoiding conflict, Marcus nodded and smoothly turned to Carol, who proudly obliged. She spoke about her brother's dedication to his work, his love for his daughter, and how close she herself was to him. Stella snorted derisively at this.

"Stella," Carol scolded under her breath, before continuing. "Albert and I grew up raising our younger brother,

Gabriel, together. We were completely dependent on one another..."

"Doubtful," Stella murmured.

"...losing Gabriel in the war was difficult enough," Carol continued, ignoring her niece's snide remarks. "But now, with both brothers gone, Albert's passing is a great loss for all of us."

"Or gain for some..." Stella muttered again.

Ben looked over at her incredulously. Her resentment toward her aunt cast a dark and ruthless shadow over Albert's pleasant memory; every well-bred bone in Ben's body was unsettled by the audacity.

Marcus stood beside her and decided to take action. Or, at least, make an attempt. He touched Stella's arm gently and whispered something in her ear. She merely rolled her eyes and sighed in exasperation.

Her aunt prattled on, thankfully maintaining the attention of the majority of the attendees. One of Albert's younger colleagues, from Harvard, had been gazing at Stella since the beginning of the service, and her crass comments had captured his full attention.

After Carol had finished, Reverend Jamison concluded the service and left time for anyone who wished to approach the casket or share consoling words with one another. Everyone mingled, chatting about Albert and those happy memories they all shared.

Ben felt out of place, for he had known the man before any of them, save Marcus and the family, but he hadn't been there for any of Albert's Harvard stories. And so he stood, hands awkwardly hidden in his trouser pockets, lips tightly closed, and anxious eyes wandering.

Albert's colleague's, young and old, paid their respects to Carol—and aimed to do so to Stella as well. She, amusingly enough, decided she was done with her part of the funeral. She perched herself on the edge of her father's casket to check for small rocks she had felt rolling around in her shoe.

The young colleague whose attention she had stolen was flirting whole-heartedly with her, and she shamelessly returned the attention, tucking the folded flag under her arm. When she sat against the casket, however, the young man was taken aback and unsure how to respond. She put him at ease by continuing their conversation as casually as before. She laughed at his witty comments too loudly.

Ben's anxious eyes watched as she stood back up, and used the young man's shoulder for support while she balanced on one foot to return her shoe to its proper place. She smiled widely and left her hand affectionately on his arm. Considering their recent nuptials, Ben was unsure of just how much responsibility he held in confronting and correcting her behavior.

Ben was not the only one watching her inappropriate display. Carol stood only a few feet from him and had engaged in haughty conversation with one of Albert's older colleagues. As soon as she spied her niece's behavior, she approached Ben with a mind for scolding, perfectly clarifying his husbandly responsibilities.

"Mr. Caverly," she said to him ferociously. "You need to control your wife." She put a spiteful emphasis on her last word, verbally shoving him toward the duty which already made him so uncomfortable.

Clearing his throat and contemplating the most diplomatic solution, Ben approached the fire. He touched her arm and gently pulled her away from the hopeful suitor. Suddenly noticing the pair's matching wedding bands, the young man slowly stepped away, nodded at Ben, and made his way to his other colleagues.

"Could I have a word with you?" Ben asked Stella.

Stella rolled her blue eyes. "What do you want? I was having a gas talking to whatever-his-name-is over there."

"You realize where you are, right?" he said, in a discreet tone. He pulled her aside, attempting to take her out of immediate earshot. His reprimand didn't need an audience.

"Excuse me?"

"You are at your father's funeral. The least you could do, Stella, is give the respect he deserves," Ben told her. He kept his tone even and peaceful but firm. She appropriately perceived the undertone and took offense.

She inhaled deeply and looked him directly in the eyes for the first time since they met at the hospital.

"Don't you dare tell me how to show respect to my father," she threatened him, every word punctuated with malice. "He's *my* father. And I have every right to behave however I wish."

Marcus, from across the grave site, heard the exchange and sensed the tension. In a few swift strides, he was at Ben's side. Stella drew another deep breath, ready to continue her rant in a rather coarse fashion. Marcus cut her off.

"Stella," he warned quietly. "Listen to him. If there was ever a time for you to actually behave yourself, this is it."

"Oh please," Stella scoffed. "My father isn't even in there." She pointed at the coffin with a finger that trembled slightly. "It's only a body. One that he left thirty-six hours ago. You think this funeral is for him?"

"Stella..." Ben pressed, trying to lower the volume of her voice.

"Funerals are for the living," she said, bitingly.

And she was right. The dead don't think much of funerals—in fact, they typically don't even attend their own. Seeing such sorrowful faces is bound to bring you down, so they believe it's wise to just skip out and tune back in later.

"He knows me well enough not to take offense to whatever it is you think I'm doing that's so *disrespectful*." Her tone thickened with mockery and contempt. Her eyes were dry and, to the ignorant observer, she seemed unaffected by the loss she had endured the last day and a half.

"Stella, I think ya need to go home and pack," Marcus suggested.

There was an edge to his nerves since Albert left. Stella's disciplinarian had left them. Every word he spoke was a tender step around a bomb he feared would explode at any given moment.

Stella pursed her lips and took off both of her shoes defiantly. "I'll pack when I'm ready to pack, Frank."

Without another word to either of them, she turned and walked away barefoot from the cemetery with her shoes held tightly in her grasp.

"Do you know where she is going?" Ben asked Marcus.

He shrugged. "Her house is a couple blocks away. When she's upset, Albert always used to say she would hide in their rose garden."

"Their rose garden," Ben repeated.

"Yeah. One of Stella's old nannies was quite a gardener. Apparently, with Carol there, the rose garden is just about the only place Stella spends her free time."

Marcus sighed and turned to look at those who remained mingling at the site. Several people had left shortly after the reverend's portion of the service ended, and more people were beginning to leave after speaking with Carol and giving the appropriate condolences.

"Ah, Stella will be okay," he concluded. "Albert was the only person she ever listened to. Now she's a bit of a loose cannon—ya know, the way she is the rest of the time when Pops ain't around."

"Hm."

"Can I ask ya something, Ben?"

"Of course."

"Why'd ya agree to this?"

Ben paused before answering. He slipped his hands into his pockets thoughtfully. Why had he agreed to this? The only answer that came to him was the truth. "For Albert."

Marcus smiled. "Good. I think, for the next six months, ya should keep reminding yourself of that. It'll make it easier."

"I am sure it will."

Marcus chuckled softly. "'Cause she certainly won't."

And she certainly did not.

# 4

## THE LADY OF CAVERLY MANOR

Why'd you agree to this?

The question repeated itself in Ben's mind for the majority of the flight back to England, despite reminding himself of the answer.

*For Albert.*

Albert had trusted him with the single most important thing in his entire life. He would never do anything to disappoint or betray Albert, but strangely enough, repeating his own answer didn't put him at ease either.

Then he looked over at his new wife.

She sat across the aisle from him in first class. Her legs were tucked under her. She was curled up against the seat and had been asleep since the plane took off. While her chest rose and fell in the rhythm of a peaceful sleep, the evidence of her unbearable pain was written all over her face. Her lack of tears fooled the funeral party into believing her indifference—

something which came so naturally to her—but now her unguarded expression betrayed the truth.

Ben suddenly realized why he had agreed.

The pain she refused to show was the pain he felt. She needed him, and perhaps he needed her. True, he had married a woman he knew almost nothing about, but they had a very significant connection: the man who changed their lives. And now he was lost to both of them. If he cared for Albert at all, he would be able to care for his daughter for as long as was needed. The short life expectancy of the marriage eased him a little. He could only imagine what was going through her head and what had made her agree to such an arrangement.

His mind would not settle for the duration of the flight. When they arrived at Heathrow airport in London, he gently woke his bride and guided her off the plane. She was eerily quiet for the entirety of the drive to Oxford, leaving the awkward silence hanging in the air up as they walked through the doors of the Caverly family home.

Sir Walter Caverly–knighted for his contributions during the War, you see–passed away when Ben was studying at university. Ben inherited Walter's much larger estate in London. He hated London. Ben had lived and worked in Oxford for most of his adult life, there occupying and running his own property. Pained by memories, he promptly sold his father's home and took the belongings and a few of the loyal staff members with him to Oxford.

And such was Caverly Manor as Ben affectionately called it. Actually, it wasn't really much of a manor at all. In fact, it was a simple, yet substantial, cottage just outside of Oxford. It sat cozily on four acres of land, and was maintained by a small grounds staff.

Flower beds surrounded the front of the house and led back into the remarkably extensive garden, kept up personally by the housekeeper, Patricia Milton. She was a very prim and austere woman, with a heavy amount of femininity which she never failed to bestow upon Ben's household. He tolerated it very amiably, however, as was his nature. She had worked for the Caverly household since Walter inherited the estate from his father before she had the honor of changing Ben's nappies.

Patricia was waiting at the front door to welcome them. She walked toward them as the car pulled into the stone driveway and greeted Ben with a warm smile.

"It is lovely to see you home again, my dear." She helped him lift the suitcases out of the trunk of the car, but her cheerful warmth turned cold once her gaze fell on Stella, who climbed out of the backseat of the town car.

"Ah, Benjamin, this must be the lovely Miss Towson you told me about on the telephone," she said stiffly.

"Yes, and she is to be given every courtesy afforded to the lady of the house." He handed Patricia one of Stella's lighter bags while he stacked and carried the larger ones.

Stella helped herself through the front door of the cottage, to acquaint herself with her new home. It was warm and welcoming for the residence of a bachelor. Patricia was apparently an avid cleaner. The living room was vacuumed within an inch of its life, and all the books Stella could see, which were great in number, were immaculately dusted and organized along shelves, tables, and even on the mantle of the fireplace.

A long, brown sofa stretched along the farthest wall in the room, right beside the archway that opened into the dining room. To the right of the archway, and down a wide hall, with a couple rooms tucked away on the side, was a large staircase leading to the equally spacious second floor. Stella, in her assuming way, imagined her bedroom would be amongst the others, so she lightly skipped her way up the stairs and curiously approached every door. They were all painted a shade of beige with dark blue doorknobs, with all but one already open.

The first bedroom was Ben's, as she could see by the number of bookshelves that lined the wall, as well as the pressed suits in the closet. Making her way along the hallway, she found that most of the others were guest bedrooms, save Patricia's large sewing room. The one closest to Ben's, however, was the only door closed. As she curiously reached to open it, a sharp cough struck her from behind. She turned around to see Patricia glaring judgmentally at her.

"That is not yours," she said, shortly.

Stella crossed her arms with authority and smirked. "Technically, it is."

Patricia's lips curled in distaste. "Your bedroom is down the hall." She pointed at the open door on the opposite end of the hallway, as far from Ben's as possible. "Mr. Caverly called ahead for me to make arrangements. I'm sure you'll be pleased with it."

Stella walked down the hall and glanced at her room. "It's satisfactory, I suppose," she nodded condescendingly.

"Dinner will be served at six sharp," Patricia said through politely clenched teeth. "That should give you plenty of time to settle in and...attempt to make yourself presentable, Ms. Towson."

She then turned sharply and returned downstairs. Stella wrinkled her nose and mockingly muttered her best imitation of Patricia's accent and tone, "*Ms. Towson.*"

"What sort of solution is this?" Patricia pestered.

She set the table with frustration while Ben sat in his seat at the head of the table, pouring over the paper he had missed while he was away. You see, a truly educated man is not only well-read on events of the past but also the present.

"It's all a bit archaic if I say so myself," she continued to fume. "I'm sure the girl agrees. It's nonsensical. I mean, what was the man thinking? Really."

"He most likely wanted her to be stable before coming into this amount of money but didn't anticipate it all happening so soon. It was his best option, Patricia," Ben replied idly. He had put the discomfort of the issue out of his head and chose to focus on other matters at hand—a task which seemed much more plausible for him than for Patricia. "And it is only for six months. I think we can all manage."

"Do you realize what damage a woman like that can inflict in a matter of six months? I remember Mr. Towson's letters. I'm familiar with her antics, Benjamin."

Ben glanced up for a moment. "Albert's letters? You read my personal letters?

"This is not the time for that," Patricia waved off his accusations, then she stopped and gripped the remaining dishes tightly in her hands. "I may even take my sister's advice and try that new Valium drug for my nerves. I have a feeling that I may very well need it. This is all quite unsettling!"

Ben returned to his paper. "Life will continue as before, Patricia. We simply need to adapt to Stella's presence. If it is too much of a problem for you, feel free to be on holiday for the next six months."

"Now, Benjamin, don't you mock me," she warned. He just smiled, only half-joking. "I know why he did this..." she continued, almost to herself, "He wanted to trap you into marrying his daughter so that she could be twice as wealthy. Old money loves old money–that's what this is."

"Patricia," Ben snapped, his paper slamming against the table before him. "I will not allow you to speak of Albert like that."

"Neither will I," Stella concurred vehemently, standing at the bottom of the staircase. She was refreshed and dressed for dinner, curiously listening to their conversation.

Patricia exhaled sharply in embarrassment. Looking at Ben apologetically, she finished setting the table and retreated to the kitchen to serve the food. Ben stood politely as Stella entered the room and pulled out the chair beside him for her to sit.

"Erm, how is your room?" he asked, trying to change the conversation.

"Clean." Stella faked a smile, taking her seat.

Ben chuckled. "Yes, one of Patricia's many talents. You'll never live amongst disarray in this house."

"So I've gathered," she said, noticing the exact arrangement of the dishes on the table.

Ben cleared his throat uncomfortably. "I...I do apologize for Patricia. She never knew your father, so she does not understand the way he thinks...uh...thought."

"Don't apologize. Nobody ever does."

The tension in the room was excruciatingly thick, as it was on the ride from the airport, with the addition of Patricia's apprehensive stare at Stella. The food was delicious enough to keep Stella quiet and content, being deceptively low-maintenance as she was. Patricia, however, sat with her food untouched, scrutinizing from across the table.

"So..." Patricia began carefully, testing the water. "You've been living with your Aunt...Carol, was it?"

Stella glanced up at her in amazement that the woman was speaking to her unnecessarily. "Hm," she mumbled while a mouthful of beef made its way down her throat. Once she swallowed, she washed the bite down with some water before answering. "She lived with us, actually."

"Ah, I see. It must have been hard, though," Patricia continued, still ignoring her own meal. "Your father having been away so much."

Stella stared at her as she chomped another bite.

"Did anyone call while I was away?" Ben asked, trying to change the subject.

"Sir Bevington stopped by, but he said he would visit another time," Patricia recited dutifully. "Would you have been more comfortable remaining in Boston with your aunt, Ms.

Towson? I should think you would have hardly noticed your father's absence..."

"What kind of a woman—?" Stella spat, but Ben cut her off before she could finish her crude remark.

"Patricia, please eat in the kitchen."

"No, no need," Stella assured him. "I've finished anyway." She stood up and briskly walked out the back door without another word.

The garden was larger than Stella initially thought. It had stone pathways woven throughout, curving through a wide variety of flowers and bushes. In the center was a koi pond with lily pads gliding across the ripples. Dozens and dozens of big, beautiful flowers surrounded her, but no roses. Such an absence made her feel so cripplingly alone. She crossed her arms firmly across her chest and rubbed her arms in a vain attempt to comfort herself.

And then it came.

The first tear since her father left her.

She wasn't sad about his absence; she had grown too accustomed to that while he was alive. What frightened her was thinking he wasn't out there somewhere waiting to come home to her. She somehow felt safe, even when he was away on business, just knowing that he was thinking of her and couldn't wait to see her again.

He was gone.

She had faith she'd see him again, but it would be such a painfully long time. She couldn't bear it.

The tears rolled down her cheeks as her shoulders heaved, no matter how hard she tried to hold them still. She hated this place already. And her father wasn't there to hold her. No one was.

Six months...six long months and she could be free of it all. Or could she? *What comes next?* Stella wondered. She would have her inheritance, but she still wouldn't have him. She would just be alone...again. Her soft cries grew into heavy sobs as she tried her best to suppress them.

For a moment, she thought she felt someone behind her, but as Stella turned to look, she found she was mistaken.

And then, that was it.

Stella knew she was alone.

# 5

## A Secret Affair

Two weeks passed as painlessly as they possibly could. Stella and Patricia were always discontent in one another's company, but it was doubtful that any amount of time would change that. Ben had returned to work, his stable teaching position at Oxford, and life seemed to return to its relatively steady pace. In his eyes, at least.

Stella made attempts to explore Caverly Manor, but Patricia was sure to keep her on a tight leash. Whomever, or whatever, dwelt in that closed room seemed to be a secret Patricia and Ben were keen on keeping from Stella.

The cryptic housekeeper bustled in and out of the forbidden room occasionally, but only when she thought Stella wasn't looking. The curious creature tried to catch a glimpse through the door but to no avail. So, to keep herself occupied, and with Patricia pressing her to leave the house, Stella made a habit of visiting the campus every other day to deliver the lunch Patricia would set out for Ben.

Once in town, the stroll through Oxford was very calming and allowed her to clear her head. Unfortunately, once on campus, this trip included her enthusiastic interaction with the attractive, male graduate students who bustled through the courtyard and in and out of Ben's office.

Stella figured that if she had to endure an icy and emotionless six months, the very least she could get away with was the occasional innocent flirtation. Oliver was one of the more studious of Ben's students and also happened to be one of the more physically appealing. He styled his blond hair to the side, being sure not to block his charming brown eyes with his bangs. As he passed her in the hallway leading to Ben's office, he flashed her a flirtatious grin.

"Did you get in trouble and have to stay after class?" Stella teased.

"Always." Oliver winked.

Stella giggled softly and waved at him before turning the corner. Ben was sitting at his desk, buried behind piles of books and folders overflowing with graded papers. A lovely, young, redheaded woman with her hair pulled loosely into a bun held by no more than a pencil stood leaning over the desk and pointing at something Ben was reading.

"He needed you to sign there and be sure to bring it with you to the next board meeting," she told him, leading Stella to assume she was Ben's secretary. As the woman stood there, Stella performed her examination. The loud, chevron print of the redhead's dress was a transparent attempt to get attention, she decided. When she saw Stella standing in the doorway, holding a bag of food, she straightened her back immediately.

"Oh, you must be Miss Stella?" She held her hand out to shake.

Stella shook her hand politely, studying her. She was a beautiful girl, Stella thought. No wonder he's so uninterested in me; he has his very own ginger to look at all day. "And you are...?"

"Emily," the woman said. "Emily Grayer: the department's secretary. It's so nice to finally meet you, miss. I have to be going, though. I have a lot of work to do. I'll see you at that board meeting in the morning, Professor Caverly."

Ben smiled at her sweetly. "Uh, yes. Nine o'clock."

"Right." Emily beamed once more before leaving; her suede pumps clicked against the floor as she walked.

Stella chuckled. "She's a cute little thing, isn't she?"

His focus returned to the papers stacked across his desk. "I suppose so. I don't usually notice."

"You suppose so..." She raised her eyebrows doubtfully. "I'm sure you didn't notice her tight little dress either...which is fine, I guess, since you're a married man anyway." She was having a bit too much fun teasing him, but he didn't seem to notice that either. He just smirked and quietly continued going through the papers, setting some aside, and flipping through more. "Here's your lunch." She handed him the bag.

"Um, thank you. Have you, uh, already eaten?"

"Yes, I ate before I came."

She aimlessly glanced around the office soaking in the environment. It reminded her of Ben's study back at Caverly Manor, as well as the living room, and his bedroom–books stacked on furniture, often stuffed with papers bearing haphazard scribbles. It was glaringly obvious that the man was a comparative literature professor. Book cases lined the office, containing the more organized publications waiting on their alphabetically sorted shelves, waiting for their turn to be annotated, as they were at home.

In many ways, Ben reminded her of her dear father; his passion for literature and his strategic mind had made him and Albert kindred spirits. The thought made his cold, emotional distance from her more bearable. Since the wedding, they had barely made physical contact, not even so much as a handshake. They spoke to one another only when necessary and hardly glanced in each other's direction.

"Oh, I have something to show you." His head suddenly perked up.

He rose and walked over to an armchair that was placed beside the only window in the room. On the armchair was a cardboard box with shipping addresses plastered all over the side and the edges held together with packaging tape. Ben opened the top of the box to display the contents.

"What's this?" she asked, following him to the chair. She peered in the box and saw a thick stack of leather-bound books, topped with a folded, well-worn leather jacket. "That's...that's my father's."

Ben nodded. "Yes, it is. Frank sent it, as per Albert's request. Apparently, this is my inheritance."

Her eyes widened in curiosity. The leather jacket was one she had seen every time Albert returned from a business trip. The man hardly took the thing off. She picked it up and felt the old, cracked leather between her fingers. It still felt the same. Ben watched her as she brought it closer to her face.

"It still smells like him," she said softly.

She was speaking to herself, with a smile on her face that was the sweetest, most childlike expression Ben had perceived on her since he saw the childhood portrait Albert kept on his desk. "Like old books and fresh ink."

Ben chuckled softly. "Yes, that was Albert."

She smiled to herself again, nodding nostalgically. She lowered the jacket back into the box but didn't let it go. "What are you going to do with all these?"

"Read them, I suppose. When I get the chance. There are quite a few, so it may take me a while." He chuckled again, gesturing to the plentiful number of leather-bounds which filled most of the box.

Stella chuckled as well. "He wrote down everything. I hope he doesn't burden you with the tedious history of my toilet-training."

They both laughed together. It was nice being able to reminisce. It reminded them both of their only real connection. When the laughter ended, a bit of the discomfort returned to fill the silence.

"Um...you can keep that if you like," Ben offered awkwardly. He noticed her hands hadn't loosened their grip on the jacket. He gave her a small smile, which she returned with pleasant surprise.

"Really?"

"Of course. It might fit you rather poorly, but...at least it was his."

Then without warning, and for the first time in their entire acquaintance, Stella reached up and wrapped her arms gratefully around his neck. "Thank you," she whispered in his ear.

Stella smelled like a mixture of sweet, rosy perfume and Patricia's gardenias. She had clearly been spending some time in the back garden, but with this degree of closeness, Ben found it both refreshing and relaxing. He decided that he liked her scent and warmth, but soon shook the thought from his head to return to reality.

When they separated, he cleared his throat nervously. "I, um, I had something else I wanted to speak with you about."

"Yes?"

"Patricia and I..."

Stella release an irritated groan.

"...we thought, given the circumstances, it would be best if we referred to you as my cousin...visiting from Boston."

Stella just stared at him. "Your cousin."

"Yes," he simply nodded. "Considering the short term of this, um, arrangement...I think it would be wise for both of us to keep it between the few who already know."

She began to laugh, but not a pleasant laugh. It was more of a release than an expression of amusement. She wore an exhausted smile as she shrugged.

"Well, at least it's only for the next five and a half months. You've probably already told your colleagues that I was your cousin, so why not?" Discreetly, she removed her wedding band behind her back and slipped it into her sweater pocket only then noticing that he had not been wearing his.

"If you are not comfortable with this, Stella, we can—"

"Comfortable?" she repeated quietly, shaking her head. "I don't even know what that means anymore." She took the jacket back out of the box and wrapped it up in her arms turning to leave. Before she walked through the office door, she turned back to face him and with her usual nonchalance she taunted, "Don't you worry, I'll keep our secret."

# 6

## SILLY COUSIN STELLA

As any man would be in his situation, Ben was at a loss. He knew Stella was suffering, but there was only so much that could be done. He was never really one for warmth or comfort, or understanding emotions in general which is why he fit so well in academia He was a pragmatic man, one who only saw what was in front of him and didn't always understand it. She was an enigma. Uncharted territory. He imagined her grief from losing her father, but her biting frankness and rebellion were very different than he had expected. Of all the times he visited Albert at home, he had seen and interacted with Stella only a handful of them. He knew she was bright, curious, inquisitive, and bold—but all he knew of her was from Albert.

He had spoken to Ben about his daughter frequently, praising her outstanding traits. And, oh, how he praised her. The angelic way in which Albert depicted his lovely daughter would never lead one to believe she had any faults at all. He wasn't blind to them, for he was as discerning as anyone would be, but he willfully overlooked them. He only ever winked at her difficult personality and obstinance—of which, Ben thought, a warning would have been most helpful. This made it challenging for Ben to see the Stella that Albert always saw. As I said, Ben only saw what was in front of him.

Six months.

Was it worth getting to know her if she would be leaving so soon?

As frustrating as it was, he still found a certain magnetism about her that he couldn't explain. The kind he was certain Albert had never experienced, but one that every other man she encountered inevitably did. A magnetism that would soon prove more spellbinding and potent than he initially imagined. Somehow, Ben was able to remain aloof and detached, treating the situation as he would any other business arrangement. If he treated it any differently, the attachment would only grow more complicated for the both of them.

So, for the next several days, Stella kept to herself in her room or the garden, making the occasional retort toward Patricia and smiling at the inevitable reaction. She was livelier than when she had first arrived, but her intractability remained the same. Stella didn't want to be there, and she made sure it was no secret. Enduring the incessant banter with Patricia, the coldness from Ben, the restriction from even properly exploring the house in which she was practically imprisoned, and the loneliness of her overall condition wore on her, but she only fought back with more resistance.

She hadn't slept much since her father's funeral. Her eyes would close, and her consciousness would drift, but startling nightmares would haunt her, yanking her out of any temporary rest or relief. Nightmares are dreadful things; quite a ghastly contrast to pleasant dreams that lure dreamers into the pleasures of slumber.

Stella's nightmares, sadly, were even darker than the norm, laced with hellish eyes and venomous shadows which did all they could to block any hope of light. Dark circles slowly began to form under her eyes and, in vain, she attempted to blend just enough concealer to brighten her visage. Every small effort did its part.

The garden was beautiful, though the place lacked the comfort of roses. The journey to and from the university gave her the fresh air she needed, though twinged with discomfort, given the company that awaited her. The one taste of home that came her way was several weeks after her arrival. Ben held a small, private dinner party for a select few of his colleagues from the university, along with their wives, in celebration of Professor Burkham's impending retirement. Her father frequently hosted dinner parties, whenever he was home, and she adored them. Of course, she loved any opportunity to showcase her charm and sparkling wit.

"Do you have an appropriate dress for the occasion?" Patricia questioned Stella when she informed her of the dinner party.

"Of course I have an appropriate dress for the occasion," she countered mockingly.

She chose to wear her father's favorite dress—a plum, satin, knee-length cocktail dress. He had always said whenever she wore it she looked the most like her mother. Beaming at herself in the mirror, she wished she could have seen the comparison. Albert would always take her by the hand and twirl her about like a ballerina after seeing her in the dress calling her a princess. She smiled in spite of herself, for the first time in a long time.

Once Stella reached the foot of the stairs, she did a quick ballerina twirl and asked Ben how she looked. He wasn't quite sure what to say. She looked as if she would give some of his older colleagues a heart attack before they could even reach retirement. She was indeed stunning, and that he couldn't deny.

But, a simple, "Lovely" was all that his disciplined mouth would allow to escape.

"Thanks." Stella sighed, letting her arms bounce gently against her thighs as they fell from pose.

The dinner party arrived soon after. Five men and two women, excluding Stella and Ben, filled the parlor, chatting cordially like old friends. Three of the men worked with Ben at the university and were introduced to Stella as Professors Burkham, Smith, and Granger. Professor Burkham, the guest of honor, was an older man with very little hair and very large spectacles that covered most of his small face. He was hunched slightly over but supported upright by his sturdy wife. His son, Thomas, had also accompanied them, standing on the other side of his father. He was a younger, pleasant-looking man, only a few years older than Stella, and wore a very cheerful and friendly grin aimed hopefully in her direction.

Ingrid, the wife of Professor Smith, was the most talkative woman Stella had ever met. She chattered on the entire evening about nonsense to which no one paid much attention. Professor Smith himself was precisely what Stella had expected. She had seen his sort many times in many universities. He was tall—about Ben's height—and smartly dressed, with spectacles and a mustache, peering at everyone arrogantly as if gracing them with the honor of his presence. He was very different from Ben, she noticed. Ben had a much more approachable demeanor. Professor Granger stood beside Smith and was someone Stella had recognized as one of Ben's good friends. She had seen him frequently in Ben's office and found him friendly enough. He was shorter than Ben, and a bit older, with streaks of grey throughout his dark red hair.

The fifth man introduced himself, to Stella directly, as Sir Reginald Bevington. She remembered him being the one Patricia had said visited while Ben was away. He was a very close family friend, apparently, and had been good friends with Ben's late father. He seemed very friendly, making quite an effort to speak with Stella throughout the evening. He even went as far as asking for the table settings to be rearranged so as to give himself the opportunity to sit beside her at dinner. Her attention, however, was directed toward the younger Mr. Burkham.

"I thought I knew most of Ben's family," Bevington remarked, intruding on their personal conversation. Everyone had convened to the parlor to mingle while Patricia served the tea. "Are you from Rupert's side or Anne's?"

"Yes, I am," Stella answered vaguely. "Now, if you don't mind, Thomas here was in the middle of saying something."

Thomas coughed nervously. "Erm, no, it's fine."

"And Ben said you lived in the States for most of your life, is that right?" Bevington continued on, paying little attention to the intimidated young man.

"But it's not fine, sir." Stella smiled ironically. "He was speaking to me first. I'm sorry, but you'll have to wait."

"Excuse me?"

"With all due respect, Mr. Bevington—"

"Sir," Patricia snapped from behind her as she picked up the saucers and cups. Stella's impertinence alarmed her, but she tried her best to bite her tongue in front of company.

"Sir Bevington," Stella corrected, overemphasizing his title with veiled annoyance. "Thomas and I were in the middle of an enjoyable conversation. If you want, I'm sure Mrs. Smith would be more than happy to talk to you."

"Well, I dare say, young lady," Bevington gasped, taken aback by her boldness. "You did not inherit the Caverly grace; that much is certain. You must have been in the States for a very long time."

"Long enough," she said bitingly. "Now, if you'll excuse us." She then took a stupefied Thomas's arm and led him out into the garden. Patricia gave Ben a hard nudge as he and Granger had engaged in conversation with Professor and Mrs. Smith on the opposite end of the room. Ben glanced Stella's way and saw her leave with Mr. Burkham, abandoning a very offended Sir Bevington alone by the fireplace.

Inhaling deeply, summoning his strength, Ben excused himself from the conversation to do some damage control. He approached Bevington and gave his sincerest apologies.

"I am truly sorry, sir. My cousin, she has not adapted well. She is —"

"Rather fiery," Bevington finished for him. "Benjamin, while I have always fancied women with fire, I must say, hers must be tamed if she is to make it anywhere." He patted Ben on the shoulder and shook his head. "I am not at all surprised that you have shielded her from the general public. Anne has always been a great judge of character, particularly to those she welcomes in her home. It only disappoints me that you would expose the young lady at a time when your poor mother is unable to come to your family's defense."

"Sir, as insubordinate as Stella may be, you can hardly blame her for speaking her mind," Ben spoke candidly. He found it a challenge apologizing to a man who would so quickly slander his family's reputation, particularly that of his dear mother.

Bevington looked at him with an almost pitying expression. "Ah, Ben. I don't doubt your intentions, nor hers, but I think it is time for me to leave. It's been an...interesting evening. I thank you." And with that, after giving his best to all those still in the room, he left.

Patricia took her master aside after the remaining party bid farewell and didn't hesitate to make her opinion known. "Benjamin, this cannot go unpunished," she advised. "Not only did she treat such a high-ranking friend with gross disrespect, but she secluded herself in the garden with a young man to

52

whom she paid an inappropriate amount of attention to for the entire evening."

Ben sat himself down in his armchair and breathed heavily. "Patricia, this is hardly your concern."

"No, but it is yours, sir. Whether she is posing as your wife or your relative—she is still capable of ruining you, and she is succeeding!"

"Patricia," he warned. "Calm down and fetch her for me."

She inhaled sharply and turned to retrieve the miscreant. Within moments, Stella descended down the stairs and stood before Ben with her arms folded across her chest. He could tell that she knew what was coming, and her defenses were raised. In all of his experience relying on his mind, nothing could have prepared him for the mental power he found necessary for reprimanding Stella.

"Yes?" she said with all the petulance of a child.

Ben cleared his throat. "I'm sure you can imagine what I need to discuss with you."

"Mm, no, I can't imagine." She shrugged. Her expression was unchanged, annoyed, and even a little smug.

"Your behavior tonight was...unacceptable."

"Unacceptable?"

"Professor Burkham is one of the most beloved professors at the university, and Sir Bevington is a very old friend of the Caverly family—the level of respect that both men are warranted may be something that you are unaccustomed to giving, but as long as you are my wife, it is the level of respect you will give." His words were very succinct and controlled, and his tone remained steady.

"But I'm not actually your wife anymore, am I? I'm just your embarrassing cousin." While her stance remained the same, her frustration caused an alarming escalation in volume. "And how exactly did I disrespect Professor Burkham?"

"You secluded yourself in the garden with his son, to whom you paid an inappropriate amount of attention for the entire evening."

"I'm not allowed to let people know I'm your wife and now I'm not allowed to behave like the single lady I'm supposed to be pretending that I am!"

"Single women can still behave with decorum and propriety," he answered evenly.

"Wake up, Ben, it's the sixties—not the 18th century."

"Stella, if you are seen as a member of this family—whether it is as my wife or cousin—you must behave like one. Your behavior must be more conservative and—"

"My behavior! I think it's only fair that if you can ogle your hotsy-totsy assistant in her tight little skirts, I think I can have an exclusive conversation with an attractive gentleman at a private dinner party."

"My what? Emily has nothing to do with this conversation, Stella. This is about you."

"Yes, because all of this inconvenience is my fault. You did agree to this too. But, of course, only I'm to blame. Perhaps you should just keep me locked up—like whoever you have imprisoned upstairs. Who is it—a crazy ex-wife or something, Rochester? It seems to work for them, however cold and cruel it actually is. Out of sight, out of mind, right? Until the prisoner sets the house on fire."

Without giving Ben the chance to respond, she turned curtly on her heel and started for the staircase. Before stomping up the stairs like a child, she turned her head back toward Ben. "Next time you see Sir Bevington, apologize on behalf of silly cousin Stella, will you?"

# 7

## THROUGH THE PAGES

Stress lines were beginning to creep onto Ben's face. As he sat alone at breakfast, the argument from the night before played through his head on an unending loop. Perhaps it hadn't been fair to make Stella put on a charade. The arrangement itself was already tricky enough. But, as Patricia frequently reminded him, he did have his family name to uphold. A six-month marriage for purely financial reasons would not look the least bit acceptable. It was best to keep it discreet, he concluded.

Had he been too hard on her? Was he to blame for the conflict? Had taking Patricia's advice only caused more problems? The past couple of weeks weighed uneasily on him, and he could feel an ulcer forming in his gut. He decided to push all of his domestic problems out of his mind and focus entirely on his work in that cold way he did.

*Cold and cruel*, he thought. Those words seemed to sting the most. But, he tried to put himself at ease. She had not known the entirety of the situation. She was only speaking out of rage.

He assured himself that she was grieving and would eventually regret her words. Stella would work out her own problems alone; pushing her would accomplish nothing. He—quite accurately, might I add—imagined an exasperated Albert giving her space quite frequently.

However, a comment Frank Marcus made at the funeral suddenly struck him. Albert was the only person she ever listened to. He then remembered Albert's gentle touch that seemed to tame her. His expression had been filled with so much love, which she responded to in kind. Perhaps that was the cause of her discontent now; the lack of affection she had received throughout the past couple of weeks. He had been so sure not to put an excessive amount of emotional attachment into the arrangement, not that he had been initially tempted. A strong bond between them was not necessary, given the relationship's life expectancy, but perhaps he could make more of an effort in making her feel comfortable and at peace while living in Caverly Manor.

He needed a gentle touch. He needed diplomacy and grace. But most of all, he needed to try to see what there was to love.

Stella slept in late, trying to sleep off her anger and forget their last conversation entirely. Her only regret, however, was her tone. She never did seem to have control of her temper; something her father voiced as her greatest disadvantage. Whenever the two had argued, which was quite rare, he was always capable of remaining calm and thinking clearly. Ben, apparently, had an unnerving amount of control, and she hated him for it. His dry, mechanical responses only fueled her frustration.

Patricia's disruptive knocking on her bedroom door just made Stella squeeze her eyelids shut. She pulled the covers up over her head and pretended not to hear.

"Ms. Towson, I need to change your sheets," Patricia called impatiently. "And it's almost noon." She sounded disapproving, which made Stella smile. She knocked once more, louder this time. When there was still no answer, she let out a profound and dramatic sigh of exasperation. "Fine, I will check in again in a few hours. And those sheets had better be ready for me."

Stella groaned, rolling over to face the nearest window. The sun was very bright, echoing Patricia's reminder that it was already midday. She decided that if she didn't get up now, she might as well never get up at all, but the noises from her stomach reminded her that she had missed breakfast.

After getting dressed, she snuck into the kitchen to see if there was something for lunch. The only thing that seemed remotely appealing was a lone apple that sat on the top of the fruit bowl. She snatched it up and wandered aimlessly around the house. She was still angry, but with Ben at work and out of sight, it was considerably easier for her to remain calm. As long as she didn't run into Patricia, she knew she could think through things clearly.

She found herself wandering into Ben's study. It was one of the two rooms in the large hall, after the staircase, and it was usually kept closed. As hidden away as it was, Stella found it very welcoming. There was a large armchair a short distance from the desk, and, as was prevalent in all of Ben's rooms, bookshelves lined the walls.

He was a creature of habit, she observed. She recognized that the bookshelves, extending even as far as his workplace, seemed to be a sort of security blanket.

She couldn't particularly blame him. Growing up with a father such as hers, it was a comfortable setting for her as well. Despite the very stiff, angular arrangement of the furniture and bookshelves, it made her nostalgic.

Sitting on the armchair was her father's leather bomber jacket. She remembered leaving it hanging on the banister the night before. Ben must have stowed it away so Patricia wouldn't hang it up in the closet with the rest of the coats. It was respectfully folded and placed in the center of the cushion. Stella held it up to the light from the window and envisioned Albert wearing it.

Every story he ever told, he told while wearing the jacket. Every happy memory, every promise of adventure—all of those moments happened in this jacket. Instinctively, she put it on and wrapped her arms around herself. It was too big for her, but the warmth was still there. It still felt like him, still smelled like him. Breathing in the essence of it, Stella felt her father's memory calm her mind.

She started by walking through the garden and then made her way down the empty country road, the comfort of the jacket enveloping her.

She could hear her father gently chiding her:

Behave, Stella. Give the man a break. It takes extraordinary people to handle you sometimes, my love. You

59

know that. He's trying. He took you on, for my sake. Now, ease up on him, for my sake.

She almost rolled her eyes, but then remembered that there was no one actually there to see. She must have walked for at least two miles while allowing her father's voice to prance around in her head. It was better than letting him leave altogether, even if she didn't entirely care for what he was saying. It was utterly silent, with the exception of the light tapping of her Mary Jane's against the paved street.

The jacket suddenly grew warm, tingling against her skin. She stopped in her tracks and touched the outside of the leather gingerly with her fingers. It was almost as if a subtle current of electricity was coursing underneath. The tingling only intensified at her touch, and the leather began to glow a subdued, bluish shade.

Stella froze in panic.

"What—?" she exhaled sharply.

She blinked only once and, when she pried her eyes back open, she was standing in the middle of a vast, round room. In an instant, she collapsed in shock, her knees hitting an aged wooden floor. Her blurry, confused eyes could only make out the vague details of the room.

There was no ceiling, just walls reaching so high that they disappeared into the sky— they weren't quite walls at all, in fact, but neatly-filled bookshelves. For a moment she thought she had somehow reappeared in Ben's personal library, and then she considered her father's in Boston. Albert had always arranged the furniture and bookshelves in quite a circular fashion. There were even houseplants and flowers placed sporadically amongst the neatly shelved leather books. This room was familiar—with the exception, she uneasily noticed, of the lack of doors and windows.

From what unseen source did all of this light come? How did she get there and, more importantly, how would she leave? There were no visible doors, no windows, no means of escape.

Stella searched her surroundings frantically, seeking some sort of explanation. There were three leather armchairs—the exact shade of the leather jacket she now wore—which were arranged around a fireplace on the farthest side of the room, facing each other as if engaged in conversation.

The fire was a strange translucent shade of blue and didn't quite seem real. A winding staircase lined the walls tightly, crawling up into the mysterious oblivion above Stella's head. And every fifth shelf or so, the stairs leveled out to create a platform for a book-seeker to walk across to grab the book of choice. As far as Stella could tell, however, the room was empty.

Not a soul in sight.

Her heartbeat couldn't decide if it was excited, panicked, or madly curious.

"Don't forget to breathe, silly," a little voice giggled from somewhere above her.

Stella exhaled deeply in an attempt to steady her breathing. She stood up quickly, her head whipping around anxiously to find the voice's owner.

Still, she saw no one.

"Who—?" she croaked.

She then heard the patter of small footsteps make their way down the winding staircase. As they came closer, she could make out the bobbing head who owned them. A young girl, no older than eight years old, Stella guessed. She had a curly, blonde mess of hair and the clearest eyes ever to be seen. The child's countenance was nearly as bright as the room in which they stood. She almost reminded Stella of someone, but she couldn't quite recollect.

"Just breathe," the girl said again. She skipped over the last few steps and danced her way over to Stella, and stopped a few steps cheerfully in front of her. She wore a white, cotton sundress with a pair of white sandals and a bow in her hair. "You're different," she giggled, after studying her for a moment.

"I'm different?" Stella repeated, struggling to process.

"Oh, please don't traumatize the poor girl even more, Alice," another voice said.

Stella followed the voice to one of the platforms above her, where a small man sat at a desk covered in parchment and manuscripts. He appeared to be writing something, toggling his intent eyes from his work to the small, circular glass—a looking glass, in fact—that sat on the right end of the desk.

At first, she assumed he was studying his own reflection until she looked a little harder and found that the mirror wasn't reflecting anything at all. It was playing images, like a television set. The small man peered down at Alice and smiled warmly at Stella.

"Isn't she different, Clancy?" the girl asked. "She's not like any of the others."

"Well," he considered. He appeared to be the nervous type, shrugging uncertainly and fiddling with his hands. "She surely isn't. But I-I'm sure there's a reason. Just...don't you overwhelm her. Remember what happened to poor Mr. Dodgson the last time you decided to over-inform."

"Charlie," she giggled emptily. "It's okay. It can still be fun. I'm Alice."

"Alice...Charlie Dodgson." The girl's resemblance suddenly struck her. "As in...as in Lewis Carroll...Alice in Wonderland..." Stella remembered drawings in her old picture book of the peculiar character, but never imagined a real-life similitude.

The girl held up a hand to stop her and shook her head amusingly.

"Wonderland was a cover story—" Clancy explained.

"An excellent one," Alice chimed in, smiling widely. "And you're Albert's daughter. I like him."

Stella blinked hard. She still wasn't able to understand what was right in front of her, nor how this young girl...Alice from Wonderland...knew who she was. How could this be real? Those nightmares must have drained her into a heightened state of sleep deprivation. It was the only possible explanation for what was happening.

"Where—?"

"The Arkis," Clancy answered. He had stood up from behind his desk, but remained on his platform as if some sort of invisible wall kept him locked in place.

"Arkis?" Stella mumbled.

"Of course," Alice giggled. "This is the part where they usually grab a book."

"What?"

"The ladies and gents that come in here. This is where they grab a book and leave. That's not yours," she pointed at Stella's jacket. "You're not the one, but I think you're still allowed."

"Allowed to do what, exactly?"

Alice placed her hands on her hips and sighed. "I already told you. You have to pick a book."

Stella pulled the jacket tighter around her.

*You have to pick a book.*

She looked around at the millions of books around her, trying to make out all the titles. One book, in particular, stood out to her. It was different from the others. It had a certain allure that was difficult to describe. While seemingly ordinary, it wouldn't allow her to look away. And though all of the books had a distinctive presence to them, somehow, this one felt more alive, drawing her in. A light whooshing sensation could suddenly be heard in Stella's ears, as if she had placed a seashell to her ear.

Strikingly, the book's binding showed subtle signs of decay. This seemed unusual for a library that was apparently so well-kept. It was only slight corrosion, but enough to spark intrigue.

She glanced back at Alice before walking toward it, and seeing her eager smile, she stepped closer to read the words along the spine of the book.

*Le Morte d'Arthur* by Sir Thomas Malory.

"Touch it," Alice urged, squealing softly in excitement, ignoring Clancy's warning,

"Now-now be careful down there."

Stella crinkled her mouth to one side, thinking hard in confusion. "Why—?" But it was too late. She grabbed the book, opened to a page at random, and felt the jacket tingle once more.

In the blink of an eye, she was somewhere else.

Her body jolted in shock, like a small earthquake had moved the very ground out from under her. The wooden floor beneath her feet had become patches of grass and soil. The peaceful silence of the Arkis was broken by the abrupt clanking of metal and chattering of passersby.

Shock initially blurred Stella's vision, but as focus gradually returned, she found herself behind a large beige tent. Several tents just like it were lined ahead of her, as well as behind. The top of each tent featured a variety of colorful flags bearing insignias for the respective owners. Stella's eyes, though still unsettled, followed the rows of tents to the end of the vast walkway they bordered, leading her to the source of the clanking metal.

An arena, the stands of which were filled with boisterous spectators, was nestled in what she assumed was the midst of these apparent tournament grounds. Men in full suits of armor and wielding long lances were positioned on opposing ends of the arena, facing each other atop their noble steeds.

Peasants donning linens and nobles donning fine silks all bustled to and fro. Had they paused for even a moment to notice our puzzled Stella, they would have been quite surprised to see the contemporarily conservative contrast her blue cotton dress from Woolworth's provided against her medieval surroundings.

Stella certainly noticed.

Her calves and ankles, though covered in pantyhose, felt bare compared to the floor-length gowns donned by her counterparts in this foreign land.

Almost instinctively, Stella lowered her panicked arms to shield her legs. It was only a brief attempt at modesty, as her continual observation of those around her pulled her attention away yet again. Several knights with squires, preparing for the games and passing her by, continued to take no notice of this strange girl.

"Wow," was all she breathed.

Stella began to wander absentmindedly. Lost in the grandeur, she paused and took a step backwards, bumping into the horse of a knight who had been riding past with his friend.

"Oh, sorry," Stella apologized, distractedly. The knight glanced down at her with a smile.

"No need to apologize, my lady," he said sweetly. His face was kind and handsome, though aged with the experience of a man who'd seen his share of bloodshed.

Stella felt that she knew him, that there was something familiar about him. She was certain she had never seen him before, but given the context, he gave her the strangest sense of déjà vu.

He and his friend both wore armor and carried shields, just like all the others. What set this knight apart was the richly-colored red kerchief dangling from his saddle. It was the sort a gallant knight would wear in honor of a lady fair–his good luck charm while in battle or in a tournament. He must have placed it there until the tournament, where he would attach it to his helmet.

"May I offer you assistance?"

Stella stared at him, unable to form words. What little concentration her mind could muster was dedicated to attempting to place both his face and his red kerchief.

His friend cleared his throat and nudged him before she could respond. "We must find our lodgings, my friend."

"Right." The knight smiled. "I bid you good day, my lady." He gave her a chivalrous nod and trotted off toward the row of inns leading into the small town.

A disruptive thud boomed, causing Stella to snap her head back to where she had first appeared. Two haphazard gentlemen had suddenly taken her place on the ground behind the beige tent that was now several wandered footsteps behind her. While not quite as anachronistic as Stella herself, their panicked state certainly matched hers upon arrival.

Slowly she approached them, hoping that if they weren't locals, they could possibly lend some explanations. One of the men was dwarfish, perhaps the height of a smallish donkey, at the withers. I say donkey, you see, because the donkey is infamous for obstinacy, naturally brought about by a highly developed sense of self-preservation.

But more on that later.

This dwarf wore a very colorful, tweed cardigan with a dark gray undergarment. The entire ensemble, including his trousers, were faded and patched. His hair was a light brown and messy on the top. His eyebrows matched, both in color and disarray, framing his dark beady eyes. His big, bearded mouth was spewing profanities at the older gentleman with whom he had been wrestling. The older man looked as though he had fallen out of the sky, or perhaps fallen with the dwarf, and landed on top of him. They were stumbling over one another, arguing and wrestling as they tried to free themselves from one another and stand.

As she neared them, she heard the small one shove the larger man and exclaim, "Would ya get off me?!" He had a peculiar accent that Stella couldn't immediately identify.

The older gentleman, however, was even more exotic. "You will not best me this time, knave!" he croaked, regaining composure and breathing heavily from the exertion.

He straightened his back and drew a flimsy sword from its rusted sheath. He was dressed like a knight but in a childish, makeshift way. His armor was rusted, and mildewed, barely staying in one piece. He wore a small, matching headpiece with a cardboard neck guard and strips of some sort of thin metal sticking out of the bottom, apparently lining the inside.

His appearance made Stella chuckle, but the intensity of his expression was disturbing. Neither man looked like he belonged here, anywhere, or even together at all. The two men came from completely different time periods, and two very different parts of the world. *Well, whatever world that might be*, she thought.

"I demand you return what was stolen from myself and my squire," the old man insisted, holding his sword to the dwarf's chest, as he laid on the ground, staring and irritated.

68

"You're mad!" the dwarf spat, pushing the sword away.

The older man became suddenly aware of his surroundings and spun around in confusion. "Where—where have you taken me? Is this some sort of witchcraft?"

Spanish, Stella decided. His accent was Spanish. He was frantic for a moment, before noticing some knights who walked a short distance from him. "Ah, here there are fellow knights-errant. You may have saved me, fiend. But where is my squire? Sancho?" He spun back to face the beady-eyed dwarf and held his sword even closer to the man's chest. "Has he been slain by your hand?!"

"I didn't slay anyone, you moron!"

They had captured the curiosity of a small handful of idle knights passing by. As the knights approached them, Stella hid behind the corner of the nearest tent, observing the whole scene. Two of the knights, who were not yet in their jousting armor, tried to settle the dispute with diplomacy.

"What seems to be the conflict here, my good man?" the younger knight asked politely.

He walked with an arrogant swagger, as did his partner. The older, taller one yanked the dwarf away from the aimed sword with disregard, while the younger knight raised his hands peacefully. He hadn't drawn his own sword; Stella assumed the situation had been deemed not dangerous—or the old man's madness appeared harmless enough.

"The games haven't even begun, my friend. If you are so excited to begin early, Sir Kay and I would be more than happy to oblige. But this man is unarmed, and there is no sport in that."

The Spaniard lowered his sword slightly. "I thank you for your concern, sir knight—"

"You may call me Sir Mordred," the younger knight insisted.

"Sir Mordred. This is between myself and this thief. He has stolen from me and slain my squire. He has dishonored me!" He brandished his sword in the tiny man's direction, causing the dwarf to back away and cower behind Sir Kay.

Sir Mordred finally drew his sword and pointed it at the Spaniard. "What has the dwarf stolen from you, sir?"

The Spaniard seemed a little confused and still disoriented from the earlier scuffle. He staggered, his sword arm flailing a bit and was unnecessarily blocked by Sir Mordred. Before Stella knew it, the two men were awkwardly dueling. As dignified as Sir Mordred seemed to think he was, he wasn't too much better in swordplay than this old, confused, pseudo-knight.

In the midst of the ridiculous sparring, Sir Mordred seemed to have been struck, but from Stella's angle, she couldn't say for certain how it happened. Mordred collapsed to the ground with a gaping side wound, and the Spaniard stood over him, deliriously victorious. He defeated him—he didn't understand how, but he didn't seem to care. He grinned proudly and turned with gusto to Sir Kay. Kay fell to Mordred's side to find that his friend was no longer breathing. The wound had killed him almost instantly.

The sight of the gushing blood made Stella feel queasy. The cries of the surviving knight, exclaiming his friend's death loudly, made her eyes sting with tears. It was all so overwhelming.

She must have let out a whimper, for the old victor's eyes snapped alertly in her direction. His face suddenly fell as if he had only just realized the extent of his actions. He hadn't intended to kill the knight, and judging by the look in his eyes, he wasn't even sure what he had meant to do. He seemed just as mad as the cowardly dwarf said, but in a much more pitiable sense.

Stella covered her mouth and staggered backward, stepping directly into the path of a young woman carrying a bushel of apples behind her. The apples toppled to the ground, startling Stella further.

"Careful!" the young woman exclaimed. She scrambled to gather them, apparently oblivious to the scene that had just occurred. "You've gone and bruised them."

The young woman glanced up, moving her rust-colored hair out of her face to scold Stella once more, but she immediately stopped at the sight of her. As the woman stood straighter, clutching an apple or two in her hands, her sea foam green eyes slowly looked Stella up and down, settling on her jacket for a few moments before connecting with Stella's flustered gaze.

"Easy there, love," the woman said, in a much gentler tone than before. "Are you all right?"

"I'm–I'm so sorry," Stella blubbered. "I'm so sorry, miss."

"Ava," the young woman smiled. "I'm Ava. And you have nothing to be sorry for. You're clearly distressed. Where did you come from, love?"

"I'm..." a sudden catch came to Stella's throat, preventing her from answering. Her answer didn't matter, in any case.

Within seconds of Ava posing her question, the jacket tingled, Stella blinked twice and jolted forward. And before Stella knew it, she was once again in the Arkis.

Alice sat cross-legged on the floor, simply waiting. There was a book open on the floor in front of her, but she wasn't reading it. Instead, she was staring ahead at the exact spot in which she knew Stella would appear.

Stella gasped quietly. When she looked to Alice for further explanation, all Alice did was smile as before. "Don't worry, I talked to him about it. You're not the one. But you'll come back—you just can't come back alone."

Before Stella could breathe another unanswerable question, she was back on the streets of Oxford. She collapsed again and heaved the deepest breaths her body could handle. The road was cold and wet, and her mind was utterly blank. Nothing that had happened made sense. And, just as part of it began to, she felt a hand touch her back. Spastic, she flung her arm up defensively, hitting the police officer trying to help her in the face. He swayed backward, holding his jaw in shock. The helpless woman crumpled on the country road in distress had struck him with surprising strength.

"Just—" she managed to wheeze. "Just, don't touch me."

"What happened to you, miss?" the officer asked, hoping that her explanation was as simple as intoxication.

"The guy...killed the guy...and the knight...his sword was...I don't..."

# 8

## THE CLEVER BEAUTY

For the duration of Stella's little adventure, much less excitement was occurring a short distance away at the local university. With Professor Burkham's retirement around the corner, the department held luncheons in his honor for the week leading up to it.

Social settings such as these were a bore to Ben, but he suffered through them as he had his whole life. Since his father died, the social events lessened, but his academic career brought some of them back as a necessity. Most of the time, he just stood and vaguely listened as his colleagues droned on and on.

"...frankly, I thought she wasn't entirely in the wrong. Men like Sir Bevington think they're so entitled to whatever tickles their fancy," Granger rambled. "I hope you didn't scold her too harshly."

"Hm?" Ben jerked out of his reverie. "What?"

"Your cousin, Caverly. I hope you didn't scold your cousin too harshly for the whole dinner party debacle."

"Oh, I don't believe I did."

"I mean, once you get past that mouth of hers, she's actually quite charming."

"You think so?" Ben contributed nonchalantly.

"Indeed! Oh, but of course you don't. Believe me, as a completely unrelated gentleman, she is quite the catch. Did you ever meet her mother?"

"Hm, no."

"I heard from your housekeeper that no one really knows who she was. Must be a great family mystery, eh? I can only assume pretty Stella inherited your aunt's aesthetically pleasing features. I can only pray her mother wasn't obese, then there may be hope for the daughter. She is quite fine. Physically, at least. I mean, I didn't talk to her much last night. She could be as dumb as soup, really. But if you don't care about intelligent conversation, that's easy to overlook. It's almost expected though, I suppose. All the pretty ones are dense—"

"No, she isn't," Ben interrupted, with more earnest than he intended to convey.

"What?"

"Dense. Stella is actually quite intelligent."

Granger smiled and nodded. "Is she now? A clever beauty. Well, in that case...how would you feel if I asked her to dinner?"

Ben scoffed. The thought settled in his mind, becoming rancid almost immediately. "I know better than to allow you to date any relative of mine."

"Oh, you'd love to have me in the family, old sport, and you know it."

Ben chuckled and rolled his eyes.

"How 'bout her? Would you object to my asking her to dinner?" Emily Grayer had woven through the luncheon to speak with Ben, and Granger set his eyes on her from the moment she entered the room.

"Hm," Ben hummed curiously. "I'm hardly standing in your way, my friend."

"Professor Caverly," she greeted. Her expression was lacking in her usual cheerfulness. She wrung her hands in hesitation, carefully gathering her words.

"Emily," Ben pressed. "What is it?"

"A man called from the police..." she began. "Something has happened."

Granger leaned in closer to hear, but Emily pulled Ben aside, farther away from Granger's curious ears, before continuing the message in a low whisper.

"The police found Miss Stella—she's fine now," she assured him, seeing the rise in his shoulders. "They took her home, but they want you to be there before they leave her. Mrs. Milton was insistent that you come home immediately."

Ben sighed deeply and looked over at Granger in exasperation. Granger raised his eyebrows, waiting for an explanation.

"What is it, Caverly?" he asked.

"The clever beauty."


As soon as the officer left, Ben shut the front door and dismissed Patricia. Stella sat strangely solemn on the sofa before him. Her hair was a mess, falling out of the bun that was once on the side of her head. Her hands were in her lap, nervously tugging at the long sleeves of the oversized jacket.

Her expression was peculiar.

It wasn't defiance.

It wasn't disdain.

It wasn't anything he had seen on her before but a strange concoction of fear and utter confusion. She was dazed, staring at nothing. Patricia's brief scolding about impropriety and tarnishing the family name had no effect on her. Not a single sardonic remark escaped her lips. Only resigned silence.

The officer had informed him that she was found on the side of the road and struck him when he attempted to offer assistance. The officer was gracious enough not to press assault charges but strongly suggested that Ben see that she is "*dealt with*" as soon as possible.

Before leaving them, he declared she had gone "*stark mad.*" Ben had his doubts about his unwarranted diagnosis, but he was beginning to believe Patricia's well-voiced theory of Stella's hunger for attention.

"What happened?" he asked her, trying to be gentle.

"The police officer told you," she answered without looking up.

"Yes, and now I am asking you. What happened to you?"

"Will you believe me?"

"I will most certainly try."

Slowly and apprehensively, she lifted her head and looked him directly in the eye. "I went into a book."

Ben frowned and placed both hands on his hips, straining for patience. "You went into...a book."

"The jacket...it tingled, and then I was in a huge library, and I met a little girl...then I—I opened a book that was humming and it sort of sucked me in. There was a wild dwarf—"

"A wild dwarf," Ben repeated softly.

"There were knights, and this Spanish fellow killed some other knight. There was...so much blood..." she stopped, swallowing hard.

"You went into a book," he said again, enunciating every word. Steadily, he inhaled. "Stella...I am trying exceptionally hard to be patient with you. But, you are making it quite difficult."

She didn't respond, but her eyes shifted from his.

"I sincerely hope that this—this acting out for attention ends very soon. Otherwise, this is going to be a very long five and a half months."

Still, no response.

Ben's shoulders fell.

"Stella," he snapped. His impatience was beginning to overpower him. "Are you understanding me?"

Her eyes suddenly snapped back up at him. "Yes," was all she said.

"Do you have anything to say in your own defense?" he demanded. "Anything at all?"

His tone startled her. He had moved past diplomacy and sounded out of character. His volume was raised, his expression tightened. She recognized that she just placed the last straw on the camel's back and it was breaking.

"You don't believe me," she muttered.

He hesitated, examining her face. Her story was outlandish and exaggerated, at best—how could he believe her?

"No." He shook his head. "You are overcome by your grief and frustration and...I...don't know what to do with you anymore."

Defeated, Stella's eyes returned to her hands. "I'm sorry." Without saying another word, she took off the jacket and handed it to him before leaving the room.

He stood holding the jacket, alone. He had never been so uncertain. He seldom lost his temper and rarely raised his voice—particularly to a woman. He was a commonly mild gentleman. What was it about Stella that changed him?

A migraine began to form in the back of his head. Deciphering Stella was a mental challenge for which he was not adequately equipped.

Before going to her room for the night, Stella lingered on the stairs, clutching the banister as she listened to Patricia consult with Ben. She was done fighting. *The incident*, as Patricia now called it, would brand her. Everyone would believe she had gone insane. And maybe she was, Stella considered.

No, she wasn't.

Stella knew what she saw, what she felt, what she heard. It was real. The blood, the blades, the confusion. All of it was real.

"Insulting dignified guests in your home is one thing, Benjamin—but inventing ridiculous stories and practically being arrested for assaulting a police officer! That is more than I can bear. As your housekeeper, and old friend, I strongly advise you to consider an earlier annulment," Patricia rambled passionately.

"Hm," Ben mumbled. Stella couldn't see him from where she stood, but she imagined him rubbing his forehead, the way he did when something was clawing at him. "The way this woman handles grief, Patricia...I am at a complete loss."

"Annul the marriage," Patricia urged.

He wasn't paying her much attention. "I mean, this is beyond anything I would have expected from her."

"She'll ruin you and your family name, Benjamin. If your father were alive, he would—"

"Well, he isn't, is he?" Ben cut her off. "This is my problem. If only Albert...I can't say I anticipated quite this much difficulty when I agreed to this."

Patricia sighed deeply. "So what will you do? Clearly, you won't go through with my idea."

"I'm a man of my word, Patricia. And I'm not going to let Albert's only daughter live in destitution. I think...the only thing we can do is...let her grieve. Wait it out. She could just need time."

*Time*, Stella thought to herself.

Was that all she needed?

She disagreed.

She needed a sincere ear to believe her. She needed her father. But, knowing that option was not available at the moment, she just needed to survive. As Ben said, there were five and a half months left in the arrangement.

Five and a half months of being perceived as mad.

Five and a half months of unanswered questions.

Alice had given her even more of those, and a less than satisfactory assortment of answers. *You're not the one*, she told her. Who was the one? And *what* was the one?

She said that Stella would come back again, but not alone. What did that mean? Who would go with her? *Certainly no one here*, she thought. *Not as long as they think I'm mad.*

She could almost hear Alice's voice quoting from her own "cover story," as they called it:

"You're mad, bonkers, completely off your head. But I'll tell you a secret. All the best people are."

After all the lights in the manor went out, Stella crept down the stairs like a shadow. Blending into the darkness and adapting to the silence, she swiftly moved through the door of Ben's library. With a fairly pristine memory as her ally, she lit the closest lamp—being careful not to draw Patricia's attention from down the hall—and hunted for the right title.

Given the vast number of books there were for her to choose from, *Le Morte d'Arthur* was surprisingly easy to find. Stella promptly opened the book and flipped through its dusty pages.

### Page 766

**AND THEY RODE SO LONG TILL THAT THEY CAME TO CAMELOT, THAT TIME CALLED WINCHESTER; AND THERE WAS GREAT PRESS OF KINGS, DUKES, EARLS, AND BARONS, AND MANY NOBLE KNIGHTS...**

As she scanned further, past the jousting, past Launcelot's wounds, past Gawaine discovering Launcelot's identity...still nothing. Nothing regarding an old Spanish knight, and certainly nothing about Mordred's death. Skipping to the end, she confirmed what she suspected: Mordred kills King Arthur.

But how could that be, if that old man murdered Mordred right before her eyes? *Perhaps he was only wounded*, she thought to herself.

No; his wounds were too deep and far too bloody for him to have survived. Clearly, something was wrong. Something she alone couldn't fix.

# 9

## THERAPEUTIC TRAGEDY

The first few weeks after the incident, rumors began to spread like the plague. Word of Stella's alleged mental breakdown made its way around the university but eventually simmered. The rumormongers let it all pass as an excusable event caused by her grief and seclusion.

Ben had not publicly connected Stella and Albert Towson, you see. No, instead, he told his colleagues that his unnamed uncle had merely passed away for fear that some would recognize Albert's name and unravel the charade.

Regardless of the sort of grief others believed her to have, Stella did not particularly appreciate the rationalization. But, in time, she too let it pass.

Everything around her returned to normal.

Everything but her.

She was more controlled, more silent, more reserved, and even behaved herself stoically on the few occasions she attended Ben's social events. Ben was rather unsettled.

Something was wrong. Her sky eyes no longer sparkled, and instead seemed to dim with submission. As happy as Stella's new behavior made Patricia, something did not sit right with Ben.

He was pleased to see the avoidance of further social blunders, but her soberness seemed just as unhealthy as her believed hallucinations. He noticed she spent even more time in the garden, thinking, reading, and keeping to herself. She only left the cottage grounds when Ben explicitly invited her to social events, and she only spoke when spoken to. She rarely smiled, and instead adopted a more reserved, contemplative countenance. For the first time in Ben's life, the silence was killing him.

He had forgiven the incident and regretted his initial treatment of her. He pitied her, but in a strange way. He found himself longing to see her smile again, and hear her laugh. It was what Albert would have wanted for her, but now it was becoming what Ben wanted as well.

The distance that had developed in the past month or so was even further and more torturous than when the arrangement first took place. He remembered the way she embraced him when he had first given her the jacket and how warm it felt. What little warmth there had been between them was now completely gone, and the jacket now rested in its previous home, on the armchair in his study.

Sitting in his office at the university, Ben decided that perhaps now was the time to finally look through Albert's box of books. He had been foolishly procrastinating, telling himself that he was too busy with work and dealing with Stella.

Admittedly, he was only afraid of what he would find. Stella's hallucinations had made him uneasy. The way she spoke of the incident reminded him of the way Albert spoke of his work. Though, if you had seen all that Albert had in his particular field, you would be just as passionate. But, as far as Ben was concerned, the man had been a simple Classics professor.

Regardless of Albert's renown in certain circles of the academic world, his work wasn't as serious and world-altering as he portrayed. He spoke of it with such reverence and devotion; some considered him "the amusing sort of mad". The time had come, however, for Ben to peer into the madness and discover what there was to revere.

"I don't think it's right."

Granger interrupted his study session with Albert's journals to suggest going out to lunch, as Stella had discontinued her university visits with Ben's homemade meals.

But, Ben was in no mood for a restaurant setting, so Granger bought some takeaway for the two of them and brought it to Ben's office. He sat with his legs crossed, in the way he did when he'd make a point.

"I'm serious, Caverly. I don't think it's right for a woman like that to be locked up in that house the way she is," he repeated, emphatically.

"She is not locked up," Ben assured him, continuing to pour through the journals on his desk and only half-listening to Granger's babble. "She stays at home on her own accord."

"Do you think that has anything to do with...the *incident?*"

"I think it has everything to do with it, but it's hardly your concern, Granger. She's, um, moving past it on her own."

"Hm," Granger said thoughtfully, leaning back in his chair. "I knew a lass like that once. She lost her brother, never recovered. Stayed in her room all day and all night. Maybe she should go through some sort of therapy."

"Yes, I think therapy would do your friend a world of good," Ben said, listlessly.

"No, Caverly. Stella. Maybe she should seek some sort of counseling."

Ben glanced up at him from the handwritten pages that were beginning to strain his eyes. "Stella is the last person in the world who would agree to see a psychiatrist. Trust me."

"Well, that's just because she doesn't do well with people who aren't familiar with her. What if she were to speak to someone she already knows? Someone she trusts and who knows her?"

Ben shut the journal and gave Granger his full, but skeptical, attention. "And who did you have in mind?"

An enlightening smile crept across Granger's face. "You may remember that I started in psychology, my friend."

"You can't be serious."

"Of course I'm serious. She already knows me. I wouldn't pressure her, you have my word. I'd just be someone with whom she can talk through her feelings. Someone completely objective."

Ben considered this. It wasn't a horrible idea. She certainly wasn't confiding in him, so perhaps by some chance, she would confide in Granger.

A foolish assumption, of course, but most of us learn these things through trial and error. The possibility of her trusting Granger more than Ben caused a twinge of envy, but he quickly pushed it aside, reminding himself that it was for her well-being.

So, that night, Granger accompanied Ben home for dinner. Granger tried his best to engage in conversation with Stella over the meal, but she was short and terse, as she had been of late, and resisted all of his pursuits. After they finished eating, Ben retired to his study in order to allow Granger a few moments to speak with Stella alone in the parlor. Patricia, being the nosy housekeeper she was, kept a close ear on the two of them from the dining area as she cleaned up.

"That Patricia is quite a cook, isn't she?" Granger commented, vainly endeavoring to trap her in conversation.

Stella shrugged but didn't reply. She sat down on the sofa and grabbed the nearest book. Ben didn't have to explain the reason Granger wanted to speak with her alone; she was raised an intuitive and observant woman. Granger had been trying to coax out her story since the incident occurred, but a keen woman can spot smarm a mile away.

She imagined he found her new vulnerability attractive and inviting, but she was far from obliging. Noting her disinterest, Granger sighed and sat down beside her. She glanced at him from the corner of her eye but remained unmoved.

"Ben tells me you're having a rather difficult time adjusting," he said plainly.

"Really," she muttered, turning the pages idly.

"And I'm sure you've been told," he continued, "Talking about it does help. So would you like to discuss it with a completely objective and understanding friend?"

At this, she shut the book and tilted her head in his direction. "Discuss what?"

He inched closer to her. "Whatever it is that you need to discuss. What's happened that has hurt you so deeply? Please, tell me your story."

After a long, scrutinizing moment, she sighed. "I suppose it would be best to finally confide in someone."

"Of course." His posture became more eager, thinking he finally passed a barrier.

Stella intertwined her fingers gravely and cleared her throat. "It's my husband."

Granger sat back in astonishment. "Your husband? I had no idea you were married."

She merely nodded; she could hear Patricia startle and drop a dish against the counter in the kitchen. "It has been a blissful marriage, but lately I've been very disturbed. You see, my husband has been convinced...by a friend...that I am having an affair."

"Well, who is your husband?"

"He's a General in the army. He thinks I'm unfaithful with his second-in-command."

"No!" Granger said, supportively. "Who could think that of you? Who's been telling him this?"

Straight-faced and sincere, Stella said, "Iago."

Stella watched Granger's face fall with the realization she was taunting him. Granger tried to contain his frustration and not roll his eyes. Instead, he sighed deeply and leaned a little closer.

"My, my, you truly are damaged. Well-read, to be sure. But....tragic."

He placed his hand on her thigh, where her eyes immediately followed. She cleared her throat threateningly. Looking back up at him while making bold eye contact, she took one of his fingers and pulled it back as far as she could. As he yelped in pain, Stella heard Patricia scrambling in the direction of the study, dutifully fetching Ben.

Stella stood up and backed away from the sofa. He quickly followed suit to apologize. "I'm sorry if I've offended you, Stella. My intent was only to comfort. In whatever way you need." He took a step forward, but before he could, Stella kneed him in the groin, causing him to crumble back on the sofa in pain.

Ben soon came hurrying into the room to see Stella standing over a clearly incapacitated Granger. "What is this?"

Stella straightened her back, preparing for the disappointed scolding, but to her surprise, Ben walked over to the sofa and lifted Granger roughly by the arm. He led him to the door, muttering something to Granger in a low, aggressive tone.

"Alright, Caverly!" Granger shook him off wildly when they reached the threshold.

"You lay a hand on her again, and you'll regret ever stepping foot in this house," Ben swore to him quietly, but menacingly.

Granger scoffed. "You know, Caverly—"

"Get out," Ben snapped, shutting the door powerfully behind him.

Turning back to the parlor, he saw that Stella looked uneasy and was almost cowering. "I'm sorry," she mumbled when he walked back into the room. "I should've handled that better."

"No," he stopped her. He put his hands on her shoulders, alarming her a bit, and looking tenderly in her anxious eyes. "Are you alright?"

She slowly nodded. "Yes. I'm fine."

"I am sorry. I shouldn't have left the room. I trusted him to talk to you, but I didn't think him capable of...well, you can see I am clearly not the best judge of character."

He stepped back to give her some space. He felt like a fool, not seeing his good friend as the scum he was, and justly so —for I am sure that you, as the reader, could have foreseen such idiocy. But, let's not dwell on Ben's lack of discernment; aren't we all so commonly blind to the faults of friends we care for and trust?

"I don't know, you're not so bad," Stella assured him.

He looked up at her. She gave him a small smile, which he couldn't help but return.

"You saw through me, didn't you?"

"No, I didn't," he nervously chuckled. "I still don't."

She nudged his arm and continued smiling. "You'll get there. If you're lucky, it'll be just in time for the annulment."

Her smile then faded, as she suddenly remembered the roughly four short months remaining. She had finally started feeling relatively comfortable. Ben made her feel safe and, over the course of the last two months, he had been so gentle and patient with her, despite the frustration he must have felt. She was sure he would be eager, pen at the ready, when the six-month deadline arrived. Stella has caused him so much trouble; she wouldn't blame him. She, however, wasn't sure she was ready to leave.

Stella studied her husband's face as he looked at her. When she first saw him again in the hospital in Boston, nothing about him really struck her. He had grown into a fairly average-looking man according to her typical standards. But, now, standing in front of her was a man who had proven himself to be far more honorable and caring than she expected. It's funny how quickly attraction can hit you, and on a face you've seen so ordinarily before. He was suddenly handsome, with caramel brown hair and beautiful blue-green eyes.

Then, the reminder of that foreboding annulment flashed once again in her mind, causing her train of thought to abruptly derail.

"I think I need some air," she nodded gratefully to him before heading out to the garden.

The moment Stella was out of earshot, Ben called for Patricia. She was by his side in a matter of seconds, as she was conveniently  around the corner since the moment Granger left. She proceeded to pick up the book Stella had been reading, which had fallen on the floor during the scuffle. She tidied up the parlor while muttering her inevitable opinions.

"That scoundrel," was the first thing she said. "I hope you gave him a piece of your mind, Benjamin. That is simply appalling. Poor girl."

"Patricia," he started. "I need you to do something for me."

"Of course, what is it, dear?"

"Have, um...have some rose bushes put in the garden."

# 10

## ANNE'S BEEF WELLINGTON

Stella breathed in the comforting aroma of the new roses in the garden. Something about the smell took her back to early childhood, surrounding her with soothing nostalgia. She sat for hours on a sturdy wooden bench and soaked in the scent, the feeling, and the clarity of the garden. It was her haven. She gazed at the beautiful rose bushes surrounding the bench, thinking about the past few days.

She didn't think Ben took much notice of her or her daily habits, but his ordering Patricia to add roses to the garden was indeed curious. Her mind dwelt on it for a few moments before her gaze shifted to a second-floor window. Patricia had opened the curtains to let in the sunlight and was babbling cheerfully to someone.

For the majority of the time she had been at Caverly Manor, Stella had given up on sneaking into the forbidden room upstairs—whether because of the distraction of all that had occurred or because of Patricia's constant, hawk-like surveillance. Now, her curiosity finally got the best of her. Once Patricia's indoor chores were finished, and she started for the garden to weed, Stella snuck upstairs like a mischievous child.

All of the other bedroom doors were opened, as usual, to be aired out for the day. She saw the light from the window coming out underneath the mysterious door, but there was no movement. Slowly, she opened the door, holding her breath in anticipation.

Unlike the rest of the house, this room had only one small bookshelf. It was an immaculate, tidy room with more of a feminine touch. Accessories, such as a changing screen, a matching dresser, and vanity, made it clear that this was the room of a lady.

"No need to be shy, dear." A woman rested weakly in the queen-sized bed in the center of the room. She looked a bit like Ben—gracefully angular, aristocratic features, golden brown hair, and blue-green eyes. She was roughly Patricia's age, or perhaps a bit older, but with a much kinder face. She looked as if she could be Ben's mother. The woman smiled faintly, but sweetly, from the head of the bed. "You must be this Stella I've heard so much about."

Stella stepped further into the room but maintained her grip on the door behind her. "And...you must be the Mrs. Caverly I've heard nothing about."

The woman chuckled. "My dear, you are just as charming as Ben described."

"Charming?" Stella repeated in confusion, mirroring Mrs. Caverly's chuckle. "I doubt that."

Mrs. Caverly lifted her hand and beckoned Stella over to the bed. Stella slowly obeyed, smelling the fresh lavender that sat on the bed table beside her. "I would have greeted you ages ago had it not been for my....poor health."

"You're ill?" Stella innocently inquired.

"Oh...my health has not been the same since...I lost my dear husband. Some days I can hardly sit up in bed, let alone leave my room. Ben does his best to boost my spirits, but I admit, I have the tendency to be absurdly stubborn. The dear boy thought it best to keep us away from one another—apparently, he fears that such a short-lived attachment would not do well for my nerves....he means well....."

Stella remembered calling Ben cruel for locking someone away in this room all day. A dreadful feeling of guilt formed in her stomach, and she regretted her own foolishness. "He takes good care of you," she noted.

Mrs. Caverly smiled. "Yes. I have been blessed with the most compassionate son. He takes very good care of those he cares deeply for." She touched Stella's hand gently. "You seem much happier than Patricia described."

Stella looked down at her hands and chuckled in spite of herself. "Well, I've been trying."

"So has he."

Stella glanced up at her. "Trying what?"

Mrs. Caverly lifted herself slightly against her pillow with much effort. "Ben," she grunted, "has difficulty expressing himself—something his father was cursed with as well."

"Yes, well, lucky for him he only has to fake a smile for four months and a week longer."

Mrs. Caverly raised her eyebrows as a sly gleam flickered across her face. "You think Ben is counting down as you are?"

"Oh, I'm sure he is."

"Ha, Stella, I can assure you....my son is a much worse liar than you believe him to be."

"What do you mean?"

"Ben is a man of few words. He doesn't waste time talking about subjects he doesn't consider important to him." Stella stared at her strangely. As if answering her unspoken question, Mrs. Caverly smiled at her again. "I have heard many splendid things about you, Stella—and I think you know they didn't come from Patricia."

Stella laughed. "No, I'm sure they didn't." Fiddling with a loose thread on her cotton dress, she released an uncertain sigh. "Ben's just...being a good sport. If you left this room, Mrs. Caverly, you'd know. I'm quite a handful."

"Please call me Anne, my dear," she insisted. "And, you are continually wrong, you know. I haven't formed that impression at all."

"That's sweet, Mrs...Anne. But, he's probably just trying not to bother you."

"Don't tell me what my son is trying to do," Anne scolded with a smile. "I raised the boy, you know. Like I said, he is a horrific liar. He may seem reserved and distant, but he does feel. Quite deeply, in fact. He deals with emotions very privately. Hardly lets anyone in, even his own mother. It took losing his dear father for him to begin confiding in me. Though I don't think I should say anything further, or I'll embarrass him. Such a sweet boy," she said softly to herself and folded her covers over.

95

She didn't seem ill enough to be bed-ridden, in Stella's opinion, but she imagined her weakness was more psychosomatic than physical. Anne's emotional state did seem to change through the course of the conversation.

"Yes..." Stella's eyes returned to her hands, thinking of the roses in the garden. "He really is, isn't he?"

Anne stroked Stella's cheek lovingly, the way Stella imagined her mother did when she was very young. It was a knowing touch—for Anne Caverly knew, just as I have come to realize: human beings need one another. As much as an individual may try to deny it, the truth remains the same. And it was a truth that both Ben and Stella would soon learn. Then, without warning, Anne flung her covers back and sat up straighter.

"What are you doing?" Stella asked in confusion.

Anne flashed yet another sly smile. "Ben will be home in a few hours. We are going to make supper for your husband."


Pouring over Albert's journals all day, without so much as a lunch break, took much longer than Ben intended. Stella had not exaggerated when she said that Albert recorded everything. His accounts were detailed and lent considerable insight into life in the Towson household. He came to better understand everything from Albert's relationship with his daughter to the decades of grieving he had done after suffering the loss of his precious wife.

The one thing that he did not intend to discover, however, he stumbled across shortly after missing his last lecture of the day.

It was a leather-bound journal, like all the rest of them, but this one was different; it was battered, and the leather was much more faded than the others as if it had left the safety of Albert's office more often than not. In fact, a leather strap was wound around it, making it ready for travel. The binding remained strong and intact, but the pages were ragged and stained.

The entries were nothing like any of the other journals either. The first entry was dated as far back as the year 1939, at the start of the Second World War.

According to the entry, Albert came in contact with a strange man who told him a peculiar story. It was a story about a trader who conned a young man with some magic beans, but soon paid the price for his greed and was given a chance for redemption.

"*Keepers of happily ever afters,*" Ben whispered to himself. That's what Albert called them. It sounded like a fairytale, a bedtime story. Sorcerers and magic cloaks and all sorts of fanciful things. Yet, something about it felt familiar to him.

Albert mentioned the leather from the trader's ill-gotten gains and the significance of it. He said that the old man had enchanted it. The sorcerer had enchanted it. Ben fumbled through more pages in an attempt to find a reference to the source of this fairytale but in vain. Albert wrote about it just as frankly and honestly as he had of his daughter's life. As if it were fact. Ben liked to think that Albert was incapable of insanity, as wise and intelligent a man as he was, but at first glance, his story seemed more than implausible.

Still, he read on.

The more he read, the clearer the stories became. He seemed to learn just as Albert did. The man had told Albert to put on his cloak and, after Albert had done so, an eerily familiar thing happened. Suddenly, Stella's hallucination seemed less like fiction invented to gain attention.

The two accounts were nearly identical—a library, a little girl, magic books. Ben couldn't understand it. If he were to believe what he was reading, he would have to believe Stella's story. Perhaps she wasn't quite so mad. Because, if she was truly mad, then Albert was mad—and, based on every conversation he had ever had with the man toward the end of his life, Albert was nothing less than sound of mind. And to that, I can most certainly attest.

Toward the middle of the last half of the journal, the parchment changed. It became less aged and even smelled fresh. It was a peculiar thing, but all the more peculiar were the words he read. "*I have always thought that weather was a curious thing...*"

The deeper he dove into the words before him, the more confused he became. He read his own name, as well as Stella's and Albert's—much like you have done, reader.

How was this possible?

The journal had been in Albert's box throughout the entirety of the most recently recorded events, with no logical way of anyone transcribing them on these pages. Even Stella's alleged mythical experience was laid out in words before him, affirming the truth she had told him. As he anxiously continued, even nearing the final few pages, a knock came at his office door. It was soft but no less interrupting.

Ben rose from behind his desk and, almost in a daze, answered his door. A tall, dark sandy-haired man with deep, clear eyes stood in the doorway wearing a very gentle smile and a scholarly tailored suit. Ben stared for a moment before coming to his senses.

"Um, can I help you?" he asked.

The man just chuckled softly. "Perhaps."

His voice was very smooth and comforting. Without saying another word, the man walked past Ben and directed himself into the room. Ben spun around to follow him in surprise when he saw something that bewildered him even more. There, in the armchair in front of his desk, appeared an elderly fellow with a discerning brow. He looked very much like an aged edition of the first man, with the exception of his short beard and wiry spectacles. His hair was a light grey, and his eyes were just as deep, clear, and friendly as the other gentleman, giving both of them a rather distinguished presence. Anyone would have assumed they were just another pair of academic colleagues walking the halls of the university.

"Um, excuse me, but I am quite busy at the moment. I am sure if you contact the, um, department secretary, she could set you up with an appointment," Ben scrambled for words.

"You say that quite a bit, don't you?" the elderly gentleman asked. He sat very comfortably in the armchair as if it were his throne. Much like the other man, his voice was smooth and melodic, almost as silk.

"I, um, I beg your pardon?"

"That's it," he nodded. "Um. As if you're not sure if what you're saying is worth saying."

Ben wrinkled his eyebrows in confusion. "I don't usually say it if it isn't worth saying. And, um—I'm sorry, who are you?"

The younger gentleman chuckled again. Something was apparently amusing to him, something that Ben was missing altogether. He idly roamed the room, reading the various titles on all the books throughout. "Comparative literature," he commented, in his curious way. "Admirable field."

"Yes...thank you."

"There is something about literature, don't you think? One can become so empowered by simply throwing themselves entirely into the words on a page." The elderly man smiled.

"Indeed," his younger friend replied. He then wandered closer to Ben's desk, moving around its puzzled owner. "This one is probably my favorite," he added, picking up the worn journal that lay open.

"Who are you?" Ben repeated, more firmly this time.

"Albert is one of my favorites, as well," the elderly man remarked, fondly. "Never takes anything for granted. Belief comes so naturally to him—it has from the beginning."

"No it wasn't, father. He had quite his share of obstacles first."

The older man sighed. "Yes, well, not everyone is quite so teachable."

"You knew Albert?" Ben looked from one man to the other, surprised yet eager to mine them for information.

The old man nodded slowly, his smile never fading. Something about him calmed Ben, dissolving all suspicion and discomfort. "Yes, of course, we know Albert. And he always speaks so highly of you, Ben. He all but knew it would come to this."

"Come to—come to what? Are you talking about the book? Keepers? All that is real?" Ben suddenly became very excited. Something about these men assured him that all of his thousands of questions could finally be answered, considering his only other hope of explanations died nearly three months ago.

The old man's eyes glistened a little as he looked at the younger man, who was apparently his son. He mumbled something in a language Ben didn't recognize before turning back to face him. "I believe Myk, here, could answer all your questions much more simply than I could."

Ben turned to Myk, who only put the journal down and looked back at him expectantly. "I think he knows it all now," he said. "He just needs to work on believing it. Tell me, Benjamin, what did dear Albert leave for you before he left?"

"Hm," Ben pressed his lips together. "And here I thought it was pronounced '*Mike*'...Myk...Mykolas. *The most fierce, peaceful warrior I have ever met.*"

Myk smiled. "Oh, I'm flattered."

"That's what Albert called you." Ben then pointed to the elderly man in the armchair. "Which would make you..." he struggled to say the words, "...Yonas. The Author. The High King. Creator of the Keepers. You are the old sorcerer from Albert's story." Ben frowned. The old man didn't seem quite as decrepit as the sorcerer he had pictured from the story.

Yonas just kept smiling. "No, no. That was this old boy here." He gestured to Myk, who had returned to skimming through Ben's bookshelves.

Ben frowned, glancing over at Myk. While Yonas was far from feeble and crippled, as Albert had described, Myk was even farther. There was more than could be seen on the surface, apparently. Ben remembered references of shapeshifting and the manipulation of a beholder's perception, but his mind was still attempting to sift through the words and their meanings.

"But you can't be real, can you?" Ben chuckled nervously.

"Can I not?" Myk asked, still distractedly browsing. "I don't think you have as many questions as you think you do, Benjamin. Because, against your better judgment, you know. And I don't think we have to prove anything for you to know it because that isn't why we stopped by."

"Then why are you here?" Ben looked to Yonas. The old sage merely shrugged and turned his own attention to his son, who answered,

"We feel it customary to personally welcome every first of an era since their predecessors are rarely around for their orientation." Occasionally, Myk reached for a book, only to idly flip through the pages and return it to its shelf. "Embarking on a new era can be a rather daunting task. So we like to show our support." Finally he glanced at Ben with a smile. "We're quite courteous in that way."

"Indeed we are," Yonas agreed.

"We would have been in earlier, but we had some business to attend to. Thankfully Stella's little adventure adjusted our schedule. The timing was right, as usual."

"What...." Ben exhaled softly.

"I thought you read the book, Benjamin," Yonas mused. He smiled cryptically as if waiting for something wonderful to happen.

"I....thought so, too."

"Small doses are necessary, Mykolas." Yonas casually took off his spectacles, cleaning them with the sleeve of his sweater.

"Yes. Well, what do you actually remember then?" Myk prodded.

Ben looked at Yonas and then back at Myk again. Myk was right. Against Ben's better judgment, he couldn't deny what was in front of him. And if he couldn't deny what was in front of him, he couldn't deny what he had read.

"I know..." he breathed, shaking his head and whittling down to the basic truths he gathered from the many journal entries. "Albert saved stories."

"Realms," Myk corrected. "And he was quite good at it." He tended to gush about his friend, of course. He and Albert had grown particularly fond of one another during Albert's Keepership, though they had quite a rough beginning. But I've found that initial friction can often prepare the soil for the most blooming friendships.

"Once he moved past his personal crusade, Albert was unstoppable." Myk placed his hands in his trouser pockets, leaning back in reminiscence. "He protected more realms on his own than any single Keeper."

"Protected them from an evil sorcerer with a grudge," Ben continued.

"Korbl is far more than simply an evil sorcerer with a grudge, Benjamin. He is much more dangerous than that."

Ben rubbed his forehead, closing his eyes thoughtfully. "Clearly. He orchestrated the death of Albert's wife and destroyed her entire realm–if the story proves accurate."

"It does. I was there."

"Does Stella know about that, by the way? Who her mother was—what happened to her?"

"No, she doesn't; Albert never told her. But she will know, in time."

"And everything in there is true?" Ben pointed at the journal. He still grasped helplessly for further verification that he was not losing his mind. "Korbl invading other books— realms? Keepers and their magic jackets and destinies?"

"It is all true. Everything. Toward the end, I think, he knew it'd be you. He'd read too much Arkis literature to deny the similarities between..."

"What? What would be me?" Ben asked in alarm. He retreated slightly, leaning up against the end of his desk for support.

"Well, the next Arch Keeper, of course," Myk gestured to him, encouragingly.

"Arch Keeper?"

"Yes, Benjamin. A leader of Keepers. Destined to—"

"Yes, yes, I read that part. But...it isn't me."

"It is," Yonas contributed, suddenly very reverent and emphatic. There was a momentary silence as Ben digested all of the information. He rubbed his head again and looked at the ground. "I know what you're thinking, Mr. Caverly. There is no shame in thinking you are inadequate. It is something all true heroes encounter."

"Thinking is the talking of the soul with itself. Even if it's lying," Myk chimed in.

"Lying horribly, in fact," Yonas agreed.

Myk placed his hands in his pockets again and sighed. "There are writings of you in the Arkis, to be sure, but I do believe Albert would have figured it out without them. He always had a feeling about you. The curse of mortality is the inability to see true, full potential, but he saw it." Momentarily, Myk glanced down at Yonas and added, "I can't deny seeing a bit of myself in him, you know." Then, turning back to Ben, he continued, "He's been preparing you from the beginning, you know. Nudging you toward studying literature, teaching you to open your mind—even Stella."

Ben's eyes shot back up to Myk's deep face. "Stella? What does Stella have to do with this?"

This time, Myk's cryptic smile only provoked more questions. "You will soon begin to understand."

"At least tell me why—"

"Benjamin," he cut him off. "I swear to you, you will know all, in time. Why don't you pace your understanding, for once in your life? Your busy mind will thank you." Myk then picked up the journal and handed it to him. "Just don't lose this."

As Ben stared down at the book, he heard nothing but silence. The two men were gone.

*Just don't lose this.*

Albert knew it all—it had to all be in here, he thought to himself. All the answers to all his questions. Without doubting it, or anything he had just experienced, he sat back down behind his desk and reread every word.

It was later than he expected when he finished rereading the entire journal, but he decided to walk home anyway and took the chance to ponder further on the events of the day.

He now understood Albert and was beginning to understand Stella as well. His mind was burning with curiosity, which only heightened when he got to the front door of Caverly Manor and inhaled a strong scent of fresh biscuits and his mother's famous Beef Wellington.

Patricia had never mastered his mother's recipe for Beef Wellington and had given up on trying long ago. The only explanation he could conjure was a bit improbable. Slowly, Ben opened the front door in anticipation.

At this point, he thought nothing could possibly surprise him, but he found that he was once again wrong. The dinner table was set for three, candles in the centerpiece lit the room, and his own mother sat at the head of the table in mid-conversation with an unseen voice.

"...and I did say that you wouldn't over-cook it, didn't I, my dear? You're a very quick study. It's a wonder you never bothered going to school," she was saying, straining her neck toward the direction of the kitchen.

"Mum?" Ben mumbled.

She glanced over at him, slightly startled, but smiled enthusiastically. "Ben, dear! You're later than we expected."

He gradually dropped his coat and briefcase in the hallway and made his way toward his shockingly exuberant mother. She shot up from behind the table and glided to kiss him affectionately on the cheek.

"You're...downstairs," he observed.

"Excellent observation, darling," she teased. "Now, what took you so long?"

"I-I stayed after to finish up a bit of work. What's going on?"

"You sure this isn't over-cooked—?" Stella entered the dining room, carrying a tray of Beef Wellington, but froze when she saw Ben. "Oh, Ben. I didn't hear you come in." She looked nervous, but he couldn't quite understand why.

"Your wife made you dinner," Anne informed in a very matter-of-fact tone.

"My—"

"Now, sit down, dear, and we'll get started."

Ben allowed Anne to lead him with childlike obedience to the head of the table. Stella finished setting out the food and sat to the right of Ben. After saying grace, the three of them indulged in the meal Stella had carefully prepared while Anne went on about how Stella was such an eager and absorbent student.

"She's simply a natural, Ben. And she mastered my recipes much quicker than poor Patricia..."

Ben nodded throughout her story, chewing on the surprisingly successful Beef Wellington and fresh bread. "Have you been up all day?"

"Well, yes, most of it. Stella and I had quite an afternoon, didn't we, my dear?" she reached across the table to rub Stella's hand encouragingly. Stella gulped down her glass of water, nodding in agreement. "Doesn't she look lovely tonight, Benjamin?"

Ben smiled at his mother's affectionate nature. Though now soaking in Stella's appearance, he did notice a certain brightness about her. She had even put on her light blue dress which, he noticed, was her favorite. She was also wearing a tasteful amount of makeup that made her big, stormy eyes even more striking than before. They were a little brighter now, those eyes. A silly smile lingered on his face as he managed to say, "Yes, very lovely."

"You know," Anne continued, pushing the conversation forward, "I knew Albert quite well. He was a pleasant-looking fellow, I suppose, but I must say—you look nothing like him, Stella."

Stella cleared her throat and shrugged. "What can I say? I used to joke that I was adopted, but my father didn't seem to like that very much."

"I'll bet you look just like your mother. Do you remember what she looked like?"

"Oh no, she died when I was very little."

"That's right, she did. I'm sorry."

"It's not your fault," Stella answered, absently cutting her meat into smaller pieces.

"Well, your father was an exceptional man, to have raised you so well," Anne smiled, gently.

Stella smiled back. "Yes, he was pretty wonderful."

Another moment or two passed while the three of them chewed quietly in comfortable silence. The reason escaped him, but Ben could no longer focus on the wonderful Beef Wellington. Instead, he couldn't take his eyes off of Stella—so many thoughts and questions and conclusions ran through his head, connecting her, and the incident, to everything Myk had confirmed.

After they all finished eating, Stella stood to collect the dishes, but Ben stopped her.

"I can get them," he told her. She crinkled her mouth to one side, hesitant of how to respond, but then smiled.

"How about we both do it?" she suggested.

He chuckled lightly. "I suppose that's acceptable."

Anne sat back and watched the two of them clear the table, all the while grinning in satisfaction. "Why don't the two of you take a walk—perhaps to the cinema? I can finish up here."

"You are going to do all of the dishes?" Ben questioned.

"Oh please, Ben. I gave Patricia the night off, but I'm sure she'd love to finish them up in the morning when she returns." She walked toward both of them and guided them ambitiously toward their coats. "You two should get some fresh air and exercise. It's always healthy after a good meal."

"Alright, alright, mother. We're going," Ben assured her. He helped Stella with her coat, being sure to grab Albert's old leather jacket and tucked the journal safely in its pocket.

With his hand at the small of her back, he led Stella out the door and onto the sidewalk. They started for town, conversing casually and a bit uncomfortably about a variety of subjects, ranging from dinner to her appreciation for the rose bushes in the garden. All was well, but Ben yearned to discuss her father and his journal.

"Did you ever accompany your father on any of his business trips?" he pried.

She smirked, sticking her cold hands in her coat pockets. "Um, no," she answered, startled by the frankness of his question. "I never accompanied my father on any of his business trips."

"So...you never actually knew where he went?"

"He always told me, but I never went with him." Stella slowed her pace, suspicious of where the conversation might be heading.

"What did he tell you about your mother?"

This made her stop completely. She stared at him, trying to figure out what sparked this line of questioning. "Why?"

Ben hesitated, feeling the journal in his coat nagging at him. "I have just...been reading a lot—a lot about your father's...work. How much did he tell you about it?"

"Why are you asking all these questions?"

"I'm just..." he cleared his throat, "...I'm just trying to figure out how much you knew of what your father really did."

Stella crinkled her mouth to one side again and then resumed walking. "Why? Was he a commie spy or something? Look, I know my father didn't tell me everything, but he never lied to me."

"I know that. In fact, I think he may have told you more than you realize."

"What do you mean?"

This time, Ben stopped to face her. "I need you to tell me everything that happened to you the night of the....uh, *incident*."

Stella slowly shook her head in disbelief. "You didn't care before. I've tried not to talk about it for weeks. If you're mocking me—"

"No, no, no," he put his arms out carefully, preventing her from stepping in front of him. "I would never mock you. I am entirely serious. I need to know every detail."

She paused for a moment, eyes darting back and forth, studying his face for any sign of guile. "Okay," she breathed.

And she told him. Every detail, as he requested. He knew the story. He read it. But hearing her describe it made it seem even more real. In his mind, her story was in line with Albert's, with a few notable differences, of course.

"Wait," he said when she finished. "You went into *Le Morte d'Arthur*?"

"That's what it said."

"And the knight you saw killed. What was his name, again?"

"Mordred."

Ben frowned. "Mordred is intended to kill Arthur. He couldn't have died at the tournament."

Stella shrugged. "I know. I don't remember that as part of the story either, but it happened."

"Tell me again how it all happened."

"Mordred being killed?"

"No, no. The actual going into the book. You said that the jacket tingled?"

"Yes, sort of. I was wearing it, and it got really warm and then started to....tingle. It's a little hard to explain."

Ben started toward a nearby bench they had reached just outside of town and took off his own coat and the blazer he wore underneath, setting both of them on the bench. He then put on the leather jacket he had been carrying on his arm and turned back to an amused Stella.

"You put it on like this?"

"Yes, that's how one usually wears jackets," she giggled.

"Well, I just...I was just curious," he said softly, slightly embarrassed. "How long did it take to start tingling?"

She stepped closer to him and made her crinkled expression again. "Mmm...it took a while, actually. I think I walked about a mile before it did anything. But when it started —"

"Warm and then tingly or warm and tingly all at once?"

Stella cocked her head to one side. This was beginning to feel silly. "Well, it was sort of a warm feeling that became tingly."

Ben's expression suddenly changed. It went quickly from curious to alarmed. "Like this?" he asked, holding out his arm for her to touch.

She touched the jacket sleeve gingerly and felt a rush of that newly familiar feeling. She looked earnestly at Ben, with a face that knew exactly what sort of excitement was soon to follow.

# Part Two
## Something is Starting

# 11

## A Keeper of Happily Ever Afters

Ben couldn't quite understand how it had happened. All he could recall was the leather of the jacket tingled and glowed, and in a second, they were somewhere else. Stella pulled herself closer to him, her body jolting forward from the transit. Ben's grip around her shoulders was tight and uncertain. but once he became aware of their new surroundings, he didn't let go, no matter how uncomfortably close they stood.

Stella exhaled, laughing at his utter dismay. "This is what I told you about!" She tugged on his arm excitedly, like a child at a zoo. "We're in the Arkis!"

Still in a daze, Ben only vaguely heard her excited chattering. He tried to cognitively focus on everything around him, telling himself that it was real. The shelved walls, the winding staircase, the platforms, the houseplants, the armchairs, the desks...the books!

They were unlike any books he had ever seen. Each had a presence of its own, like little souls resting comfortably in rows.

His eyes were drawn to the fireplace, a short distance from where they were standing. And there sat the little girl, with her messy blonde curls, intently reading a book on the floor in front of the burning, blue flame.

"What...?" Ben muttered, finding himself speechless.

A Keeper's first time in the Arkis can be quite jarring. I, myself, unintentionally held my breath for almost two full minutes before I remembered to exhale.

"That's exactly what I said," Stella whispered. She followed his gaze to the little girl and smiled. "Alice, I think I found the one you were talking about."

The little girl was slightly startled when she heard Stella's voice. She spun around and ran toward them with her arms open. She hugged Stella's legs tightly, squealing, "Miss Stella's back!"

Stella was taken aback by Alice's enthusiasm, but rubbed the girl's head affectionately, peering up at Ben. "This is Alice."

"I see," he responded hesitantly.

"Clancy kept telling me you would come, but I'm not very patient," Alice told him, now hugging Ben's legs. "He said to keep an eye out for you because you're very important. Mr. Albert told me so many good things—and all of them true! He told me how tall you were, the color of your hair, and how Miss Stella looks so much like The Lady—I never met Miss Stella's mum, so I pretend she looks like her too. And now you and Miss Stella can both have such fun together—oh!" she suddenly exclaimed. "I kept the book out for you."

She then bounced back to her spot in front of the fireplace like a young puppy playing fetch. She picked up the book she had been reading and brought it back to Ben. "Here."

"This is—"

"*Le Morte d'Arthur*," Stella finished for him. "Thank you, Alice."

Ben sifted through the pages studiously, trying to remember what Stella and Albert had said was supposed to happen next.

"Myk said to hurry up. So there it is," Alice pointed at the book obviously.

"But how do I—?" As he began, the book burst with life and the jacket tingled once more. Stella's eyes lit up again, and she instinctively grabbed Ben's arm.

Something to note concerning the jacket: of its many qualities, it also tends to be quite oracular. Not only can this phenomenon transport someone from one realm to another, but its timing and location are always divinely expedient. For example, when Ben and Stella entered Le Morte d'Arthur, they didn't just appear in any old place. They appeared precisely when and where their presence proved to be serendipitous.

In this case, that precise when and where suited the poor, old pseudo-knight's necessity. In an open clearing of the forest, an enemy patrol of sorts had traveled far too close to the borders of King Arthur's kingdom. They carried no identifying insignias, nor did they wear any special emblems suggesting their origin. To an ignorant onlooker, the beings that filled this glade were as generic and untraceable as could be. And our Spanish friend, after miraculously escaping the onslaught of Mordred's angered comrades, found himself wandering into this unfortunate clearing.

The five armed beings were adorned in black cloaks, with thin dark armor contoured with light grey lining. Their thick hoods covered their heads, while a small section of armor hung delicately in front of their faces, shielding any hope of recognizing discernible features. All that could be seen were their fierce glares—some bright and piercing, but most clouded with peculiar staining of the skin around the eyes. They spotted the knight and advanced with their weapons drawn. The Spaniard's pathetic sword was all that stood between him and his inevitable defeat.

But here, however, is where Ben and Stella fortuitously appeared—directly between the brave knight and his attackers. Still stunned from travel, Ben momentarily adjusted to what was now in front of him and almost instinctively grabbed the most dangerous weapon he could find: a long, thick branch that dangled off of a nearby tree. With skill and agility that came almost naturally, Ben warded off the aggressive foe, strategically defending Stella from any harsh blows. Just as instinctively, Stella searched for her own means of defense. However, their Spanish ally had different ideas.

"No, my lady!" he shouted chivalrously over the ruckus, stopping her from picking up a branch. "We shall defend you!"

He fearlessly, however gracelessly, fought by Ben's side. His flailing limbs occasionally intersected Ben's offenses, but they were patiently averted. Stella stood reluctantly on the sidelines, dodging when they dodged and mirrored what she thought should have been their every move, now and then exclaiming, "To the left!" or "He's on your right!" She watched the Spaniard with particular amusement. His foolishness and humor seemed so recognizable to her, but she couldn't place it.

Her attention, however, was ultimately drawn to Ben. She had never viewed him as combative or even proactive, and yet he fought with such vigor and stamina that she couldn't help but be impressed. Ben's stances were strong, properly protecting himself from every offensive maneuver that came his way. The fencing lessons forced upon him in his adolescence finally came to his aid.

He masterfully kept the five soldiers at bay, but they soon viewed the Spaniard as the easier target and zeroed in. The first assailant lunged his sword toward the Spaniard's weak armor, but Ben quickly stepped in front of him, blocking the strike with the thick branch. Unfortunately, the branch was no match for the man's sharp sword, and the blade connected with its target.

Stella jumped and released a soft cry as she heard Ben grunt. She covered her mouth with her small hands, completely stupefied. She saw the Spaniard gasp wide-eyed, but more in amazement than remorse. Stella craned her head to better see the horror.

But Ben still stood. The assailant turned pale, swaying as if faint.

Ben's wound was nowhere to be seen.

It was only then that Ben looked down to see that the leather jacket he wore had somehow transformed into a vest of fitted leather armor. It was unlike anything he had ever seen. The leather was thick, to be sure, but how could it be so impenetrable?

His opponent stared, astounded, at what he saw before him. I suppose astounded is not quite right. His expression leaned more to the side of momentarily caught off guard due to a lack of updated information.

Whoever these men were, they had not expected the man in the magic leather to arrive quite this soon. Remarkably, as the attacker stepped back, Stella observed a much more shapely figure than she expected from a soldier. Without so much as a single verbal order given, all of the attackers retreated, scurrying their way back into the trees.

Stella ran to Ben, who was still frozen. He didn't know what had shaken him more, the miraculous blow or the sinister look in the attacker's dark eyes.

"Are you alright?" he asked her.

His voice was slow and precise, as it was when he was filled with uncertainty. He had never witnessed anything so miraculous in all his life.

Considering her own previous experience with the jacket, very little surprised Stella. "Yes, I'm fine," she chuckled. She couldn't help but smile. The jacket had never conformed to her body as it did to Ben's. She even more firmly began to believe that he was the one to which Alice referred. "Are you okay? That was amazing!"

Ben nodded, but his eyes were still full and contemplative, scanning the leather vest. "I don't know—"

"Truly, you are a god," the Spaniard broke in. He dropped his sword and reverently knelt at Ben's feet. "Or a sorcerer sent to guide me on my quests."

Embarrassed, Ben lifted the knight up by his arm. "Oh no, please. I have...no idea how this happened..." he lied. He knew exactly how it happened. It still sounded bizarre to him.

"It was my father's jacket," Stella said plainly. "I guess he wasn't kidding when he said it was your inheritance. Fits you perfectly."

"But, I can't be a Keeper, I—"

"A Keeper?" The word felt so fitting on her lips, it made her smile again. Albert's familiar words returned to her mind. "...of happily ever afters."

Ben sighed, relaxing his shoulders and dropping the broken tree branch. From the sound of it, he didn't have much left to explain. The expression on Stella's face was both reassuring and intimidating. Without having any formal knowledge of all that sentence entailed, she already understood more than he did.

The Spaniard, in blissful ignorance, stood eagerly, sheathing his sword. "Truly, my lord, you are destined for greatness."

"Stella, I—" Ben's explanation was cut off by a sharp voice behind them.

"Stay where you are!" the voice barked.

The three of them froze.

"Identify yourselves."

They turned to see four knights adorned in bright, silver armor. They were appropriately regal, wearing emblems on the saddles of their horses and the fronts of their shields. Their polished swords were wielded and aimed in unison at the strangers.

When no one replied, the commanding knight repeated himself threateningly. "Speak! Who are you?"

Stella watched Ben inhale deeply before he stepped forward with unprecedented confidence. "I am Lord Caverly, and this is my wife, Princess Stella of Faegrian."

The word wife incited a strange feeling as he said it, but Stella seemed more alarmed by the title he suddenly bestowed upon her. She scrutinized his face, but it betrayed nothing. No sign of guile, nor sarcasm. He said it so easily as if he weren't bluffing.

"I've been promoted to wife, huh?" she mumbled under her breath. Ben cleared his throat.

The speaking knight returned his sword to its sheath and bowed his fair head respectfully. His eyes were like ice, much like his words as he spoke. "I am Sir Agravaine. My apologies, my lord—princess," he nodded toward Stella. "I am afraid, by orders of the king, you have found yourself in the company of a wanted man. Wanted for the vicious murder of a Knight of the Round Table."

As an aside: it is quite nice when medieval characters accommodate the modern story-traveler, isn't it? Not nearly as many "thees", "thous", and "thines" as you might expect. If by chance, you were curious, in such cases as French or Spanish or any other foreign literature, part of the advantage of the enchanted leather is the language accommodation. Whatever the native tongue of the traveler may be, that is the tongue in which the natives within speak.

But, I digress.

"Sir knight, I am Don Quixote de La Mancha," the Spaniard proclaimed proudly. "And I will not have you slandering my honor."

"No," Stella said softly in disbelief. Trying her best to keep quiet, she tugged at Ben's arm. "Don Quixote....from *Don Quixote*."

Immediately recognizing both the knight's name as well as that of the Spaniard, Ben spoke up again. "Sir Agravaine, I can vouch for this man's character. He only just, um, saved the princess and me from an enemy patrol. We owe him our lives."

Don Quixote beamed at this.

"If your king," Ben continued, "wishes to bring this man in, I must insist that we accompany him."

"An enemy patrol, you say?" another knight questioned. "So close to the border. The king must be informed."

Sir Agravaine paused for a moment in consideration and then grimaced in defeat. "As you wish, my lord." He turned his horse toward their new destination and gestured for the other knights to follow suit.

The second knight who spoke nudged his horse in Stella's direction and lowered his arm. "And perhaps a proper ride for Her Highness," he offered with charm. He was a very handsome man, with dark hair and a kind face; a legendary man, whom we will soon know as Sir Gawaine.

The smile and wink as the knight lifted Stella onto his steed made Ben's gut wrench—as did Stella's grinning, eager acceptance. The remainder of the knights surrounded them, herding them along toward the correct path.

And so, patiently and submissively, the two remaining gentlemen traveled on foot, with the ever grateful Don Quixote never ceasing to praise Ben's knightly demeanor and bearing. The journey to the castle was not a long one—thankfully, for Don Quixote's feeble legs were beginning to tire.

The castle, most commonly known as Camelot, is most uncommonly known in description outside of its realm. Words read on a page never quite do justice to such an architectural vision. Words never do when describing a heroine's beauty, a villain's terrifying presence, nor in this case, the grandeur that is Camelot. Sure, a wordsmith might try as he chooses, but the reader must ultimately act on a little faith.

That said, I shall stick to the most basic facts.

The castle, built with hundreds of large stones and a legacy that will be remembered for ages, sat on a stately hill. The height of its spires cast long shadows down the grassy slope, reaching the busy traffic at its base. Camelot was a bustling metropolis of sorts, what with its thriving trade and semi-functional feudal system.

All surrounding villages had a physical path back to the epicenter of the legend itself. All highways met just outside of Camelot's borders and wound their way to the castle. The main dirt road leading to the castle was peppered with peasants pushing carts, staggered animals crossing, and the occasional beggar.

One particularly grubby peasant with a single, emaciated lamb passed Ben closely on the narrow path and looked up at him with a folksy grin.

"Beggin' your pardon, my lord," he gleamed; his teeth were slimy, crooked and yellow. Ben nodded passively, cringing on the inside from the putrid smell. "Come, come, for the love of all," the peasant nudged his lamb forcibly.

"Ah, love," Don Quixote sighed dreamily. Ben looked at him sideways. Clearly, the word was taken out of context. "Love is my Dulcinea. For she is every bit as good as the noblest princess on earth—even so noble as the fairest Princess Stella."

Ben cleared his throat. "Uh, yes. How exactly were you separated from your...Dulcinea?"

The Spaniard inhaled proudly, twinged with a hint of imagined regret. "I ventured forth as a knight-errant to honor her name and bring praise to the power of our love, as did the knights of old."

At the corner of his eye, Ben noticed Sir Agravaine raise an eyebrow in confusion. The funny Spaniard hailed from a realm where chivalry and questing knights were long outdated. In his own land, Don Quixote was seen as mad for believing he was destined to seek out medieval adventure—and in this land, he was seen as mad for his deliriously overzealous nature.

Ben could sense that there would be no winning for this poor chap. Holding back a chuckle, he nodded and quickly continued. "Yes, well, I meant from your...realm. How were you taken out of your realm?"

The poor man didn't have a jacket, as Ben had, so something else remarkable must have happened. In fact, as an aside, only one has the authority to utilize the particularly enchanted leather which Ben now possessed, while others might possess their own facsimiles. But, more on that later. For now, we shall return to our Spanish friend's response.

"Realm?" Don Quixote tripped stupidly as he attempted to dignify his stride. "I don't know what you could mean, sir."

"Your homeland? Your...intended quest? Sancho—?"

"You know my man, Sancho?" he stopped in his tracks.

"Erm, yes." Ben paused beside him. "Well—I know of him. What happened to him?"

"A scoundrel—"

"Move along, gentlemen," a harsh voice boomed from behind them. One of the knights grimaced down at them impatiently. He was the one Stella saw in her earlier adventure, known as Sir Kay. The testy Sir Kay inched his horse around them, careful not to trample them, but determined to move on ahead; all the while, he eyed the Spaniard venomously.

Ben took Don Quixote's arm and led him forward, urging him to continue.

"A little scoundrel," the Spaniard proceeded, "attempted to rob us blind just after we came upon those vicious giants."

"Hm, the windmills," Ben said softly, reminding himself of the particular scene in Don Quixote's story. The simpleton imagined large windmills were giants and, against his squire's protests, he had attempted to fight them off.

"...I apprehended him, and he used some sort of black magic to conjure me into this strange land."

"What was the little scoundrel's name?"

"That I know not—but, on my honor, I will find him, and he will rue the day he—"

The man halted again, just inside the gate of the citadel. This time, he stood in a hostile stance, eying an obscure face in the crowd of peasants making their way through the town square.

"Avast, ye villain!" Don Quixote shouted, wielding his weak sword and brandishing it in front of him.

Alarmed, Ben followed the Spaniard's line of sight. He was a weaselly, beady-eyed, dwarfish man in a colorful tweed cardigan. It didn't take Ben very long to realize that this peculiar man must have been the little scoundrel of whom Don Quixote spoke so vengefully. Among the chiefest evidence of this was the Spaniard's hysterical rage. He lunged forward through the crowd, startling everyone in his path, and flailed his arms about —as was his most consistent sword-fighting technique.

Sir Agravaine and Sir Kay lept off of their horses to restrain the spastic man, but he was far too frantic for them to maintain their grip. Sir Gawaine and his other companion, the good-natured Sir Bors, came to their assistance, each holding one of Don Quixote's arms. Ben quickly studied the dwarf from a short distance and, in a moment, Stella was at his side.

"That's him," she said in a low tone.

"The little scoundrel, yes?"

"The one that came with Don Quixote before he killed Mordred. I haven't figured out where he's from..."

Ben imagined the man in a variety of settings, none of which entirely fit his physical appearance. Of course, this is generally common with nomads. Their appearance is only one of many aspects of theirs that typically takes on various qualities of their ever-changing surroundings. Their accents, just to name another, usually sound much like an accumulation of several other distinct dialects.

"My lord," Sir Bors called to Ben. The men had successfully subdued the poor old Spaniard, holding his limp yet struggling body back away from the beady-eyed dwarf, who cowered behind Sir Agravaine. "This man was traveling with you —what do you wish to be done?"

"Hold on, um," Ben began, formulating a variety of possibilities in his head.

"Who are you?" Stella confronted the dwarf.

The little scoundrel straightened his back hesitantly. "I'm not quite sure I want to answer that."

"Answer the princess," Gawaine growled threateningly.

Agravaine placed a stabling hand down on the nomad's shoulder, holding him in place. "Sir Kay, was this the man quarreling with the Spaniard before my brother's death?"

"Murder," Kay corrected roughly, under his breath. "That was the man."

Our dear Spanish friend attempted to lunge toward the man once again, but he submitted to the knights' restraint upon hearing Ben call out to him.

"At ease, Don Quixote. This man will be brought to the king as well so we can hear his story." It was more of a general proclamation to the entire company. Ben nodded to Agravaine, silently instructing him to keep hold of the dwarf.

"Impressive, Lord Caverly," Stella quietly teased.

# 12

## FIX THE STORY

As a rule, legendary characters tend to be faithful to the words on the page. That is just how they were created. However, in the flesh, they each exhibit various idiosyncrasies and expressions that are not easily—or even bothered to be—expressed on paper. I myself have only met King Arthur in passing but I did happen to notice a certain depth in his face when he stumbled upon something remarkable. It was almost as if the muscles in his face were thinking just as intently as his mind, for they all pulled together so elegantly. Pensive, yet invested. Knowing, yet curious. Expectant, yet surprised.

Of course, the human mind has a sadly difficult time visualizing an expression like this based purely on words. Unless you happen to meet the man himself, you'll just have to take my word for it.

In any case, such an expression crossed the good King's face when he soaked in the sight of Lord Caverly and Princess Stella as they stood before him in the Great Hall of Camelot. A certain level of expectant understanding had enlightened something inside him. Past cues, which would eventually be discussed, began to connect in his mind. Don Quixote, of whom he had heard too much from his knights, had been taken directly to the castle's dungeons below, along with his dwarfish foe.

"To what do I owe the pleasure of your lovely presence in my realm, princess?" the king grinned.

He gingerly kissed Stella's hand, causing her to giggle girlishly. She could not believe she had just been kissed by King Arthur. He was more handsome than the descriptions she had read about him—again, words can hardly lend a reader the full experience.

At the height of his reign, he was most likely in his mid- to late-thirties, but his face only slightly betrayed such mileage. He was fair-haired with somber, yet energetic blue eyes. Hardships within his Round Table had worn on him, as well as the expected stresses that come from being king, but the smile lines on his face proved his resilience.

"Oh, just passing through," Stella beamed.

"Sir Gawaine tells me you hail from Faegrian," he went on, turning to Ben.

Arthur stood a few inches taller than Ben, but the warmth in the king's smile evened their ground. Habitually, Ben put out his hand to shake in introduction, before correcting himself and proceeding to bow. The king chuckled. No one else, save the small handful of royal guards, were in the hall with them during this private audience, but that did nothing to alleviate the pressure of addressing a king.

"Um, Your Highness, may I ask what is to happen to Don Quixote?" Ben got right to the point, which the king seemed to appreciate.

"The Spaniard?"

"Yes, sir."

The king sighed diplomatically. "Yes, I understand he was your traveling companion."

"Well, um, not exactly, sire." Ben stepped forward to explain. "But I am curious as to how he got here. He and the uh...the other one. I imagine they arrived in your realm around the time Sir Mordred was killed."

The king furrowed his brow. "My men tell me your Spanish friend maliciously slew Sir Mordred at the tournament."

"Maliciously?" Stella blurted. "It was self-defense. If anyone was malicious, I would say it was Mordred. He was a little too arrogant for someone so....unskilled."

Her opinion, of course, was biased—after all, one tends to have preconceived views of characters when they know how their story is supposed to end. She quickly caught sight of Ben's warning glance and silenced herself.

"Did the princess attend the tournament?" the king asked in surprise.

"Um..." Stella wasn't sure how to even begin to explain her previous presence in the book. "Sort of. I saw what happened, but I didn't...I didn't stay long."

This only confused the king further. He had noticed the couples' peculiar attire when they entered his hall, but he had only assumed her short cotton dress and Ben's black slacks were common in Faegrian. "Self-defense, say you?"

"You don't think he's a Keeper like you, do you? I mean, he kind of just appeared like we did," Stella muttered softly, hoping only Ben would hear.

Unfortunately for her, King Arthur had impeccable hearing. Well, almost impeccable. He really only heard the suggestion of the word "*Keeper.*"

"A Keeper?" he repeated, his attention peaked. "I have heard many stories of that race of sorcerers from Merlin, but I had never given much thought to their possible existence in England. However, this does provide an explanation for his mysterious arrival. Is this what you believe, Lord Caverly? That this Spanish knight is a Keeper?"

All eyes now rested upon Ben. Stella knew she had said too much, but she was just as curious about Don Quixote's purpose in being there as King Arthur.

"Um, no," Ben began. "I haven't quite figured out how he got here. But, my lord, I think his being in your realm could explain why we are here."

"I do not understand."

Ben inhaled deeply, bracing himself for more questions unable to be answered. "I am the Arch Keeper," he slowly released, allowing his new title to roll off his tongue.

King Arthur's face was frozen. "An Arch Keeper," he mumbled.

The king was confused—no, more astounded than confused. He had heard stories of various Keepers Merlin had come across during his travels, but the Arch Keeper, as he understood it, meant something much, much more.

131

"In Camelot? In England? My realm? But how—" he paused for a moment. "You are here, then, to..."

"Fix the story," Stella finished softly.

Ben glanced back at her and saw a smile on her face. Whatever subconscious understanding she had was starting to come together. Ben was a Keeper—as her father was, she presumed—and now he was to save the Arthurian legend. What was once a childhood bedtime story was now very much reality. Stella slipped her hand in his, stepping closer to his side. Ben nodded to her and returned a more hesitant smile, before turning back to the confounded king.

"You have been sent to be my guide, surely," King Arthur continued to mumble. He paused thoughtfully for a moment before looking to Ben again. "Merlin has left my side, but has sent the chiefest Keeper of legend to guide me in my reign, to help me vanquish my foes, keep peace in this realm, and fulfill my destiny."

Ben wanted to stop him from assuming he was capable of more than he believed himself to be, but that's the curse of most heroes: underestimating themselves.

"I will certainly do the best I can," the humble Keeper shrugged. "But, sire, I have to assume that I'm only here because someone else got here first—someone much more dangerous than Don Quixote. And whoever he is...he is here to see that your kingdom is destroyed."

The king pursed his lips, thoughtfully. If there was anything more alarming to a king, it was learning that his beloved kingdom was endangered. Luckily, for Sir Thomas

Malory's written realm of England, the Arch Keeper had made his entrance.

As would be expected of a king called Arthur, he thought it best to further discuss the matter of the impending threat with the rest of his Round Table. And, being a reverent admirer and respecter of the legendary Keepers, the king naturally extended a royal invitation for Lord Caverly to join them.

Stella, on the other hand, was graciously introduced to her very own handmaid, Ava. She was a uniquely pretty, darkly redheaded girl with green eyes, the color of sea foam, and a broad smile. She was perhaps a few years older than Stella, but with a lilt in her step that suggested youthful innocence.

"You look like you're feeling much better, Your Highness" Ava smiled when they were introduced.

It took a few moments for Stella to recognize the rusty hair and resting smirk, but she soon remembered their last meeting.

"Oh! Yes, I am," Stella returned the smile. "So sorry about those apples."

"Please, Highness." Ava shook her head, good-naturedly. "Don't even think of it."

As ordered, Ava took Stella directly to her beautiful room, furnished with a very feminine taste. It had all the trimmings, so to speak—a hardwood bench, vanity, and large wardrobe, with deep purple drapes to match the canopy of the king-sized bed. Something I've always admired about royalty is their propensity to never settle for anything less than class and quality.

Within the large, wooden wardrobe, the king provided her with a countless number of gorgeous gowns. On principle, it took her several minutes to finally select the most suitable option. With the help of Ava's humble input, Stella settled on a red, satin gown embroidered with white petals and trim.

She eagerly shed her blue cotton dress and slipped into the soft new fabric. After taking a few moments to admire the intricate needlework of the silky pink gown she chose, Stella decided it was time to explore the castle. This part was expected, I suppose, seeing as how well you, as the reader, now know Stella Towson. She's an inquisitive soul, a trait she inherited from her mother, I've always thought. And like every curious soul, she is no match for the temptation of a medieval castle.

And so, Stella, with her inquisitive soul and searching sky eyes, left Ava to clean up the disarray left in her room. Commonly, I think, the first place that the average individual would care to explore would be halls and corridors closest to their accommodations. Yet, Stella is far from the average individual. Her first investigative urge led her down to the dungeons, where she had overheard Don Quixote and the mystery man were being held.

They were dark, the cells that filled the dungeons. One bored guard kept watch at the entrance, while lazily fiddling with a leather strap on his loose belt.

"Excuse me, miss." He stood abruptly upon seeing Stella. "Can I help you?"

"Uh, yes," Stella said. She quickly thought of an excuse to be there. When she couldn't find a believable one, she decided to be plain with him. "Could I speak with those...gentlemen?"

He turned his head to give a quick look in the direction in which she gestured. "I'm sorry, miss, I was told those men are prisoners awaiting a trial with the king."

Frustrated, Stella placed her hands on her hips in defiance. "Look, I'll be sure to keep it brief, alright? I won't even tell anyone you let me pass."

"I'm sorry, miss. I can't help you."

"But I'm a guest of the king," she pressed.

"And what might your name be?" His tone was becoming mocking, and Stella did not like that.

"Princess Stella of Faegrian," she grinned, hoping her fake title would be able to pull some weight. Thankfully, it did. The guard's eyes widened, and his stance humbled.

"I'm so sorry, Your Highness. I did not recognize you—if I had known, I would have never dared disrespect the wife of the Keeper," he apologized, bowing.

"Wife of the...Keeper. Of course," she chuckled under her breath.

Ben must have been a very revered mystical figure for them to honor her status as his wife more than her title of princess, she thought to herself. It suited her just fine, however, so long as it gained her access to the prisoners.

Without further hesitation, the guard stepped aside and granted her full access. Don Quixote and the mystery man were kept in opposing cells, facing one another in the very back of the dungeon. Don Quixote was sleeping restlessly on his wooden cot, but that didn't matter to her. Stella rapped on the cell bars of the mysterious traveler. The dwarf sat in the corner of his cell, trying to fall asleep as well, but clearly to no avail.

"Hello," Stella called to him. "Hey, you, sir."

His eyes shot open and stared directly at her. His face was somewhat wacky, in her opinion. His messy, light brown hair swooped inelegantly to one side, barely skimming over the top of his unkempt brows. The look that crossed his face was a combination of confusion and intrigue–as if he recognized her, but not in the present context.

"I presume you're the princess the guards won't shut up about." He slowly stood and advanced toward the bars of the cell.

"I presume you're the midget no one knows anything about."

"Dwarf," he corrected. "And I'll let that slur slide this time, princess." He pursed his lips as he examined her, before nodding in decisive conclusion. "You look like the princess type. Those big doe eyes."

"You have a lot of experience with princesses? Oh, now I get it. You're one of Snow White's dwarves. Which one are you?"

"Snow White's dwarves? How do you know I'm not Cinderella's charming prince?"

Stella lifted a skeptical brow.

"You've got an awful lot of assumptions, princess. You think you know things. But you don't, because if you did, you would know me as Riddock. A man without a story."

Stella wrinkled her mouth in thought. "Riddock," she repeated. "Why are you here? How'd you get here with that other fellow?"

"The delusional buffoon. It is a mystery, isn't it?"

"But...how'd you do it? You don't have a jacket."

"Ah, now I recognize that lovely mug," he chuckled. "From the tournament. What'd you say your name was, princess?"

"I didn't. Stella Towson—" she stopped herself. "Caverly."

"Towson," he repeated. "What did you do then? Steal daddy's jacket and go on a little adventure?"

"No," she snapped defensively—before, of course, remembering that he was not wrong. Instead of admitting anything, she leaned in closer and lowered her tone. "What do you know about my father's jacket?"

"Ooh, what do *you* know?" he mocked, chuckling at her responding glare. His expression soon began to melt, however. It was a bit difficult to be cruel to her, no matter how arduously she may behave; it was an unfair advantage she had had since childhood, and one she most certainly inherited from her mother.

"Plenty," she said. "So is this just what you do?"

"What?" he grimaced.

"You just jump around from story to story?" Her hands went straight to her hips again, her patience with him running thin.

He paused. "It's a lifestyle choice."

"Just for fun? Are you working for someone? Intentionally meddling with the flow of things?"

Riddock's arms fell to his sides in defeat. "Oh come on," he defended, as if to a reprimanding parent. "Your father turned a blind eye. I'm not really hurting anyone...usually."

Stella's eyes brightened. "So you did know my father?"

He sighed, so exasperated. "Yes, of course, I know Albert. He lets things slide because he knows I'm too thick to cause serious trouble."

He said that last part too quickly before realizing he had insulted his own intelligence.

"Erm...that's just what he tells me. Not actually true. I'm not too thick to cause serious trouble—I'm too good of a man." He flippantly waved his hand, dismissing any feigned conviction in his statement. "Now, he wouldn't happen to be here, by any chance, would he? I imagine that'd be very advantageous for me."

When her face fell, Riddock understood. She didn't have to utter a word of explanation. As someone who had been around as much—and as long—as he had, he caught her meaning.

"I see. Well, that would explain it. My condolences, my lady," he said, in the most polite tone she had yet heard from him.

"What do you mean?" she frowned.

He raised his eyebrows again. "Um...Alby has...passed, am I right?"

"Yes, but you said 'that would explain it'. Explain what?"

"Oh. Explains why there's another one."

"You mean Ben?"

"Ben...your brother or something?"

"My, uh, husband."

"Lucky man. Havin' a Companion who looks as good as you." He paused again. "Wait, how long have you and Mr. Keeper been here?"

Stella stared at him. His tone wasn't as sarcastic as it was before. Something changed, bringing earnest. Was it something she said? "Not long. We just got here."

He nodded slowly and took a few steps back. The weight of his previous statement was beginning to settle on him.

*It explains why there's another one.*

Even a fool such as Riddock knew the gravity of those words. When you travel as much as he does, you inevitably pick up pieces of information that prove useful to you. Riddock may not have had all the information Stella was after, but he had enough to know when his presence was no longer needed—or rather when his presence was in the line of fire, and he felt the need to remove himself.

It's where he excelled, you see, self-preservation.

"Korbl's already here, then." A shadow was cast over Riddock's face, a shadow of fear. He glanced quickly to his left, upon hearing the squawk of a raven which had flown through a window, and then looked back at her.

"Hold on, whose side are you on?" Stella asked hastily. She pressed her body against the bars of the cell in her urgency, but he was retreating even farther back. There was nowhere for him to go, she observed, but he seemed ready to go...somewhere.

He gave a crooked smile and scratched his nose. "Whichever side keeps me safe. Your little hubby being here and all...something is starting, and I have no intention of being here when it does. I typically try to avoid jumping into realms in the middle of a war."

"What do you mean?"

Instead of answering her, Riddock grinned again and disappeared in a flash—but not before Stella noticed a leather band on each of his wrists. They bore a striking resemblance to the leather of Ben's jacket, with two notable exceptions: the color was darkly stained, and the texture was seemingly scaly. Being the sharp woman that she is, Stella lept to the correct assumption. That was how Riddock got into this realm, and Don Quixote must have had hold of him. And this Korbl must have been the true reason she and Ben were needed.

The little information she had obtained was falling into place.

# 13

## FLEETING WORDS

"No one," King Arthur firmly planted his fist on the canvas map. His present knights, as well as his new Keeper ally, stood surrounding the large wooden table the map was spread across, in the center of the Council room. "Your description of the patrol in the forest matches no known enemies of England. At least none I've ever encountered."

His tone was frustrated, and a small part of it may have been directed at Ben. For a Keeper, his presumably infinite wisdom revealed itself a little slower than the king had hoped.

Ben rubbed his jaw, deep in contemplation. Nothing in his memory of the book lent him any sort of insight. Arthur's physical enemies were well-known and easy to identify. They could have been rogue knights, of sorts, but their apparel and techniques were far from knightly. They were almost fluid and mildly delicate. The looks in their dark eyes suggested they were full of purpose, a dark purpose.

No, this enemy did not belong.

"I don't think," he started cautiously, choosing his words with care, "that the patrol was from around here."

Sir Gawaine frowned. "I don't understand."

Ben breathed deeply and attempted to answer in terms they would understand. "A larger force is working against you. One that I am still understanding, but I—"

Suddenly the doors swung open, and Stella marched in, ignoring the guards who foolishly tried to slow her down. Several of the knights cleared their throats and mumbled to themselves of their shock at her indecency. Ben's face grew hot with embarrassment. Decorum escaped her in her own time; he could hardly expect her to maintain it now.

"Would you stop?" she exclaimed to the guard who dared to grab her arm. "I just need to tell him something."

"Is there a problem, Your Highness?" the king asked her patiently.

"Yes, *him*." She shook off the guard. Gawaine chuckled at her brashness.

"Stella," Ben warned.

"Princess, I assure you, you may have an audience with me after we've sorted matters here," the king tried to appease her. He nodded to the guard, who listlessly made another attempt to escort her out of the room.

"Riddock said it was Korbl!" she blurted quickly before he could grab hold of her.

The king froze, and this time Ben replied.

"What?"

"The little man who came with Don Quixote. Riddock. He said—okay, you can let go now," she hissed at the guard and

142

his tight grip. In his shock at the outburst, he had forgotten his hold on her. "He said that Korbl's here; he arrived before we did, which is probably why we're here in the first place."

"Bring the man up for questioning, immediately," the king ordered. But, before any of his men could leave the room, Stella stopped them.

"That will be difficult. Apparently, he isn't there anymore."

The king looked at her expectantly. "And where might he be?"

She just shrugged. "I don't know. He disappeared. Sort of like we did, except...a little differently," she added to Ben.

With a sigh of exasperation, the king took Stella gently by the arm and guided her to the table. "If you would, princess, enlighten us? Who is this Korbl, and why does he wish to see England crumble?"

Stella looked around and saw how many curious eyes were on her, eager to learn more. Her heart sank a bit; depression found in a lack of knowledge was a genetic defect of sorts in the Towson family. She wished that Korbl had been explained to Arthur in those stories of Keepers, but Merlin had apparently failed to give such details.

"I...don't really know," she admitted, glancing at Ben.

He watched her intently, but with a puzzled expression. She couldn't decide if he was embarrassed by her again or if he was confused by this new information. Part of her secretly hoped he was taken aback by the sight of her in the beautiful red gown, but she knew he had more severe matters weighing on his mind than a woman in a dress.

"You don't know," Arthur repeated.

"All I know is that he said *something is starting*."

"Korbl is the reason Keepers exist, sire," Ben contributed. And once again, the attention returned to him. "The devil of all devils, as it were. He's an attacker of...realms," he attempted to recite from the journal with accuracy.

Something stopped him from saying stories. *These people don't know they're inside of a book*, he realized. Most mortals believe that their realm of understanding is the only one that truly exists—and that is perfectly acceptable. Most of them could not handle the sort of apprehension that Ben now possessed. A heightened level of awareness calls for one to watch their tongue.

I feel it necessary to remind you, reader, how much more there is to an individual beyond the written description—and the same applies to a spoken description. There is only so much Ben could express regarding this new adversary for King Arthur to understand just how immensely wicked and complex a villain such as Korbl could be. In your time, I believe, this would be referred to as the *reader's digest version*.

Ben folded his arms in front of his chest and went on,

"He is very dangerous, ruthless, and powerful. His preferred method of destruction is tampering with fate. Destiny. Your destiny, Your Highness. He is trying to destroy your destiny, as well as the destiny of your Round Table—which ultimately results in the fate of England. And, because of Mordred's death, the course of your destiny is no longer the same. He will use that, somehow."

Arthur listened, engrossed. "Then what, Keeper, do you predict is his next move?"

Ben considered this, but no idea was coming to him. "I don't presently know. Give me the night to sort it out, and I could have an answer for you by morning."

"I hope so, Keeper. You've had a long journey, surely. You must rest. Even the all-knowing can grow tired."

Stella smirked. *Not so long a journey as you would think*, she thought.

"I shall give you until morning to devise a plan of action, and we shall then reconvene," the king nodded decisively. "Food shall be sent to your rooms, so all of us may rest for the night."

Delicious private meals were delivered to their chambers, as the king promised. The Caverly's were given adjoining rooms, as was expected from the publicly married. Toward the end of her meal, Stella faintly heard the sound of Ben leaving his room. His door closed softly, and his quiet footsteps headed down the corridor.

In her curious way, after she hastily swallowed her last bite, she followed him. It amused her to find he had discovered the palace gardens before she did. He was walking deliberately, rubbing his jaw again, deep in thought. His leather vest, she noticed, had its jacket form, but a much more medieval style than before.

"That's quite a fashionable convenience," she said aloud and surprised him. Ben turned to face her and gave a tired smile. "I never saw it do that on my father...but I guess it was meant to look like a bomber jacket when he was home."

145

"If only he had mentioned more of its nature in his journal," Ben said.

*That was it*, she thought. The journal somehow filled him with more anxiety since the meeting in the Council room.

"I just...I don't understand how I've missed so much. I mean, I read the blasted thing twice through," he rambled on. "I...don't understand."

"Did you try taking notes?" she suggested.

"It doesn't help," he snapped.

"Okay," she surrendered. She stepped closer to him and touched his arm in the most soothing way she knew how.

He quickly corrected his tone. He wasn't frustrated with her, and he knew it was unfair to punish her for what he couldn't manage to figure out. He sighed. "I'm sorry, it just...changes."

"Changes?"

"The words, they, um...it's almost as if they change every time I read it. I could have sworn I had gotten so much from it the first two times, but nothing—there's nothing I can find about defeating this Korbl character. What am I supposed to do? Throw the book at him? Who answers to him? What are his methods? How will he attack the realm? Why is he attacking the realm? How can such simple words be so changeable? It doesn't make any sense."

Stella chuckled. She had never seen him so helpless. His mind just couldn't easily wrap around an opponent he knew so little about.

"I...don't understand."

"Yes, you said that," she whispered.

He looked into those sky eyes of hers. They were swimming with a sort of power and belief that he understood even less about than the journal. Somehow, though, they gave him a little more hope.

"Maybe the words aren't changing," she said thoughtfully. Her voice was even and smooth, without a hint of sarcasm or mocking. "Maybe what's changing is what you need from them."

Ben paused for a long moment, just staring at her. "I, um, I never thought of that."

She smiled. Her disarming smile was beginning to weaken his knees more than he would have liked along with those doe eyes of hers. "Well, what did you get from it the first few times?"

"He's a disgruntled sorcerer...sort of. I think, he may be Yonas's son..."

"Okay. And who's Yonas?"

"He's the, um...I don't know, the king of...all of whatever they are."

She wound her arm around his and started walking with him around the garden, continuing to coax the information out of him. Her touch was warm and almost distracting. But, it was working; everything he had read was gradually resurfacing and forming graspable concepts.

"So Korbl's disgruntled," Stella established. "Is he magical?"

"Beyond belief," he nodded. "But not–I don't think–as powerful as Yonas."

"And he wants to ruin the story, right?"

147

"In a manner of speaking."

"Just for fun?"

Their pace slowed as he thought about this. He hadn't even considered Korbl's motivations. "He craves power, like every other mad villain. He's just more...more. More intelligent, more powerful. His purpose runs deep—he's far from petty—I just don't fully understand what exactly that purpose is."

"Did my father ever deal with him directly?" she pressed.

"Only a couple of times, I think. He encountered him in person once when he was first made a Keeper. Korbl seemed to prefer working through manipulated characters already in the given realm."

"So Riddock dragging Don Quixote into all of this was a bit of a monkey wrench for both sides then," Stella concluded.

"Yes, but—"

"But what?"

Ben squinted, in confusion. "His goal isn't always control or destruction. That's often the inevitable result, but his objective could lead anywhere. Perhaps the Round Table is some sort of threat. Perhaps it's Arthur himself. Sometimes his objective revolves around the Keeper. In Albert's case, when he visited *The Sleeping Beauty*..."

Something changed in Stella's face, making him trail off. It was recognition.

"That's why it was different," she whispered. She pulled his arm a little closer, pressing the side of her body against his as they kept walking. "He told me that story when I was a kid, but he always had a hard time finishing it. He used to think I fell asleep before the end so he wouldn't have to. I made up my own ending once."

She wore such an innocent, reminiscent beam as she spoke. She felt so warm inside. It felt as though her father were there with them again. "How did Korbl attack him in that story?"

Flustered by her closeness, he had trouble focusing on what he remembered. "I'm, um....if I recall, Korbl knew Albert's strengths and weaknesses—as if he were in his head. He knew what was...in his heart. And he used that against him." A sudden sadness washed over him. "That's how he manipulates characters. He knows them too well."

And then, all at once, it hit him. He stopped in his tracks and turned to look Stella square in the eyes. Holding her by the shoulders in front of him, the pieces were matching up quickly.

"The one thing that ultimately weakens King Arthur, in the book, is Guenever's betrayal with Launcelot. Perhaps Korbl's counting on the affair still playing a role in his downfall."

Stella made her thinking face, wrinkling her mouth to one side, and nodded in agreement. "I would think so."

"But, Sir Mordred was meant to be one of those who exposes the affair," Ben continued. "He causes the conflict, and then later kills Arthur. Without him...only Agravaine stands to really care enough to expose the affair. Which means that..."

"Korbl could have Agravaine—or really anyone—kill Arthur," she finished. "He could basically do what he wants since Mordred's gone. And, if it could be anyone...that means that anyone could be a traitor?"

"Agravaine is always a good candidate. Arthur has his share of enemies; that's expected. But everything has changed now. Nothing is predictable anymore."

"Well," Stella sighed. "If the affair is something he's going to use, maybe we should go wherever that spoiled brat is."

Ben smiled. "Guenever?"

Her lip curled in distaste, making him laugh. "Yes, her."

His hands fell to his side, and it didn't take long to miss the touch of Stella's warmth. He looked into her eyes again, but this time an excerpt from the old man's journal struck his memory.

*I don't think I've ever been so confused by a woman, as I am now. Every woman has apparent flaws that make them human and approachable. Not this one. The gift of beauty, the gift of virtue, the gift of love, and the gift of wit. I think those fairies played a dirty trick on humanity. They've created a specimen so perfectly intoxicating that despising her is entirely out of the question. Every man is a fool who can't look away—and can't avoid loving her.*

These words were depicting Albert's late wife, Rose. *Intoxicating.* It was funny; Ben had once used that exact word when thinking of Stella—but in a very different context. Watching her face brighten throughout their conversation, he began to see a personification of Albert's description. The women in Albert's immediate family had enchanting genetics that made them more susceptible to being loved by men in particular. Ben couldn't fathom how someone so ill-behaved and wild could become so lovely and enticing. Maybe it was the heightened bond between them due to their situation. Perhaps it was his new understanding of her, her strengths, and her resilience.

Whatever it was, he was apt to agree with the young Albert—and the feeling terrified him.

He could have stood there all night. In fact, he wanted to. He wanted to say something. Anything. He wanted to tell her about her mother. About how much more there was to Briar-Rose. But she didn't give him a chance. Still beaming, Stella stood on her toes to kiss him on the cheek with her soft lips, more intimately than in any other encounter since they said their vows.

"Good night, Ben," she wished him before heading back inside to her chambers for the night.

While it may have been a good night to Stella, Ben's mind was not yet ready to call it a night. He went straight to the king's chambers to give him word of his decision. Tired-eyed, but eager, the king quickly agreed. They were to return to London in the morning.

# 14

## THE LEGEND OF THE AEREST

And so our story continues, shifting its weight from Camelot to London.

Traveling is massively dreary, being comprised of walking, riding, running, more walking, more riding, and more running. That said, I will only relay the necessary details of their journey.

At the king's insistence, Stella was placed in a covered carriage with Ava, while the men followed on horseback. Much to Ben's chagrin, Sir Gawaine was most insistent on traveling closely beside the carriage to ensure Princess Stella's safety and comfort.

Don Quixote was ecstatic to be released from his cell and invited to ride alongside Ben and the other knights. His continuous praises of Ben's honor and heroism were a refreshing relief from Gawaine's incessant babbling. Ben couldn't recall Gawaine's character being so unbearably chatty in the book, but he then reminded himself of the limited conversations that were actually written. The boisterous knight proudly boasted his exploits and was sure to speak loud enough for the women in the carriage to hear him.

*Honorable quest* this, *good king Uncle Arthur* that. Naturally, Gawaine skipped over his many failed endeavors, which Ben didn't hesitate to add under his breath. Sir Gawaine had once fought another knight to whom he showed no mercy and was cruelly victorious. He neglected, however, to mention how he unintentionally killed the knight's fair lady as well. Nothing could tarnish his spirits. Gawaine either ignored or missed Ben's quiet amendments to his tales and proceeded to entertain himself and the listening ladies.

When the party arrived in London, Gawaine lept to assist Stella from the carriage. Stella appropriately reached for Ben's arm,to be led up to the castle doors.

Anticipating their arrival, the queen was waiting for them near the doors. Her purple, embroidered gown fluttered across the stone floor as she gracefully approached her returning husband. Seeing all men fixate upon her, her beguiling eyes twinkled. She was stunning, as expected, and fully aware of her allure.

Ben could certainly understand why Arthur chose her as his bride. Her poise and manners were substantial evidence of her aristocratic upbringing. She had a small attendance of knights surrounding her—including the friendly knight Stella had run into at the tournament during her first adventure in the realm. His handsome face was slightly pale as if he were recovering from a wound of some sort. In fact, he was.

He did his best to mask the pain of recovery. But Stella took notice. The friendly knight was then introduced to them shortly after the queen. Sir Launcelot, was one of the king's most trusted knights. And the queen's secret lover.

Stella's diplomatic propriety was somewhat lacking. She wrinkled her nose in disgust as she curtsied for the queen, and wrinkled even more so when she saw the way in which Sir Launcelot gazed.

"It is indeed an honor, princess," Guenever said. "I do believe we will become good friends."

Stella snorted until she caught the warning glance Ben was throwing her way. "We shall see, I guess."

"From whence do you hail?" the queen asked curiously.

"Fagan—"

"Faegrian," Ben corrected under his breath.

"Faegrian," she rectified with confidence.

"Hm," Guenever pursed her lips, studying the specimen before her. "We must do something about your wardrobe. A princess in my court should be presented with much more...well, it's nothing that cannot be remedied."

Stella raised her eyebrows. Smoothing her own gown, Stella snidely smirked. "Oh? The king chose this dress himself. Sir Launcelot sure seems to like it."

Slightly embarrassed for being caught staring, Launcelot cleared his throat and diverted his eyes with a smile.

The queen, however, was not smiling. "Hm," was all she said.

"You look lovely, princess." Launcelot nodded politely, his cheeks still blushed.

"So do you," Stella smiled. "I've heard a lot about the legendary Sir Launcelot. Noble, brave, and the most beloved of the Knights of the Round Table."

The blushing did not cease. Launcelot humbly kissed Stella's hand and bowed. "The princess is too kind. I am sure there are many who speak so highly of you, as well."

"I see why you're such a hit with the ladies—"

"I think our guests need rest, dear," Guenever cleared her throat.

Ben agreed; he knew Stella's flirtation was motivated by an irritated desire to get under the queen's skin, but it had already been such a long and tedious journey already.

"Quite right," the King cheerily chimed in. "Why don't we have you shown to your rooms, and this evening we shall have a feast in honor of our guests."


When a king is intent on throwing a feast, even amid tension and sorrow, one tends not to argue. Royalty spares no expense when entertaining guests.

The great hall of festivities was arranged with an angular table that bordered the walls, the high table in the front of the room being specially set for the king and his queen, with two long tables branching along the room on either end. These tables were covered with delectable dishes prepared with the greatest care and flair. In the center of the room, court musicians performed, significantly contributing to the general atmosphere of gaiety.

Lord Caverly and Princess Stella were afforded the finest clothing, presented as the guests of honor, and granted a special place near the high table. As the feast was served, the king turned to the Keeper he had strategically seated next to him.

"Now, Lord Caverly," he began, "tell me more about this attack on my realm."

A funny thing about royalty: they are bred with life handed to them and are not particularly accustomed to asking nicely. Even Arthur, who had been raised by a mere knight, had adapted quickly to this idiosyncrasy.

Ben swallowed hard. How could he explain something he himself did not understand?

"I, um, I'm not sure what more there is to tell, Your Highness." He focused a little more energy into cutting the tender meat on his plate. Patricia's cooking certainly couldn't compare to that of the King's kitchen staff. "The attackers were already advancing on Don Quixote when Ste—the princess and I arrived."

"And what is your verdict on this Spaniard?" Arthur lowered his tone in an attempt to avoid any eavesdroppers.

Don Quixote was seated farther from the high table, being the more inferior of the guests of honor, and thankfully entranced by the surrounding knights' tales. Sir Gawaine was especially animated, of course, in continuing his narratives. As previously shown, he was a man with a lot of character, good or bad, and no hesitation to share it.

"Don Quixote is as honorable as they come, sire. If he—"

"—and then that was it! There's just no stopping a legend, I suppose!"

Ben was momentarily distracted by the greatly exaggerated exploits of Gawaine as well as Stella's engaged laughter. He doubted Gawaine was funny enough to warrant such a laugh from her, but he turned back to the King and went on.

"If he is responsible for Mordred's death, it was unintentional. Based on Princess Stella's story, Don Quixote was disoriented—and Mordred instigated the duel. All in all, Don Quixote did nothing wrong. He acted honorably in the forest, protecting the princess and...assisting me," Ben almost chuckled remembering Don Quixote's clumsy technique. "I'm comfortable vouching for his character."

Arthur smiled, sipping his wine. "Well, he certainly speaks highly of you. He told me of your bravery as well as your powers of invincibility," he said this with a wink as if sharing a great secret.

Not knowing how to respond, Ben stupidly shrugged and focused a little more energy on cutting the meat on his plate. His anxious grip slipped, scraping the knife against the porcelain dish instead, but it was hardly noticed. Clearly his throat, he said, "One of the perks of being a Keeper, I suppose."

"And I can hardly wait to witness others during your time with me." Arthur took a few bites of his meal and watched the performers. After a few moments, he took another sip of wine and turned back to Ben. "The moment I heard news of a peculiar happenstance at the tournament and...I had a feeling, one that I couldn't understand."

He took one more sip.

"You are here to guide me to my destiny, Keeper. I only wish I knew what that was. Why else would you enter my realm? Why else would I need a sorcerer, one as powerful as you, to guide me?" he inhaled slowly. "A great evil is coming that much is certain."

Ben set his own utensils down and pressed his fist against his lips, deep in thought. "How do you know? What exactly did Merlin tell you?"

Arthur looked at him strangely. As far as he was concerned, the Keeper knew all. "Merlin often spoke of your kind. Especially of the Aerest Keeper—I only wish he had dwelt here long enough to meet you face to face. Of course, were he here, he'd have been the first to recognize you. Your presence was prophesied. A new era, Merlin called it. A new era of three, I believe."

Ben vaguely remembered reading over this in the journal, but it hadn't quite stuck with him. Myk had even, just as vaguely, mentioned another name for what Ben was, but he couldn't quite remember. "Did, um, did he tell you what exactly *Aerest* means?"

Arthur applauded the performers as they ended a tune. As they began another, he sighed in recollection.

"I believe he said it was from an ancient tongue. The tongue of an ancient race he referred to as *Galdere*. *Aerest*, I believe, meaning *first*. Appropriately, I suppose, as you are the first of the alleged new era."

*That was it*, Ben recalled. *Aerest* referred to the opening of this very era in particular. I take keen interest in this period

158

of Keeper history for obvious reasons. It is, after all, my given occupation.

"Did he tell you about the other two?" Being the scholar that he was, Ben was burning with curiosity. Unlike this current record, Albert kept the journaled details of the final three to a minimum. At least, as far as Ben had presently known.

"Only the titles which he called them. *Haeleth* and *Fulendian*." Arthur took his final sip of wine when Sir Kay appeared behind him, asking for a private word. Before ending the conversation and rising from his chair, the king emphatically added, "You have my word, Keeper, as long as I reign, this court will honor and follow your wise counsel. Merlin wouldn't have had it any other way."

As the king rose, Sir Kay gripped his arm, urgently leading him to the hallway. The guests in the great hall continued feasting and being entertained, but not everyone was quite so jovial. There was a darkness to Kay's countenance that troubled Arthur. He had noticed Kay glaring all night and feared where this conversation might lead.

"What is it, Kay?" Arthur asked, noting Kay's remaining grip on his arm.

"My king, there should be no celebrating until Sir Mordred's murderer is dealt with," Kay rasped with passion.

Arthur sighed. "Kay..."

"Sire, he was your own flesh and blood—whether you accept that or not."

"Watch your tongue, brother," Arthur snapped, pulling his arm away. By nature, Arthur was not one to deal with situations that caused him discomfort; being reminded of his ignorantly incestuous sin and the offspring that resulted caused him such discomfort. "Mordred was as valued a knight as any other, and his death is unfortunate. But, he was defeated in a duel which he himself initiated. Justice has dealt with itself."

Kay threateningly crossed his arms in front of his chest. "And you believe that to be justice? Let revenge be sought, Arthur. Revenge for Mordred's death. He was a knight of the Round Table, and that cannot be cast aside."

"Revenge?" Arthur repeated, almost mockingly. "The fight was fair, Kay."

"You don't think his brothers would wish to seek vengeance?"

"We are all brothers here."

Arthur looked Kay straight in the eyes as he said this, making sure he understood him fully. The bond of the Knights of the Round Table was strong, though Ben could sense wavering.

Kay understood. He stepped back respectfully but refused to back down from his cause. "His kin will want vengeance."

Arthur sighed again and waved his arm in the direction of the great hall. "Have a look, Kay. Do his kinsman seem at all concerned with avenging their brother's death?"

Kay grimaced at the sight of such neglectful knights. Gawaine had hardly noticed much since the arrival of the princess. Agravaine was also distracted by the princess' handmaid, Ava. Gaheris and Gareth were otherwise occupied with correcting Gawaine's tall tales. Kay's jaw clenched. He loathed that Arthur was right.

Arthur gave Kay's shoulder a comforting squeeze and adopted a more congenial tone. "Mordred had his share of enemies, brother. We are all sorry for his loss, but his end was brought about by his own doing. There is time to mourn, but the Keeper has brought hope to the kingdom that is worth celebrating."

Kay inhaled sharply and took another step away from Arthur. "There should not be merry-making after the loss of a knight."

And perhaps Kay was not entirely in the wrong in believing this. After all, Knights of the Round Table were meant to be tight-knit and loyal to a fault. That was their purpose. Regardless of Mordred's intended destiny of killing his own father and helping along the downfall of the kingdom, Arthur was unaware of this.

So, you see, Kay could be justified in his anger if his following actions had not been so wicked. As if on impulse, Kay reached for the dagger on his belt.

At that moment, the foolish Don Quixote had rudely interrupted the private conversation, eager to inquire of the king to let him join the Round Table, and found himself between the king and the sharp blade.

There was an outcry and the Spaniard fell against the gob-smacked king, clutching his side as the blood began to flow.

Kay staggered backward, both shocked and incredibly disappointed that he missed his mark. Arthur's eyes shot from the wounded Spaniard to the bloody weapon in Kay's hand. He knew he was the intended victim of the dagger's point.

For a moment, he could only stare while his heart fell. This man, this brother, this kinsman with whom he had been raised had tried to kill him. Kay had his faults but never had Arthur imagined him capable of such betrayal. He shouted to his knights in the great hall.

Seconds later, Kay was gone.

# 15

## A WORTHY OPPONENT

In the realm of Middangeard—the name given to our own world by an ancient race of sorcerers; perhaps you have heard it before, or something like it from various forms of mythos—ancient Europeans believed ravens brought bad omens or were  incarnations of damned souls or even the devil himself in disguise.

This is silliness, of course, but their superstitions are rooted in truth. While ravens may not be the devil incarnate, they do make beneficial assets to evil. They are incredibly intelligent, monstrously devious, and strangely communicative. When trained and controlled by a dark being, they can be quite ominous, I must say.

To Kay's advantage, a small battalion of these dark birds was ready and waiting for him outside of the citadel. After his failed assassination attempt, Kay bolted to the stables, pushing aside the stable boy and jumping on his steed. The poor nag hadn't run so quickly since he had first been broken.

The ravens led the way, far into the woods and away from the lights of the castle. Luckily for them, the light was hardly a necessity for the dark beings who awaited them. Near a dense cluster of trees, nestled outside the mouth of a large cave, Kay's horse slowed its pace, possibly out of apprehension, just as these dark beings came into view. The shortest and darkest of the beings stepped forward with a sneer.

"You don't seem as victorious as I expected," the man snarled. Kay dismounted, breathing heavily from rage and exertion.

"I failed—that moronic Spaniard!" Kay seethed. "And that Keeper! With Mordred gone, how are we expected to—?"

"Oh shut up," the shorter man muttered.

He was a sturdy fellow with a face resembling an over-sized rat. His large, sallow eyes were fringed with a sort of shadowy stain on the skin. The man waved off the circling ravens, sending them into the trees until their next assignment. With a humorless chuckle, he then gestured for the three men who were with him to take Sir Kay's horse into the cave.

Once he and Kay were alone, the man snarled again. "The king will be dealt with in due time."

"Perhaps it is the Keeper that should be of greater concern. He appears to be more than capable of outwitting you," Kay spat.

"Watch it, boy," the man growled. "The Master's put me in charge of this enterprise, so I'll be takin' no lip from you."

Kay rolled his eyes. "My apologies, Spyros. Forgive me for assuming your master knew what he was doing."

164

Kay had a knife held against his throat before he could draw his next breath. The man called Spyros had thrown him aggressively against the outer wall of the cave.

"Never doubt The Master," he hissed. "He always knows what he is doing."

"Is that right?" Kay challenged. "And how does he intend to dispose of the Keeper?"

Spyros released a raspy chuckle. "You know so little, it's laughable. You think the Keeper is his target. His plan is already in action." Kay raised his eyebrows laggardly. "When attacking an opponent, one must target their greatest vulnerability."


Arthur insisted on maintaining the daily training for his Round Table knights —he personally preferred sparring to any other form of therapy. Within a few days following Kay's escape and banishment, the knights gathered in the training yard, where their manservants fully armored them for practice and where the ladies stood simpering in their little cluster around the queen to gawk at the men.

Stella tried her best to keep her distance from the queen, for Ben's sake more than anything. She knew that spending too much time with Guenever would lessen her ability to filter the crass comments that had a tendency of running through her head. Fortuitously, Don Quixote was more than happy to provide her with a distraction from the queen's attempts to catch her attention. Though recovering from his recent stab wound, he would not be deprived of witnessing the excitement of the day. Comfortably, he sat next to Princess

Stella, granting her his most informative commentary of the sparring at hand.

Arthur began leading the training exercises, wielding his legendary battle sword Excalibur, with a duel against Sir Gareth. The other knights watched his form and Gareth's defensive maneuvers carefully, as they always did. Arthur was not a noted fighter, but he excelled in strategy—an area all of his knights thirsted to perfect.

While the contesting pair were studied by onlookers, Sir Agravaine was still awaiting the arrival of the remainder of his armor. His manservant's mother was ill, so he had a bit of a rough morning. When the king's sparring failed to hold his attention, he decided to strike a conversation with the court's honored guest.

"Quite a spectacle, isn't it?" he asked casually.

Ben was leaning against the side of an outdoor stone staircase, uncomfortably adjusting his armor. His own assigned manservant assured him that chaffing was to be expected, but he hadn't anticipated quite so much sweating. When reading stories of knights, he had an image of how weighty their armor must have been, but the heat was an unexpected factor, particularly with the added layer of thick enchanted leather he was sure to wear underneath. "Um, yes it is. Very impressive."

"Try not to think about it."

"Think about what?"

Agravaine laughed. "The heat. It won't bother you so much if you put it out of your head. Just think about how many amorous glances you'll get from the fairer sex. They always love a man in battle armor." He winked, glancing quickly in Stella's direction. She was sucked into a conversation with Lady Katrina, one of the queen's ladies-in-waiting, and Sir Gawaine.

Ben chuckled. He didn't follow Agravaine's gaze and instead tried to settle his discomfort. He decided to take Agravaine's advice and stop thinking about it. Shifting his weight, he said, "I guess you're right."

"Oh, of course, I am." Agravaine's face took a reproachful turn. "Even the married ones," he added slowly. His eyes again went to the princess, who giggled at something Gawaine whispered in her ear.

"Mhm." Ben's eyes, however, went to the queen. The ardent and commanding stolen glances she shared with Sir Launcelot from across the yard were so treacherous. Ben wondered how Arthur had not realized what was right under his nose. Something so dangerous that it would become a deadly blow to the strength of his kingdom.

"Yes, I think my brother enjoys certain aspects of knighthood a little too much," Agravaine said in a low voice, readjusting one of the straps of his armor.

Finally, Ben followed Agravaine's train of thought, leading him to notice Gawaine's ability to captivate female attention. Despite Stella's gentle reminder of Don Quixote's convalescence, Gawaine had chivalrously volunteered to help Don Quixote refine his techniques in swordplay and quickly experienced the diverting fashion in which Don Quixote flailed his sword about. The ladies watched in giddy amusement; girlish giggles escaped Stella's lips every time Gawaine flashed a smile in her direction.

Agravaine stepped in front of Ben's line of sight and, in a way that seemed like an old friend, he leaned in with a somber, sympathetic frown. "I think it fair to say, Lord Caverly—and it may very well be nothing—last night, I heard what sounded like my brother outside the princess' chambers. I would hate for a fellow man of honor to be cuckolded."

"Lord Caverly!" Sir Bors called from across the yard. He waved his arm, gesturing for Ben to join him. "Let us see if you're a worthy contestant!"

Ben raised his eyebrows knowingly at Agravaine. *Of course, he would be concerned*, he thought, *considering how aggressively he was supposed to fight to expose Launcelot and the queen.*

"Yes, well, I'm sure it was nothing," he assured him. He gave Agravaine's shoulder an encouraging squeeze and nodded in gratitude. "Thank you for your concern, but the princess is playful by nature. So, I'm not worried," he lied. He forced a smile and excused himself to join Sir Bors.

Like the well-seasoned knight that he was, Sir Bors proved to be a challenging opponent; just accommodating enough to take it easy on Ben, but too skilled to let him win. Within minutes, Ben was on the ground. A mixture of cheers and chuckles rippled through the training yard. Bors himself wore a wide grin with a twinkle in his eye.

"That was quite impressive," he said heartily, offering a hand to help Ben to his feet. "You almost had me for a moment there."

Breathing deeply to regain composure, he wiped the beads of sweat from his forehead. *This armor is certainly not getting any cooler*, he thought. "It's not quite fencing, but it'll do."

"Excellent form, sir." Bors continued to praise him until the two of them were discreetly angled away from curious ears. "Do not worry, my friend; Agravaine's opinions should not be given much merit."

Ben's brow furrowed in feigned confusion. "I don't know what you mean."

The greying knight gave Ben's back a gentle pat and replied with a knowing smirk. His eyes did not earn those wrinkles without learning something along the way.

"Lord Caverly, your expressions are not always as guarded as you undoubtedly intend. You seemed unusually pensive and troubled after speaking with Sir Agravaine. Don't let his words weigh too heavily on your mind." Then, stepping back into the open yard, he added in jest, "And maybe Sir Agravaine's swordplay has finally caught up with his mouth!"

Winking at Ben, Bors chuckled and pointed his sword playfully in Agravaine's direction. "Are you up to the challenge, Agravaine—do you think you can match the skills of the Keeper? He cannot beat me, but I think he may easily defeat you, sir!"

Agravaine stood up from the step he had been sitting on and responded proudly. "Indeed I would be up for the challenge —but, sadly, I am not yet fully armored, Lord Caverly. Perhaps Sir Gawaine would be a suitable substitute."

Hearing his name, Gawaine's head snapped away from his spirited conversation. Encouragement was hardly required, but the king himself, and those standing around him cheered on the idea. Gawaine glanced at Stella, whose eyes were now on Ben. Gawaine then puffed up his chest, proudly accepting the challenge.

"It would be an honor," he returned. He unsheathed his sword and took his place in the middle of the yard.

Ben's enthusiasm, however, had died. Suppressing a grimace, he stepped forward and braced himself.

I'm sure you've noticed this amongst animals or hot-headed youth: when the favor of a female is involved, an entirely new instinct takes control. It causes one to wholly and rashly lose authority over one's faculties. This bestial change happens to the best of us, and is one of the beautifully consistent aspects of reality—no world outgrows irrational decisions. Even intelligence and practicality are sorry defenses. It's one of the downfalls of feminine wiles.

Ben, a sensible and level-headed man by nature, found himself putting a little more aggression into his technique than intended. Apparently, it was effective because, this time, the cheers and chuckles were in Ben's favor.

Stella rooted loudly, whooping and clapping her hands together in her adorably unrefined way. The queen and her ladies grinned and whispered words of approval. The king exclaimed his support by matching the volume of Stella's shouts and cheers. I suppose the training had successfully distracted Arthur from his many problems.

Gawaine himself stared up at Ben, from his now grounded vantage point, with a combination of shock and admiration. As Stella cheered, he remembered his intent in dueling the Keeper and was suddenly embarrassed to be seen on the ground. Swallowing his humiliation, he quickly stood and shook the clumps of dirt off of the back of his legs.

"Well..." he began, holding out his arm for Ben to shake. "Well done, sir. You are certainly worthy of your title, Keeper."

Ben nodded in acknowledgement, still surprised with himself. "As are you," he replied amiably.

It was an honest compliment. Ben knew Gawaine was not inherently horrid, and he could hardly blame him for his attraction to a woman like Stella. Ben scolded himself for allowing his emotions to so brutishly defeat a knight like Gawaine, for he knew he was too rational a human being to allow such loss of control. Such irrationality was a sign of weakness in his eyes. And his guilt was only enhanced by a congratulatory embrace from Stella as well as the unending adorations from Arthur. He did not allow Ben to forget how blessed and honored the realm was to have a Keeper such as him to guide their leader to a victory over his enemies.

With his faith in the Keeper maintained, King Arthur insisted on meeting privately with Ben at the end of the day to deliberate possible threats. Obediently, Ben hurried to his chambers to quickly re-skim the journal for the sake of his confidence, but his jaw dropped at the sight of the empty desk drawer. In a panic, he rummaged through his trunk of new clothes, beneath furniture, behind his wardrobe, and even peered under his mattress.

The journal was gone.

# 16

## THE MAY DAY RIDE

Several weeks had passed since the banishment of Sir Kay. The journal was still missing, and Ben was still frantic. He was too cautious and slightly embarrassed to bring the journal to the king's attention for fear of the repercussions should Arthur find it and decide to read it.

Stella, upon learning of the journal's disappearance, encouraged Ben to accompany the other knights on hunting trips and training exercises to distract him from his anxieties and stress. She tried to calm his worries of being completely lost and lacking in direction, but men like Ben are difficult to placate once their minds are fixated on a particular problem.

Nevertheless, he humored both Stella and Arthur by participating in the usual knightly activities. He quickly gained the respect and admiration of all those who ever doubted him. He was now a revered member of the Round Table as well as Don Quixote's key to gaining the knightly prowess for which he yearned so desperately.

Meanwhile, dear Stella had reluctantly engaged in a strange friendship with the queen. Despite Stella's best efforts to avoid it, Guenever managed to trap her into spending almost every moment with her. To any other woman in the kingdom, this would have been an immense honor, but to Stella, it was more of a test of personal fortitude.

The Queen was one of those unique souls who fails to understand when a person shows her any form of dislike. For a woman so accustomed to being loved and adored, Guenever was intrigued by this princess and her unique way of expressing opinions. In all fairness, the two women shared many traits, and this could have very well contributed to the contentious nature of their friendship. At least on Stella's part.

With the exceptions of Ben's nerves and the underlying tension against their former brother-in-arms, there was a general mood of peace throughout the kingdom. However, deep in the darkest part of the woods, Kay and his allies were far from at ease.

Taking advantage of the temporary lull, Arthur insisted that they move along, business as usual, until the Keeper deemed it necessary to take action, which only added to the pressure of an already harried Ben Caverly.

According to Thomas Malory's records, Queen Guenever planned on taking her traditional May Day ride, as the beginning of May was soon upon them. At a quiet, private dinner with the royal couple and the Keeper and his lovely wife, the queen presented the idea to her audience.

"Given the circumstances, my dear, I think it best to proceed with my May Day ride tomorrow morning," Guenever touched her husband's arm in the most subtle form of manipulation known to women. Of course, as his gender seems to require, Arthur agreed without argument.

Having a sudden recollection of the events which transpired on the recorded May Day ride–the ambush, the abduction, and the rather risky rescue mission–Ben held up a questioning hand.

"Um, do you think that is such a good idea, Your Highness? We still don't know where Sir Kay is hiding."

Wiping a smudge of food from the side of his mouth, King Arthur cleared his throat. "I don't think—"

"It is perfectly safe, my lord," the queen waved Ben aside. "It is only along Westminster. And we will be escorted by a good number of knights. Besides, it has been over a fortnight, and we have received no news of Sir Kay. I am sure he is hiding somewhere far away, wallowing in regret."

Arthur inhaled and gradually began to nod. "Very well, my dear, if you insist upon it—"

"I do."

"—then you shall go."

"And Princess Stella shall accompany me," she added, beaming at Stella and taking a sly sip of her wine.

The unsuspecting princess nearly choked on the cheese tart she had been eating. "I'm sorry, what?"

"Your complexion could use a bit of sun, princess, and we'll stay the night with a good friend of mine I should dearly love to introduce to you."

To the surprise of everyone at the table, instead of biting back a snide retort, Stella made her thinking face and nodded. "Sure, why not?"

Ben stared at her, trying to detect sarcasm, but failed. Stella never ceased to astound. Even as a child, not a soul could predict just quite what she would say next, not even her father.

The queen broke into a wide, triumphant grin. "Wonderful."

Shortly after the surprising dinner, all commenced to their chambers to prepare for bed. Ava helped Stella out of her gorgeous, burgundy gown and into a soft cotton nightgown. A woman never considers herself in need of help getting ready for bed until the option is available. Stella enjoyed Ava's company, surely above that of the queen's. In the weeks they had been in the realm, Stella had grown rather attached to her maidservant. Back in Boston, her father had one maid who only cleaned on Saturdays; having an attendant following Stella around felt a bit strange at first, but she found it suited her.

Ava took the pins out of Stella's hair and began combing through the long, wavy locks. Ava's rhythmic combing was quite soothing and Stella felt her eyelids become heavy while she sat in front of the vanity. Stella jolted out of her therapeutic lull when a knock came from the chamber door.

"I shall get it," Ava assured her, setting the comb on the vanity and hurried to the other side of the room to answer the door. Stella closed her eyes again, trying to regain that serenity. She then heard some low mumbling, Ava's obedient response, and then felt Ava back by her side. "It is your husband, Lord Caverly, my lady. He wishes to speak with you."

"Oh," Stella opened her eyes and wrapped her lace robe around her nightgown. "Let him in, and you can go to bed if you want."

"Are you sure you won't be needing anything?"

"I'm sure," Stella nodded and ushered her out.

Ava slipped past Ben, who was standing in the door frame with his arms crossed in front of his chest. He straightened his stance when he saw Stella, and he seemed somewhat surprised to see her in a nightgown.

"Um, hello, could I have a word?" he managed to say.

She smiled. "Yes, sure, come on in." She held the door open wider so he could enter, and then quickly tightened her robe, suddenly feeling self-conscious. "What is it?"

He turned to face her with hesitation. "I...don't want you going on the May Day ride."

Stella frowned. Thick pieces of her hair fell in front of her face, so she walked back to her vanity to pin it back while she replied. "Why not?"

He shifted his weight nervously, remembering the last time he attempted to order his wife around. "I don't know how much of the book you remember, but I don't want you getting hurt."

Leaning against the chair in front of her, she squinted at him with curious interest. "You're worried about me getting hurt on an overnight ride through the countryside?"

Ben cleared his throat. "Guenever is supposed to be abducted by an ardent and dangerous admirer. I don't want you going."

"Why didn't you say something at dinner, before I agreed to it?" Her hand was now at her hip, mildly defiant.

"I didn't know whether the characters are meant to know what's supposed to happen to them or not."

"Ben, they're not characters anymore." Stella stepped forward aggressively. "They're real people, with real lives. They aren't just names in a book."

"What does that even mean?" Ben shot back, his general irritation rising to match her tone.

"You can't treat them like clueless idiots just because you've read their stories. Do you even know how much of the book is actually going to happen?"

"I don't know. I don't know anything!" he exclaimed.

His frustration had hit its limit. She knew he was stressed because he very seldom raised his voice. He didn't even raise his voice during his scolding back in Oxford. But this wasn't an angry tone. It was desperation. This softened her; selfish as she may seem, Stella was not without compassion. She lowered her defensive hands and relaxed her shoulders. He put far too much pressure on himself. The stress lines on his face were growing deeper, and his posture was taut. Without the journal, the one thing holding his world together in this outlandish adventure, he was beyond lost.

"Okay," she spoke gently. She reached out and touched his arm, causing him to ease ever so slightly. "Why don't we just let things play out?" she suggested. "And only interfere when

177

Korbl does. That is why you're here right? We don't make a move until he does. Until then, just let these people live their lives. We can't hold their hands—they still have to make their own decisions. That's the way life is, right? I imagine it's no different for them."

He looked at her, looked into those deep eyes, and breathed slowly. He knew she was right; but his knowledge pushed him in the other direction. He knew too much about each character's fate, and the more friendships he made with the individuals, the more he wanted to tell them. More urgently weighing on his mind, however, was protecting Stella without arousing the suspicion of the principal characters in the realm. He couldn't rightly tell the queen to not go on her May Day ride because she would be abducted.

The temptation to rig the game is a trial every Keeper encounters, particularly when loved ones are involved. The more he looked into Stella's understanding face, the less he wanted her to go on the ride tomorrow.

"I would prefer it if I went along."

Stella sighed. "Ben, you have to stay with Arthur. You're the Keeper—you can't nanny everyone. Don't worry, I'll be armed. And we'll have knights with us, and maybe I could even ask Gawaine to—"

"No," Ben said quickly. "I mean, the knights in the book make no difference. They are all wounded or killed, and Meliagrance still gets the queen."

"Hm," Stella crossed her own arms, deep in thought. "Well, is the queen hurt when she is abducted?"

"No, I don't think so. The abductor is in love with her."

"Does she get out of it?"

"Yes. She gets a message out to Launcelot. He saves her and kills Meliagrance."

"See," she nudged his arm. "We'll be fine. We just have to let it play out, okay?"

Stella gave his arm one more encouraging rub and walked him to the door so she could get some sleep. He gave a nervous chuckle at her persistence but left without any further argument.


The travelers rose early the next morning to prepare for the ride. As promised, there were ten knights, accompanying a total of ten ladies, who were attended by ten squires. In addition to this, twenty yeomen joined the ride. All rode horseback, and all were cloaked uniformly in green. With Sir Kay in exile, the position of the tenth escorting knight had yet to be filled. Luckily, the noble Spaniard felt relatively healed from his stab wound and eagerly volunteered.

"The wounds received in battle bestow honor, my lady. I insist," he pressed when Stella showed concern for his recovery. "I shall take upon myself the charge of your safety. To gain my noble knighthood, I once bested many a foe to protect my armor at the castle's trough—for there was no chapel. No sword nor flying stone kept me from my post. And so shall I defend you, princess."

Stella stifled a laugh and nodded to him graciously. "Of course you should come then, Don. I mean...Quixote?" Before she could decide on which part of his name she should use, the queen gestured for all to fall in line and begin the ride.

The jovial Spaniard didn't seem to notice her ignorance. He rode closely beside her, with Sirs Ironside and Persant closely behind, while Queen Guenever and Sir Agravaine took the lead.

The queen maintained control of the conversation for the majority of the ride, and none of the attending ladies surrounding her seemed to object. Stella, however, grew anxious with boredom. She managed to tune out the queen's chatter and entertain herself by watching Don Quixote attempt to imitate the posture and mannerisms of the other knights. After a while, she almost forgot that the queen had been talking and interrupted Her Highness by striking conversation with the funny knight.

"What made you want to be a knight?" she asked Don Quixote.

He seemed honored that she had asked, for his chest puffed and his face beamed. "All of the wrongs to right, grievances to redress, injustices to repair, abuses to remove, and duties to discharge. My lady, how could I not claim my calling as a knight-errant? I knew I must expose myself to peril and danger from which I may reap eternal renown and fame. Who would not yearn for their name to be immortalized as heroes of old: Palmerin of England, Amadis of Gaul, the Knight of the Burning Sword—and, of course, Reinaldos of Montalban! I only mourn the loss of my squire and my noble steed, Rocinante." He patted his new horse's head, reassuring her that she was still suitable. "Oh, he was comparable only to Bucephalus, for he was the best bit of flesh that ever—"

"—*ate bread in this world*," Stella finished with a smile. She giggled to herself. "You know, yours was the first full book I ever read on my own. Without pictures, at least. It was always my favorite. So funny...."

Don Quixote stared at her, his mouth slightly opened. When she suddenly realized what she divulged, she locked her lips closed. Guenever had loudly continued her own conversation, so all who seemed to hear her blunder were Don Quixote and Sir Agravaine, whose inquisitive ears twitched as he tuned in.

"My book?" The Spaniard's eyebrows were raised in avid curiosity. "There are already books accounting my exploits?"

"Um..." Stella's mind desperately grasped for words. "I didn't mean 'book.' I meant...prophecy," she said slowly. "Keepers, they're privy to all sorts of...prophecies. And-and being the Keeper's wife, I've heard a couple."

"What sort of prophecies?" Agravaine shot over his shoulder.

Stella blinked nervously. "Oh, you know...the normal kind of prophecies. Destinies and stuff."

"You know of my destiny, princess?" Don Quixote pressed excitedly.

"Well yes, but I can't tell you. That would be...breaking the rules." She cleared her throat, growing more confident in her lies. "I mean, they're just words, after all. *It is not in the stars to hold our destinies, but in ourselves*," she quoted. It seemed safe to quote her father's use of the words of the great William Shakespeare, as they had never heard of either gentleman. Thankfully, it put the matter to rest with ease.

"How profound, princess," the Spaniard praised. "You are correct, of course. We must choose our own path..." and he continued on.

As he jabbered on, the sky seemed to gradually grow darker. Agravaine was the first to take notice. He glanced cautiously about and stopped his horse in its tracks. They were within seven miles of Westminster, and the woods that separated them from the city itself seemed denser than he remembered. Surrounded by the flowers and mosses the queen loved so much, the riding party was pleasantly distracted until Agravaine's resistance to move forward suddenly captured everyone's attention.

"What is it, Agravaine?" Guenever asked him softly.

His eyes were alert, as were those of his steed. Before he could speculate, a loud rustle sounded from the woods ahead of them. Within a few short moments, those rustles seemed to materialize into dark figures creeping from behind the trees. Over a hundred dark riders were well-harnessed for battle, eightscore of them donning the crest of Meliagrance.

All of the queen's knights surrounded her and her party of ladies, with their nervous swords drawn and at the ready. While they were each honorable, good-hearted men in their own right, none had yet seen a battle. They were merely selected to be part of the Queen's Knights because she had taken a liking to them. All they knew was the general purpose of a sword and the usefulness of their white shields. Beyond that, they were no more warriors than Don Quixote.

So, as the terrifying enemy advanced, the poor, unschooled knights shook in their armor. It all happened so quickly; Meliagrance's men and the dark host with whom they worked attacked with such ferocity that Agravaine and his men stood no chance.

As she had promised Ben, Stella was armed with a long dagger she kept sheathed under her dress. Her face was hot and her blood burned with a cocktail of anger, fear, and confusion. The knights' line of defense was breached in five heavy heartbeats, and all that stood between the women and their attackers were the exhausted swords of Sir Agravaine and Don Quixote.

The wicked knights surrounded what was left of the party in a circular formation, their weapons trapping them aggressively. Once resistance relaxed and Agravaine saw their chances slimming to none, the adversary's leader in the attack guided his horse past the barricade his men created. The rider chuckled evilly and barked for the cowering survivors to dismount.

Agravaine signaled for the women to obey the orders, but to stay close to him. Don Quixote bravely stuck to Stella's side, keeping his weapon aimed at the opposition and only slightly wavered when his old stab wound became irritated.

The rider gestured for his men to take the horses as he dismounted. In one grand motion, he removed his helmet to reveal the smug visage of Sir Kay. Agravaine's face twisted in rage and all the womenfolk gasped softly in fear.

"Your Highness," Kay smirked, mockingly bowing to the queen. "There is someone who is eagerly awaiting your arrival."

Agravaine stepped in front of the queen defensively. "Why don't you crawl back under the rock you came from and die?" he suggested bitingly.

Kay chuckled again, swiftly striking Agravaine's head with the hilt of his sword. Agravaine grunted and crumbled to the ground, clearing Kay's line of sight to reveal Stella standing firmly beside the wounded Spaniard. The handle of her dagger was slick with sweat, which only increased as Kay's eyes narrowed in on her.

"You," he stepped forward. "What a great fortune seeing you as well, princess."

# 17

## THE OTHER SIDE

Agravaine was left unconscious and bleeding from his wounds on the ruined field. Queen Guenever was hysterical, wringing her hands and weeping. The other nine women who attended her felt inclined to follow suit.

Stella did her best to calm them, but she had difficulty being convincing, as she was fighting her own fears. Don Quixote's stab wound had been re-opened, as Stella suspected, and gradually drained his energy. He leaned up against Stella as they stumbled along between the walls of black horses. He battled consciousness but was determined to stay alert enough to protect the fair ladies.

"Ben was right," Stella mumbled quietly to herself. "Why didn't you listen, Stella? Oh, I know, because you thought you were right. You should probably stop doing that. He knows what he's talking about—when he says you're going to be abducted, you should probably believe him. He actually read this book. You only skimmed it once in school..."

"What are you saying?" Guenever whispered loudly.

Stella rolled her eyes. "Nothing. We shouldn't have done this. Ben warned us about Kay, but you insisted, Gwen...and now we're captured by villains."

Guenever raised her brow at the impertinence, but it only made it easier for Stella to lay blame her way. "I beg your pardon? This is not my fault."

"Shut up," one of the grumbling knights growled.

The queen covered her mouth with a shaking hand, suppressing a whimper. The captives were taken to that darkest part of the woods. A wooden pen, with soldiers standing guard, was set up especially for them. They were herded into the enclosure like cattle awaiting slaughter. The terrified women cowered as far from the entrance of the pen as they could, leaving Stella, Don Quixote and Guenever standing their ground in the front.

All of the dark soldiers bore the trademark stains around their eyes, sending chills down Stella's spine, but none of them reached the magnitude of chills their dark general evoked.

*Spyros*, they call him; Kay's vertically challenged ally. Stella was uneasily reminded of a wild rat when she caught a glimpse of his face. His very presence formed a massive pit in her stomach. He rode through the encampment with a new companion the queen seemed to recognize immediately.

"Meliagrance," she grimaced, almost in annoyance.

"I should hope next time you will not be so quick to doubt the Master's word," Spyros seethed to Sir Meliagrance.

Meliagrance dismounted the moment they approached the pen of prisoners, eying the queen with an eerie gaze. "It is not your master I doubted, Spyros—it was you. But you saw it through."

He seemed pleased beyond measure. He reached out to kiss Guenever's hand, giving a derisive welcome that was not well received.

"You shall pay for this!" the queen slapped his hand.

Rubbing his hand, the wicked knight was unabashed. "Hm, I wished to see you in better spirits, my queen. No matter, we shall make do."

"You traitor," she said venomously, standing defiantly in front of the group of prisoners. "You are the son of a king—and to bring such disgrace upon your family and title...you bring dishonor to your position in the Round Table. Were the king to learn about this, you would surely be—"

And the brute slapped her across the face, causing her to stagger backwards almost into Stella's preoccupied arms.

"It may have escaped your notice, Highness," he gripped her face and held it viciously close to his own. "But I have the advantage at present. If I were you, I would carefully consider this before insulting the man in whose mercy you find yourself."

Stella shifted her weight uncomfortably, noticing her arm falling asleep under Don Quixote's weight. The queen was now shaking. All resolve she held a moment ago disappeared, and she surrendered to the terror before her.

Stella sat Don Quixote gently on the ground beside her and pulled Guenever away from Meliagrance's grasp. The wicked knight quietly watched, not taking his eyes off of the horrified queen.

"Your knights are dead," he straightened his back to tower over them. The courage he felt, knowing dozens of armed men stood behind him, gave him the smugness to gloat freely to his captives. "All you have, my queen, is a herd of helpless women and a foolish Spaniard—which hardly works in your favor," he added with a scoff.

Stella grimaced and looked down at the discouraged knight. "He's an idiot; you're not foolish," she told him softly. "You're a noble warrior. And you did your best to protect us...considering."

This caught the evil general's attention. Spyros narrowed his gaze and slowly walked up to the curious blonde rebel. With a peculiar expression on his face, he stared into her eyes, as if looking for something. Those big, sky eyes.

All of a sudden, his body tensed and his hand immediately clutched the hilt of his sword. Something in her eyes blinded him, alarmed and threatened him. Stella swallowed hard and looked at him, perplexed. He merely cleared his throat to regain composure.

"Take the queen to my tent," Spyros barked at one of his soldiers. Meliagrance's face fell. He forcefully held his arm out to stop the soldier.

"Wait," he challenged. "Spyros."

A stern but silent communication passed between them, resulting in the two stepping aside for a rather heated re-establishment of terms. The mumbling was subtle and low, but Stella and her keen skills of eavesdropping managed to discern the words "*King*", "*instigate*", "*distraction*", and an emphatic "*the Master knows what he's doing.*"

Through the bits and pieces, Stella assumed that the purpose of their abduction went beyond Meliagrance's mere fancy of the queen. With Spyros' involvement, the intent was to hit the king where he could do the most damage. Apparently, the affair wasn't moving things along fast enough. Taking the queen would start a war; Stella supposed all villains thrive on conflict, so the explanation was simple. However, she couldn't quite figure out how distraction played into the scheme. Distraction from what?

Spyros breathed an obvious threat to Meliagrance, and an agreement of some sort was made. Meliagrance gestured to the nearest soldier, who then promptly grabbed the queen's arm. Guenever's eyes widened as she vainly resisted.

"What are you going to do with her?" Stella intervened. The book said the queen wasn't harmed, but an alarming rush of panic reminded Stella that the book no longer applied. This evil goblin-man was as much a monkey wrench in the plot as she and Ben were.

"Silence, woman!" Kay snarled, raising his arm to strike her.

Spyros forcefully seized his wrist with aggressive strength. "Who is this woman?"

Kay's lip curled. "She is the Keeper's wife."

"The Keeper's wife," the rat-faced man repeated prepensely.

"I also go by Stella," she contributed, with that reckless spunk of hers perfectly intact. "Or, Princess Stella, to you."

"She's of no real use to us." Kay drew his sword. His agitation toward Stella went beyond the burden of a hostage;

every ounce of his hatred of Ben seeped through to Stella in his penetrating glare.

Spyros merely rolled his eyes. "Oh, shut it, Kay. You have no clue." He snorted grossly before continuing. "She needs to live."

This made very little sense to Stella. In her mind, killing both the Keeper's wife and the queen seemed like an effective way to wage war against the forces of good. But, for one of the rare moments in her life, she decided to keep her lips sealed. Something told her that if they needed her alive, the queen's life would be just as valuable to them.

Guenever would be safe.

The thought repeatedly ran through Stella's mind as she watched them take the queen to a tent in the center of the encampment, guarded by two heavily armed sentries.

Just after sunset, all of the captives collected around their only beacon of strength: the beleaguered princess. With the queen being held separately, Stella was the closest person they had to a figure of authority as she sat stalwart against the wooden fence with the huddled women and Don Quixote falling asleep around her.

Her own eyes refused to close; her posture may have been lazied by the effects of boredom, but her mind remained alert. She kept a wary eye on Don Quixote's wound; she managed to clean and redress it, with the fabric she tore from one of the many layers of her dress. The bleeding had finally slowed, allaying only a minuscule fraction of Stella's stress.

As the night continued to fall, the dark watchmen relaxed in their stance. Spyros and Meliagrance were apparently convening to discuss their dealings in a tent on the other side of the encampment.

The sound of hoof-beats coming through the woods caught the attention of all those still awake. Stella flinched, almost knocking the head of the soundly sleeping Spaniard off of her shoulder. The horse came into view as it neared the cluster of tents, giving Stella a glimpse of its rider.

The man was dressed in dark fabrics, as expected, and from what the lights of the torches revealed, even his fair hair and skin had a singed shade to them. That feeling of dread Stella experienced earlier toward Spyros was now returning. Her first suspicion was that this rider could, in fact, be Korbl himself.

Shortly following him were eleven other riders, adorned in black cloaks and thin black and grey armor. Unlike the previous sighting of these riders, Stella caught sight of their faces. Their thick hoods were down, revealing very delicate, feminine features. Those piercing stained eyes struck Stella with the memory of the attack outside of Camelot. The warriors who had surrounded Don Quixote—she knew their forms were far too shapely for the average knights. The first rider had his own personal battalion of female warriors and the way they followed him only supported Stella's developing suspicions.

As Stella narrowed in on the rider's identity, a cry from the sentry outside of Spyros' tent announced the rider as "Bastien" thus dashing Stella's hopes that this was the evil sorcerer Korbl. Spyros slowly emerged from his tent with a grimace across his face. He was not pleased to see this visitor.

"Well you clearly haven't accomplished too much, my friend," the rider chuckled darkly. "You look far too fat to be working hard."

Spyros rounded his shoulders back defensively while self-consciously sucking in his gut. "Says you, rogue," he sneered. "Matters are taken care of here. What do you think you're doing on my turf?"

The man called Bastien smirked. He proudly stood a head taller than Spyros, and his confident demeanor threatened the rat-man's dominance. Stella couldn't help but smile at the satisfaction this gave her.

"Did you not hear? Our assignments have crossed. I have a message for you," Bastien went on. "From the Master himself. He says to play nice and stay out of my way."

The tents were several yards away and even straining, she couldn't quite catch the whole of the conversation, as the two men turned away from curious ears. She sighed in disappointment; it was proving to be much more difficult than last time. She did, however, hear her own name mentioned. Spyros seemed indignant, exclaiming that he had everything under control. His authority meant nothing to this rogue, who stood skeptically.

"Just leave." Spyros waved an outraged hand in the air. "Tell the Master all is taken care of on my end. If anything goes wrong, you're the one to blame."

Bastien chuckled darkly. "Oh, he knows who's to blame. I'm sure he just wanted to remind you, in case stupidity became your primary trait."

In two swift seconds of rage-fueled stupidity, Spyros had a knife to Bastien's throat.

Chuckling again, Bastien grinned. "Relax, friend," he said with irony. "I'll give the Master an accurate report. And I brought you some help in your next endeavor. Perhaps they'll ensure you don't spoil my assignment too badly." He waved a hand to the women on the horses behind him. The woman in front nodded to Spyros with a smirk on her face.

"I didn't call for you, Medea," Spyros insisted.

"I'm here for my share. You won't be depriving me now —you can't have them all," the woman chuckled.

If only I could adequately portray the unhinged nature of the timbre of this woman's grating voice. If her name is not enough to suggest her story, just bear with me, reader, and further acquaintance with her will follow in accounts to come.

Spyros released a frustrated sigh as he conceded and gestured for the lady riders to continue past him. And with that, Bastien the Rogue smoothly remounted his horse and rode off, never losing his smirk at seeing Spyros' displeasure. Stella pretended to doze off when Spyros glanced in her direction before he lumbered back into his tent. Korbl's men must not get along on principle, Stella thought. She imagined being grumpy is a prerequisite for being a villain.

Stella's last interaction with Ben kept popping up in her head. As much effort as she put into trying to fall asleep, her mind refused to quiet down.

*I would prefer it if I went along.*

She was beginning to agree with him. She had to be stubborn, and she couldn't forgive herself for that. Everyone in the camp was fast asleep; no one saw her growing anxiety. She was terrified. Any previous discomfort she had once felt around Ben had disappeared. He knew so much more than she did, his instincts were sharper, and he made her feel safe with his calm demeanor. She promised him that the riding party would be safe and that nothing would happen. The worst she had expected was some teasing from Meliagrance, some shaming from Guenever, and then Launcelot would come and...

She finally remembered that most crucial detail. Guenever was to send a message to Launcelot and would therefore be saved.. The only obstacle now was Spyros separating Guenever from contact with the rest of them. The attending maidens were sleeping on one another's shoulders, slightly relaxing in their slumber. Don Quixote's head had slipped off of Stella's shoulder and now rested on the wooden fence. He snored loudly, occasionally twitching and muttering nonsense in Spanish.

"Don," she whispered. When he didn't respond, she lightly nudged his heavy arm. "Quixote—wake up."

"Hm?" he stirred. He rubbed his dirty hand across his face to wipe off the drool. Lazily, he opened his eyes and quickly came to attention upon seeing Stella's face staring at him. "Princess," he recognized, too loudly.

"Shh," she hushed him. "I have a plan to get out of here. But I need you to do something for me."

He attempted to straighten his back, but the flesh in his abdomen was still too tender, causing him to wince in pain and groan. "How may I serve you, my princess?"

"I have a quest for you."

Being so conditioned as Don Quixote was, through an overabundance of books featuring brave knights and adventures, the idea of a quest of his own naturally delighted him.

The narrator of his own tale, dear Miguel, wrote *"for me alone, Don Quixote was born and I for him. His was the power of action, mine of writing."* And too true, in fact. The Spaniard was a man of action. He leapt at the excitement of the possibility of a quest before knowing what it entailed. Of course, the symptoms of his avid reading causing his brain to be *"dried up"* might give one pause. His enthusiasm could easily be mistaken for madness. But, in any respect, whether it be lunacy or passion, Don Quixote was willing.

"It'll be an adventure," Stella began. She felt as though she were mocking him, speaking as if to a child, so she shifted her tone. "I mean, it probably won't be as exciting as those giants probably were, but..."

"My lady," he assured her, "Any errand for a fair princess cannot be anything less than noble. I shall take this quest upon myself with vigor and—"

"Okay, okay, shh," she hushed him again. "I need you to get a message to Sir Launcelot. You need to tell him what happened and have him bring some knights to come kill these... whatever they are."

Before the Spaniard could protest with something regarding his own qualifications, Stella made him swear to follow her orders to the letter. Puffing his chest with pride, he dutifully swore. Thankfully, the guards had made their rotations, and there were only three presently on duty. They stood leaning against the posts of the fence; one guarded the gate in the front, and the other two were stationed evenly along the round enclosure.

It took calculation and timing, but Stella eventually found a small portion of the fence, toward the back, that could be wide enough for Don Quixote to squeeze through—as long as he took her advice to "think thin." The guard responsible for that particular area was starting to doze off, lowering the risk factor to a more reasonable level. The Spaniard took off the top layer of his armor, as quietly as he could, and held his breath before making an attempt.

Triumphant, he grunted loudly as he stumbled over to the other side. Unfortunately, the guard stirred and snapped his head in the knight's direction. Almost instinctively, Stella clenched her arms around her stomach and groaned loudly. She stepped in front of the guard's line of sight and began dry-heaving.

"I'm sorry," she croaked. "Do you have any...?" She quickly stopped herself, momentarily forgetting she was not in the 1960s anymore and could not ask for her usual antacid. Frantically, she tried to think of a more archaic alternative. "...bread?"

The guard's face seemed alarmed, especially as she proceeded to dramatically gag and turn an unhealthy shade of red. In her childhood, Stella perfected the art of feigning illness, so as to be freed from attending school or dull social obligations with horrid Aunt Carol. The guard seemed to struggle between his commitment to being cruel and his preference for keeping his clothes vomit-free.

"Um..." he muttered in hesitation. He held his arms up, defensively keeping her at a safe distance. For the first time, something familiar caught Stella's eye. Almost identical to Riddock's, the guard wore a scaly leather wristband. "You should...uh...get back over there and...uh...walk it off...?"

He attempted a light shove to push her farther into the pen. Stella was barely moved, still staring at the wristband, but she only lingered long enough for Don Quixote to clumsily disappear into the woods.

# 18

## THE FOOL'S NOBLE ERRAND

For the first time since his abrupt pilgrimage to this new realm, Don Quixote was swelling with his trademark enthusiasm and determination. Finally, he could embark on a noble quest he had only dreamed about.

In all the books he had so erratically and thoroughly studied, those honorable knights made their legacies on such pursuits. The pride in the Spaniard's heart overshadowed any pain that might have lingered in his side. He was filled with dignity and purpose. Nothing could deter this man. He journeyed, ever so resolutely, only stopping when he stumbled upon the aforementioned battleground. A pale, groaning Sir Agravaine still lay wounded, with half of his life drained out of him.

The soft soul hurried to his wounded comrade's side. "Dear sir!" he exclaimed, lifting Agravaine's head. Having come to only a few moments before, the man was almost too weak to even flinch at Don Quixote's painful, but well-meaning, assistance. "Truly you are as strong as an ox—we thought you had fallen by the sword! Your living breath is miraculous."

With a groan, Agravaine glanced up at the eager new hero. "It is more than miraculous. The enemy has kept you and the others alive?"

Don Quixote nodded. "Yes, indeed. I have escaped embarking on a quest for the princess. I am to gather my fellow knights as reinforcements to free the fair maidens from the enemy's wicked grasp."

"Princess Stella sent you?" Agravaine inquired. He managed to lean against Don Quixote's arm to sit up a bit straighter.

"I am to deliver a message from her to Sir Launcelot, yes. Shall I take you with me?" he mindlessly grabbed Agravaine's sorely bruised arm in an attempt to lift him.

"No!" the knight gasped sharply. When the Spaniard released him in alarm, he corrected his tone. "No. My strength is gradually coming to me. You must fulfill your mission, my good man. I shall seek out the princess and the queen and ensure their safety on my own."

This appeased Don Quixote. He watched as Agravaine rose on his own, displaying his growing strength. The small gash on his forehead had dried up, from where he had been knocked unconscious, while the various nicks from his enemies' swords left only superficial wounds. Despite the concussion, his energy was moderately restored; the hope of the women still being alive seemed to revive him.

"Go," Agravaine ordered. But, before allowing the Spaniard to leave, he firmly gripped the fool's arm and locked eyes with him. "And, Don Quixote—if you should find Launcelot unavailable, seek out Gawaine to deliver the princess' message. She would trust him to come to their rescue just as well as Launcelot."

It took Don Quixote nearly all night before he staggered through the castle gates the following morning. Adrenaline is undoubtedly a force to be reckoned with. This convalescing human somehow managed to travel to his destination without so much as stopping for respite. It was quite remarkable to witness.

Equally remarkable was that, contrary to Agravaine's intentions, Don Quixote happened to stumble upon Ben Caverly in the courtyard instead of Sir Gawaine. Ben had been pacing the yard idly—clearing his head of what, at the time, he believed to be foolish worry over Stella's safety—when he ran into the winded knight. Sir Launcelot sat leisurely nearby and lept to attention at the first mention of Guenever.

"What is this of the Queen?" Launcelot pried desperately.

To the best of his ability, Don Quixote abridged the adventure that was the May Day Ride for the eagerly attentive heroes: "...and I was commanded by the princess to summon Sirs Launcelot and Gawaine. Together, we are to assemble a noble battalion of knights to regain our ladies' fair."

Panic quickly rose within Ben, and his heart sank. "Wait, Stella told you to fetch Gawaine and Launcelot?"

"Where is the Queen? Where are they keeping her? Is it that demon, Meliagrance?" Launcelot verbalized every question that ran through his head.

Don Quixote blinked; his excitement and fatigue triggered momentary, short-term memory loss. "Um..."

"Never mind," Ben shook his head. Technicalities hardly mattered. Stella had cleverly thought through the best solution, but it would all be in vain if they didn't act quickly. He knew Launcelot was meant to save Guenever and take down Meliagrance himself, but this was personal. He couldn't sit back and allow Stella's fate to lie solely in Launcelot's hands simply because the original text demanded it. And yet his loyalty demanded he remain with Arthur.

Calm and determined, as was his nature, Ben accompanied Launcelot and approached the king with the situation. Within those next few hours, Arthur promptly organized the rescue party.

Don Quixote refused to stay behind and recuperate. After a decent nap and having the court physician redress his side-wound, he squeezed his way into the ranks before they headed out. The king was hesitant, but his protests fell on deaf ears. Ben assured him that there was no point in trying to battle with the Spaniard over the issue—steadfast, quest-seeking heroes are notoriously stubborn. This quality incidentally provided Don Quixote with the necessary vigor to keep up as our team of heroes rode off to the rescue.

The sun came up, with no rescue in sight. Stella was beginning to regret sending Don Quixote on his own. Everything she remembered from his book didn't inspire much confidence.

What if his wound had reopened and he bled out? What if he suffered the same fate as Agravaine? What had happened to Agravaine? She dreaded the thought. Interrupting her thoughts was Spyros, with an ultimatum: their lives for their allegiance.

"Scada always take care of our own," Spyros promoted.

*Scada*, the wicked label, applies to any and all humans and creatures alike who take on the particular dark oath, binding them to the very beacon of all evil. In contrast, those who resist this evil are pleasantly referred to as Alden or those under the authority and care of Myk.

Returning to our hideous Scada commander, he stood in the center of the encampment with Medea and several of his own guards. The coward couldn't face the women alone for fear they'd get the better of him. With armed escorts on either side of him, he stood proud and confident. He wore an expression that seemed a comical attempt at a compassionate smile. He was there as a friend and potential comrade, not the sniveling rat he indeed was. "It has been nearly twenty-four hours, and there has been no response to our letter of ransom. Your king has abandoned you, and I'm sick of wasting time."

Stella was no fool. She had been on alert for anyone leaving or arriving, and he sent no such ransom letter. Sure, Don Quixote would have expectedly taken quite a while traveling back to the castle, being in his wounded state, but she refused to give up hope of rescue.

"Before the next sunset, you will die. But...as I said...we take care of our own. Those who are against us will die. However, the wise ones, those of you who think this through, will be spared."

He was horrible at sweet talk, but his speech was apparently convincing enough to sway the minds of the majority of the women. He gestured for those in agreement to follow Medea out of the enclosure.

Of the ten original attending women, only four remained. Secure in their defiance, they looked to Stella—the most defiant of them all—for additional strength. The insurgents stood behind her, but as reinforcement to their leader, no longer cowering in fear. What little they knew about Spyros was enough to feel the darkness that came with accepting his offer.

The recreant fool seemed more relaxed when only five stood against him.

"And you, princess?" he spat, advancing. He stopped only inches from her face. She could hear her allies behind her shift uncomfortably, but she didn't even flinch.

An advantage to being an insolent child is the tendency to revert back to blatant and fearless obstinance with ease. As frustrating as it could be, it does prove to be a useful defense mechanism in situations such as these.

"No, thank you," she rebutted. In her peripheral vision, she could see the weak ones being taken into the tent across from Guenever's. Shortly after the tent flap closed, unintelligible mumbling could be heard. "You can just go ahead and kill us."

He scowled, harshly wrinkling his eyebrows together. "I look forward to it," he hissed and turned around sharply.

"Why not do it now?" Stella called out. He froze at the entrance of the enclosure and faced her slowly. His expression darkened with disdain. Emboldened, she taunted him further, "You said you're sick of wasting time." She stepped closer to the gate with a smirk shining across her face. "Unless you need special permission. You're not actually in charge, are you? You're just an underling."

Within seconds, Spyros had his knife to her throat. Clearly, she struck a nerve. "I am no underling," he growled.

"Really? Then what's stopping you?" she whispered. His breath smelled horrible, but the knife was an easy distraction from the stench.

Gutsy as the antagonism was, it achieved what she intended: the truth. He didn't have the authority. He may have been the leader of this attack, but he was not in charge. He wouldn't kill them until he was given the proper instructions. This gave them time. At least, until sunset.

He reluctantly withdrew his blade, hating every moment. "Sunset," he reminded them viciously. Lumbering out of the enclosure, he threw a commanding gesture toward the gate guard.

Spyros's vain promise left a certain shadow hanging over the camp. Stella could feel it lingering when, in fact, it was much more. This oath I mentioned was such an affair that it bid the presence of a very special guest.

He did not stay long but slithered into Spyros's tent visibly enough for Stella to catch sight of him. He crept out of the darkness of the trees, making no noise, and even flashed Stella a curious, sinister glance. He was of average build. Handsome as he was, his dark eyes made Stella inhale sharply in fear. The strange familiarity she felt ran through her in cold chills. And then, just as smoothly, he disappeared past the tent flaps, never to resurface.

It wasn't long before the weak ladies emerged from the tent. They were given new clothes and a new purpose. As the traitorous women walked by the fenced enclosure to their newly assigned posts, their eyes flashed in Stella's direction. Their expressions were of fading regret and renewed confidence. They felt they had won, looking down on the foolish ones still held captive like animals. In these falsely arrogant faces, a dusky shadow stained the skin around their eyes, much like that of their new rat-faced commander.

Stella looked away quickly; the lack of light gave her a terrifying chill. Whatever happened in that tent, it changed the women forever. Adorning their wrists were those familiar leather wristbands. Stella assumed they were a mark of allegiance.

Now, there are naturally varying levels of evil. As Medea formerly claimed, she took her share. Not all of the weak ones partook in the oath that binds the soul, and the wristbands, and the eye stains. No, indeed. In fact, three of them emerged from the tent in relatively sound condition—following Medea's lead to the horses and only gained brass cuffs on their arms of a uniquely winding design: the details of which Stella could not make out from a distance.

The differences between them and the newly ordained Scada women were distinct but no less disappointing.

Time was running out. It must have already been noon, for Stella's sense of urgency was heightening quickly. There was no certainty that Don Quixote made it to Launcelot. She had to act. One of the guards, she noticed, was the same one she nearly fake-vomited on, so she decided to invest in that connection. He was a scrawny man with rotting teeth and an eye patch. She knew she could easily muster a conversation.

"Hey there," she leaned up against the portion of the fence he was guarding.

He glanced at her idly, and then looked away in indifference.

"So...what do they call you?"

"Havelock," he said shortly. His voice was much deeper than expected for a man of his frame.

"And from whence do you hail, Havelock?" doing her best Guenever impersonation.

He didn't trust her. His one eye looked at her strangely. "Neverland."

She nodded, pretending not to recognize the name in order to build the conversation. "Ah, good old, Neverland. What's it like?" He ignored her, but she wouldn't give up. She inched closer to him, aiming to annoy. "Come on," she pleaded. "It is so boring in here. I'm sure you're bored too, just standing there all day."

"Mangy," was all he said after a prolonged pause.

"Huh?"

"Mangy. With too many children."

"What did you do for a living? You know, before you...enlisted?" She wasn't sure what to call signing up to follow a raging warlord through various realms.

"I was a sailor," he said.

"Was there...magic in your realm, too?"

206

Pausing for a moment, he scratched his behind before answering. "A bit, yes. I didn't get none of it, though. Only the fairies and that blasted kid."

"Blasted kid," she agreed. "So you worked for Captain Hook, I presume?"

Havelock's eyes snapped to her abruptly. "You've heard of the Captain? Oh, I suppose bein' an Arch Companion you know all sorts o' stuff."

She shrugged humbly. "A bit, yes."

Suddenly, his voice became hushed, and he leaned in closer. "Tell me something...did the Captain beat the kid?"

Stella was surprised. This evil henchman, whose job was to defeat and discredit the Keeper, was asking Stella to confirm her ability to know his realm's fate.

"Well..." she started. She had no knowledge of the actual state of the man's realm—every story she ever knew was just recently challenged by this entire adventure. To maintain his interest in the conversation, however, she feigned insight. "Peter is the realm's hero so...he sort of won."

In Neverland's most recent state, Stella was mistaken. However, in fairness to her claims, Captain Hook hadn't claimed victory over the realm either. So, in a sense, she was not entirely wrong.

The pirate frowned in disappointment and annoyance. "Of course he did."

"Is that why you joined Korbl? Because you were tired of being on the losing side?"

He didn't reply, but his face gave her the answer.

207

"Wouldn't it just be easier to switch sides again? You know, to the one that's winning?" It made too much sense to Stella, but because she'd never experienced the other side, she couldn't quite understand his blind allegiance.

"You lot don't win all of them," he protested. "Besides, we take care of our own."

He sounded like a drone who had ingested too much of Spyros's propaganda. Stella wasn't buying it. She respected that he was standing his ground—he was just standing on the wrong ground.

"How long have you worked for Korbl?" she asked conversationally.

"Long enough."

"Long enough that you didn't get to see how your own realm turned out?" she pointed out.

He glared at her insinuation.

"Korbl didn't even conquer your realm, did he? How did you end up here?"

Grunting, he adjusted his weapon on his belt and gave his section a dutiful, cursory glance. "Spyros was there takin' recruits."

"So...he didn't even think your realm was worth conquering?"

"Of course it was!" Havelock snapped. Stella raised her hand apologetically. "He said it just weren't the time."

"It is all about timing, huh?"

He gave one quick nod and then tried to continue ignoring her. It was not as productive as he had hoped. She prodded his arm obnoxiously.

"Hey, how'd you lose your eye?"

He lifted a dagger to her, threateningly. "I can show you."

She retreated, only slightly. "Sorry, I just thought you would have a really fun story to go along with that eye patch."

He squinted at her, trying but failing to understand her. She was terribly chatty, but he was far too dense to think of what she could be trying to accomplish. "It was an accident."

Stella stared at the dark patch, formulating possibilities. "Was it just incredibly itchy and you asked Hook to give you a hand, but he accidentally gave you a hook instead?"

"I was capturing that blasted fairy, and the wretch threw pixie dust in me eye. Blinded me forever—but just in the one eye," he explained, ignoring her ridiculous theory.

"Did she get away?"

"No, I was too fast for her," he said proudly.

"Of course you were," she patted his arm in praise. This seemed to stroke his ego just enough. "Stupid fairies. Hey..." she added in a whisper, "...do you think you could get me into the queen's tent? These other ladies are starting to smell."

"No."

She pouted a little. "Come on. Could I at least talk to her?"

"No." He seemed vehement on the matter.

"Okay. You know what? You can go ahead and kill her— I don't really like her that much anyway, to tell you the truth. But, do you think the rest of us could slip out? You really only need the queen."

"No." It was clear that the friendly discussion was over. Havelock was closed off to any other schemes she may have had up her sleeve.

The new batch of guards brought the women a meager bread-crumb lunch. There was no use wasting food on hostages scheduled for death. Stella refused to give Spyros the satisfaction of complaint, and she ate the breadcrumbs silently. As the women ate, a sudden urge overcame Stella.

*Run, now.*

She couldn't understand it. The new guards were still alert enough to keep an attentive eye on them. The situation was far from ideal. She decided to ignore the urge until the henchmen had relaxed lazily into boredom.

Run, now!

It was stronger this time, overcoming her senses. Attempting once more to push the idea to the back of her head, Stella made a humorously confused face, catching the attention of one of her fellow captives.

"What is it, my lady?" the young woman inquired.

"I don't..." Stella trailed off. "I need you to do something."

"Anything, Your Highness."

Breathing steadily with resolution, she took the woman's hand and looked at her earnestly. "When I give the word, take the other three and run straight for the castle—without stopping or looking back."

As she said these words, part of her doubted every syllable. With so many of Spyros's men surrounding them, there was no remote possibility of them escaping.

Apparently, despite her personal doubt, Stella's words had such power and conviction behind them that the young woman trusted every word. She nodded faithfully and gathered the other three without question. The four of them stood at the ready near the side of the fence from which Don Quixote had previously escaped. Stella kept a wary eye on the guards, who became abruptly distracted by a sudden shout from Spyros's tent.

"Go," Stella gestured frantically.

Unbelievably, all four women swiftly slipped under the fence and dashed out of sight with ease. In the height of her excitement, Stella quickly leapt over the fence herself and darted across the camp. Miraculously, she also went utterly unseen. A passing henchman brushed against her as she approached the queen's tent, looking directly at her. She held her breath and braced herself for what was next. It was in vain, however. As if she were invisible, the guard moved on without so much as a blink. She could hardly believe it. By some miracle, she had managed to walk through enemy territory without raising any sort of alarm.

With her head held high, Stella slipped quietly into Guenever's tent.

The tear-stained queen yelped in alarm.

Stella promptly threw her hand over Guenever's mouth to silence her. "Shh, be quiet," she hushed firmly.

"H-how did you get in?"

Stella started but realized she had no explanation. "I, uh, I don't really know. But we need to leave. Now."

She grabbed the queen's shaking hand and dragged her behind. Just as before, they quickly walked through the camp undetected. Keeping the queen close, Stella gestured for her to remain silent. The queen reluctantly obeyed. However, the moment they passed the borders of the camp, and far enough from earshot, Guenever didn't hesitate to challenge Stella's plan. It is generally a female attribute to question every detail, but this particular female weighed even more quickly on Stella's nerves.

"What if they notice we're missing?"

"Then they'll notice we're missing. Walk faster."

"But how did they not see us? We were so close to—"

"Would you just shut up, you nagging brat!" Stella snapped. She stopped in her tracks and turned abruptly to face the nuisance. Thankfully, they were deep enough into the forest to be easily hidden from passersby. "Can't you just take it as the miracle it was and let it go?"

Indignantly, Guenever crossed her arms in front of her chest and pursed her lips. "How dare you speak to your queen in such a way!"

"You are not my queen, lady. You're just a—" the loud rustling of slow hoof-beats cut Stella's retort short. Before the queen could squeal nervously, Stella's hand covered her mouth once more. "Not a word," she whispered threateningly. She dearly hoped that the two of them were somehow still invisible.

The hoof-beats neared them and then came to a stop. Upon seeing the rider, Guenever pushed Stella's hand aside and smiled with relief.

"Agravaine!" the queen exclaimed.

The knight dismounted and bowed to them gracefully. "My ladies, are you well?" he inquired. "I have searched for you through the night in the hope that you survived. I am...beyond relieved that you have. Now I will return you to London. We mustn't worry the king."

He chivalrously gestured for the women to ride his horse for the journey back. Stella quickly thanked him and began to mount, but Guenever petitioned for sympathy of which she had been sorely deprived.

"Oh Agravaine, we have been through such an ordeal!" Guenever whined.

As she whined, Stella's leg brushed against the outline of a strange object in Agravaine's saddlebag when she mounted the horse. With its owner preoccupied, Stella sifted through the bag. Her fingers swept across a recognizable leather binding.

"No," she exhaled softly.

She swiftly pulled the object out of the bag and nearly gasped when she recognized her father's journal. It seemed Ben had been right in suspecting Agravaine of treachery. She didn't dare confront him quite yet; for the moment, her safety rested in his hands. Instead, she subtly slipped the journal into the belt that once held her now-confiscated dagger, and draped her green cloak over it. With luck, it was safely concealed by the time Agravaine turned to lift Guenever onto the saddle in front of Stella.

"Are you sure you should walk, Agravaine? You are still wounded," the queen pressed.

"It is but a mild head wound, Your Majesty. I shall manage. It is much easier to keep you safe while you have the advantage of riding horseback."

"But are you certain you wouldn't rather—"

"Just shut up and let the man walk," Stella rolled her eyes. The queen finally smiled in satisfaction, but Stella couldn't conceal a distrustful grimace.

Agravaine chuckled. "It seems this venture has worn your patience thin, princess."

"You have no idea," she muttered.

They trotted along for a time, as quickly as Agravaine could follow. Just as the forest began to thin, rustling and the echo of the hoof-beats of the enemy's search party surrounded them. The dark faces slowly became visible through the trees with weapons drawn and kill orders given.

"How did they find us?" Guenever whispered. "Why are we not invisible like before?"

If Stella had ventured a guess, she would have suspected Agravaine's presence had something to do with it. But she hardly had time to speculate. In a similar fashion as before, Sir Kay emerged from the midst of his ranks with an eye of vengeance.

"We must not let this become a habit of yours, dear Agravaine," he chuckled.

"Not again," Stella moaned.

"If you had just died the first time, you would have been spared the humiliation of being defeated twice," he went on, ignoring Stella's complaint.

"Maybe you should've just made sure he was dead the first time instead of conking him on the head like a careless moron," Stella shot back, louder than she intended.

Kay raised his eyebrows. "Captivity has not dulled your spirit, princess. Unfortunately, you and Her Highness have an appointment you can't afford to miss." He signaled for his men to advance, Kay himself charging for Guenever.

Guenever dodged his first blow and kicked him, as hard as she could, off of his horse. Ignoring Agravaine's order to stay on the horse, Stella followed Kay to the ground and grabbed his sword before he could reach it. Guenever shouted for Stella to get back on the horse, but swords were pointed in her direction as well. Agravaine disarmed the closest attacker and vigorously defended the queen, endeavoring to form a sort of wall between the queen and the enemy.

With Stella's help, Agravaine fought off the assailants. Only Kay remained. The odds seemed to be in their favor, but things are not always as they seem. For even though Stella had seized Kay's sword, Kay retrieved a dagger from his boot and aimed it at Guenever's heart. She stood at a defensive angle behind Agravaine and had momentarily stepped aside as Agravaine killed his last opponent. While her heart was narrowly missed, the blade sliced past the queen's upper arm, just above her elbow, hitting a critical vein.

Agravaine chased the survivor back into the forest and turned back just as Guenever fainted into Stella's arms. Her color was fading fast. Her arm was bleeding profusely. Stella fell to the ground, holding tightly to the dying queen. She gently set her head on the ground and desperately tried to apply the needed pressure to the wound. Stella's mind was racing so frantically that she hardly felt herself crying.

"What do I do? What do I do..." she cried to Agravaine. He ran to her side and knelt urgently near the queen's head.

Guenever's eyes slowly closed, the life draining out of her. Stella felt helpless and regretful. She found herself surrounded by entirely too much death. She had absolutely no previous regard for the dying queen, but a sudden rush of sorrow overcame her and prevented her from suppressing her tears. The queen whimpered softly in fear as she lost consciousness. Agravaine fell backward in defeat.

He had failed.

Stella was not quite so quick to give up. Keeping a firm hand on the wound, she practically shouted words of encouragement, ordering Guenever to open her eyes and continue breathing.

Sadly, the dying are not always obedient.

# 19

## THE DESIRED EFFECT

In spite of Don Quixote's prolonged message delivery, Ben and Arthur wasted no time coming to the rescue. Within hours of departure, the party came upon a fatigued, but alert, Agravaine. He stood leaning against the broad trunk of a tree, his sword drawn. He was pale, but not from his wounds. He couldn't bring himself to handle the body of the unfortunate queen, so he had agreed to stand guard while Stella gathered her wits.

"My king?" Agravaine started. He looked up to thankfully acknowledge Arthur, Ben, and their companions. Gawaine and Launcelot stared searchingly, expecting the worst. The king, not seeing the women behind the large tree nearby, dismounted and hastily confronted Agravaine. Ben, Gawaine, and Launcelot promptly followed suit, leaving Don Quixote watching curiously from atop his steed.

"Where is the queen?" Arthur pressed.

"Where is Stella?" added Ben.

Agravaine hung his head low and weakly gestured to the other side of the tree trunk. Ben's heart quickened with dread. Everything on Agravaine's face suggested tragedy. All four men held their breath and stepped forward to see a crestfallen Stella still holding the queen's shoulders heavily in her lap.

Stella's face was still moist and her heart heavy. The front of her dress was drenched in Guenever's blood; her hem was torn, in an effort to create a tourniquet, but in vain. When the drained caretaker saw her rescuers, she quickly rose and tried to wipe the remaining blood off of her stained hands.

"I couldn't stop the..." she trailed off, losing the need for an explanation. She ran into Ben's arms and buried her face in his chest. He held her close, exhaling in relief. Watching King Arthur fall to his knees at the sight of his wife's lifeless body, Ben felt a twinge of guilt—he couldn't help but be grateful it hadn't been Stella.

Arthur wept, clutching Guenever's hand and praying desperately that what he was seeing was a lie. Launcelot staggered backward, reaching out for the tree trunk to steady him.

"I should have been there..." he mumbled faintly. "Had I ridden with her...I could have saved her..."

Arthur looked up at him strangely. Naturally, Agravaine didn't hesitate to contribute. "Perhaps she should have more appropriately been saved by her husband, and not her lover."

In a moment of unthinking, raw rage, the king drew his sword and lashed out in Launcelot's direction, Agravaine's comment evidently confirmed Arthur's suspicion. The knight dodged the attack; Arthur was thankfully impeccably average in his skill, and even more so when emotionally compromised. Before Arthur could take another swing, Ben lunged to grab his arms and restrain him.

"She was my wife, Launcelot!" Arthur shouted, fighting off Ben's constraint as the tears ran down his cheeks. "And you, a Knight of the Round Table—where was your honor!?"

"I—"

"He had none!" Agravaine stepped in, standing between the king and his rival. In addition to his apparent desire to stir conflict, Agravaine had a small and strange sense of loyalty to his uncle, Arthur. "You have no right to weep over the loss of the queen—she was not yours to lose," he growled. "No matter how much she may have thought so."

"Indeed," Gawaine agreed with his brother but stepped in line with Stella. "But is there not a better time than this to—"

"Do not dare lay blame on Guenever," Launcelot interrupted, guilt-ridden. His breathing deepened with overwhelming despair. He had betrayed his king and lost his ladylove. "She is not to blame."

"But you are," Agravaine grimaced. "Had you any love for Arthur and respect for your knighthood, you would have ended the affair, you faithless—" he raised his sword aggressively.

"Stop it!" Stella hurriedly cried. Agravaine froze. She stepped beside him just as he was about to strike. "Do you think adding another body over the queen's is going to solve anything?" she hissed.

He slowly lowered his sword, strangely obedient as he looked into those captivatingly stormy eyes. In surprise, Ben loosened his grip on the king, relaxing his arms and keeping his eye on Stella.

With a threatening glance, she had secured the attention of every flaring temper. She moved, imbalanced, to Guenever's side.

"Neither of you is innocent in any of this," she stared down Arthur and Launcelot.

Gawaine backed away, giving her a straight line of sight to both male participants in the legendary love triangle. The king was alarmed by this accusation, but before he could interject, Stella continued forcefully.

"Arthur," she stepped closer to him. "I don't condone anything that Guenever and Launcelot did in betraying you—they definitely deserve to be punished—but you need to understand Guenever's situation."

Ben subtly raised his eyebrows, interested.

"A woman pushed into an arranged marriage, as the queen was," she went on, "would be very easily tempted to fall in love with another. When you're unhappy, you're unhappy. Marriage is hard enough with someone you love, but it's even harder with someone you don't. She was already in love with Launcelot before you chose her. She should have known better, but you couldn't expect her not to have wandering eyes when you forced her into marriage."

Ben swallowed hard. Her words seemed a little too personal to be fabricated for the sake of calming the conflict. He briefly glanced at Gawaine, who was entranced by Stella's charisma, and then looked to the ground with a glower.

"But, Your Highness—" Agravaine spoke up.

"Let her finish," Gawaine snapped.

Without skipping a beat, Stella then approached Launcelot, still maintaining complete control of the situation. "But you...you should have known better." The good knight hung his head in disgrace. "You both knew better. I know you loved her, but she was not yours. She was married to another—and quite frankly, she treated you like dirt in any case—so you should be ashamed of your actions. You and Guenever were both guilty."

Launcelot looked regretfully into the eyes of his king. Stella's scolding was most effective. Launcelot was the first to step forward. His face was more contrite than any man I've ever seen. Despite his heart betraying him, Launcelot was a man of honor.

"My Lord," he softly spoke. "You are my king. And my friend. I offer you my deepest and most sincere apologies...and condolences. Guenever was a strong queen, and her memory will forever live on. I pray we can put this regretful ordeal behind us and move forward with dignity." He lifted an amicable hand, and all eyes turned to Arthur.

The king was hurt as any cuckolded man would be. But, somehow, the words of the Keeper's wife held such power that Arthur was now filled with understanding and forgiveness. He saw her happiness with Launcelot and regretted not providing it for her himself. As despicable as her sin was, Arthur could not hate her for it. Nor could he hate the humbled man standing before him.

With a presence of peace, Arthur took Launcelot's hand, and the two men mourned the woman they both loved.

The queen's body was carefully wrapped and rested atop the king's horse for the ride back to London where she would be buried. Word of Guenever's murder spread quickly, sending the entire kingdom into mourning. Hundreds attended her funeral, paying their respects to the deceased. Putting aside her previous disdain, Stella behaved herself for the duration of the funeral. King Arthur was silent through the entire ceremony, merely nodding as guests bid their condolences.

"This was intentional," he whispered to Stella. "You said Kay fled after the queen was wounded?"

She nodded. "He didn't bother sticking around to see if he succeeded."

"They wanted to hit Arthur where he's most vulnerable. They want to start a war."

It may have sounded like a drastic conclusion to draw, but Ben felt with great certainty that the May Day Ride abduction was carefully planned and executed for just that purpose.

"When they had us," Stella informed, "Spyros said something about a distraction. Do you think that's what he was talking about? You think Korbl's starting a war to use as a distraction?"

Ben considered this. "Yes," he said decidedly. "But a distraction from what?"

Stella shrugged. Gawaine spotted her from across the courtyard and began making his way toward her. Ben rolled his eyes and stepped just a little bit closer to his wife. Young Gawaine, however, was not one to easily register hints.

"Maybe Korbl is after the one thing in the realm that can take him down," Stella suggested, lowering her tone. She angled herself to face him head on, blocking his view of Gawaine's advance. "You," she added for clarification.

Ben sighed doubtfully. "No, if he were after me, why hasn't he attacked me yet?"

Stella shrugged again. "Maybe he has, and you just don't know it. He could be testing your strength. Maybe a know thine enemy situation." And with that, she turned to meet Gawaine halfway, engaging in an appropriately somber conversation.

Ben cleared his throat and shook off his fears. He wasn't there to worry over Stella and Gawaine; he was there to help Arthur. The grieving king stood with his hands intertwined in front of him. His face seemed to have aged a hundred years.

"Sire," Ben gently prodded.

"The queen is dead, Keeper," the king replied mechanically. "And that means war."

# 20

## THE TALE OF THE AUTHORS

Nothing quelled the fury of his heart more than preparing for war. King Arthur couldn't spend another moment of mourning—he was a man of action. He sent word out to his various citadels, ordering the knights stationed there to scout out Korbl's forces and gather as much information about Korbl's bases as they possibly could.

Arthur's passion and intensity in his cause incited alarm amongst his knights, but Ben encouraged them to follow orders and not to interfere. He could only imagine the pain motivating the king. I can testify of the utter anguish that overwhelms every facet of one's being when suffering the loss of a beloved spouse. The king was not in his sound mind. His rage was implacable. Korbl deserved what was coming to him.

Some of the scouting knights sent word that Kay had retreated northward to a castle they had never before seen. Its craftsmanship was terrifyingly detailed, too meticulous to have been created in such a short amount of time.

"Korbl must have built his own fortress," Ben concluded. "He wanted this war. It makes sense that he's more than prepared for it."

The king pressed his fist against his lips thoughtfully. The two were posted around the Round Table, which bore a large map of the land, as they had done before. Ben suggested they meet privately, should a traitor still be among them. "It was not there the last time I visited Launcelot's castle to the north. How can such a monstrous structure be built so quickly?"

"Sire, Korbl is more powerful than you can imagine. He can level a village with a snap of his fingers—he can build a fortress in less than a few minutes."

To the king's ears, Ben sounded so experienced and informed, but he spewed only facts he read from Albert's journal. At least the ones he could recall, lamenting the loss of the journal. Still undecided as to their next move, Ben and Arthur took a recess from their war council. As he left the grand hall, Stella met him in the corridor.

"Can I talk to you privately for a second?" she asked, hiding an arm behind her back.

"Of course." He guided her gently by the elbow until they came to a large enough nook in the wall for the two of them. Luckily, the other knights were training while the servants were busy attending to duties, leaving them quietly alone. "What is it?"

She glanced around, making sure the corridor was indeed empty. Once clear, she took her hand out from behind her, in it held Albert's journal. Ben's face lit up with excitement.

"You found it," he breathed with disbelief. He took the journal and ran his fingers down the spine as if making sure it was real.

"In Agravaine's saddlebag," she explained. "You were right about him. I think he's trying to sabotage you. The affair has already been exposed, and Arthur and Launcelot didn't do each other in as he expected. He probably wanted Arthur to lose his mind and kill off the rest of his Round Table in the process. It was a little presumptuous, but who knows what he'll try next."

"Yes, you seem to have spoiled his plans on that one," Ben chuckled. Suddenly, an idea came to him. "He was expecting Arthur to be on the offensive."

Stella stared at him. "Yes...that's basically what I said."

"No," he grasped her shoulder firmly. "Korbl is expecting the same thing. He had Guenever killed to start a war, and Arthur's rage is too predictable. We can't be on the offensive yet. We have to wait Korbl out." Inspired by his new realization, he swiftly kissed her forehead and turned to reconvene with the king.

"Wait, wait, wait," Stella grabbed his arm. "I figured it out."

Ben paused, momentarily confused. "Did you want to tell the king yourself?"

"No, not that." She beamed adorably at him, with that knowing smile of hers. "I skimmed through the journal. I know...I know why my dad could never finish the story."

Ben knew the story. And, so do you, I presume. The most beautifully tragic tale ever untold. *Briar-Rose. The Sleeping*

*Beauty* as recognized by some. This was the moment Albert always dreamed of; his daughter could finally understand.

"She was my mother."

No remorse, no anger from being left in the dark was within Stella. In that age, Korbl was on what was eventually named the Fairytale Crusade; fairy tales brought hope and that was dangerous to him. She understood that. It was who she was.

"That's why you called me a princess," she added softly.

Bashfully, Ben looked at his hands. "To be honest, I actually forgot about it at the time."

She smiled sweetly and kissed him on the cheek. "And now I know what Faegrian is."

The journal did not include a glossary, but considering the importance of Briar-Rose to his family, Albert gave quite a detailed account, including the realm's ancient name.

"Uh, yes." Cheeks still red and flustered, Ben added, "You know…I, uh, didn't realize it the first few times, but I've finally recognized what Korbl targeted to get at your father."

"What was that?"

"His Companion. Your mother."

"She was the threat," Stella pieced together. "She sounded like quite a lady. Korbl was probably afraid she'd kick his pants."

Ben laughed. "Yes, she certainly could have. I should…go tell the king what we've come up with."

"Oh, yes," she nodded. "You should do that. Ava scheduled for me to get fitted for a new dress."

Before returning to the king, Ben felt prompted to think his plan through thoroughly. He sat at the large desk in his chambers, staring at the pages of the journal, half-hoping a more comprehensive answer would reveal itself. The silence of his room was agitating him, keeping his mind from being fully engaged. And so, as most brilliant men do, he paced the room. He knew what Korbl was expecting: a vengeful full-frontal attack. A furious king is not always a wise king.

But what would Korbl not expect?

"That is a dilemma, isn't it?"

Startled, Ben nearly tripped over his own feet. "Myk?"

"How have you held down the fort while I've been away?" the cryptic man inquired casually, leaning against the door frame.

He had no desire to synopsize the adventure, and he had a feeling he didn't need to. "Where exactly have you been?" Ben asked instead.

Myk smiled. "I've been about. There were other matters to attend to. I see you've learned quite a great deal. Good to see you held on to that," he nodded to the journal.

"Well, if you're here, you can destroy Korbl," the Keeper gestured to him expectantly.

Myk held his palms up, calming Ben's assumptions. "It cannot work that way."

"Why not?" he questioned, with an edge of irritation.

"You are the Keeper."

"But you're just as powerful as Korbl—even more so." Ben was frustrated. The seemingly convenient solution in front of him merely looked away before stepping beyond the threshold.

"Benjamin," Myk patiently walked forward. "You don't understand. I cannot kill one of my own. Not truly. And if I did, it would void the very purpose of this war."

Ben frowned. "What do you mean?"

"Let me tell you a story...."

"Myk...."

"Humor me, Benjamin." Myk took a seat at the desk and leaned back comfortably in the chair, preparing himself for his own story.

"It is the tale of fifteen beings—beings of great, unspeakable power at their fingertips—Authors, we'll call them. These Authors discovered something beautiful and powerful: the magic of creation. With this new magic, these beings imbued words with such magic. The sentences, paragraphs, pages–every drop of ink were emboldened to create worlds. After the birth of these realms, the greatest and most powerful ruler of the Authors organized his people to protect them. They were precious and vulnerable, and there was one who sought to gain control of them.

"The Author's Bane, we'll call him. He slowly darkened others in order to claim the realms in their charge. As he gathered and beguiled followers, he led a rebellion against the ruler of the Authors. A terrible war took place, drawing lines between brothers and sisters. The Author's Bane claimed many— but only those who fell willingly.

"A safe haven was made to house the stories under the supervision of the Authors. The Bane took his new army to dwell in a realm too dark to name, a realm kept from all light. While the Author could not force the worlds in his care to stay loyal to him, he could arm them, if they chose, with the power necessary to protect and defend against the Bane's influence and violent crusade for control. Power, of course, along with the assistance of some of the Authors' own kind. Each of the divine beings took mortal forms and prepared themselves to defend the Author's precious realms when their time came....your time."

"You took that from Albert's journal," Ben commented quietly.

"Yes, I did. And he took it from another scribe I had the privilege of bringing to the Arkis. She always saw things more poetically than others. I couldn't have told the story better myself. But her account was accurate."

"It's a lovely story, Myk, but it doesn't answer why you can't take on Korbl yourself."

"Oh, but it does. You see, Korbl....the Author's Bane, as she called him....didn't just corrupt, he challenged. If they were to given life, he—well all of us, really—had the divine right of dominion and control over every living thing within each mortal realm." Myk glanced down at his hands. "He sought to assert this sort of control, to prove that dominion."

Ben leaned against the wall nearest the desk, wrinkling his brow in contemplation. "And that assertion of control inhibits your own?"

"We're fighting for autonomy, Benjamin. Autonomy, agency, free will—whichever descriptor you choose. If these worlds we created choose to allow Korbl's influence to reign, there is little we can do to prevent it. If the mortals allow it, we cannot stop him. We can only offer maintenance and rescue. Hence Yonas's strategy."

"The strategy of you doing nothing?"

Myk smiled a little. Ben's tone was far from accusatory. It was inquisitive, puzzled, searching for a reasonable explanation.

"Let them fight for their own freedom. Those Authors I spoke of are also known as Galdere. Korbl, Yonas, myself and others....we cannot be killed. We are immortal, sorcerous beings. This war can't simply be won by me engaging Korbl in hand-to-hand combat—and believe me, it has been attempted. He must be brought down by a force greater than that. He must be defeated by the mortals he seeks to control."

"Forgive me," Ben sighed. "But they didn't ask for this."

Myk nodded slowly, watching the Keeper. "You're right. But their creation was unavoidable. That creation magic I mentioned has destructive tendencies when left unchecked. The Council's decision was intended to preserve as much as possible. I don't expect you to remember that quite yet. You've been overwhelmed enough, I think. The coalescence of magic was inevitable; the future of the creations was...optimistic."

Ben straightened his back. "Expect me to remember...?"

Clarification didn't come, however. There was a silence between them as Myk glanced down at his hands, in deeper contemplation. Ben put himself at ease by considering further study of the journal.

"It's a nuanced war, to be sure," Myk finally continued. "The battle ground Korbl chose was a vulnerable one. The mortal element required the handicap of a mortal shell for the majority of our agents. But that is why you've been granted an exterior source of Galderean magic." Myk gestured to the jacket-vest Ben still wore. "Gives you a fighting chance.

Myk squared his shoulders to finish his explanation. "So, you see, this war is not solely my own. I cannot win this war alone any more than I can conquer your portion of it for you. However," he added, as Ben's face fell, "I can help you if you'll let me." He strolled to the side of the desk and picked up the journal. "I see Stella took a turn with the journal."

"How did you..." Ben trailed off.

"Korbl is distracting you," Myk restated the obvious and ignored Ben's confusion. "I'm here to tell you from what."

And so, the cryptic Galdere stood and perched himself on the edge of the desk to continue his explanation. Ben intently crossed his arms in front of his chest.

"Korbl cannot be killed in the traditional sense," Myk clarified. "Even if he could, you would not be the one to to strike the final blow. His fate will be at the hands of the Fulendian, so it's not entirely your concern quite yet. What is your concern, however, is the fate of this realm. It's been claimed by Light in the past and, so long as the ruler of the realm concedes, Korbl must be banished. As the Aerest Keeper, you're entitled to certain tools for your personal arsenal, which I'm inclined to assist you in acquiring. I have been visiting a specially beloved sorceress." Ben could have sworn he saw Myk blush, but he couldn't be sure. "She resides in a particularly notable lake in this realm."

"The Lady of the Lake? Isn't she dead? Beheaded?"

"Temporarily left the realm. You will need to seek her out. The earth beneath her lake contains material of a celestial nature, originating from the stars. It's provided an ideal treasury for the first of these tools: the Soter Stone. She also knows the location of a Regent Keeper called Merlin—"

"Merlin is a Keeper?"

"Regent Keeper," Myk corrected. "Poor soul does his best, but he isn't quite the caliber needed in an Arch Keeper."

Having met Merlin personally, I can tell you that Myk's lamentations about Merlin's capabilities are accurate. No one is perfect, but some are further from perfection than others.

Sensing Ben's confusion Myk continued, "Regent Keepers are less powerful than Arch Keepers but more powerful than the average mortal. They too are given Galderean magic and noble assignments but are typically overseen by Arch Keepers. Going unsupervised can lead to scenarios of a chaotic nature. Regrettably, the adulterous circumstance of Arthur's conception was a result of Merlin being left unattended. Alas, it resulted in the temporary suspension of his Keepership, ending an era of Regents."

Ben nodded his head, which was now swimming with mental notes and references to research as he hung on Myk's every word.

"In any case, finding Merlin will lead you to find the second addition to your collection: the Sword."

"Wait," Ben stopped him. "The Sword and the Stone? As in...the stone Arthur pulled the sword from?"

"Yes. Well, not the exact stone, no. The Soter Stone is far more significant."

Ben frowned. "But the king already has Excalibur. Why would we need Merlin?"

"Excalibur is not the Sword. There are two. One gave Arthur the authority to rule and the other, the power to vanquish his enemies. Before Arthur received Excalibur from The Lady, Merlin took Caliburn—the sword from the stone— and hid it somewhere safe as he was instructed. Korbl knows you possess the jacket and have entered the realm; he's now working to keep you from uniting the Sword and the Stone as well."

"Agravaine stole the journal," Ben told him, though he guessed Myk already knew.

"Ah, yes. Another important addition to a Keeper's arsenal."

"What would the enemy want with it? What threat does it pose to him?"

"Oh, words have inconceivable power, Benjamin. Korbl knows that." He set the journal back on the desk and stared Ben square in the eye, ensuring he had his undivided attention. "You must go, Ben. Go to the Lake and—"

"Ben, I thought about what you..." Stella walked right into Ben's chambers, unaware she was interrupting. She was silenced, however, by the sight of Myk. A striking familiarity bombarded her eyes, causing her to clutch the handle of the door she had just swung open. She felt she knew his face, but she couldn't hope to produce a name. "Sorry," she mumbled.

"Stella," Myk grinned.

Her misty eyes widened. He knew her by name. This did not alarm her. Instead, it calmed her. She released the doorknob and relaxed. He slid off the edge of the desk and moved so smoothly as if gliding.

"He was always right about your eyes—like the entire sky trapped in glass. You certainly didn't get it from Albert—his are too dark, like his father's. Definitely inherited them from Rose. I work with your father," Myk explained, resting a few feet before her. "I'm Myk."

Albert Towson may not have divulged much to his daughter before departing, but Stella had sworn she once heard her father mumble that name before flying off on a business trip. Myk.

Without hesitation, Stella embraced him. Ben was taken aback. It felt as though she were embracing her father again. He even smelled of old books, as Albert always had. She didn't want to let go. She was safe, comfortable.

He chuckled warmly. "I'm going to need to borrow your husband for a little quest, Stella."

After they separated, he briefly explained the necessity of the three keys a Keeper needs, leaving nothing out. She understood perfectly, as he knew she would. Lovingly, he took her hand and reached for Ben's shoulder. For a moment, they both felt a surge of energy through his uniting touch.

"But I swear to you, my dear," Myk added in a soft tone, "that I will see that Ben returns to you safely."

Content with this promise, Stella left them alone once more. As soon as the chamber door closed behind her, Ben shook his head. "I think you may overestimate our marital connection."

A smirk flashed across Myk's face. "For now, perhaps. Just be sure to assemble a band of knights and meet me at the Lake, Benjamin."

# 21

## A HERO'S JOURNEY

Being a Keeper in a realm where your kind is generally revered and lifted atop pedestals certainly has advantages. Whether you know what you're doing or not, those who follow you will take your word as gospel.

Auspiciously, for Arthur, Ben's counsel came directly from Myk, so the king's faith in Ben was well-placed. Ben relayed Myk's plan, explaining the sorceress at the Lake and the help she would give. He was careful to use vague words, still unsure of just how much Arthur would understand regarding the three keys and such. Arthur readily agreed and assembled a great collection of knights to accompany them.

"I must stay in London," Arthur lamented. "As much as I should dearly love to ride with you, Lord Caverly, I must await word from the remainder of my knights. They are still scouting the northern regions to bring me a more accurate map of Korbl's defenses. I wish you success."

He presented Ben with a map to the Lake as well as his hand-selected team: Don Quixote (for he had proven himself capable and honorable in his aid to Stella in the May Day ordeal), Gaheris, Bors, and Agravaine. Ben was a bit unsettled at Agravaine's joining the expedition. He was torn—should he warn Arthur of the traitor? He decided it best to keep Agravaine at his side instead of leaving him in London where he could wreak havoc for Arthur. He planned to confront him privately, far from the king, and deal with the knight then. Knowing the other three knights were allies calmed him.

Just inside the gates of the citadel, our heroes prepared for their quest, strapping their horses with the necessary supplies and bidding farewell to the fair ladies seeing them off.

Don Quixote, in his noble way, approached Stella as she finally broke away from a loquacious Gawaine. "My lady," he began, taking her hand. "I vow to ensure Lord Caverly's safety to the best of my ability."

A beam of admiration stretched across Stella's face. Flashing another smile in Ben's direction, she placed her other hand atop the Spaniard's and lowered her voice. "Thank you, sir. I shall hold you to that. But, take care of yourself too."

He cheerfully pledged to do so and moved along to see to his provisions. Stella was left alone, watching Ben. She wasn't sure how she felt about him leaving her like this, especially after the May Day ordeal. He seemed too pensive, and that worried her.

"Need help?" she offered, bouncing to his side. He looked up quickly from his saddlebag with a start.

"Um, no I think I have everything," he patted the bag and straightened his back. "Could you, though, look after Arthur while I'm away?"

Her mouth twitched with a smirk, hearing Don Quixote fumbling onto his horse behind her. "Only if you agree to look after Don over there."

Ben chuckled.

The levity soon died, however, when he caught sight of Gawaine offering Don Quixote assistance. He had tried to ignore the knight chatting up Stella moments before. The way she laughed and smiled at his witty remark...Gawaine seemed a little too eager for Ben to leave. Ben's eyes fell back to the saddlebag he had checked twice already.

*Relax*, he told himself. *This was meant to be temporary.*

Stella sensed the fall in enthusiasm and shifted her weight anxiously. "Ben," she said softly. "Are you sure you can't just have someone else go instead? After everything, I think I'd feel much safer with you than without you."

He glanced up at her with a solemn smile—only briefly because he found it difficult to look at her. "You'll be safe here," he assured her. Then, with a hint of unintended spite, he added, "And...if anything should happen to me, I'm sure Sir Gawaine would take very good care of you."

An indignant expression darkened her angelic face. She stepped closer to him, ready for an argument she was sure to win. "But I don't want him to take care of me. I want you to take care of me."

His eyes shot up at her in surprise. Ben had lost track of how many times since their Boston reunion that Stella had

239

surprised him by her behavior. And this was no exception. Benjamin didn't know what to think. All he could manage was a boyish smile. Seeing that the other men were ready to leave, Stella surprised him yet again, touching his hand and standing on her toes to give him a quick, but tender, kiss. As she kissed him, he felt her slip something into his leather vest. When they separated, he saw it was a beautifully preserved rose, faded with age.

"I found it in dad's journal," she explained, still touching his hand. "It's not a handkerchief, but I figured I might as well go along with the whole medieval thing and send you off with a good luck charm." Slowly, she stepped back to let him mount his horse, her lovely but sullen eyes reluctant to let him go. "Just...come back, okay?"

Ben could hardly focus on following the map Arthur had given him, still reveling from his wife's kiss. Bors chuckled to himself at Ben's lack of faculties and did his best to guide them as they went.

As they rode up a rather steep hill, unbeknownst to the five travelers, a stranger made his way to the back of their party. He wore that smug expression you would most recognize from the enemy's camp. Bastien rode behind them silently on his dark steed, careful not to draw attention to himself until the opportune moment.

And when that moment came, the knave strategically slipped a comment into a conversation between Don Quixote and Sir Gaheris regarding the late queen.

"It was a shame," Bastien casually contributed. "I'm sorry to have missed the funeral. I'm sure it was lovely."

Instinctively and in perfect synchronization, the knights turned on Bastien with weapons drawn.

"State your business," Sir Bors demanded, pointing his sword aggressively.

Bastien chuckled darkly. "Oh please. My business is easy enough to guess." He turned his dark eyes to Ben and gave an acknowledging nod as if to an old friend. Ben held his weapons defensively, certain he had never met the man before. "Love the vest," Bastien sneered. "It suits you well enough."

His tone was dripping with derision that nearly spilled over onto his own leather armor, which bore a striking resemblance to Ben's, but for the deep stains that covered it. Ben hardly recognized the resemblance of the man's vest; it had been so defiled.

Seconds later, Bastien needed only to flick his wrists, and all five men were thrown off of their horses by an unseen force. They each bravely attempted to retaliate but to no avail. Four of them remained motionless on the ground, static with bewilderment.

It was at this time that Ben, the ignorant Keeper, stood from the ground and spoke words that were foreign to his lips. He couldn't recall even quite what he said, but whatever the words, he raised his sword to Bastien with confidence.

Instantaneously, the very atmosphere around Ben bent to his subconscious will, throwing Bastien off his horse and hard to the ground. He nearly rolled down the hill but caught himself with another flick of the wrist, which forced the stable soil in

241

the side of the hill to further push a protruding rock out of the earth for him to latch onto. The knights remained frozen on the ground in awe of Ben.

The only other instance Ben had experienced such magic was when the mystic leather protected him from being impaled. It was miraculous and, had he allowed himself time to digest, he would have been just as frozen as his comrades. The adrenaline prevented even a moment of registration.

Assuming his sword was the source of the magic, Ben lifted his sword again and started for his adversary. Within a matter of seconds, Bastien had climbed his way back up the hill and blasted a polluted, dark red smoke from his fingertips. The air around him swirled and blackened with dust and shadows. It was as if his hand tainted the very air around it, forcing the smoke into a honed, bullet-like weapon to be shot dangerously in Ben's direction.

The Keeper's arms quickly raised themselves instinctively, forbidding the smoke from touching him.

Bastien glared with incredulous fury and lifted himself from the ground. His rage began to boil. He charged Ben with his mortal weapon drawn. And they dueled treacherously close to the edge of the steep hill. It was a location at which I would personally try to avoid any sort of conflict, as the surroundings were not at all ideal for safety.

Sword clashed with sword, aggression ever-growing. Bastien knew he stood no chance against Ben's level of magic, so he took advantage of his opponent's inexperience by relying on the blade. But it was short-lived—Ben was quicker than he expected. After a swift blocking movement with his sword, Ben realized that the power he was feeling wasn't coming from his sword, but his hand. He tossed the sword aside and aimed his hand, with a hopeful heart, at Bastien.

Down the hill the evil one fell, but not before drawing a short dagger and digging it into Ben's leg, dragging him down with him.

Ben howled in pain, lumbering down the hill after his foe. Agravaine was the first of the four to recover from the shock caused by the magic. He ran to the edge as quickly as he could. The knight peered down the side of the hill to see the deep ravine where shadows clouded his view. Though, clouded as it was, he was able to make out the two figures at the bottom.

The two rivals both rose from the ground, despite Ben's fresh and excruciatingly painful wound. Weapons were no longer in sight, just magic versus magic. Ben cast Bastien so strongly against the side of the hill and heard several ribs snap upon impact. As a last defense, Bastien retaliated with even more force. Ben was thrown into a seemingly shallow cave where Bastien expertly blasted a sizable boulder nearby and caused a cave-in which no mortal could possibly survive.

A strange and cryptic grin stretched itself across Agravaine's face as he watched. It quickly changed to a remorseful expression, however, as he turned to his fellow knights and announced his findings.

"The Keeper is dead."

# Part Three

## Hope is Born

# 22

## THEIR SOLEMN RETURN

Stella felt an awful disturbance in the pit of her stomach as she watched the knights unexpectedly return to the palace empty-handed. She stood at Arthur's side, on the steps of the palace. The king sensed and shared her expectant trepidation. Ben was nowhere in sight, and the knights' expressions were dreadfully less than hopeful.

Agravaine was the first to speak, taking the lead of the party as they approached their king. "The Keeper has been killed," he reported sorrowfully.

The dismounted soldiers joined him in his somber report, hanging their heads respectfully. "He was crushed by a boulder thrown at him by one of those dark warriors. There was no hope of recovering his body for proper burial, sire. He was killed instantly."

"No, he wasn't," a numb Stella spoke. The knights before her stood uncomfortably motionless. Each of them looked to her sincerely, and yet she still shook her head. "He didn't."

Arthur put a consoling arm around her shoulder, his own face fallen with despair. Having only just suffered the loss of his own spouse, the king's immediate concern was Stella's emotional welfare.

"The Keeper can no longer help us, Your Majesty," Agravaine added. He fell silent upon seeing the king's earnest expression.

All she could do was stare.

Everything inside of her collapsed.

If it hadn't been for Sir Bors and Don Quixote silently confirming Agravaine's tale, she would not have believed it. With a chilling silence, she turned away from the messengers and walked stoically to her chambers.

Her face was dry, but her heart was flooding. The moment her doors closed behind her, she slid down them and collapsed on the floor. She couldn't even cry. Every ounce of her wanted to. She wanted to fall apart. She felt as if she were, but something was stopping her. Only a few heavy drops were permitted to fall from the clouds in those sky eyes.

She felt Myk taking her hand all over again.

*But I swear to you, my dear, that I will see that Ben returns to you safely.*

Why would he say that? Why would he say that and then take him away?

It wasn't fair.

It wasn't right.

Something wasn't right.

All those witnesses— notably the few she found reliable —said he was gone. But how could he be? The facts suggested...the facts...those things Ben once relied on so heavily, and they now worked against him. Flashes of Ben ran through her head: the wedding, the funeral, the scoldings, the expressions of disappointment, the smirks, the chuckles, the impressive instincts. Suddenly she stopped breathing. His jacket once saved his life, she thought. He was impaled and yet remained unscathed by the blade.

Distraught females—well, either gender, really—tend to think irrationally and emotionally, jumping to dangerous conclusions. This led Stella from hoping the jacket had saved her husband to fearing that she'd never get home without Ben and his jacket. But, as you've seen before, the calming words of a father can prove to have a remarkable effect.

Albert's soothing voice hummed in her ear. *When Myk promises something, he sees it through until the end. You carry on helping Arthur until Ben needs you.*

She wanted to scream, but the words ran through her head once more.

*Just do it, Stella.*

Finally, she took the deepest breath her lungs could accommodate, rubbed her face clean of her sorrow, and stood up. A part of her was still devastated by the thought that she would never see Ben again, but that part was trumped by her faith in Myk's promise being fulfilled. If you couldn't trust an all-powerful being with endless wisdom, who could you trust?

That evening, Sir Gawaine escorted Stella to supper. He was gracious enough to respect her loss and keep his distance, so his flirtatious attentions were held to a minimum. Gawaine was never notably chivalrous, but Stella seemed to bring out the best in him. He and the king were very reliable sources of support. Whispers of the events surrounding the Keeper's tragic death were spread throughout much of the kingdom.

While very few ventured to question her plans as a new widow, speculations were made well within her earshot. Stella hardly went a meal without overhearing some conjecture of which Knight of the Round Table she should attach herself to. Gawaine's name came up more times than she could count.

She resented this.

As far as she was concerned, nothing had changed between them. After all, for those last several weeks, she had not pretended to be Ben's silly cousin. She was his wife. She stood by his side; she supported his decisions, and she advised him as needed. While their relationship, on a personal level, may not have been entirely marital, the role she fell into when they entered this book made her feel otherwise. And that was not something that could be cast aside so easily.

In spite of the knights' general acceptance of this grievous turn of events, Sir Bors took careful note of Stella's demeanor. He began to have his doubts about what he thought he had witnessed.. It was never spoken, of course, but her behavior following the reception of the news suggested indifference or disbelief. Many perceived this as confirmation of her alleged romance with Sir Gawaine, but Bors knew better. The princess must have known something that no one else did.

# 23

## THE BELATED BEN CAVERLY

Ben had not, in fact, met his end.

The great ones never really do.

For just as Bastien launched that final blast, Ben fell through a shallow gap in the cliff and landed in a deeper cavern. The ground was mossy and cold; though Ben hardly noticed the details of his surroundings as the adrenaline wore off and reminded him of the excruciating pain in his leg. He groaned loudly, tears stinging his eyes. Bastien's knife cut him deeply, tearing skin and muscle as they fell down the cliff. His open leg wound had collected a disturbing amount of grass, dust, and dirt from the tumble down the hill, causing it to sting even more.

While Ben groaned and clutched his bleeding leg, a rather alarmed old man sat hunched over a small fire not too far from the Keeper. The flame flickered, illuminating the old man's quizzical eyes and large ears. His surprise was beyond reckoning; no one had entered his cave since he had been trapped inside.

Despite all confusion, the good soul wasted no time in hurrying to Ben's aid. Instinctively, the old man pushed Ben's shaking hand away and cradled the leg in his own hand. Placing his other hand directly on top of the wound, he mumbled incoherently and a sharp sensation shot through Ben's leg. The bloodied flesh aptly cleaned itself and mended the torn edges. Ben's pain began to dissipate. .

Never before had Ben seen flesh heal itself so rapidly, without so much as a bandage or cauterization; he merely stared at the old man, awestruck.

"You...how did...that was..."

"I'm Merlin," the old man answered the vague questions cheerfully. "And who might you be, my mysterious friend?"

Ben turned his hazy focus to his freshly-healed leg, still a bit breathless from the fading pain. "I'm...um...wait, Merlin?"

The old man raised a skeptical brow. "No, I'm Merlin, dear boy. You must have your own name."

With labored breath, Ben tested Merlin's work and attempted to stand, using the wall of the cave as support. "No, of course. I'm, um, Benjamin Caverly. Myk sent me to find—"

"The Aerest Keeper?" Merlin interrupted.

His eyes widened in recognition. The man needed no further evidence; Merlin smoothed his old, grey robes and knelt reverently at Ben's feet.

"I spoke for decades of your arrival, but I quite honestly had my doubts that I would ever personally make your acquaintance." He slowly rose and looked around the cave with discouragement. "It is unfortunate that you should have landed

251

in this cursed cave. It's rather difficult to save the world from down here."

Waving his hand in the direction of his small flame, he brightened the inside of the entire cave.

"There's no getting out, you see." Merlin returned to his spot in the corner and invited Ben to join him. "This is my punishment, I suppose, for sharing my knowledge of magic. I was too good a teacher. Nimue...she was too good a student."

When an especially perceptive student excels past your own level, I believe it's wise to move on to another student, or you are more likely to end up trapped eternally under a rock. Of course, imprisonment probably would not have been necessary if the teacher had known boundaries. Merlin was a particularly attentive suitor, and no respectable young lady would tolerate that, including one as scheming as the sorceress Nimue. Ben understood his new ally well enough and didn't care to hear the details of his lewd transgressions. He had other issues pressing more urgently on his mind.

"Myk said you have the Sword," Ben began, awkwardly joining Merlin on the floor. His leg was still a bit tender, so he propped it on a nearby stone. "I was supposed to meet him at the Lake before nightfall, so if you could tell me where the Sword is, it would be much appreciated."

"Ah, the Sword," Merlin idly stoked the fire. "That which gave Arthur the authority to rule the realm. My one charge. Guide Arthur, but protect the Sword. You know, I couldn't seem to get either of those quite as right as I should have."

Ben frowned. "You don't have the Sword."

Merlin peered up at him like a child caught doing something naughty. "Not exactly—in my defense, however, I hid it to keep it safe from my pupil. Those who are beautiful cannot always be trusted. Never trust them. The ugly ones are the more trustworthy folk. They have nothing to exploit. The pretty ones know their power—imagine a woman with both magic and physical appeal. Very dangerous, my friend. Being sent to a realm with its own magic was truly a test to my fortitude. My downfall was a pretty face interested in magic. I was sunk from the start, I'm afraid...what were we talking about? Oh yes, the Sword! As far as I know, it still may be safe and sound. It's only a matter of finding it. Of course, I couldn't take you to the Sword, even if I wished to. This desolate cave is forever my prison. 'Tis a shame, too. The Sword is relatively close by..."

This brand of jabber caused even the patient Ben Caverly to roll his eyes in exasperation. Clearly, this man had gone too long without speaking to another human being. As he rambled, Ben sincerely hoped Myk would come looking for him when he didn't show up at the Lake. He was still unsure of the extent of Myk's knowledge, but he dearly prayed it went as far as locating Keepers in places more obscure than King Arthur's palace.

"...but wait!" Merlin started excitedly. "You said that you were meeting Myk at the Lake? I was not aware he's also returned to the realm! My, so much happens when you live under a rock," he added in jest.

Ben nodded, gingerly rubbing his sore leg. "Yes, he is. And hopefully, he'll find us...eventually."

253

"If anyone could break the bonds of an eternal prison, it is Myk," Merlin proclaimed, rather emphatically. His conviction in this statement impressed Ben.

"How well do you know him?" Ben asked curiously.

Merlin bowed his head in regret. "Not as well as I should, but enough to know what he is capable of. He set the standard for Keepers, after all."

Ben gave him a strange look, so he went on.

"I should think an Arch Keeper like yourself would know, but Myk was one of us for a time. Gave up being a Galdere to serve his time, as it were. In fact, part of his time was served in this very realm. It's rather funny how things come back round, isn't it?"

Still looking strangely, Ben questioned, "But, why?"

"Well someone had to show us how it's done, you know. Galderean magic is strange, powerful, and complicated. We, mortals, need instruction, I suppose. Some of us more than the rest..." he trailed off, intently staring at the flames before him.

"Was he...the first Keeper?" Ben could only picture the characters from Albert's story of the sorcerer and the cow. He found it hard to imagine Myk as the selfish trader who conned the poor boy with those magic beans.

Merlin smiled softly. "No, no, but he was the most important."

They both fell silent for a moment. Ben felt a little silly not knowing Myk's story. Albert could only fit so much information into the pages of his journal—and even so, only so much information can be presented at one time. It was only now that Ben noticed the leather waistband that was worn beneath the sorcerer's grey robes.

"Is that your, uh...?" Ben asked, gesturing to the waistband.

"My conduit leather? Yes, indeed it is," he patted the trusty leather.

"Conduit?"

"Conduit, of course, to access Galderean magic, and the like. It's the only thing that sets me apart from the average sorcerer in this realm. Heavens, there are so many of them. Still, it's something. Of course, mine isn't quite as powerful as yours is, especially following my suspension, but I suppose—"

"The man who attacked me," Ben cut him off, "he wore one. But it was...different. It was a sort of vest."

Merlin's visage suddenly changed. His eyebrows wrinkled together in concern. He didn't chatter on, and he didn't stoke the fire; he only wrinkled his brow. "He wore conduit leather? He could not be a Regent—I was the only Keeper before you entered the realm. You say he attacked you?"

"Yes, with a kind of...I don't know...smoky magic."

Merlin pressed his lips tightly together. "Hm. Dark magic. It is tragic when they take one of our own. He must be an old one."

"He looked no older than I do."

"Traveling through realms does tend to slow aging greatly. His enchanted apparel reveals his era, however. Each Arch Keeper has a style differing from the last. For the most part, Regents appointed by an Arch were given a variation of this belt." He gestured to his waistband. "There was one—of whom I've heard great things but never had the good fortune to meet myself—who optimistically aimed for his Regents to develop Arch potential. O'Leary, I believe he was called. His Regents were given vests. I suppose he thought the more leather they wore, the more powerful they'd be. Who's to say? They were believed to be elite, as far as Regents go. This dark sorcerer must have been one of O'Leary's boys. Such a shame; I don't know if any of them turned out quite as expected. Was the leather discolored, stained?"

Ben nodded. "Yes."

"Ah-ha, a corrupt O'Leary Regent," Merlin shook his head. "I must have been trapped down here longer than I thought. Myk will not be pleased."

Merlin stood and frantically tried to blast the ceiling of the cave, breaking small pieces of rock that avalanched in Ben's direction.

"What—what are you doing?" Ben stopped the sorcerer's increasingly counterproductive attempts. Merlin had a new eagerness to him that was more than slightly alarming.

"You—" he suddenly pointed energetically. "You are an Arch Keeper! Surely you could move the rock!"

The lingering pain in Ben's leg was starting to disappear, but he was beginning to feel a faint pain forming in his head. He made an effort to blast the rock but to no avail. Neither Keepers' powers were sufficient enough to destroy the obstacle. The timing of their fruitless endeavor was impeccable, however. For just as they staggered back in defeat, the giant boulder was raised from its socket and placed gently beside the opening of the cavern.

"You didn't strike me as a man of tardiness, Benjamin. But, at least you've been productive," a comfortingly familiar voice chuckled.

Ah, Myk.

It didn't take him long to sense Ben's difficulty in making it to the Lake, nor did it take him long to find Merlin's rock prison. At the sight of him, Merlin instantly fell to the ground in penitence. He blubbered apologies for his shortcomings, and gratitude for their rescue, but Myk laughed lightly.

"Relax, Merlin," he lifted his old friend from the ground and embraced him. "I think you've been trapped in here long enough. And you seem to have taken good care of the Aerest." Myk nodded toward Ben's freshly healed limb. "Perhaps, if he sees fit, the Aerest might even re-institute your Keepership. That is one of his duties now."

Myk stared encouragingly at Ben for a long moment before the Keeper realized that he was expected to answer.

"Re-institute?" Ben repeated.

"Regents are nearly nonexistent since Albert's day when the Regent Purge left them slaughtered or inactive. It seems you'll be in great need of them, and I'd suggest you take advantage of all who are willing. You are willing, aren't you Merlin?"

"Naturally, sir—willing and eager to have another go!" Merlin nearly lept in excitement.

"Okay then, and....how, um, how would I do that, exactly?" Ben stammered.

Chuckling, Myk patted Merlin on shoulder, holding out a hand to the repentant wizard. On cue, Merlin removed his conduit belt and handed it to the Galdere.

"Simply by saying so, Benjamin," Myk explained. "You have the authority—so use it."

Ben cleared his throat. "Oh," he started. "Okay then. Um, consider yourself re-instituted, Merlin."

Myk handed Merlin's belt to the Keeper and waved for Ben to return it to the expectant Regent. The moment Ben touched the leather it glowed, much in the same way as Ben's jacket. With a beaming smile, Merlin accepted the belt and returned it around his waist.

The Arch Keeper had officially gained the first Regent Keeper of the new era. As Myk mentioned, since dear Albert's death, Regents were, for all intents and purposes, extinct—which can be credited to Korbl's active fear for the arrival of the final three.

But now, as Myk revealed, that was about to change.

"I am forever indebted to you, Ben Caverly," Merlin bowed as the two men stepped back. "I shall never stray again. Or I shall try not to, at the very least."

"Come on then, the two of you," the Galdere beamed. "We have an appointment to keep."

"Ah, yes," Merlin nodded.

Once out of the cave, he then proceeded to engage in a number of common tracking methods—licking his finger and holding it up to the wind, feeling the ground for signs of movement, etc. Though, how these tricks helped him find the Sword's hiding place, I do not know. Apparently, the cache was so secret that he nearly forgot it himself. He comically inspected every nearby tree trunk, knocking on the bark and listening carefully for a hollow echo. Once he found it, his face lit up, and he giggled like a victorious toddler.

"A-ha, Caliburn!" he exclaimed. He broke off a large chunk of bark and reached his hand into the hole he created. Myk and Ben followed him expectantly, only to be equally disappointed. The excitement in Merlin's eyes dimmed as he retracted his arm, empty-handed. "Myk, I swear to you, it was here. Someone must have..."

"Nimue," Myk affirmed. He crossed his arms in front of his chest solemnly. "This only delays us slightly. Ben, how much do you remember of the sorceress Nimue from the original text?"

Leaning against the exterior of the cave, Ben struggled to recall the rigorous details of the book. His memory was impressive, but not exact. And, it had been some time since he had read it.

"Um...Nimue...trapped Merlin under the rock and then married Sir Pellinore or something."

"Sir Pelleas," Myk corrected. "Yes. He does not live far from here. That's where we shall find her."

Myk waved his hand, beckoning three horses to come forth from the forest. He guided one to Ben and then offered the other to Merlin, who cleared his throat in reluctance.

"If it's all the same to you, Myk, I'd rather not—"

"Oh, but you will. Your duty is to assist the Arch Keeper, and assist him you must." There was no arguing with Myk. The three mounted their horses and Myk gestured for Merlin to lead the way. "I'm sure you know the way, my friend."

Disgruntled by his own entanglement, the sorcerer sighed and rode in front. Confronting an old paramour was difficult enough without a history involving attempted murder. Every man must earn penance in his own way, I'm afraid. I do not envy Merlin his.

He unhappily guided Myk and Ben through the forest and across the plain, grimacing with every trot as they came closer to the homestead of Sir Pelleas. His castle was very modestly perched on a small hill.

Interestingly enough, as if fate had intervened, Sir Pelleas was not where he was written to be in the original text. You should have had the pleasure of meeting him much earlier—during the May Day Ride—but he was prompted by his wife to stay home that day and send someone else in his place. It's very comforting to recognize the forces of good working in the Keeper's favor; if Pelleas had in fact ridden with the queen, he would have risked being counted among the slain and would be unable to lend assistance to our hero. Thus, the good knight was precisely where he needed to be, precisely when he was needed.

As they neared their destination, a mounted peddler and his cart, along with an apprentice of sorts, passed our travelers on the dirt path leading to the castle. He wore a charming grin, while his apprentice anxious avoided eye contact.

"Timo," Myk nodded to him.

The peddler smiled, stilling his horse and gesturing for his apprentice to pause. Playfully, he then glanced at Merlin. "Well, well. That cave aged you, old friend."

Myk sighed. "Now, now. Leave him be."

"Come on, Myk," Timo chuckled. "I've missed Merlin's quizzical brow."

Merlin chuckled back nervously, rolling his eyes. "Is she there?"

Timo shrugged, and then laughed at his apprentice's suddenly widened eyes. Their recent trade with the lady Nimue and her husband had left the apprentice overwhelmed by his choice in occupation. It was only then that Ben noticed the apprentice wore a lute across his back and a flute on a leather cord around his neck.

"She spent a pretty penny," the apprentice commented. "Wasn't happy with anything. Didn't even like my performance."

Timo waved off the apprentice's low self-esteem and shook his head. "Alan exaggerates. She has particular taste, but I never leave a customer unhappy with their purchase. I have a reputation to uphold."

"But she–"

"You didn't bring your best to the performance," Timo promptly dismissed, bringing an end to the commentary. He was far too busy staring intensely into Ben's eyes to bother with Alan's list of complaints.

The musical apprentice sighed at the rejection of his search for sympathy, but Timo hardly noticed.

"Who's your friend?" the peddler nodded to Ben.

Merlin answered before Ben's lips could part. "He's the new one. Ben Caverly's his name."

Timo's eyebrows lifted.

"Caverly," he repeated. His eyes shifted from Ben to Myk and back to Ben. "Pleasure to meet you, Mr. Caverly. But,

I'm afraid we must be on our way. Opportunity waits for no man, and we have business elsewhere."

Timo waved a hand in Alan's direction and the two prompted their horses to pull forward, continuing down the path, away from the castle.

"Myk," Timo nodded politely as he passed the Galdere.

"Timo," Myk returned. He pulled the reins of his own horse, moving up the path once again.

"Who was that?" Ben inquired, nearly the second they were out of earshot.

"An old friend," Myk answered plainly. "But never mind him. It seems we've arrived."

And they had.

Before them were the ornate gates of the house of Nimue and Sir Pelleas. At last, Merlin thought his redemption was complete.

"Here we are," he passed on. "I wish you the best of luck, my friends."

Myk smirked. "Hm, I will wish you the luck, I think."

"Oh Myk," Merlin groaned. "How many beatings must a man's pride endure?"

"As much as it can take. I shall stay with the horses and wait for your return with the Sword." Myk took the reins of Ben and Merlin's horses and retreated farther from the gate. "Go on then. And be wise about it."

Merlin sighed. Ben obeyed, laughing quietly at Merlin's agony, and together they approached the gate. Two guards stood on either side, soberly manning their posts. It was clear that very few visitors passed this way regularly. The guards appeared to be dozing off. Merlin explained to them that they came to see the lady Nimue. While the guards opened the castle doors, Ben leaned over to his companion.

"Do we just ask her nicely for the Sword, then?" he guessed.

Merlin shrugged passively. "Your wish is my command, Aerest. But I think, for the success of this endeavor, it may be best for you to do the talking."

"Yes, you're probably right," the Keeper agreed.

The guards let them pass through into the great hall where Sir Pelleas stood waiting to greet them. He was a man of humble countenance. He was relatively young, perhaps only a bit younger than Ben, but had seen a lot of heartache in his time. However, now he held his head high, a new man healed by love. He welcomed them both with a smile.

"To whom do I owe this pleasure?"

Ben looked at Merlin, who only looked right back at him. He caught the hint. "Lord Caverly," Ben introduced himself.

"Ah, yes, of course," Pelleas kept smiling. "The king's guest. We met briefly before. It is truly an honor, sir."

Ben bowed his head congenially. "And this is Merlin."

Pelleas' smile sank. "Merlin? The sorcerer?"

Putting his palms in the air defensively, Merlin stepped behind Ben, anticipating what was to come. This was a safe maneuver, as Nimue had walked into the hall and froze at the sight of him.

"How did you...?" she started. Pelleas turned around, prepared to stop his wife from doing anything rash.

"Someone more powerful than you set him free," Ben explained with haste. "I'm Lord Caverly, the Aerest Keeper." He dearly hoped that title meant something to her for the sake of the innocents experiencing this awkward exchange. Lucky for him, it did.

"The Aerest Keeper," she replied, eyebrows raised.

"I'm here for the sword Caliburn."

"Caliburn?"

"Yes."

She crossed her arms in front of her chest. "And what makes you think it is here?"

Ben moved closer to her, but respectfully stopped when he came to Pelleas. "We know you took it from the tree where it was hidden. I've come to get it back."

Sir Pelleas looked to his wife, silently verifying her involvement with this alleged sword. She merely sighed. Nimue was no villainess. She only took the Sword out of spite. But she knew the authority it held, and she was not about to hand it over to the first man who claimed to be the Aerest. Arms still crossed, Nimue held her head high.

"If you are the Keeper, you must prove it to me," she challenged. "You must complete an insurmountable quest. I am sure you have heard of the sorceress, Morgan Le Fay."

Clearing his throat, Ben nodded. He knew her to be one of Arthur's most bellicose of foes, and he feared just how involved she would be in this quest.

"She has made several attempts on King Arthur's life, one of which I was able to prevent," Nimue went on. "The murderous witch stole Excalibur and replaced it with a duplicate. Exact in every respect but its power. She gave the real one to her lover, at the time, Sir Accolon—whom she arranged to duel and kill Arthur. The king was badly wounded. Thankfully, I arrived in time and, with my enchantment, he was able to regain Excalibur.

"Accolon died of his wounds, but not before he confessed Morgan's involvement. Arthur sent Accolon's body back to her with the message that he had reclaimed his sword and its scabbard. You see, Keeper, Excalibur's scabbard has magical properties, much like the sword itself. It forbids the wounds of the bearer from bleeding." She stepped in line with her husband, continuing her exposition. "That is why the good King Arthur survived his wounds. But, in Morgan's anger, she stole the scabbard, and it was never found again."

Merlin frowned. So much excitement occurs without you when you're believed to be dead. "And you would like us to find it?" he presumed.

"Not you," she corrected. "Him. If you are the Keeper you claim to be, you will find the scabbard and bring it to me."

"He does not know the lands," Merlin protested on Ben's behalf. "And if its location is as unknown as you say, it could take years to find."

Nimue stared straight through Ben. "Not for a Keeper. You, Merlin, will sit waiting for him in our dungeons. If you do not return with the scabbard, Lord Caverly, your decrepit friend will rot in his cell. Do you accept this quest?"

"Decrepit?" Merlin resented.

Ben exhaled contemplatively. "Well, you don't give me much choice."

"You always have a choice, Keeper," she countered. "You should know that."

She spoke the truth; Ben did know that.

Just as Arthur proved his worthiness when he drew it from the Stone, so must Ben prove himself before acquiring the Sword. Nimue, as skeptical as she was, knew this as well, and she was only too happy to provide him with such an opportunity.

"Then I accept," he stood tall.

"Where will you begin?" Sir Pelleas inquired with curiosity. Every knight was intrigued by a good quest—especially one considered insurmountable.

"Could you bring me any maps you have of the land?" Ben asked him. Pelleas complied while his wife watched Ben in eagerness. "When Morgan Le Fay took the scabbard, Arthur chased her," Ben rehearsed from his knowledge of the legend once the maps were laid out in front of him. "He chased her into plains until she realized she could be caught. She decided that if she were captured, she still didn't want her brother to have the scabbard, so she tossed it in a nearby lake before he caught up to her. This lake was next to a valley covered with large stones. She turned herself and her men into stones to hide from Arthur's men. And it worked because she managed to escape to Gore for a while."

It's extraordinary how the proper information can come to your recollection when you most need it, almost divinely. Nimue and Pelleas were dumbfounded by Ben's omniscience. This information was only known to the narrator of their story, so Ben's knowledge of it was positively awe-inspiring.

266

"Well, tracking the location on a map is one matter," Nimue masked her admiration. "It is another to acquire it. Now shall we see if your prophetic inclinations are the only manifestations of your powers?"

# 24

## The Quest for the Scabbard

Ben was given enough supplies to last his journey. As he passed the castle gate, he saw Myk sitting on a stump beside their three horses. He explained to Myk the stipulations of the quest as well as Merlin's absence. And Myk simply laughed.

"Of course he's imprisoned. Again," he added in good humor.

Without standing to join him, Myk handed Ben his reins and wished him luck. It was a journey he must take alone, unfortunately. The company of a Galdere would have been most helpful, but that would be cheating, dear reader.

Ben followed the maps Pelleas had given him, and it took only half of a day's ride to come to the plains. And, as expected, there was a valley of stones within walking distance of the lake. Ben dismounted at the water's edge and stood with his hands thoughtfully on his hips.

Now what?

He knew the scabbard had been thrown into these very waters, but...where?

The lake was not a small body of water like a pond or a creek. It was wide, and it was deep. Dredging every inch of this lake would take him days or even weeks. The water was murky and unclear, which would have made it even more difficult. But, Ben was a Keeper. And this is how he was to prove it.

The scabbard itself was bejeweled and heavy, which is why it sank to the bottom of the lake when Morgan Le Fay disposed of it. How would he find it? He sat down to rest and watched his horse drink from the lake. He began to consider ways that Albert used his magic, according to the journal. He took the journal out from his vest and fingered through it once again. A particular passage caught his attention:

Wrong or right, the surge of power I felt consumed me. The ground shook as I faced him, and I swore I saw a brief moment of his inner panic. The air around me gathered, guided by my hands, and blasted the demon against a nearby boulder. In retrospect, I probably shouldn't have felt so much satisfaction at hearing his back break, but my rage was guiding my every action. Trees moved at their roots when I stepped closer, awaiting my command. The nearest willow collapsed easily on top of him at the simple flick of my wrist. I doubt I will ever again experience the power I felt that day. I trapped the devil with the tree trunk and made sure he knew I was winning. I may have been smug, but I was broken. I am broken. I find solace in knowing that I rid the worlds of such an evil. That, I think, is the only reason for my being strong enough, while I was so overtaken by my own grief and rage, which would have otherwise stifled any hope of Myk allowing my authority and magic to take effect.

Blasts of air, pulling trees down to the earth, and shaking the ground. All blatant exhibitions of power...but how did it work? Air, roots, earth...they all seemed to be various manipulations of his surroundings. Matter, and therefore, the energy within. The nature of Galderean magic heavily influences matter, you see. It seemed that the very basis of Galderean authority was command over the matter throughout each realm. Through the management of a Keeper, for example, the matter utilizes its energy as directed.

This understanding began to form in Ben's mind.If Keeper magic worked through a command of such universal foundations, then what was to stop Ben from commanding the lake itself?

Aiming his palms, he tried with all his might to move the water. Nothing happened. He tried again, equally steadfast. Only small ripples appeared.

"I assumed  you'd need me."

Ben turned around to see Myk standing over him wearing a knowing smirk. "I have to do this alone, Myk."

"Yes, so I heard. But can you?" Myk sat down beside him.

Something was different about him, Ben noticed. Something in his face.

"You are trying to control the lake," Myk went on, "and as it is, you are not powerful enough. But I am. If you'll let me, I can get the scabbard, and we can be off on our journey. We are wasting time here."

Ben studied his friend without replying. This seemed an odd thing for Myk to say. Myk knew Ben must do this alone, and yet, here he was, tempting him with his assistance. Seeing Ben's apprehension, Myk leaned back, propping his back up against his arms.

"I already made you a Keeper, Ben. What more do you have to prove?"

Ben chose his words carefully. "Everything. That's why I have to do this on my own." He stood and reevaluated his tactics. Examining the lake before him, Ben decided to proceed according to his level of capability. Instead of harnessing control of something as vast as the lake, he focused his energy on a target much smaller.

Holding his palms to the lake once again, he summoned the sheath itself. But he did not use words so common and ordinary as simply saying "Come on out now, scabbard, old boy".

No. Not Ben Caverly.

Not the Aerest Keeper.

Without foreknowledge of any kind—for the language he needed was too divine to be recorded by anyone, even Albert —foreign, ancient words came from his lips with such intensity that the scabbard flew out of the depths of the water and onto land, startling Ben's horse.

"Hm, well done, Keeper," a new voice commended. Myk had turned into the true form of the sorceress Nimue, sitting judgmentally on the ground. "That was most impressive, indeed. You certainly have the powers and brains of the Aerest."

"You could have just asked to come along," Ben sighed. He stepped forward to reach for the sheath, but an unsettling rustle in the distance caught his attention. For a moment he froze, scanning the stony surroundings for an audience beyond the sorceress. Seeing nothing, he decided Nimue would be the only one to show herself, picked up the scabbard, and faced her to display his victory.

Swayed by Ben's ability, she lightly applauded. "And you did it all on your own, which shows integrity; something that's been greatly lacking in this corrupt world. Shall we travel back to your Merlin then?"

Gallantly, Ben helped Nimue onto his horse, without asking how she got there in the first place, and the two traveled back to the castle.

Shortly into their journey Ben and Nimue came upon two knights and a maiden. It didn't take much time for Ben to unravel the situation. It seemed the young maiden was attempting to elope with the younger knight.

The elder knight, apparently the maiden's father, was quite against it, thus inciting a duel. This sort of thing happened quite regularly in this realm. It was not uncommon for questing knights to come across scenarios such as these.

It was now Ben's turn.

The poor father begged his daughter to see the knave for what he truly was—a usurper of purity and manipulator of youth. The rascal's lies confused the poor girl, and she watched in consternation as her father fought for her honor. All of this, Ben gleaned from the bantering back-and-forth between contestants.

"Should we pass on?" Nimue whispered in suggestion.

Listening for a moment, Ben gripped the scabbard tightly in his hand. He was inclined to help the poor old knight in his noble cause, but he knew it would accomplish nothing if the daughter did not see her father as the hero. But the father was no swordsman of note. Ben was reminded of the pitiful Don Quixote's proficiency. Given time, he would surely be defeated. In a moment of short recess, the father leaned exhaustingly against the nearest tree, where his daughter dutifully observed.

"Sir," Ben approached him. "Put this on your belt." He handed him the ornate scabbard. The man seemed confused. He did not know who Ben was, nor could he imagine why he was giving him such a bejeweled sheath. But with his enemy advancing, he quickly obeyed and returned to the fight.

Nimue observed this occurrence with acute wonder. The father fought off the rapscallion, never suffering a single wound. When the other knight's blade sliced the father's skin, no blood was spilt. Out of fear, the enemy soon fled, leaving father and daughter victorious.

"What sweet magic is this?" the father marveled.

"It protected you so you could do what needed to be done," Ben explained simply. The father returned the scabbard to the Keeper and thanked him profusely.

"It seems you've passed my third test," Nimue told Ben when he returned.

"You can't tell me you arranged all of that," he said skeptically.

"Oh no, but it did suit my purpose," she winked. "Now, I shall give you Caliburn."

When the two of them returned to Pelleas, Merlin was set free. From its case, Nimue retrieved Caliburn and placed it reverently in Ben's hands. "You have proven your Keepership to me, Lord Caverly," she said. "If you are ever in need of an ally, please call upon myself and Sir Pelleas, and we shall come to your aid."

Ben tried to give her Excalibur's scabbard, but she refused. "I have no more use for that than I do for Caliburn," she said to him. "Return it to King Arthur, where it belongs."

Merlin bid the lady a brusk goodbye, after Ben thanked them gallantly, and they departed from their presence. Myk—the real Myk—was still waiting for them outside the gate and stood when he saw the sword.

"Finally," he sighed. "Now you can wield the sword Caliburn. The Keeper is almost ready." He dusted his hands in finality.

"You're not leaving now," Ben feared. He was beginning to tire of being left on his own. And I hardly blame him.

Myk laughed. "Not quite yet. There is still the Stone to acquire. Besides, I promised your wife I would see you home safely, and I intend to keep that promise."

# 25

## THE LADY OF THE LAKE

The journey to the Lake was not long, and time passed more easily now that Merlin felt liberated from his misgivings and could return to his jovial, entertaining self. It's fascinating; in Malory's original text, the old boy never explicitly names this sacred lake, nor does he intricately describe its surroundings. However, the closer one came to walking on the enchanted ground, the more easily Ben recognized it. The soil was softer, the air was freer, the shadows were brighter, and the trees seemed to whisper to one another in smooth, melodic tones. Sunlight had dimmed, allowing the starlight to sparkle as it peeked through the leaves above. The clear water winked back at the stars as if in response to a delightful conversation. The mistress of this lake is often given the name of The Lady of the Stars, for her magic transcends the pure powers of the earthly lake, and the present stars bore witness of that.

Merlin laughed gleefully as they approached the Lake. The closer they came, the more the silky surface of the water

275

rippled. Myk's very presence was compelling and caught the attention of every moving thing in the glade. When one has the power to command the elements, the elements respond. They are much more reverent than human beings, I find.

Sitting gracefully on a large rock along the stony beach was a breathtaking figure. Her hair was a warm golden blonde, and her skin was so fair—as was everything about her—it radiated a clean, bright aura. Her features were majestic and fiercely beautiful, easily surpassing all expectations. The gown that draped her body was a delicate golden fabric that seemed to flow in rhythm with the waters around her. Her harmony with her surroundings made her seem at home in this world. Magic in any realm seldom cares where one is from; it only cares whose authority they exercise.

Her flawless mouth stretched into a charming beam upon seeing Myk approach. "Mykolas," she greeted in her melodious tone, descending from her perch. The two affectionately embraced, Myk kissing her lips with tenderness. As she angled her head, Ben noticed a sparkling earring that crawled up her slender earlobe. It almost glowed, as if made of the stars themselves.

"And he's here," she commented, moving her gaze to Ben and noticing his stare. Myk nodded and stepped back, inviting Ben to come forward.

"My Lady, this is Benjamin Caverly. The Aerest Keeper."

Her bright face lit up and then deepened with understanding. Ben gently kissed The Lady's hand, as he felt was appropriate, given her visible divinity. She was much more heavenly than Nimue and was undeniably the purest and most powerful of the ladies of the Lake.

"Welcome back," she grinned. Ignoring Ben's sudden wrinkled expression of confusion, she looked once more at Myk. "It is finally time, then."

What happened next was remarkable, if not surreal. The fair Lady took Myk's hand and, following his lead, stepped to the water's edge. Conjuring that same command over his surroundings, as has already been so openly displayed, Myk lifted a hand toward the Lake.

It was only then that Ben noticed, as Myk's sleeve slid down his arm, that the noble Galderean wore a thin silver cuff around his wrist, with the subtle engraving of a rising sun along the bottom. The subtlety did not last, however, for just as Myk raised his hand, the engraved sun began to glow in conjunction with the glow of his Lady's star earring.

At once, the water seemed to scurry into hiding places under the wet sand along the rim. The waters subjugated to Myk's will so easily that Ben was almost envious. The bottom of the Lake was bare and exposed. Beneath the water was not the expected lake bed, with algae and mud; instead, the ground was a solid, marble-like material which shone as the sunlight hit it. This celestial element spanned across the Lake, concentrating heavily in the center on a small, raised island, which had been previously concealed by the water.

With his Lady at his side, Myk proceeded to walk toward the center of the marbled Lake. The two Keepers watched from the beach, Ben curiously straining his neck to see more clearly. Myk and his Lady both slowly raised a hand to the small island, rupturing the cap of the enclave until an untouched fragment separated itself from its host.

It was all incredibly magnificent to witness.

Somehow Ben's defensive magic in acquiring the scabbard seemed dwarfish in comparison to Myk's formidable abilities. Maybe it was the force he dominated, rather than the way he did it, but Myk's magic was controlled and strong—that much was clear. The modest stone made its way into Myk's hand, where it stayed until the Galdere and his Lady returned to the beach.

"Here you are, Caverly," Myk said reverently, handing Ben the stone.

It was no bigger than the palm of his hand. As Ben examined it further, he noticed strange markings that covered the stone, markings which were slender and precise, telling a story of their own.

"It's our native tongue," The Lady contributed as if reading his mind. "The Galdere. It seals the Stone's power." Placing her soft touch over the Stone, The Lady looked into his eyes and said, "Never lose this."

Ben mentally added it to the list.


Now that the gathering of Ben's arsenal was complete, the Keeper must also correctly comprehend his own weapons' efficiency. But do not forget, our Keeper is mortal. And, as with all mortals within Myk's dealings, Ben must be left to figure things out on his own.

What was the significance of the Stone?

What was its purpose?

Frustrating as this was, Myk left Ben to his own mind as the three travelers started back for London. Giving Ben all the answers at once spoils the fun, I suppose.

If it was any relief to Ben, this cryptic treatment of Keepers was simply Myk's way. He was no respecter of persons. No one has ever been excluded from this sort of fun, not even I.

The Stone was burning with questions in the goatskin pouch around Ben's waist. The journal was bursting with possible answers, nestled securely in the pocket inside Ben's vest. With Myk only footsteps away from him, Ben saw no need to revisit those pages.

To his chagrin, naturally, Myk's answers were short and enigmatic, producing even more questions. Merlin was of no help; he followed aimlessly behind them, apparently still dazed by the orphic experience with the Lady of the Lake.

As night began to fall, Myk stopped.

"We shall make camp here," Myk decided. "The sun is nearly gone, and we should get a fire started. Merlin, I think you and I should gather firewood while Ben takes another gander through that book."

Merlin obediently complied, while Myk illuminated the way ahead of them with a luminous orb floating above his hand.

Ben took off the belt that held Caliburn and placed it beside him as he sat on the ground. Left alone, he conceded to follow Myk's advice and have another read through Albert's journal. Perhaps it would prove more generous with answers than Myk himself.

*Myk referenced the significance of the final three Keepers in this war. They're all coming together very soon, apparently, and I'm expected to prepare for them.*

*Not too much has been said, but I have an inkling that I have already met the Aerest. He's the one who starts it all. He's the leader.*

And then there will be the Haeleth. He's the fighter.

And finally, the Fulendian will come. He's the victor.

*This calling is difficult enough as it is—I do not envy these poor chaps and the harrowing roles they will play. They will have help, naturally, but knowing when to utilize that help will be the trick. Those who live through this new era, this new age, will undoubtedly be the most resilient and sturdy of all of the Alden, by necessity.*

Myk will undoubtedly have to choose wisely. But, I trust he knows what he's doing. He's been doing it for quite some time now.

This information was not new to his eyes, but the way Albert talked about his inkling regarding the Aerest made Ben shake his head with a small smile. The old man knew. His intuition was so very accurate. And his predictions concerning the Keepers to come seemed inspired. Ben coveted how much Myk presumably revealed to Albert.

He continued to cursorily skim the pages when a startling jolt suddenly shook him. The air around him became tight and noxious, with a darkness that went far deeper than the night air around him. A dark figure appeared before him, but kept a considerable distance, lingering only in the trees around the small camp. The feeling was overpowering, but Ben conjured enough strength to draw Caliburn from its sheath. It was then that a deep, gravelly voice crept through the darkness and into Ben's ears.

"You've been well-prepared, Caverly," the voice crooned ominously. "That certainly didn't take long."

The dark figure paced slowly, with a smugness, but remained in the shadows. Ben strained his eyes to make out a face. Briefly, he could make out the shape of a man, but he couldn't be sure.

The voice then chuckled, "I confess, I seem to have overestimated my readiness for the arrival of the Aerest Keeper. Towson's curse took him much faster than anticipated—I am constantly underestimating my agent's abilities. She's amusing that way."

Ben stood alert and defensive, Sword in hand. The dense air made it difficult to breathe, but the tighter he held Caliburn, the more strength he felt surge through him.

"Thankfully, your weaknesses have been fairly transparent..." the voice went on. "...and those of little Stella. I appreciate straightforward opponents. I really do."

Ben tensed when he heard him speak her name. He didn't have to ask because he knew. He felt the answer with every accursed word emanating from the blackness.

*Korbl.*

A new fury boiled within our hero, an fury so overwhelming and intense which he had never before experienced. His jaw was clenched so tightly that words were forbidden to seep through.

"That's fine, don't speak, Caverly. You don't have to. Allow me. All was going so well...the traitorous fools...the

281

pervasive doubts...the illicit affair...ah, the affair. Everything in place for Arthur's fall."

Korbl's voice took an eerie pause.

"Sir Gawaine was such an easy mark," he hummed.

Suddenly Ben realized that the demon was not referring to Guenever's infidelity. "Gawaine?" Ben exhaled.

"The passionate usually are," Korbl went on. "Alas...they are not always reliable. I don't mean Gawaine, of course—some men's passions are easily predictable. No, what was not expected was being burdened with a Creator who had so quickly fallen in love with her Keeper. It's been quite the recurring inconvenience, in my experience. I can empathize with your doubts, however; knowing the threat of another stealing your lover's affections...it can be crippling. As it happens, I was hoping it would cripple her as well."

Ben's heart skipped briefly before swelling with pride. Korbl was counting on Stella's infidelity; a feat he clearly thought was easy enough, considering the loveless origins of their marriage. This also surprised Ben, however.

*Fallen so quickly in love with her Keeper.*

This sounded so strange to him, but his mind quickly switched gears and reminded him of the one weakness of Albert's which Korbl also viciously attacked.

She was the threat.

*His Companion*, Albert called her.

However, Korbl referred to Stella as a *Creator*. It was a title Ben hadn't heard before. Whatever the semantics, Korbl was afraid she'd *kick his pants*. Ben smiled, remembering Stella's words. Like mother, like daughter.

"Clearly, you don't know Stella," Ben retorted bravely.

"And, clearly, neither do you," Korbl murmured, echoing through the trees. "Not as well as you should."

He sensed more of that doubt he spoke of, and this pleased him. Korbl thrived on doubt. It made him bigger than he was. Ben stood his ground, pushing all fears aside and assuring his stance.

"You don't know nearly as much as you should—nor will you have the chance to do so," Korbl promised so certainly. "You won't last long enough, and neither will she."

Ben felt the threat and anticipated an attack, an attack which did not come. Something stopped the dark figure. The shadows attempted to advance with a startling aggression but then retreated as footsteps sounded nearby. Ben's eyes, however, did not search for the owners of the footsteps but instead glanced down to the goatskin pouch containing the Stone.

"Ben?" Myk called out.

Suddenly, the darkness and density dissipated, leaving the air clear and light again. When the fading campfire's flame revealed Myk and Merlin's faces emerging from the trees, Ben re-sheathed Caliburn.

"It keeps him at bay," he told Myk. It wasn't a question; it was more of a conclusion based on observation. "The Stone."

Merlin frowned in confusion, but Myk understood Ben's meaning.

"Keeps whom at bay?" Merlin pried.

Myk set down his armful of firewood and began rekindling the fire. "Korbl paid us a visit," he sensed.

Merlin nodded in sudden understanding. He obediently followed Myk's lead, placing his firewood beside the fire and taking a seat on a flat, neighboring rock. Merlin picked up a thick branch that had fallen from a tree and began whittling with a small knife he had apparently been carrying somewhere in his robes.

"Is that what it does?" Ben pressed for verification.

Taking a deep breath, Myk answered, "In part. It weakens him, ultimately enabling the Keeper to banish him from a realm. With the combination of the Soter Stone and the jacket, Korbl himself cannot touch you. What did he say to you?"

"Soter Stone?"

"What did he say, Benjamin?"

Ben sat down, calmly processing. "He said he underestimated me. And Stella."

Myk hummed softly with a grin. "Of course he did. That Stella..."

"He called her...." Ben considered, "....a *Creator*. Is that what her mother was as well? What–what did he mean?"

Myk's expression hardened and his lips tightened. A sad smile poked through, but it was shrouded in regret.

"He's strategizing," he muttered. "It appears he's sized up his new adversary. Korbl's Galderean omniscience has degraded since his fall, twisting and rearranging his memories. Twisted though they may be, they are still dangerous."

While Ben was not the least bit surprised at Korbl marking Stella as a sizable enemy, the devil's fixation on her worried him greatly. "Myk....what is Stella?"

"Well, he seems to believe she's a Creator. There is one in every era, and they are twice as terrifying as any Arch Keeper, which is why they are inevitably paired with the strongest their era has to offer."

"I met the last one, as a matter of fact—ah, lovely woman. Impeccable mind, that one," Merlin threw in, reminiscently.

"She has phenomenal genetics, if I say so myself," Myk smirked.

"Is that what Stella is then?" Ben pressed.

"A Creator is more than simply a Companion, Benjamin. Creators are the beings who carried the creation magic that enabled the Galdere to bring life to countless realms. Few in number they may be, diminutive their power is not."

Ben leaned forward in his seated position, propping his elbows on his knees. "How could that be Stella?"

There was a pause in which Merlin followed Ben's lead, leaning forward, eagerly awaiting an answer as well. Myk released a considerable sigh, with a faint smile on his face.

"Creators took up arms, just like the rest of us. And with that came the potential for mortal shells. Given Stella's mortal lineage...her parents were Arches, her mother's miraculous birth being brought about by Galderean magic..." Myk trailed off in deep thought. "Re-read Albert's account sometime. It might surprise you. The evidence is definitely in his favor, I must say. And the prophecy is certainly vague."

"So many prophecies, so little time," Merlin whittled softly to himself. "One could analyze for hours if one wishes.

Some have, but of course, that is their duty and one I do not especially envy."

Interestingly, I have had such a duty, and I am here to confirm that the prophecies are countless, and all with varying levels of redundancy. A grand adventure never seems to be complete without at least one equally grand prophecy, now does it? Well, reader, time is here in abundance, and I assure you that we will again stumble upon each of these prophecies as their time comes. But for now, we shall return to the prophecy currently discussed.

"You sound doubtful," Ben pointed out. "Is Korbl mistaken?"

"Korbl is persistent. He knows that the Queen Creator chose this final era as her own, to help the Galdere bring an end to the war. All that his magic destroys can be remade, and being his antithesis from the beginning, the Last Creator will cause Korbl irreparable damage."

Accepting that he was in no position currently to receive the answer he was after, Ben settled on a more pressing question: "How far will he go to stop a Creator?"

"As far as he can. Which is why her Keeper must be most valiant. If Korbl is right, Benjamin...."

"And you know if he is," the Keeper assumed, with a slight frustration in his tone.

"....and even if he is not, keep the Soter Stone close, and keep your Companion even closer. Protect your Companion, keep Korbl at bay, and banish him every chance you get. That is your objective."

"Myk, if you just created the...Soter Stone, then how were past Keepers able to banish Korbl?"

The inscrutable Galdere leaned back against a tree, resting his hands behind his head. "Technically, I did not just create the Soter Stone. I recovered it. The Stones were a wedding gift."

"A wedding gift!" Merlin clapped his hands together supportively.

"Yes," Myk beamed, filled with the happy memory. "From the Queen Creator to The Lady and myself. It marked an allegiance made, as well as the start of a rather unconventional future for our people. As far as this war is concerned, it wasn't entirely necessary until now. Korbl once fought more directly, as was his style. He preferred to do the dirty work himself. Admirable, I suppose."

"He does have that going for him, doesn't he?" Merlin contributed. "If we're looking at the good in things."

Ben chuckled, and Myk continued.

"Within this last era, Korbl gained someone who regrettably enhanced his power. She changed the war and moved it along much faster than anticipated. He was already growing in strength—every time he gains a Scada, his power builds—but she tipped the scale dangerously in his favor. The Alden needed as much assistance as we could grant. As it turns out, Korbl and I had a rather explosive altercation which resulted in his imprisonment, so you can imagine the retaliation he has planned."

Ben's eyebrows tightened. "But if he is imprisoned, then how..."

287

"When a Galderean is imprisoned, Benjamin, only the physical immortal body is truly locked away. He is currently sitting in a dark hole somewhere, in chains, so to speak. His magic and influence remain free to spread. He still presents himself just enough to bark orders, though not in his full form. He has the appearance of a man, as he had before, but his being is much more comparable to a....wraith resembling a mortal. A movable spirit, but still tangible. Now that his body is restrained, he's allowing his followers more of his magic, to act on his behalf as he builds his strength for the final battle where he will be freed and fight in his full form."

Merlin chortled, glancing up from his whittling. "You poor fool. Life was so much easier before all of this."

Scratching his head, Myk brushed off Merlin's comment. "Regardless, your very presence has affected the war, for both sides. You've ushered in the new age, in which Korbl is growing more and more aggressive."

"Is that why you're here too?" Ben supposed.

Myk sat up straight. "Astute conclusion, Ben." He stoked the fire a bit and then leaned back again. "If Korbl feels the need for more aggression, then you can rest assured that Yonas thought of the idea first. This is why we've reached the chapter in which we will be utilizing the Soter Stones. His powers and that of his followers will need weakened and expelled from as many realms as possible."

"How many are there?" Ben questioned. "Soter Stones, that is."

Myk chuckled. "Well, there will be three of you final Keepers, remember? Each will have their own to wield, until the reign of the Fulendian, when all three Stones will be needed."

"And what exactly will happen when the Fulendian Keeper reigns?"

Myk grinned again, but with anticipant thrill. "The one thing Korbl fears most."

# 26

## A HERO'S WELCOME

Myk and Merlin walked with Ben until they reached familiar territory. When they came to the crossroads, the travelers bid their farewells.

"Keep care, Ben," Myk warned him. "Arthur would be wise to clean out the traitors in his own company before sieging Sir Kay. There are close allies who cannot be trusted...and there are distant enemies who can."

This wasn't entirely clear to Ben yet, like a fair amount of the riddles that Myk tends to spew, but give it time. Ben will soon understand.

He didn't concern himself with it presently; he was a bit distracted by Merlin attempting to summon an apple from a tall, nearby tree. The poor chump was not always the most successful sorcerer. While deceptively capable of great things, his priorities often confused his magic. One moment, the apple hardly budged, but the next moment, it shot down from its home on the branch and splattered across the dirt path. Merlin surrendered with a frown, crossing his arms like a discontent child. He isn't wholly a fool, I assure you. Only sometimes.

"What is to happen to Don Quixote?" Ben asked curiously. It was a question that had been quietly gnawing at him for some time now. "How will he get home?"

"Don Quixote's destiny will be fulfilled in the best possible way—all fates are. Never fear. However—" Myk paused dramatically, ensuring he had Ben's full attention. "Never forget how it all ends. Some fates are inevitable, regardless of your efforts as a Keeper, and you must accept that. You can't change their nature. Each of them is inclined to a particular destiny, for better or worse. You're here to guide them to the best of those destinies, but the choice is ultimately theirs. Decisions maketh destiny. Just...keep reading that journal and everything else will fall into place."

Myk glanced over his shoulder to see Merlin making a second attempt to summon an out-of-reach piece of fruit. "Come now, Merlin. We have other business to tend to."

"Wait, he's not returning with me?" Ben hesitated.

"It's your time now, Ben. Merlin was only here to prepare the realm. His job here is done—but the work is never over, I'm afraid. He has a new assignment. Here, before I forget." Myk tossed him a leather satchel he had been wearing across his chest. In this satchel, were three long, leather strips—leather matching Ben's vest. "Keep them close, like everything else. And you'll know when to use them."

The grin he wore as he gripped Ben's hand in parting gave the Keeper the feeling that this would certainly not be the last he will see of him.

Sometime before Myk and Merlin escorted Ben to Arthur's borders, Stella sat quietly in the garden, escaping the chatter of the courtyard and the hustle and bustle of the castle halls. She cleared her mind of all her worries—or at least attempted. Her heart ached, and her head tried to remind her of her doubts. Defying her paternal genetics, Stella had remarkable self-control when she chose to utilize it. She ignored the pain and scolded the apprehension. She was so focused that she did not notice the king walk quietly behind her.

"My lady," he addressed, trying not to startle her.

She quickly stood up from the bench and curtsied, as she had seen other ladies do when the king approached them. "Your Highness."

"Princess," he began, "I don't believe I've had the chance to say how sorry I am for your loss."

Her heart felt a sharp prick. *Everyone must stop saying that*, she thought. "Um, thank you."

Arthur held out an arm, beckoning her to walk with him. She swallowed hard and controlled her eye-rolling; a heart-to-heart gander was hardly what she needed. Nonetheless, she took his arm and tempered her sharp tongue.

"Stella, I can only begin to imagine your sorrow, as I have also felt anguish such as this," he went on. His pace was slow and deliberate. "As you know...I am without a wife...and England is without a queen..." he paused, giving Stella time to remember to breathe. "I cannot dare to assume I could replace a man such as Lord Caverly...but if we were to withstand our losses together, perhaps..."

"Arthur," she had to stop him. "I appreciate the offer, but..." Stella racked her brain to remember inventive methods of rejection she had learned from books. "...I don't think you could make me happy, and...I'm probably the last woman in the world who would make you happy." Realizing how harsh she seemed, she corrected her tone. "I'm sorry. Ben...was the only one for me. I couldn't..."

Arthur sighed. "No need to explain, my lady. I understand. Your devotion is very admirable. I only wish I had chosen a woman with such fierce loyalty. If there is anything I could do to be of service to you, you need only ask."

Stella nodded gratefully but then paused in thought. "Actually...do you think I could talk to all of the knights who rode with Ben?"

She had to know the details. As requested, the king summoned the four knights from Ben's company in the council chambers. Upon asking each of them to describe the attacker, she found that their stories matched up easily: a man on a horse, using magic, threw them to the ground and fought the Keeper before rolling down the ravine.

Agravaine confirmed that the attacker smashed the Keeper with a boulder by using magic. The other three had looked over the edge and saw the attacker walk away, victorious, and the Keeper was nowhere in sight.

"But what did he look like? What was he wearing?" she interrogated. To Arthur, she explained, "When they were holding us captive, I noticed that all of Korbl's men wore these little wristbands." As she said this, she felt uneasy movement behind her, so she faced the knights again. "Well?"

"He wasn't wearing wristbands, my lady," Bors answered. "He had dark clothes, dirty but fair hair, and a leather vest."

*The vest.*

"A...dark leather vest?" She didn't previously recognize a man in a vest, but something told her she knew him.

"Yes, my lady."

It was the rogue, Bastien. She didn't know how she knew, but she did. Her delay was longer than intended, bringing a concern to her audience.

"Do you know the fiend, princess?" Don Quixote pressed.

"Um..." she started, wringing her hands. "Yes. Unfortunately, I think I do."

Panic rose within her. She wished Ben had told her the entire plan before he left, but she had a feeling he wasn't sure of it himself. All he needed were those items from the Lady of the Lake and, as far as she knew, he didn't have them. They didn't have them. They didn't have anything. Even if they had them, she assumed only a Keeper could use them.

"Is he this Korbl you've spoken of?" the king suggested.

"No, no," Stella replied. She greatly feared meeting Korbl in person; his followers were terrifying enough. "No, it doesn't seem like Korbl does much of his own dirty work. He may be the ultimate enemy, but he's apparently the more distant threat. He has agents on the ground, like Spyros–the one who orchestrated the May Day ambush. No, the attacker at the ravine was a different...um...fiend. I think his name was Bastien. I'm not sure exactly where he fits, but I think he's quite powerful."

"I should say so," agreed Sir Gaheris. "His magic almost matched that of the Keeper."

"That's what scares me," Stella nodded. "We only stood a chance with Ben among us, he and his magic on our side—"

"And now he is gone," Agravaine contributed grimly. "My king, has this war not already taken its toll? How long must we fight this?"

"We fight until the enemy is vanquished in its entirety," Arthur snapped with passion. "Whatever the cost."

"If you don't think we can, Agravaine, you are more than welcome to leave," Stella offered, with a healthy dose of disdain. Without Ben's admonishing gaze, she no longer cared for boundaries. Not where traitors were concerned.

Agravaine cleared his throat and amended his address. "Not at all, my lady. I have full faith that the Keeper's wife is just as wise as the Keeper himself."

Before she could rebuff this, the other three knights expressed their warm accord.

"Indeed, princess," Bors assured. "We will all stand by you. To the end."


Rallying spirits and collaborating battle plans was exhausting, and Stella couldn't understand how kings and knights did so on a daily basis without collapsing. After the council meeting, she returned to the garden to clear her head again.

Meanwhile, Arthur walked through the courtyard in a light conversation with Don Quixote. The Spaniard had read so much about the great king and his Round Table of knights that any sane man would be positively giddy to have a private conversation with the legendary figure.

In his maddened mind, a personal interview with the great King Arthur was to be expected when one becomes a knights-errant. Not a great deal could shake this man's delusions.

Except, perhaps, seeing a ghost.

Don Quixote paused mid-sentence, his clumsy stroll coming to a sudden stop.

Entering the courtyard, just as the king and the Spanish knight reached the peak of their conversation, was the mighty Keeper. Ben tread through the gates with determination, straight to the awestruck king who followed Don Quixote's frozen gaze.

"Lord Caverly!" Arthur cried. He embraced the Keeper so tightly that Ben feared he would never let go. "We thought you were dead!"

"Yes," Ben struggled to reply. When the king finally released him, he promptly explained his adventure—from the enchanted cave to Excalibur's scabbard to Merlin and the Lake. He honorably handed the scabbard to its rightful owner. "So now I have—"

"Of course, of course," the king interceded. "But, first you must reunite with your precious wife! Her faithfulness must be rewarded."

Arthur then turned to a passing servant, telling him to fetch the princess, but Ben stopped him.

"Oh no, I'll go to her myself," Ben insisted. "Where–where is she?"

"She was in the garden," Don Quixote informed him. "But I believe we last saw the princess heading to her chambers."

Arthur gave Ben's arm a brotherly squeeze. "We shall discuss the Lake and your quest," the king promised with a wink. "But first things first."

And so it was.

The king was no simpleton. Ben rushed to Stella's chambers, stumbling over a couple of steps as he flew up the staircase. Stella was standing at her vanity, carefully placing a couple of freshly-picked roses in a glass vase, when he burst through the doors. He startled her so that she knocked the vase to the floor, splashing the water on the rug. She didn't seem to notice as her eyes locked on his, disbelieving what they saw.

"I knew it," she whispered. There was a slight catch in her throat as she released an emotional, relieved laugh. Without hesitation, she ran into his arms and welcomed him with a kiss.

This was nothing like the chasteness of their parting embrace. This was new. Passionate. Whole. Deep. Never in a century would the witnesses at their wedding have supposed this sort of passion between them possible. Never in a century would they themselves have supposed such meaning and longing possible.

And yet, it all was.

I am personally and dutifully impelled to remain as tasteful as possible. All I will say is that Ben Caverly did not leave his wife's room that night. Precious and sacred is the sweetness that occurs between man and wife. Up until now, there had been so little expression of love—but, again quoting my good friend Cervantes, *where there is great love, there is often little display of it.*

# 27

## From The Shadows

Sunlight spilled through the windows, reflecting perfectly in Stella's sky eyes, who beamed while Ben spoke. She hung on his every word as they lay in her bed. He told her every detail. It was the most he had spoken, at one time, for as long as she had known him. And she loved that. She rested her head comfortably on his chest, listening to his heart beat to the pace of his tale. And he loved that. He laced his fingers with hers as he regaled his adventures. And she loved that. She giggled at his witty words. And he loved that.

There was more than a fair magnitude of love in the princess's chambers that morning.

"That sounds awfully romantic," she hummed softly when he mentioned Myk's interactions with the Lady of the Lake. "Even Myk has a Companion, huh? Every Keeper needs one, right? And Merlin said Myk had his turn as a Keeper, so it only makes sense that he would need one too."

Ben kissed her forehead sweetly. "Companions are pretty crucial," he mumbled. "We'd all be lost without you."

She giggled. "We're indispensable."

"I think Korbl knows that." A sudden sadness came across Ben's face.

Stella sensed this and sat up to face him. She gazed at him with a confident and playful smile. "He's not going to win, though. We're not going to let him." And she kissed him.

He smiled in return. "You think we can do this?"

"You know what my father always told me when he got home from a trip? I'd ask him how it went and he'd say, '*They'll know I was there*'. I never knew what that meant until recently. Of the thousands of realms, you were sent here for a reason. Even if they doubt you—even if you doubt you—and you keep fighting anyway, you're winning a battle, and they'll notice. They'll know you were here, fighting for them. And that's what will count. That's where the victory is."

When his smile tugged downward into a doubtful frown, she gave him a funny look. "Hey, I've relieved myself in a chamber pot and bathed in community bathwater. I can do anything. How about you?"

Ben laughed, then kissed her back. "Only if you do it with me."

"That's the spirit," she said softly, as she cuddled up against him.

He pulled her closer and pressed his cheek upon the top of her head. She felt safe lying there with him. Their souls had finally found harmony. It was the moment Myk promised. The moment Keeper and Companion became one. Not one single individual, standing against the evil that was coming, but a combined force to be reckoned with.

Bringing a momentary interruption to this harmony, a knock came to the door.

"Princess Stella," a manservant's voice called from the other side of the oak. "Princess, are you awake?"

Stella whispered, "Can I just lie and pretend I didn't hear him?"

Ben chuckled softly, gently stroking her arm. It certainly didn't make her want to respond any quicker.

"Yes, I'm awake," she finally admitted.

"Would you happen to know where Lord Caverly might be, my lady? The king is requesting his presence," the servant explained.

Stella snorted. "No, but I can deliver the message for you."

"Thank you, my lady." And the servant left his assignment at her door.

Looking up into her husband's eyes, the princess obediently said, "Lord Caverly, the king is requesting your presence."

Ben laughed again. "Ah, I should probably meet with him." He gingerly pushed the covers aside and reached for his clothes. While he donned the enchanted leather—which had reformed into a jacket once again—he kept his loving eyes on Stella. "Come to the council meeting. I think you should be there."

She grinned. "I get to play with the big boys now, huh?"

He couldn't stop beaming. "I don't think there's any going back now."

"I'm going to take a bath before breakfast, and then I'll meet you down there," she promised. Still smiling, he kissed her once more, before grabbing the Soter Stone out of his satchel and leaving to attend to his duties.

As soon as he was gone, Stella called Ava to prepare a bath for her. The natives to this realm didn't bathe nearly as often as the Keeper's wife did. They thought her a bit odd, but her other advantages easily dismissed any severe judgment. While the princess bathed behind a screen, Ava made the bed, prepared Stella's clothes for the day, and tidied up the room as usual.

But this time, Stella heard a rustling that sounded quite different from the standard ruffled fabrics of the bedchamber. It sounded more like the quiet sifting through of hands through a bag. With as silent an effort as she could attempt, Stella reached for her robe, fastening it tightly around her, and tip-toed out from behind the screen to see Ava rummaging through the leather satchel Ben left on the bed stand.

In another life, Stella would have assumed Ava to be a simple kleptomaniac. But not here, not now, not when she noticed that Ben had left the journal in this particular satchel, along with the three strips of leather from Myk.

Ava's small hands skirted across every item in the satchel, silently taking inventory and weighing value. If Stella hadn't been self-consciously paying keen attention to everything happening in the room while she was undressed, she would have missed this highly skilled thief in action.

"Hey Ava," she called. "What might you be doing there?"

Ava spun around and ably put on a facade of innocent surprise, hiding the journal behind her back. She was so smooth that Stella almost missed the swift sleight of hand. "I'm so sorry, my lady. I was just moving Lord Caverly's things so I could properly clean the room."

Then, those enlightened eyes saw something that was formerly invisible to them: once porcelain and unblemished skin, now rimmed with shadow. Those branding stains had a vileness to them that Ava could no longer hide from Stella. Her charm, the warmth of her smile, and the kindness of her words all hid the Darkness far more effectively than Spyros or Bastien could've attempted. But it had to be more than simply deceit. Stella's eyes only now could see through the mask Ava so expertly wore.

"The Stone isn't in there if that's what you're looking for."

Ava feigned confusion. Unlike Spyros or the other Scada, Ava's eyes bore faded scars that clawed at the surrounding skin, lending her the effect of shrewd aggression—an aggression Stella could hardly believe she couldn't discern before.

"I'm sorry?" Ava pretended to fumble over her words with an innocent lilt in her tone. "If you're finished with your bath, my lady, I can help you dress for the day."

Stella stepped closer to her, jaw clenched. "Give me the journal."

The maid's expression quickly changed, dispensing all effort to sustain the ruse. Her lips curled into a devious smirk.

"Hm..." she began mockingly. Arrogantly holding the journal in front of her, Ava shook her head slowly. "You are not the Keeper. I don't think I have to answer to you. Come to think of it...I don't really have to answer to him either."

Ava was Korbl's best. Don't be too quick to judge her entirely on this one skirmish. She was not a threat to be taken lightly by any means. Stella did not know it yet, but this woman was almost as powerful a force of evil as Korbl himself. I suppose that's why they say she was his favorite.

As was her specialty, Ava had assessed the threat the Aerest Companion would pose from the moment she backed into her at the tournament.

She had Stella assessed from the beginning. It was what she was trained to do: analyze strengths, weaknesses, and threat levels. It's why she was the best. She knew Stella had no physical self-defense training of any sort and was quicker with her tongue than a sword.

That said, Ava had underestimated her opponent. Stella hastily grabbed the sharp stoker from the fireplace and brandished it combatively, slicing a clean line across the jawline of her presumptuous foe. During this befuddlement, Stella snatched the journal out of Ava's hand as Ava fell back against the bed in shock.

In an unsportsmanlike manner, resorting to her raw, but skillfully controlled power, Ava made a sweeping arm movement, blasting Stella to the wall. It was a dark magic that engulfed Stella and completely stole her breath the moment before she collapsed to the ground.

In a fortuitous twist of fate during this exchange, Don Quixote was wandering lost through the maze of corridors in the palace and, upon hearing the scuffle from behind the closed door, opened it to see if the occupants needed some assistance. Instead of retrieving the journal, Ava speedily disappeared.

When Don Quixote entered the room, Stella was still struggling to sit up. Her back was sure to be badly bruised, but her victory in keeping the journal from Ava overshadowed the pain. The Spaniard assisted the princess to her feet and, after thanking him, she hurriedly rushed him out of the room so she could change into more presentable clothing.

She had to tell Ben and Arthur. She didn't know how much Ava knew, whether or not she skimmed over the journal's contents, and what sort of an obstacle this created.

Once again, Stella interrupted the start of the council meeting, dragging Don Quixote behind her as a witness. While she was technically invited, her manner of making an entrance was becoming a trademark.

Just as she blurted out this new development, Ben simultaneously informed the king of Myk's warning that traitors were still in his midst.

"Oh, sorry," Stella apologized breathlessly. "He's right though. Kay and Ava weren't the only ones," she added, looking directly at Sir Agravaine.

The remaining Knights of the Round Table all fell silent. Sir Bors followed Stella's gaze to the uneasy Agravaine and, with caution, he placed a hand on the hilt of his sword, prepared for a fight. Soon all eyes were on Agravaine. He knew that continuing his facade would be for naught. Drawing his sword, he glared back into Stella's storming eyes.

But it was Bors who spoke next.

"My lord king," he raised his sword, "It was he who proclaimed the Keeper dead. He claimed he saw Lord Caverly smashed by the boulder."

The king was in shock, but only mildly. After the loss of his surrogate brother, his disbelief had been suspended. "Agravaine, is this true?"

Agravaine's eyes flashed to Sir Bors with tepid confusion.

"How dare you forsake the Keeper and King," Bors snarled. Agravaine raised his own sword offensively and posed to strike, but Bors was much quicker.

No more words were spoken. Because it seemed, no more words were needed.

# 28

## THE MORE REFINED STRATEGY

Skipping ahead in our tale, several weeks passed, and Arthur heeded Ben's instructions to wait out Korbl. However, they did not sit idly; Arthur wisely sent out another batch of patrols and spies, to annex further detail to their understanding of the enemy's pace and maneuvers. Apparently, Korbl's men had the same idea. They were at a standstill, but it would not last. Sooner or later, one would make their move. In spite of their stalemate, the Keeper continued to gain strength.

Naively, everyone settled comfortably in the belief that all impostors had been disposed of. Everyone, save a small few. Sir Gawaine, whose infamous loyalty to Arthur swayed his opinions of transgressors quite strongly, was perpetually in doubt of Sir Launcelot. If one would go as far as betraying Arthur on such a personal level as he had, what was to stop him from betraying Arthur on a much grander scale?

Gawaine confided as much in Sir Bors. Calming his friend's passionate distrust, Sir Bors did not wholly disagree with him. Instead, he quietly conceded to the possibility, warning Gawaine that the devil may recruit whomever he likes, making anyone a traitor. Bors stood by Ben's side more vigorously than before, actively engaging in battle plans and being particularly useful. Ben was ever grateful to have such an ally.

Spyros and Sir Kay's troops sporadically attacked small villages near the borders of Arthur's lands, testing the king's strength and fury. But, Ben was well-read and wisely heeded to Sun Tzu's acumen from The Art of War: *Appear weak when you are strong, and strong when you are weak.* Instead of retaliation, Arthur sent small troops to these villages, building a stronger defense, giving the illusion of indifference rather than rage.

Stella now regularly joined the men in the council hall, proving to be a powerful asset to the Keeper. Her input was objective and her criticism was instructive. Ben may have devised the battle plan, but it was Stella's shrewd mind that brought it to perfection. The tactical plan was on the offensive, but in a manner that Spyros the Fool was sure to discount.

Following the introduction of this refined strategy, the council chamber was thrown into yet another state of shock when a mighty blast flung the large oak doors open, tossing the standing guards to the ground. The knights unsheathed their weapons, anticipating an enemy who would inevitably come. Ben pulled his sword, Caliburn, and stood protectively in front of Stella, expecting Bastien ,Spyros,or even Korbl himself. All were surprised, you see. For it was not Bastien, nor Spyros, nor Korbl. It was an individual known by everyone in the room, save the Keeper and his wife. She was a lady, fair as any. She was a queen, an adulteress, an avenger, a lover, a hater, and one of Arthur's greatest adversaries.

"Hello, brother," the sorceress sneered.

The dark-haired beauty strutted through the chamber with an intimidating swagger, her purple cloak skirting across the wooden floor. Following in a close stroll behind her was an exotic, dark-skinned man shrouded in an indigo-colored head wrap, a long cloudy grey cotton shirt, and dark grey trousers. He leaned lightly on a tall staff as he walked, but said nothing as his more captivating companion addressed her audience.

While Light Galderean magic is actively good and pure, and Korbl's corrupted edition is actively evil and polluted, there is also a magic which hangs in between. As I've said, some realms are created with magic already in them for its inhabitants to utilize for good or evil. This native magic is not Galderean, so it is not quite as powerful. It is also not of Korbl, so it is not quite as dark. However, it is still quite effective—especially in the hands of one as studied as Morgan Le Fay. No matter how hard the guards tried to restrain her, she effortlessly kept them at bay.

"What is your business here, witch?" Sir Gawaine spat.

"Morgan Le Fay..." Stella mumbled.

The sorceress smirked. "Adorable. You've grown up so much, nephew." Her condescending eyes grazed each knight facing her, especially sparkling when they found Sir Launcelot. "Hello, handsome. It's been far too long."

Launcelot gripped his sword and tightened his lips. "Answer the question."

Her eyes then settled on her half-brother, Arthur. "I've come to make amends, in a sense. I hear a Keeper of some importance has entered the realm. And I also hear he found your precious scabbard."

Each knight began to loudly express examples of her villainy and deceit, reminding Arthur of the attempts she had made on his life. The king hesitated, his old hatred toward her resurfacing. The Keeper, however, made prolonged eye contact with the mysterious dark-skinned man and lowered his guard in intrigue. The man, though given no formal introduction, wore a silent expression that left Ben without doubt that those black eyes had seen much.

In their silent exchange, the man gave a solemn, knowing nod toward the sorceress and Ben knew she was to be trusted. Morgan Le Fay knew he had entered the realm. She knew of his importance, and had chosen this moment to create an alliance with her estranged brother. He was brought to remembrance of Myk's parting advice about distant enemies becoming allies.

Could she be that distant enemy on whom they could rely?

"Morgan," Arthur began, "I shall give you one chance to leave on your own accord before I throw you in the dungeons."

The dark-skinned man shifted his weight, gripping his staff.

"Arthur, wait," Ben interjected. "Let her speak first."

Stella stepped out from behind Ben, curiously watching it all unfold. On seeing the Keeper defend her, Morgan Le Fay suddenly turned her eyes to meet his and Ben felt himself consumed by the intensity and power of her gaze. Something in her eye made Stella shuffle her weight and clench her fist and snaked a possessive arm around Ben's.

Morgan Le Fay chuckled. "Yes, Arthur, listen to the Keeper. You have so far, and it's suited you quite well. I may have wanted to kill you before, brother, but..." She placed her hands on her hips. "I must admit, the prospect of Korbl having control of my realm was even more nauseating than you."

"What do you know of Korbl?" Arthur challenged, stepping forward.

"Far too much. And you should trust my hatred of him to surpass any rivalry I've posed against you. My apologies for wanting you dead, brother, but I recommend you accept the services we offer." Her dark-skinned friend nodded once more, remaining silent. "For the time being, you have my undivided loyalty and assistance. In any way possible."

Her words were sincere, despite her patronizing attitude. Arthur inhaled deeply and turned to Ben for assurance. Ben's eyes remained fixed on the sorceress. He perfectly remembered what she was capable of. He remembered the stories of her exploits against the king, her vengeful spirit and jaded soul.

Yet, here she stood, afraid of what would happen if Korbl gained control of this realm. Ben nodded his willingness to admit them into coalition.

A wickedly supportive grin stretched across her face. "My thanks, O' King. This should be quite a fight. Especially with this one on our side," she jutted her chin in Ben's direction. "My friend, The Lady, told me all about you, Keeper. I can hardly wait to see you in action."

# 29

## THE SORCERESS OF AVALON

The tempestuous relationship between Arthur and Morgan had the ability to turn the legendary king and most powerful sorceress back into petulant children. Particularly when childish bickering turns to vengeful rampages. A considerable amount of faith is required to forgive a dangerous sibling. An insurmountable amount of faith is necessary to let this sibling close enough to have a much greater opportunity to kill you.

Arthur's confidence in Ben's judgment was great, but what he now asked pushed him to his limit. As the wall of knights stood by his side against his sister, Arthur's jaw clenched, and his eyes darted from Morgan to Ben. The staring and silence persisted before the Companion couldn't stand it any longer.

"Why don't the king and the Keeper discuss this privately?" Stella suggested, walking toward Morgan and looking her dead in the eye. "While we wait outside."

Morgan narrowed her eyes. "As you command, Aerest."

Gawaine seethed, "Princess Stella has as much voice here as Lord Caverly."

"I was speaking to the princess, you fool," the sorceress quipped, without taking her eyes off of the Companion.

"Well, let's go then," Stella ordered her out the door, leaving her silent friend with the other men, and followed behind Morgan after flashing a reassuring glance at Ben.

The moment Stella closed the great hall's doors behind them, Morgan leaned against the opposing wall and crossed her arms in front of her chest, continuing to narrow her eyes. "Now there's no denying who you came from, is there?"

"What?" Stella spun around to face her, but then shook her head dismissively. "Never mind. Why are you actually here?"

Morgan allowed Stella to advance inches from her before responding in a low tone. "You're nothing like her, you know." Then, pausing, she considered her own statement. "On second thought....she has had moments of spunk too. Good breeding is typically effective in disguising it. Albert must've let you run wild while he was away."

Stella inhaled before responding, breathing the snide retort away. "Did you know him?"

Brief remorse swept Morgan's eyes. "Only at his beginning. I didn't hear much of him after he lost his Rose. Though I did hear he killed the monster who did it."

"Who did it?" she asked her, her pulse racing.

"Someone far worse than the rat leading the charge now."

"And did you help him?"

"Cromer was never the sort of man who could tempt me," Morgan snickered, tapping her chin with her pointer finger, which donned a curious pewter ring with a single engraved rune.

"No, my dad," Stella clarified. "Did you help him the way you claim you're here to help Ben?"

Morgan slowly grinned. "You're afraid I'll betray your husband."

"I would actually kill you." Stella's solemn expression was not to be challenged.

"I actually believe you would," Morgan blinked. "I know better than to test a loyal Companion. The Arches are the most dangerous."

"You know this from experience?"

"I liked your mother," Morgan crossed her arms in front of her chest. "In fact, I think I would've liked her even without all that perfection those Fairies gave her. Despite your obvious mistrust in me—no doubt thanks to that ridiculous Malory book —I have faith in Companions. And your mother was killed far too soon."

Morgan cleared her throat and leaned her head away from Stella, but never lowered her eyes.

"I've been around a long time, princess," she went on. "I was trained in the art of necromancy, fostered in dark magic for years before a Companion much like you set me right. I've seen enough to recognize when forces need to be rallied. Take it from me, sometimes it takes the strength of a Companion to rally support. Your mother's death rallied forces you can't even imagine, no matter how short her time may have been. No one takes it lightly when a Companion stares the enemy in the eye and welcomes her own destruction to protect another, especially one so precious to her...."

Morgan's eyes suddenly fell on Stella with such a heaviness that there was no doubt in Stella's mind who Morgan meant. "I don't even know if the poor girl understood who she was protecting...."

But she had known. Rose understood infinitely more than her single-minded Keeper. She knew exactly who she was protecting, and she fought for Albert to realize that until the moment she died. Albert, the fool, took his precious wife's wisdom for granted and he paid for that loss for the rest of his cursed life.

But that is a tragic tale for another time. For now, Morgan's following sentiments to Stella echo my own.

"Even so," she told her, "she was not the only one. I watched countless Regents stand against their enemy and face slaughter. If Princess Rose, and so many others, will throw away their lives protecting such a noble kin then so will I. You have my word, princess....while I will never claim a moral side in this war, I refuse to turn my back on the blood I am indebted to."

"Noble kin...." Stella breathed a faint chuckle. Surely she wasn't referring to Arthur. "What debt do you owe, exactly? To my mother?"

"Hmm, all due respect to Princess Rose, my debt is to someone much greater."

"The Lady?"

"You are a sharp one."

"I'm a quick learner."

315

"Just rest assured, princess, not even Korbl himself could make me break my oath to my sister. As long as The Lady lives....I will answer her call. As will the other seven queens of Avalon."

Stella's tight shoulders loosened. With anticipatory anxiety, she touched her fist to her lips. "And she's called you to fight for the Keeper."

Morgan lifted a bold brow and smiled. "Even when Towson's Regents were lost, those who answer to The Lady have always fought on the side of the Keeper, past and present."

"His lost Regents," Stella repeated. Her gaze dropped as she considered the account Ben gave of his travels. "My dad had no Regents....but Ben found one...."

Morgan's eyebrows remained raised, amused by the Companion's vocal contemplation. "Regents have their value," she confirmed.

# 30

## A NEW ERA OF REGENTS

"The enemy will have magic; I think it's only fair that we do too," Stella proposed.

Motivated by her past helplessness in Ben's absence, she took him aside the moment she and Morgan re-entered the great hall.

"We can't rely solely on you, Ben," she said in a hushed tone.

She glanced back at the mingling knights. The temporarily reconciled half-siblings murmured to one another, Morgan's eyes lingering in Ben and Stella's direction.

"We have you and Morgan....and whoever her mute friend is. I've seen only a glimpse of how many men Spyros has, and—if they all wear those wristbands—we don't stand much of a chance. Do you think it's possible to...would it be ridiculous to assume that you could...I don't know...share your magic or something? I mean, you made Merlin a Regent again. Why not make more?"

Ben considered this. He wasn't completely clear on what sort of authority he had, but something brought him back to those leather strips in the satchel Myk gave him. Something about this scenario, and the vague instructions he had been given, brought to his mind a very familiar situation.

Albert's voice reminded him of something he should have known the moment he was handed the satchel:

*I couldn't do it alone. But Myk had already planned for that. He told me as much. All it took was some enchanted leather and Myk's authority, and I made myself an ally. Otis may be useless in many ways, but I haven't met another more worthy than he is—I mean, my options may be lacking, but I think he'll prove to be a handy and loyal Regent Keeper.*

Ben suddenly knew precisely what Myk intended for them. "Belts," he said aloud. Apparently, he forgot that his process of thought had not been vocal until Stella's confused expression reminded him. "I think I can."

"How would you do that?"

"Myk gave me three strips of leather, on our way back from the Lake," Ben clarified.

She wrinkled her mouth to one side. "Okay..."

"The leather matched this," he tugged at his jacket. "They're belts. I think they could have similar magic—that may be why he gave them to me."

"He didn't tell you why he gave them to you?"

"He said I'll know when to use them. It's....my duty."

"But not how to use it?"

Ben sighed. "No, not exactly."

Stella nodded. "He's not the most straightforward fellow, is he?"

"Comes with the territory," he shrugged. "I suppose it's important for me to learn a lot of this on my own."

"Probably. So...you just give them these belts? How do you know who to give them to? There are only three, and we have a lot more than three knights."

He shrugged again. "I'll just follow my instincts."

Stella raised her eyebrows with a sly smile. "Ben Caverly following his gut. My, my, you have changed."

He chuckled warmly and kissed her forehead. "I'll be right back."

Moments later, Ben returned from his chamber with his satchel in hand. While he was fetching it, Stella explained the idea to the king, who then passed it along to his men. Morgan Le Fay sat back and watched with keen curiosity as Ben expounded on the significance of the leather and the heavy responsibility it held. Her head occasionally nodded, agreeing with his understanding.

"Now, there are only so many," the Keeper went on. "Only three of you can become Regent Keepers. That's not to say that the others are any less important...it just is what it is."

One by one, Ben bestowed the magic upon the worthy holders. First was to King Arthur himself, naturally. The man had his faults but was generally destined for greatness, and destiny cannot be ignored. The king bowed his head humbly as Ben approached him. He held this honor in similar regard to his calling as ruler of the realm. Merlin promised that Arthur would come to greatness, though he never quite explained how many ups and downs it would take to get there. In Arthur's eyes, Ben was giving him the mightiest means to achieve this greatness.

The second was to Sir Launcelot, the gallant one. Another man with faults too many to number, but his redemption was completed through his own self-deprecation. However, he was not quite so accepting as Arthur.

"No," he shook his head softly. "The Keepership should go to one worthy. If I was not worthy to obtain the Holy Grail, then I can in no way...."

"Launcelot," Ben stopped him. "I think, through your penitence, there are very few now as worthy as you."

"My Lord Caverly....I thank you." The Keeper's words incited tears to swell in the knight's eyes. He had tortured himself over his sins, and now the hero prophesied by heroes deemed him worthy of receiving such power he never imagined possible. Of all of the men in the room, Sir Launcelot was very easily the most humbled by the bestowal.

Now, the third was tricky. Ben stood directly in front of Sir Bors, ready and determined to hand him the third belt.

But something stopped him. It was a strong deterrent, causing him to draw attention to his hesitation.

Another name filled his mind: *Gawaine.*

Competition with the hotheaded knight may no longer be a rational issue for Ben, but his pride still briefly combated the prompting. *Get over it, Ben. The man needs this.* Pride suppressed by reason, Ben moved to Sir Gawaine and handed him the belt.

Gawaine was almost as surprised as Ben was. He shot a questioning glance at Arthur, who merely smiled and shrugged. In acceptance, Gawaine gave Ben a nod of gratitude, silently mending whatever rift remained between them. They were now brothers.

Despite the previous explanation of Regent Keepers being less than Arch Keepers, I feel it fair to describe to you the change in a man as the result of receiving any form of Keepership. I think it's common knowledge that magic changes you, but it isn't like those extravagant displays that you see in moving pictures. The change is much more internal. It isn't a sudden rush of maturity and prestige. It's a subtle and gradual dosage of understanding.

What is sudden is their deeper respect for Ben and the immense weight on his shoulders as the Arch Keeper. This transformation was attractively apparent to everyone in the room—particularly those who comprehended what had just transpired. Even the sorceress knew the heaviness this brought. Their arsenal against the intimidating foe was now increased to more reasonable proportions.


Once the excitement of the newly appointed Regents settled, or rather as they settled into their roles, each retreated to his quarters to process the day's happenings. Morgan had seen many a Regent in her day, but never one of her own blood. Now, more than before, she felt the need to gain Arthur's trust. He just stepped deeper into the lion's den and had no idea what he had gotten himself into. He only trusted the Keeper, as he should. But that wasn't enough for Morgan. He needed to know the allies he now had, and always had, in his own realm.

Moving her way down the corridor to Arthur's quarters, Morgan's determination was momentarily disturbed by an old friend passing her with just as much vigor.

Quickly, she turned on her heel and chuckled. "Well, when you're right, you're right, aren't you?"

Myk paused to face her, putting a finger to his lips. "Behave."

"If she insists."

"She does," he assured her.

"Very well, then," she sighed. Taking a few steps backward, she leaned against the door to her destination and flashed Myk one last smirk. "I'll do my best."

She pushed the door open, bidding Myk goodbye and interrupting the low debate between the king and Sir Launcelot on the other side.

Arthur sighed and rolled his eyes when he saw Morgan step into the room. "Must you be so intrusive?"

"I suppose not," she shrugged. "But there's little joy in good manners?"

Arthur advanced, making a threatening barrier between her and Launcelot. He aimed a stern finger at her face and said, "The only reason you are not sentenced to death is the Keeper's inexplicable belief that you won't betray us."

"As I've assured the Companion," Morgan recited, "my allegiance should not be your prime concern. You don't seem to understand, brother, just how much I have already fought in this conflict you've found yourself in." She slowly paced the king's chamber, letting her brother's eyes skeptically track her as she spoke. "I don't expect you to—I don't expect even the Keeper himself to understand. Thankfully, Lord Caverly has learned to trust the subtle nudging of that jacket, so none of you have to understand."

"How can we be certain?" Launcelot chimed in, stepping supportively to Arthur's side.

Morgan stopped just in front of Arthur's small dining table and rested her hand against it as she squared her shoulders and faced them. "It won't be much longer before your taste of this war becomes overwhelming. Believe me. A feud between siblings is so trivial; we'd both be wise to forget it."

"That's easier said than done when blood has been shed, Morgan," Launcelot growled.

"On both sides, it would seem." There was a thick coat of contempt that suddenly laced her voice.

"Neither of us is innocent in this, sister," Arthur conceded, holding up his palms.

"Indeed," she softened once again. "If it's any consolation, The Lady has forbidden me from pursuing you," she assured Launcelot. When he looked to his feet in remembrance of her attempts at past dalliances, her gaze returned to her brother. "Or threatening you...since they took your queen. And I swear to you, this war has no place for pettiness."

"Just how involved in this war have you been?" Launcelot pressed.

"One day you'll know," she promised him. "For now, all you need to know is that I pledge undying loyalty to the rightwise king."

The good knight straightened his back and nodded to Arthur. "I second that, sire. And I owe you much more than mere loyalty."

Arthur's shoulders fell. "Launcelot...you are my brother." He placed a firm hand on Launcelot's shoulder, and his voice shook ever so slightly. "We loved the same woman....but she only loved one of us. Any transgression has been settled....we both lost her."

Morgan bowed her head respectfully.

"We have suffered heavy losses since the arrival of the Keeper....and I fear it will only worsen from here. Whatever this battle will be, it is clearly part of a war much greater than ourselves. We must trust in the surviving Round Table....and its allies." Arthur took a step back and centered himself between Launcelot and Morgan. "Because, when it all ends....they will be the most powerful force left to fight against this new enemy."

Morgan was grossly familiar with Keepers who sensed their time was ending. It's incredibly common, amongst Regents and Arches alike. Morgan frowned at her brother's suspicions, but the somber confidence in his words told her he had accepted it. It's such a bittersweet ordeal to see heroes prompted toward their own demise—but alas, it is always necessary for the fulfillment of particular stages of war.

# 31

## DECISIONS MAKETH DESTINY

As has often been the norm, Myk took the time to counsel with his Arch Keeper before sending him into battle. Ben needed very little guidance regarding his battle plans—he was certainly more qualified than his predecessor. With the mind of a leader and the logic of a strategist, Benjamin Caverly impressed even Arthur's most elite warriors. Myk listened carefully to Ben's plan, and Stella's accolades of said plan, and nodded as he spoke. He sat against Ben's desk with his arms crossed in front of his chest. Stella watched every movement of his face, waiting for him to show just as much anticipation as they felt. Her mouth wrinkled to one side when she realized the Galdere had other things on his mind.

Before giving any sort of verbal approval, Myk cleared his throat and straightened his back. "There's another matter that has not been accounted for."

Ben frowned. "And what's that?"

"That scabbard requires a new home."

Stella saw Ben's face fall, but she didn't quite understand why.

"Myk...." he started softly. The one thing Myk had anticipated was Ben's reluctance to obey his next request.

"Benjamin...you and I both know the outcome of this battle." Myk stepped forward. "Arthur's fate is written everywhere his story is told, and that does not change today."

Stella finally understood. Her arms fell at her sides, and she looked to her husband, sensing his helplessness.

"You would have him die....intentionally....for your cause." There was just the slightest shade of bitterness in the Keeper's voice. He retreated slowly until sinking onto the edge of his bed.

"Many men and women have died for our cause, Ben," Myk assured. "And that will not change today. Many more will die. But every hero who falls for the sake of this cause will rise."

Stella exhaled, drawing Myk's attention.

"King Arthur will return when his realm needs him," he went on. "It's a prophecy, and we Galdere take prophecies quite seriously. He'll only be joining countless others."

"Like my mother," Stella mumbled.

"And your father," Myk nodded. "Peaceful or not, Albert died a martyr."

"His illness was Korbl's doing?" Ben shot up from the bed, prepared to console his wife. A touching gesture, but Stella was unmoved. Like her mother, she was always very quick to accept truths. She suspected the nature of her father's death. No Keeper can make as many waves as Albert did, only to die of natural causes.

"Poor Albert...." Myk's gaze fell to his hands. "He went so long serving as the only one....it's a difficult enough job, but without the support of a Companion or Regents....I knew he was only counting the days that he would finally die for the cause and gain some sort of relief."

Death is never quite as relieving and restful as one would think. In many ways, it's more exhausting than life, if I'm being honest. Definitely not the respite for which Albert had aimed. Myk knew this and only chuckled quietly to himself before continuing on a more somber note.

"But just as the deaths of Albert and Rose marked an end, Arthur's death will mark a beginning. A christening, if you will," he shrugged, in his majestic stance. "It's what is needed to complete this assignment, Ben."

"I thought the assignment was to fix the mess Riddock and Don Quixote made for the realm's story?" Stella questioned.

Myk smiled. "Oh, assignments are rarely so straightforward. Fixing one story will only have a ripple effect on another. Every story intertwines at one point or another. And chances are, it won't ever be only once. Your assignment was to prepare the realm and its heroes—everything else fell in line, necessarily, as you've done so."

Ben was silent. His mouth stiffened as he struggled to maintain eye contact with Myk. The wise one knew what was in the Keeper's mind. Ben's tendency toward obedience was being challenged, and the good man had a difficult decision to make. Myk stepped closer to him and put an encouraging hand on Ben's shoulder.

"He's become your friend," he told him in a gentle tone. "I understand that. But don't worry, either of you. Don't fear for him—he's in a realm where the dead have been known to rise and will continue to do so. The original text's promise still stands. Arthur will return....and when he does, there will be a second reign of the Rightwise King."

"Arthur will have a second reign then?" Stella asked.

"Arthur must be betrayed....it was part of his written tale and a part that will inevitably come, regardless of how altered the tale may now be."

Stella's mouth slanted in an exasperated grimace at his avoidance, but Myk was unmoved and continued.

"It will be a betrayal that leads to his death, and I'm sure you can sense how that must unfold, Ben."

Ben nodded slowly, remembering the appointment of the Regents.

"The Regent belts know a man's future as well as Yonas and I do. There was a reason you were guided as you were. Just remember—"

The chamber door opened and the king walked in, with anxious haste reflected in his eyes as well as his pace.

"Oh, I-I apologize, Keeper," Arthur stumbled for words. "I had no idea you were in conference."

"Perfect timing, Your Highness. He was...." Stella started, the annoyance still lingering in her voice. She turned slightly to see that Myk had already disappeared, and she sighed. "He was just leaving anyway." Seeing the hesitance on Ben's face, she then added softly, "And, uh....so was I. I'll be right back."

The moment Stella closed the door behind her, the king advanced with purpose. Wringing his hands, Arthur fished for words that weren't coming easily. He cleared his throat and swallowed hard. He began to warn the Keeper of what he was sure he already knew regarding his fate.

"I came to tell you, Keeper....that I have a strong suspicion this will be—"

Ben stopped him. "Where is your scabbard, Arthur?"

Arthur wrinkled his brow but reached for Excalibur, which hung reliably on his belt. Obediently, he handed the sword and scabbard to Ben, who then returned Excalibur to its hero. Ben then held the scabbard between them and spoke more to it than the king.

"This is in need....of a new owner."

"I understand."

Ben looked up and raised a skeptic brow. "Do you?"

"Have you ever had a destiny you couldn't escape?" Arthur's voice was low and contemplative. There was something in the way he gripped the hilt of the downward-facing Excalibur that seemed as if he was holding on for dear life. Ben could see that this was an individual who felt the arrival of his own judgment day. He didn't know precisely what was coming, but he did know what bearing it would have on his legacy.

"That depends on how you define destiny," Ben solemnly replied. "Who knows, for certain, what destiny is and how it ends? A higher power, certainly—only a fool can deny that. But, is a destiny what we are capable of becoming, or what we are cursed with being?"

The king's head slowly turned to face him. "You think it is a fate that can be changed?"

Ben exhaled. "Sire...I think everything is left to our own actions. Decisions maketh destiny," he quoted deliberately.

They were words spoken previously and frequently by Myk, as recorded in Albert's journal, and they were some of the first words that Ben had properly absorbed during his many studies of the text. They were the only words that comforted him when faced with the impending outcome of this battle. Arthur chose this. Arthur would choose this. The words that followed were much more introspective than Ben intended:

"Your destiny won't be anything you're not capable of—nor will it be anything you won't eventually want and accept. I think, instead of fearing it, you should have the faith that every choice you make will prepare you to be ready for it when the time comes, my king."

Arthur's mouth twitched into a knowing smile as he lowered Excalibur, almost touching the ground. "It is you who is a king, Lord Caverly."

I assume that is why Ben was chosen to be the Arch Keeper. Despite reluctance or doubt, the obedient ones were the wisest. Ben proved that from the beginning. His particular brand of perfection would undoubtedly be credited to the noble spirit in which he trusted Myk and carried out his duty. He was too modest to accept that, of course. That was simply his nature. Yet, there was a fire within him, and that much was undeniable.

Good King Arthur recognized that fire, and he did what every good king should when facing a man such as this: he humbly relied heavily upon him. "Would you....would you accompany me when I....?"

"Of course, sire," Ben promised. "'Til the end."

Arthur sighed his tension into a smile. "You have been such a dear friend, Caverly. I understand now why fate chose you as my guide. I wouldn't have asked for any other. For there is....no one more worthy of saving my realm."

Ben's eyes misted, but before he could shed a masculine tear, a knock came to the door. It hadn't taken Stella long to fetch Sir Gawaine. On perfect cue, she returned with the confused knight at her side and ushered him into Ben's chambers to face the king and Keeper.

Gawaine noted Ben's somber expression before greeting the king and returning His Majesty's smile. "You called for me, sire?"

"Um, yes." Arthur set Excalibur on Ben's desk and took the scabbard from Ben's hands. "This....this is for you. A reward for your loyalty."

Gawaine took the scabbard and frowned. He looked from the king to the Keeper to Stella. "My loyalty?"

"Yes," Stella confirmed. Ben's silence concerned her, so she slipped her hand in his and nodded to Gawaine encouragingly.

"Sire...." he turned back to Arthur and offered him the return of the scabbard. "I am not so sure I deserve this. Or to be a Regent, for that matter."

"The Keeper chose you for a reason, Gawaine." Arthur stepped aside and gestured toward Ben, passing him the torch with full confidence.

Ben's hesitation made Gawaine scoff lightly. "And I would love to know it. I don't believe the Keeper had any reason at all to choose me." Gawaine remembered the Keeper's previous hesitation just as clearly. He was not Ben's first choice, and that much was clear from the beginning.

"You're a good knight, Gawaine," Ben finally spoke, squeezing Stella's hand. "I didn't choose you. You were meant to be a Regent of your own merit. Someone with a greater perspective than I has pressed me to grant you that opportunity. And he was right to do so. But, given the time, I would've chosen you even without the encouragement."

Gawaine bowed his head slightly in gratitude. "I don't fully understand. But it doesn't matter.....I trust the Keeper. Even if he's leading us all to our deaths," he added with an adventurous chuckle.

This time Stella squeezed Ben's hand, assuring him of the jest. Thankfully, it was almost unnecessary; Ben smiled but tensed his shoulders.

"Not all of us," Arthur softly contributed.

Gawaine took note. "Sire?"

"We should see to the men," Ben said before Arthur could explain. "But, first....there's been a need for a slight change of plan."


The change in the Keeper's plans was considered classified information. After all, there were still potential traitors afoot. Nonetheless, the plan went forward, and troops were mobilized. Sir Lionel, one of the lesser referenced knights, was asked personally by Ben to maintain a small army of men to guard the citadel, should they fail, as a last line of defense. Don Quixote proudly accepted the request to join Lionel's men, claiming his duty remained with the princess.

Ah, Princess Stella.

You're probably wondering where she fit into Ben's grand plan. Well, unbeknownst to her, the good Lord Caverly made a slight alteration to the original scheme and waited to present it to her until the last possible opportunity. In fact, mere moments before leading his men out of London, Ben went to Stella's room to see her preparing for battle. The king had ordered custom battle armor made just for her, which was very well-fitted and surprisingly flattering to her figure for something so primitively masculine. Ben shook his stare and tried to focus on the matter at hand.

"Stella, you can't go with me," he said plainly.

Placing her hands on her hips Stella raised her eyebrows defiantly. "Excuse me?"

"You're not going with me. You're staying here."

Months ago, Stella would have stomped her foot and shouted indignantly. Instead, she now advanced, almost pleadingly. "I'm not going to let you go off and do these things alone anymore, Ben. You have a target on your back—and I don't want to come close to losing you again."

"I have to do this alone," he insisted. "I can't put you in danger. I owe it to your—"

"Would you stop?" Stella interrupted. "You've already done what my dad wanted you to do; you aren't obligated to

333

look out for me anymore, okay? You don't have to protect me for my dad's sake—"

"I'm not," he stood his ground. "I'm protecting you for your sake..."

"Well don't."

"And mine."

"Why?"

"Because I love you," he snapped.

It's not often that Stella is rendered speechless, but I'd say this was a special enough occasion. She couldn't even manage a response. Her sky eyes misted over, and all she could do was stare at him. When words did find their way out, they were true to her nature. "It's about time," she breathed. "Because I love you back."

Gently cupping her face in his hands, Ben kissed his wife tenderly. Of all they had been through, of all the pages of this story I have already written, it took far too long for those words to be spoken between them. Fair or not, taking advantage of this sweet moment seemed ideal for Ben's next decisive action. After the kiss sadly ended, Ben slipped her bedroom key into his sleeve and left, quickly locking the door behind him, leaving Stella both confused and enraged. She ran to the door and pounded as hard as she could, shouting and begging. Ben tried to ignore her. Don Quixote was standing guard beside the door, beginning his protective duties early.

"Don Quixote," Ben placed a firm hand on the Spaniard's shoulder. "I need you to swear to me that you will not allow any harm to come to the princess."

The good knight nodded eagerly.

"I need you to swear to me—more than you ever have before." Ben's gaze was earnest and sincere, putting all his heart into every word.

"I swear on my life, Lord Caverly."

And the good fool never broke his oath.

# 32

## A Cause Worth Dying For

Dying in battle is often advertised as tragic, yet noble and sometimes liberating. Many have done it. History and storybooks are scattered with martyrs and sacrificial heroes. Heroism is never easy, however glorious and noble the outcome and however many lives are otherwise spared in the process. Take it from me; even the simple deaths have their challenges. Whether a sword or a peaceful poison smite you, the anticipation of death lends one a certain disquiet and uncertainty. From Albert to Arthur, the imminent demise of a hero can shake even the most seasoned.

The good King Arthur's hands shook as he faced his men. Sending them to their ordered positions, with the risk of never seeing any of them again....that was the life of a soldier. A soldier and a king. He had done this many times before, every time they faced a domestic threat to the kingdom. But this was no domestic threat. This was something so much greater than any of them, and no amount of encouraging words could succor their fears. Each new Regent stood at the head of his battalion, ready for the king's signal to disperse. To their surprise, as they faced the steps that led to the castle door, Arthur took a step back and turned to the Keeper.

"Lord Caverly...." the king began. "Would the Keeper care to send us off with a few words?"

Ben, whose own hands still shook from detaining Stella, cleared his throat. "Um, Your Majesty?"

"Please, Ben," Arthur added softly.

Clearing his throat again, and acknowledging the king's unspoken fears, Ben straightened his back and moved forward. Even in school, Ben Caverly was not one for words. Give him pieces of literature, and he could tell you in minutes what the true meaning and linguistic significance was for each, but ask him to articulate his own creative thoughts into something inspiring, and he was at a loss. Suddenly he regretted locking Stella safely away, for she would have known in an instant the words these men needed. As he thought of Stella, the right words filled his mind.

"Our enemy....does not wish to destroy us merely to gain control. He wishes to destroy what we stand for....the strength, the unity....everything he has already attacked. We've been bruised by betrayal....by doubt....but still, we stand." As Ben spoke, his confidence grew and his shoulders squared. "Whether or not today is the end of us....the enemy has not succeeded and will not succeed. The blood that will be spilt will not be counted as his victory. We've already overcome him. And this day will prove that. We cannot be broken. We few, we happy few, we band of brothers; for he, today that sheds his blood with me shall be my brother."

While not an entirely original speech, the knights raised their swords in unison, proclaiming their loyalty until death. It was a moment for the history books. And it was with that conviction that this unbreakable force charged for the enemy's defenses.

The mysterious castle in the north was the base for many a foul, shadowy soldier. All of them bore the mark of their allegiance on their eyes as well as their wrists. They and their leader sat in their fabricated fortress, idly waiting for orders to strike. It's not healthy for armies to rest in comfort; it encourages laziness and gives the enemy a free advantage. For as Spyros' men lounged around unawares, a moderately large army of warriors led by Launcelot was positioned watchfully in the thick forest behind the citadel, waiting for the signal to advance.

On the other side of this dark terrain, facing the entrance of the evil fortress, King Arthur himself sat atop his steed with Sir Bors at his side. Spyros peered arrogantly over the high walls of his fortress, laughing loudly at the two pitiful horsemen.

"This is the best the great hero could muster?" he snickered. "You've come so unprepared, King Arthur."

Overconfidently, Spyros summoned his own army to gather behind the gates and, when he felt the time was right, he released the swarm. Like cockroaches, the dark soldiers scurried out of their citadel and charged for their light opponents.

Beyond the ensuing battle and farther south from the dark terrain, there waited an even larger force. The Keeper and his battalion waited patiently in the thick forest, opposite Launcelot's men on the other side of the citadel. Their numbers were the largest of the three groups but maintained the most cover. Ben tried to hush the men's restless chatter, so as to better blend in with the silence of the trees.

"Are you ready for this?" he whispered to Sir Gawaine, his general in this venture. Gawaine nodded solemnly. "You do know our likelihood of dying?"

The thought had only just occurred to Ben himself, at least concerning his future. And Stella's future. Their future. He never bothered dwelling on what would happen to them if they died in this realm until now.

A grin stretched across Gawaine's face. "Oh, Lord Caverly. If any cause was worth dying for, it is this."

This both calmed and impressed Ben. This ludicrous show-off had grown into a wise sage in such a short time. Ben was proud to have a Keeper such as Gawaine to fight by his side. In fact, he intuitively arranged the battalions in such a fashion. No Keeper, save Arthur's decoy, should fight alone.

In the distribution of assignments, Ben was sure to pass on his understanding of the use of Keeper magic. Even given the knowledge, as they readied themselves to receive Arthur's signal, Launcelot fidgeted uncomfortably with the leather belt around his waist.

"It isn't as hard as it seems," he repeated Ben's guidance to himself. "Put your hand out and take control of the energy around you. It becomes part of you. And if you don't feel it, fake it until you do."

"You're quite right, my boy," a chipper voice said. Launcelot looked to his side to see an old friend perched atop a steed of his own.

"Merlin!" Launcelot exclaimed.

"Shh, we don't want them hearing us, do we?" Merlin chided. He shifted uncomfortably in his saddle; wizards rarely needed to travel by horseback, but since the arrival of this new Arch Keeper, Merlin found himself atop one of these creatures more often than he intended.

"Merlin," Launcelot protested. "The Keeper said your time here had passed..."

"Yes, but it came back around. You didn't think we'd leave you all alone, did you?" Merlin winked at him, before pointing to Arthur's distant signal. "I believe that means it's time, does it not?"

Myk and The Lady returned to the scene with the majesty of gods. Their white steeds reflected the glow of the Galdere, while still maintaining the necessary stealth of Ben's troops.

"I wondered if you'd show up," Ben mentioned with a blend of tension and jest.

When Myk reached his side, his only response was, "You're missing someone."

Ben looked at him strangely. The Lady, moving beside them, lent no explanation.

"Well, two someones," Myk added. "Lacking them will affect the balance of this battle, Ben. Rather a lot."

The Lady nodded in support.

"Myk..." Ben started.

"Ben, I highly respect you and your desire to keep your dear wife far from any sort of harm; I understand wanting to do anything to protect the woman you love. But, this isn't the sort of battle you can fight without her."

The Keeper clenched his jaw. He knew Myk was right; but the thought of putting Stella in danger went against every fiber of his being. She was safe in London. "Who's the second someone?"

"Don Quixote de la Mancha," Myk answered, matter-of-factly. "He can't fulfill his destiny if he's playing nanny."

"I understand," Ben sighed, lamenting his mistake.

"I can't help you unless you do all you can first. And believe me, for what's coming, you will need all the help afforded to you."

The Lady smiled. "Don't worry, Benjamin. I have my best heading for your Companion as we speak, and their prime objective is to see to her safety. The greatest assets require the greatest protection."

"And she has the greatest faith in her ladies," Myk contributed, also smiling.

The Lady's gentle smile morphed into a playful smirk. "And why shouldn't I? I only choose the best. Besides, they tend to excel when paired with one of your Keepers. You chose well."

Myk chuckled, and Ben recognized the banter. Even the Galdere flirt, apparently, but as strange as it was, its purpose was served in making Ben ache for Stella to be at his side.

# 33

## THE AID OF AVALON

Hearing loud retching noises, Don Quixote burst through Stella's bedchamber door. A poor old man in his condition, he naturally felt disoriented afterward—of course, being a poor old man in his condition, he shouldn't have been capable of breaking down a solid oak door in the first place.

He found Stella with her blond head over a bucket. She was in full fighting gear with a sword gird about her waist and everything. She perked up when she heard his fiasco. "Oh, thank goodness, Don Quixote," she sighed. She quickly pretended to wipe her face with a towel and walked hastily past him. "I could've died if you hadn't barged in like...that. So dutiful to damsels in distress and all of that."

Before he knew it, she had fooled him and skirted out the door and down the hallway. Obedient to Ben's orders, he followed her as quickly as he could. "Where are we going, my lady?"

"To battle, my good knight," she answered, moving even faster. Eventually, she ran into Sir Lionel turning a corner. "Oh, hey there."

She had never paid much attention to Sir Lionel before —not that it would have made much difference now—but she suddenly became very aware of the darkness in his eyes. How had she not seen that before? How had Ben not seen it? She had very little time to figure this out, unfortunately, because he caught her staring for too long.

"Not you too," she groaned in exasperation.

Lionel drew his sword, but Stella was quicker. Their blades clashed in the narrow corridor, making any sort of footwork nearly impossible. Thankfully, Stella knew nothing of footwork. All she knew was how to block and stab, based purely on observation. She held her own like a fighter, but it was Don Quixote, in his even clumsier swordsmanship, who slayed Sir Lionel. He flailed his arm past a ducking Stella and struck Lionel sharply in the gut with his sword, bringing him to his knees.

Stella panted heavily. "Well done, sir," she patted Don Quixote's arm.

"I have sworn an oath to protect you, princess, and a knights-errant never—"

"Yes, yes, yes," she cut him off. "Keep that sword ready. We're going to war."

Don Quixote had no intention of arguing; he was yearning for more adventure. The faithful follower allowed Stella to take his hand and drag him to the stables where they acquired two of the remaining horses available to take them on their journey to where they believed the action awaited them. In truth, it was much closer than they assumed. Midway through their travels, The Lady and Myk's aforementioned chosen ones sent to retrieve the one they swore to protect.

Oddly, none were on horseback. They had no need for such means of travel. After all, their job was not to fight alongside the realm's heroes; their job was to protect the Companion. Without introduction, Stella found herself confronted by eight of the legendary Nine Queens of Avalon, lead by Morgan Le Fay herself, and accompanied by her mysterious dark-skinned compatriot.

Morgan, of course, stood at the front with her friend at her right. On either side of them were lovely and mystical ladies Stella had never before met.

A brunette woman in a dark purple dress immediately caught Stella's attention. Her presence felt familiar, as if they'd been in the same room once before. And, in fact, they had. When Stella was just an infant, this willowy fairy had launched an attack on an entire kingdom after being deprived of a party invitation. These days, Seraphina had curbed her pettiness and put her dramatics toward more productive causes.

She was the first to address the Aerest Companion. "Stella," she smiled.

Stella's wide-eyed confusion caused the fairy to chuckle and glance to the woman beside her, whose smile was much slower to appear. Instead, she tucked her coral-colored hair behind her hair and crossed her arms in front of her chest.

"She's a Towson?" the redhead muttered under her breath for only Seraphina to hear.

"Glinda," Seraphina warned.

345

"Glinda?" Stella croaked in surprise. "The...the Good Witch?"

"*Good* is relative, dear." Two middle-aged women, leaning on staffs and mumbling to one another, until the taller one, wearing a beige toga–which felt a bit anachronistic, in Stella's opinion–decided to contribute to the conversation.

"Oh, you," her shorter friend hissed and batted her arm.

A familiar face you have already met, dear reader, stepped in front of the more aged Queens to buffer the caddy deviation from the issues at hand. Nimue answered The Lady's call as quickly as Morgan had and joined her magical sisters to defend their realm. She grinned at Stella, dismissing any bickering that might have ensued behind her. The Companion's mere presence was everything Nimue would have expected for a Keeper such as Ben Caverly.

"It is an honor to finally meet you, princess," Nimue said warmly. Stella returned the smile, feeling surprisingly at ease with this new ensemble of fresh yet comforting figures.

"Well, she really does look like her, doesn't she?" another Queen spoke up.

Beside Nimue stood a peculiarly beautiful sorceress with a lavender gown and striking but pale turquoise curls upon her head, lending a start contrast to her pleasantly cocoa-complected skin. Morgan rolled her eyes as the Queen spoke.

"I heard that," the pastel Queen mumbled, glancing to the side as if speaking to someone behind her.

"You couldn't have heard that, Allora," Morgan groaned.

Allora snapped her eyes to Morgan. "And yet."

Morgan grunted, and her compatriot chuckled. "Don't encourage her," Morgan told him, but he merely shrugged in amusement. "You'll be safer if you dismount, princess," she then added to Stella.

"Safer than—" Stella began to question, but the Queens continued to bicker.

"She'll be safer on the horse," Nimue posed, challengingly.

Morgan turned away from Stella to face Nimue. "Not with the threat that's coming to her. She'll need to be completely surrounded."

"Do you have so little faith in her ability to protect herself?"

Stella considered this, even mumbling, "I can..." before being overshadowed by the continuing debate.

"I don't think she's challenging the Aerest's capabilities," a voice from behind Seraphina spoke.

A rather tan woman stood understated and subdued until selective moments. On her face, she wore a set of aviator sunglasses which sparked Stella's strong memories of Albert returning home from business trips and hanging those very sunglasses on his collar as he read her stories. When the green head-wrap she wore suddenly twitched with a strangely fluid movement, as if multiple living beings were adjusting their sleeping arrangements beneath, Stella began to wonder how Medusa managed to inherit her father's aviators.

"Why would The Lady send us if she didn't intend for us to shield the Companion from....her?"

"Morgan is not wrong, Nimue," Allora contributed.

Nimue scowled and glanced back to Stella, who was already dismounting. "I suppose she's right, princess. You'll do well to stay behind us. And your friend as well."

"Better listen, Don," Stella said quietly, watching the humorous discontent between the Queens.

Discontent or not, when the moment came for unity, the Queens and their male ally joined together and formed a wall between the abruptly approaching enemy and the precious blood in their charge.

In contrast, the personage sent to kill Stella did not come alone. The Assassin's greatest asset was the reason for such a numerously fortified defense for the Companion. Bastien knew the lengths The Lady would go to protect her own blood—or rather, Ava knew, and Bastien listened. It was why he agreed to accept Ava's partnership in this venture, though I don't imagine he put up too vigorous of a fight. Ava is quite persuasive.

The two villains strolled to confront their engagement prior to the expected battle. The Queens sensed their presence and were in readied positions around the Companion and Don Quixote before Ava and Bastien made it in sight. In her dark golden, sultry armor, Ava stood with her hands on her hips a short distance from the newly formed wall before her.

"I'm flattered," she purred. "Aren't you flattered, darling?"

Bastien smirked but knew better than to interrupt her monologue with a verbal response.

"So many to face just little old us. Do you fear the Assassin that much? Or do you finally understand what you're protecting? It must be understanding—he's highly skilled, but

348

only a couple of you could've bested him. No need for the whole crew to join the fun."

"We could say the same for you," Morgan spoke first. "You seemed to feel the need to help your little dog in his assignment against us."

"Some targets are harder to kill than others, love," Ava jutted her chin in Stella's direction. "Sometimes the Assassin needs a little help." Ignoring Bastien's visibly wounded pride as he cast his gaze to the ground, Ava added, "As he did with the last one."

Stella listened to the venomous words with a clenched jaw, but the moment Ava referenced the last one, the Companion's hands shook.

Albert.

Her father.

He was the last one.

And it was Ava who killed him.

She knew it must have been someone special; Myk confirmed as much. Never did she suspect the woman who, only weeks before, Stella had considered her dear friend. Had Morgan allowed it, Stella would have fired the cruelest of words—but Morgan had a more personal conflict of hers to address.

"Perhaps holding back on the belittlement would show some more positive results," Morgan spat, stiffening her posture. "You don't need her to carry your weight, Bastien."

Bastien looked Morgan in the eye, but her supportive words did not move his expression. In fact, they were more confused than anything. Any words contrary to Ava's escaped him and he remained silent.

"Are you encouraging him?" Allora softly murmured to Morgan. "Or have you forgotten whose side you're on?"

Morgan fell silent, slightly bowing her head. To her chagrin, Ava noted this and laughed.

"Good girl," she chided her.

Before Allora could voice defense for her fellow Queen, the Queens' ebony companion stepped in front and faced Ava directly.

"Fire Siren," he harshly called her, in his foreign accented tone.

"Easy, Zuberi," Nimue warned him.

"Hm, I've always loved that name, handsome," Ava winked at him. "Well-suited, I think."

She lowered her hands from her hips and slowly moved forward with a fire flaring in her eyes as if encouraging the moniker.

"You will not touch her," he said calmly, moving the staff he carried in front of him defensively.

Ava stopped and stood just a bit taller, impressed by his conviction. What caught her more than his words was the sight of the wooden ebony talisman that hung around his neck in the shape of a moon.

She crossed her arms in front of her chest and replied, "Well, well....not yet, it seems."

# 34

## THEY ALL FALL IN

As Ava aimed her stifled attack on the Companion, and when Spyros and his troops advanced, King Arthur and Sir Bors were meant to lure them toward Ben's soldiers while Launcelot surrounded the enemy from the rear. They were meant to be the bait.

But, as part of the newest edition of the Keeper's plan, only one was truly the bait. Bors had covertly steered the king in the direction of a carefully chosen clearing, supposedly unbeknownst to the Keeper and his plans. Just as they were alone and dismounted, minutes before they would be joined by both Ben's troops and that of the enemy, Arthur slowly turned to his old friend.

Bors had drawn his weapon, but not in defense.

"I wanted the Keeper to be wrong, my friend," Arthur lamented. "But I do believe I'm in far too deep to begin doubting a man so intuitive as Lord Caverly. You've been lying in wait since the beginning, and it took me far too long to see it." When

Bors would not lower his sword, Arthur sighed and gripped his own. "I will not be the sort of king to go down without a fight."

"There could be another way, Arthur," the corrupt knight opened his arm to welcome the king to the possibilities.

"There really can't be." The king lunged with his weapon, but training with a knight for so many years leads to predictability. Bors easily blocked his attack and moved smoothly to the side, his mouth twitching into a smile.

"You've known so little of the other side, my king." He heard his clandestine dark allies approach from behind, but used the tainted wristbands he had kept hidden from the king to signal them to stay where they were. "Merlin and the Keeper only taught you one half of this war....one half of all that is offered. The half, it seems, which requires the most restriction. Do you know the Master does not hesitate to grant his followers access to his powers?"

Arthur sensed Bors's reinforcements and caught sight of Spyros and his men in the lining of the trees. "Those are dark words, Bors. You were not always so greedy."

The expression on Bors's face suddenly changed. He was no longer mocking or smug. His mouth twisted into a bitter scowl. "Greedy? Is it greed to demand recompense for my loyalty? I have been obedient. It has gotten me nothing."

His voice grew louder as he stepped closer to the king. His sword was not aimed for Arthur; his attack was rearing to come from a very different source.

"The Master has promised me more than you could ever offer," Bors revealed. "He has granted me more than that Keeper of yours is capable of."

As he lifted his darkly banded wrist, Arthur raised his sword. But it wouldn't be enough. Even Excalibur would be no match for the sort of dark magic Korbl granted his followers. Fortunately, leaving Arthur to his own devices was not Myk's way. He's quite selective with things such as timing and resources, and Arthur's time had not yet come.

Just as the darkness began to escape Bors's wrists, Myk, his Lady, and Ben's battalion of heroes closed in on the clearing.

"Not by your hand," Myk uttered to the fallen knight.

Silently, The Lady waved her hand in front of her and magically blasted Bors to the ground. The sleeves of her silver gown blew wildly as she advanced toward her opponent. Bors quickly regained composure and narrowed his stained eyes. Marshaling every energy he could, he still stood no chance against the Companion of a Galdere. In addition to her own fearsome powers, Myk's magic surged through her very being, instantly lessening Bors's odds by immense proportions.

Not too terribly far from the established battlefield, the eight Queens and Zuberi still stood against Ava and the Assassin. Just as Ava temporarily conceded to Zuberi's proclamation of protection over the Companion, the Queens felt The Lady's attack on Bors in the distance.

The transcendent bond of the Queens of Avalon provided the type of spiritual and magical link that could call to one another from worlds away. It was part of their role as the Nine Queens.

Morgan's eye shot to her sisters, and her voice became alarmingly resolute. "We're being moved," she told them. She stepped forward and took Zuberi's arm, while Nimue and Allora took hold of Don Quixote and Stella.

In an instant, Ava and Bastien's opponents disappeared, called to the new battlefield. The witch turned to the Assassin and frowned smugly. "I do believe the fun is moving along without us. We can't have that, can we?"

Falling in line behind their fearless leader, the Queens of Avalon joined the ranks. Zuberi appeared next to Ben and gave him an acknowledging nod as he did so. Ben merely returned the nod and noted the arrival of these new allies. His eyes, however, searched for Stella. Her little blonde head appeared alongside Morgan but bobbed in his direction as she darted toward him with a big grin on her face.

"I'm beginning to really like this magic travel," she whispered to him, not wanting to break the tension between their side and Bors's gradually appearing reinforcements.

Spyros moved to the forefront, stepping over Bors's stunned body, and aimed his verbal advance at Morgan. "When was the last time you chose a side, my lady?" he derided.

"Probably the last time you had this much of a spine, sewer rat," she quipped in return. "My, it has been a while. I'm sure you're a bit rusty." Her back was to The Lady, but she could feel her sister grin. "But, I assume that's what these oafs are for, to keep that spine intact." She waved a careless hand toward his backup, before blasting them to the ground.

Stella smirked. "Okay, I take back everything I've said about her."

The reinforcements had fallen, but Spyros was not as easily conquered. He rebutted her magical blast with an equally substantial defense. The dark mist around him seemed to feed into his energy; Morgan Le Fay held her arms securely in front of her, and the other Queens followed suit. Together they formed a barrier. Spyros was a dolt, but he knew better than to take on the Queens of Avalon when their High Queen and her Galderean Keeper stood against him. Instead of casting another attack, Spyros straightened his back and inhaled deeply, steadying his men behind him.

Stella moved in line with the Queens, directly between The Lady and Morgan. Ben followed, keeping his sword at the ready. Gawaine, not wanting any exclusion from the potential action, slid smoothly between Allora and Nimue to maintain a more unobstructed view. They all felt something coming. It was not Myk, but The Lady who then called them to arms.

"Keepers," The Lady solemnly ordered. Without delay, Arthur and Zuberi also joined in the alignment of defense. "Say The Words."

"Say what, my lady?" Arthur questioned.

The Lady shot a sideways glance at Myk before smiling. "Your Keeper leather must know whom it serves before it must be used."

"What words might those be, then?" Gawaine muttered to Allora, who merely shrugged.

"You'll know," Nimue assured him.

Ben was suddenly brought to a remembrance of his altercation with Bastien, the foreign ancient tongue he spoke when he wielded Caliburn, as well as those he spoke at The Lake.

Ben's authority had been established. And now his Regents' time had come. Even a Regent Keeper has authority to be claimed, and once it is, The Words linger and need not be uttered again unless the Keeper deems them necessary.

Ben gave Arthur and Gawaine a silent nod of reassurance regarding Nimue's claim. Just as their Arch Keeper, neither man knew exactly what words they uttered that day. Words of such a divine nature cannot be recorded.. What I can record, with certainty, is how The Words—coupled with the presence of the Aerest—struck such fear into the villain's stained eyes that he had no choice but to hurry along his call to the one source of his power.

And that was when the real darkness came.

# 35

## BROTHER TO BROTHER

It's fascinating to me how a fall can alter one's appearance. In common physical scenarios, it can break a nose or bruise an eye. In the case of Myk's estranged brother, the bruising seen around the eyes of his disciples had consumed his entire visage as if a shadow was cast across his face. The familial resemblance—the high cheekbones, the deep eyes, the tall stature—was clouded by the darkness that now encompassed the clearing.

The dark shadow Ben had heretofore seen was merely a precursor to the hellishly tangible, yet not quite full form of Korbl himself. He appeared suddenly on the edge of the battlefield, stealing all attention and awe. He swaggered to the center, soaking in the fearful gazes, his own eyes searching for one reaction in particular.

However, there cannot be shadow without the light that banished it.

When Spyros' master answered his call, Myk answered a call of his own. With the aid of Merlin, Nimue, and Pelleas, and the remaining knights still alive and loyal to the king—Launcelot, Lucan, Bedivere, Gawaine, Gareth, and Gaheris—all allied troops closed in on the clearing.

"I didn't count on a family reunion, brother," Korbl smoothly rumbled. "I was under the impression you wouldn't be quite so...personally involved these days."

"You started it," Myk challenged.

The two stood facing one another in an invisible ring; no one else dared to enter. No one but The Lady herself. She glided to Myk's side, firing such a destructive gaze at the fallen Galdere, that even he briefly trembled.

Very few in history are quite sure what previously transpired between The Great Enemy and The Lady of the Stars; their confrontations have since been recorded on scrolls kept hidden in the Arkis. But those who remember this day may perfectly recall that no one terrified The Devil as much as The Lady. The fiend could hardly look the sorceress in the eyes, so he instead focused his energy on his brother. Her glowing eyes reminded him of his currently crippled state—he mourned for his whole, imprisoned, immortal form. Reduced to traveling freely as only half of an all-powerful being can undoubtedly eviscerate ambition. Not quite flesh, and not quite spirit. However, while his perennial body remained in exile, the extent of his power and influence was abounding and lethal in nature.

As if in response to Korbl's silent need for support, The Lady's dark counterpart crept from the shadows to take her place by the side of her master. Ava slithered into the scene, her dark golden armor glistening beneath the tips of her wild, rusty hair. With Ava by his side, Korbl arrogantly straightened his back and took on The Lady's glare with new confidence.

Myk glanced at his Lady's pained expression and then looked to Ava with the disappointment of a scolding parent—an expression I myself have used, and I am sure you can accurately imagine—before addressing his brother.

"Look how many are against you, Korbl," Myk gestured. "Look at how strong they are."

Korbl chuckled deeply, masking whatever fear The Lady still inspired. "Oh dear. Amazingly, I'm not too concerned. The odds are still in my favor," he took an inclusive step closer to Ava.

"I think not. They've overcome every attack you've thrown at them. None of it worked, Korbl. You're not going to win this, yet you continue to try. Your perseverance is notable, but they are still standing."

Korbl took another step, this time toward Myk. "Are they now? Because I only see the two of you standing against me, at the moment."

The Arch Keeper fearlessly stepped within the now tightened invisible fighting ring, leveling himself alongside Myk. Well, I suppose fearlessly may be a rather strong adverb. Ben was indeed afraid, but his tenacity was overshadowing.

"There he is," Ava slowly clapped at Ben's entrance.

"Good to see you again, Caverly," Korbl noted. "Did you bring that pretty little thing with you?"

*Don't step forward*, Ben silently pleaded.

But, Stella is hardly obedient to vocal commands, much less those unspoken. She stepped into the light that Myk and The Lady brought to their part of the clearing, standing at her husband's side.

"Yes, that's her," Korbl's lips curled into a wicked grin. "Pleasure to meet you, Creator."

As he declared such a title, his mistress narrowed her eyes and cocked her head to one side, scrutinizing the Aerest Companion with a fresh intensity.

When Ben felt Stella beside him, hearing her clear her throat in confusion equal to Ava's. He drew Caliburn from its sheath and held it defensively. The Soter Stone in his goatskin pouch and the journal inside his vest were on the forefront of his mind. More dark soldiers crept from the trees, catching the attention of the knights.

At the flick of Korbl's finger, and in an alarmingly dark flash, the battle commenced. Familiar faces attacked former allies with a fierceness that dominated any brotherhood they may have had. Blades screeched against blades, expressing the fury of those who wielded them. The king and his knights fought like dragons, defending one another at any cost, and slayed as many fiends as they could. A river of blood soon ran through the battleground.

The course of these events are most grievous, but such is life, I'm afraid. I've never been one to dwell on the movements of violence; I myself lean toward pacifism. Nevertheless, there are select details I must convey, despite my urge to look away from the gory scene before me.

As our heroes fought, many fell. In coming to the defense of his king, Sir Gawaine was momentarily taken down by Kay the Traitor—but without tragedy, as he still bore Excalibur's scabbard at his hip, which protected him from all wounds. When Kay recovered from his surprise, he shouted to the treacherous Bors, who once more lunged for the king. When Myk had warned Sir Bors that King Arthur would not be slain by his hand, his words rang true no matter the dark knight's efforts.

The moment Bors answered Kay's call and raised another arm toward our hero, Myk waved his hand, pulling Bors once more to the ground.

Ava, standing nearby, rolled her eyes and muttered under her breath, "Amateurs."

Ben, in the midst of a scuffle with Bastien, took notice of the vixen setting her sights on the good king and moved to intervene. But just as he bolted in her direction, Myk put an arm out to stop him. Ben didn't even realize Myk had been standing so close, but nevertheless, the Galdere shouldered him away from Ava's path. Ben froze and helplessly watched Ava deliver a deadly blow with the flick of her wrist, striking King Arthur to the ground.

On the other side of the clearing, Stella fought just as valiantly as the knights. She swung her sword, blocking and striking, with only slightly more grace than the Spaniard struggling beside her. After slaying her first few opponents, Stella noticed an odd feeling flow through her, enhancing her blows and giving her peculiar empowerment. She suddenly recognized it as the sort of Keeper magic she felt when wearing the jacket. Ben's Keeper magic was now hers as well, in a sense. Much like The Lady, Stella confidently wielded that magic with natural skill and gusto.

Once she considered her assault on Arthur satisfactorily finished, Ava thought it best to seek vengeance for her wounded ego and went directly after the Keeper's Companion. Korbl fueled Ava's strength and controlled the rest of his men from where he stood as a supercilious puppet master.

Spyros, his most loyal puppet, thought himself capable of taking on the Arch Keeper. Ben's great Caliburn vanquished Spyros's every attempt; he disarmed him and forcefully swung the blade, cutting off the rat's left leg.

Seeing his weak general nearly defeated, Korbl finally stepped in—not out of any regard for Spyros, but because such malleable help was always so difficult to find. Korbl materialized a weapon of his own making in his hand. The sword was black, long, and crooked but sharp and lethal. If not for the Stone in his pouch, Ben would have been cut down. But the Stone fed him power, which resonated through Caliburn. In one mighty stroke, Korbl was pushed backward, wide-eyed and furious.

Korbl's resolve didn't falter, however. He knew exactly where to strike. Gripping his sword in one hand, Korbl moved Ava safely out of the way and shot the sword straight for the princess's heart. Heroically, the Spaniard jumped in front of Stella, keeping his vow to protect her at all costs, and then fell to the ground with a loud thud. Stella cried out in surprise and sorrow.

Frustrated by his unintended victim, Korbl decided to try again with more accuracy. Stella felt Korbl's magic lift her into the air, blasting Ben out of his way. Advancing, he pointed his hand at her stomach.

Korbl once more chuckled deeply. "Oh...you probably don't even know, do you?"

His fingers curled into his palm as if crushing a rock. Stella screamed in agony. Something inside her was dying, slowly and painfully. The pain spread from her abdomen and immediately reached her heart. Everyone was frozen. There was no more fighting, no more clashing of swords.

Korbl had everyone's attention, just like he wanted.

He had control of the battle, just like he wanted.

And even Myk had to stand helpless and allow it to happen. A tear rolled down Myk's cheek. He understood but could do nothing.

When Korbl was finished, her screams having no effect on him, he merely let her crumble to the ground.

Cruelly, he turned to Ben. "If she didn't know, I'm sure you didn't."

Ben's rage was uncontrollable. He charged at Korbl with everything he had, but Korbl blocked his attack, keeping the Keeper's face only inches from his own.

"It's remarkable, isn't it, just how much the destruction of an unknown creation can tear someone apart," Korbl seethed.

Now Ben understood.

Stella's unborn child. His unborn child. Their unborn child.

"If it's any consolation," Korbl's lips curled into a smile as he shrugged, "it won't possibly happen again."

Ben's eyes stung with tears, and his heart raged. Shouting with fury, Ben stepped back and raised Caliburn fiercely once again. In an almighty swing and an even more almighty cry, he pierced Korbl so profoundly in the side that smoke seeped out like blood.

Seconds later, the devil had vaporized into oblivion, taking his satisfied mistress with him. Leaderless and shocked, the dark soldiers disappeared into smoke as well, leaving the surviving heroes alone in the clearing.

Ben ran to Stella, hushing her cries and kissing her tears. She clutched his vest in her fists and wouldn't let go. Her pain was no longer merely physical. She sobbed in his chest, trying to soak in his warmth and solace.

Behind them, the king staggered until he fell. His remaining strength was only sufficient enough to carry him closer to Myk and the Keeper. Myk came to his aid, congratulating him on his victory and calling for Ben. The Keeper carried the weight of his broken Companion at his side as they both staggered to the king's side.

"I'm sorry," Ben released a weak sob. He stood beside Myk, who knelt and supported Arthur's head.

"We knew what would come, Keeper. We knew....and you were...braver than us all," Arthur gasped. "Launcelot...Launcelot....."

Sir Launcelot bounded to the king's side, letting his sword fall and dropping to his knees. "Sire...."

"You have become so...." Arthur's voice waned, and he knew he didn't have enough time to express his brotherhood with this good knight fully, so he skipped to the point. "When the Keeper can no longer dwell in this realm....you must take my place as king...."

Launcelot swallowed hard. The man who made him a knight was fading before his eyes. "I can't...."

"Yes, you can. I know none more worthy to be....the Rightwise King."

It was the most endearing words King Arthur could leave with Sir Launcelot, no matter how inaccurate. Humans always acknowledge the importance of such titles, but rarely use them in the proper context.

Arthur steadfastly clasped Launcelot's hand and strained a smile. Three shallow breaths passed, and the king was dead. Ben knelt by his body, still supporting a crumbling Stella in his arms, their faces wet with tears. Myk closed the king's eyelids and mumbled something incoherent before looking up again.

"He accepted his fate, for he knew its importance," he assured them. Morgan and The Lady came up behind him, and the king's sister's face fell seeing his lifeless body in Myk's arms.

"Don!" Stella cried abruptly. Frantically, she stumbled in pain across the blood-soaked ground, searching the bodies of the deceased until she found the Spaniard lying amongst them, barely breathing. She cradled his head in her hands and spoke softly. "Don...Quixote."

"My lady," he croaked.

"Thank you...for what you've done."

"I swore an oath to protect...and a knights-errant..."

"I know, I know," she hushed, fighting the tears. "You've earned your nobility. You became a real knight. You saved a princess and a king...and now you're dying a hero's death. You are the greatest knight who ever lived."

Don Quixote died with a smile on his face. His glorious destiny, however foolish in his own realm, was accomplished here. And for that, he will always be remembered.

# 36

## ROUND TABLE UNBROKEN

In the original tale, the body of the noble King Arthur was taken to the mystical Avalon by four ladies, including the conflicted Morgan Le Fay. Well, with Myk's involvement, Arthur's parting happened a little differently. The good king passed on his throne to Launcelot, his most honorable surviving knight and dear friend. The living victors were unsure of how to proceed, so they turned to Lord Caverly, who turned to Myk. With Myk's encouragement, Ben took Excalibur from Arthur's belt and threw it into The Lady's mystical lake.

Then, following The Lady's lead, Morgan and the rest of the Queens of Avalon carried the king's body to the raft which awaited them on the lake. All who fought beside him stood on the bank of the lake, paying homage to such a great man. Stella took Ben's hand in hers. She leaned against his arm, still clutching her stomach, weak from her wounds.

"Should we say something?" she whispered.

He almost smiled. "Do you want to say something?"

She thought about it, looking at Arthur's close surviving friends, but then reconsidered. "No, never mind."

"The Round Table has not been broken," Myk spoke instead. He put a comforting hand on Launcelot's arm, seeing the pressures of the knight's recent bequeathment weighing on him already. "In fact, the king's blood only strengthens the makeup of those who keep the Table intact. You need only prepare the realm for the return of the Rightwise King."

Launcelot turned his head to look him in the eye with earnest. "So Arthur will indeed return?"

Myk smiled. "King Arthur's time will come around, as well as that of the Rightwise King."

Launcelot frowned at the vague answer, but Merlin chimed in before he could voice his question.

"And I may stay and help prepare as well?" Merlin popped up from behind Myk.

Myk's smile grew. "No, Merlin, I'm afraid you're once again required elsewhere. Somewhere where you will be both useful and well-supervised."

Stella chuckled and watched as the Queens situated Arthur respectfully on the raft before turning back to bid farewells. The Lady kissed Myk goodbye, both understanding their separate duties, and Morgan approached Ben with a deep gravity in her expression.

"I hope we meet in another life, Keeper," she said. "This is not the first time I have yielded to an Arch's authority for the sake of my realm....and now I should be dearly honored to fight by a Keeper's side again."

He nodded gratefully. "And I, yours."

There was a respectful silence while the ladies boarded the boat.

I feel it necessary now to give an excerpt from the original text of Le Morte d'Arthur:

*"Yet some men say in many parts of England that King Arthur is not dead, but had by the will of our Lord Jesu into another place; and men say that he shall come again, and he shall win the holy cross. I will not say it shall be so, but rather I will say: here in this world he changed his life. But many men say that there is written upon his tomb this verse: Hic jacet Arthurus, rex quondam, rexque futurus."*

Of course, the translation to this verse is: *Here lies Arthur, king once, and king to be.* Now, I don't know about the whole "winning the holy cross" bit, but what I do know is that King Arthur, the Once and Future King, will return. And you can be sure that when he does, he shall take up his alliance with the Keeper and see the end of this war. He has to. His destiny was not fulfilled in its entirety.

# 37

## THE BEGINNING OF THE END

The damage done to the poor princess drained all energy from her body, causing her to collapse in Ben's arms, shortly after the funeral of the great king. Even magic leaves a mark. Stella's internal organs suffered severe, unnecessary bleeding. The princess was transported back to London, along with the remainder of King Arthur's army of victors. All of the fallen were given the most honorable of funerals, celebrated for their bravery against the darkest of evils. The realm was finally at peace.

The Keeper's wife rested comfortably in her chambers, healing from her wounds. Ben refused to leave her side, stroking her forehead comfortingly while she attempted to patch up her emotional trauma.

"I'm sorry," she mumbled.

"For what?"

She looked up at him regretfully. "We can't have..."

"Shh, that's not your fault," he held her hand. "It doesn't matter."

"Yes, it does."

"That's exactly what Korbl was counting on," Myk said from behind Ben.

Stella sighed, resting her head against Ben in exasperation. "Are you always going to do that?"

"Do what?" he chuckled.

"Just show up like that."

He laughed. "One day it won't surprise you so much. Then you won't want to get rid of me." He rested a hand on Ben's shoulder and gazed down at them both.

"The depths of Korbl's damage and his dark reasoning are beyond your comprehension right now, Stella. What I can tell you is this....Korbl has only so many ways of destroying those who stand against him, and each of those ways is meant to punish me as much as it is you. He attacked your means of creation because....he feared what you might create. He feared *who* you might create. His fight is much fiercer when he thinks he's faced with a Creator. He wants you to fall, Stella, one way or another. He wants to tear your hope apart. Are you going to let him do that to you?" His voice was warm and encouraging, causing a small smile to tug at Stella's lips.

"What do you think?" she asked Ben.

Her husband smiled lovingly. "I have you; what more hope do I need?"

Growing with new confidence, Stella sat up in bed and laced her fingers in Ben's. "That's good enough for me."

The pain wasn't gone, and it wouldn't be for quite some time, but she now had something to which she could cling. And, before leaving, Myk assured them that they would have many opportunities to foster the sort of innocence and hope that was robbed from them.

When it was their turn to leave, and clinging tightly to this new hope, Ben put on his leather jacket and held his wife close. And the tingling started again. They were back in the Arkis. Clancy and Alice were there to congratulate them with open arms.

Seeing the adorable, young Alice brought a brief sadness to Stella. She imagined, if she had ever been able to have children, her daughter would look like her. But when the child embraced her, she knew that in her arms was one of those fostering opportunities Myk had promised, and she looked forward to returning to Alice many times in the future. Clancy insisted on Ben and Stella staying in the Arkis for a time to celebrate their victory.

"Every triumph should be celebrated with good food," he claimed.

And they were wise not to argue. They enjoyed the grandest feast they had ever beheld, and afterward, Clancy gave Ben a tour of all wings of the Arkis permitted for mortals, while Stella spent some time listening to Alice's long list of favorite worlds to explore. Alice had very seldom left the Arkis, you see. But, she lived her astonishingly long life through every page she turned.

Yonas joined their well-rewarded leisure. He conferenced with Ben to ensure the Keeper understood that his work was far from over. "There is still much to do," he told him.

"Yes, I thought so," Ben gathered.

"But don't worry," Yonas chuckled. "You and Stella make quite the team. With a Companion like her, I'm sure the work shouldn't be too terribly tedious."

Ben returned the chuckle. "Certainly not, sir."

They shook hands before returning to Stella and Alice. Eventually, the time came for them to return home. They said their goodbyes, promising to return as soon as they were next needed, and were sent back to Oxford.

Delight finally returned to Anne Caverly's countenance the moment Ben and Stella walked through the door that next morning. They had been out all night. Her scheme worked, just as she had hoped. Ben was holding Stella's hand, kissing her forehead, and displaying an intimacy that would have taken months and months to obtain, if not for Anne's ingenuity and infamous cunning.

"How was your walk?" she pried. She had been waiting for them, lying across the couch and dreaming of the possibilities.

Stella smiled widely. "Eventful."

"Eventful? Where did you take her, Benjamin?"

Ben cleared his throat. "We took a rather extensive tour of London."

"London? You went all the way to London?" Anne sat up in surprise. "Good heavens, no wonder it took you so long. Did you at least take a cab?"

"Of course, mother," Ben answered good-naturedly, hanging up their coats.

"And you had that much to talk about, eh?"

Her son chuckled mysteriously. "Yes, we did."

"And we made a couple of friends," Stella contributed. She was a bit eager to tell Anne everything, but she knew better than to divulge too much. It was bad enough when one of them was believed to be mad—if Ben Caverly also came down with such madness, there would be talk.

"That's just lovely. Are you going to thank me, Ben?" his mother pressed. "For putting you on such an adventure."

Stella laughed. Anne had no idea just what sort of adventure she put them on. "Thank you, Anne," she answered for him, kissing her mother-in-law's cheek.

Anne smiled congenially. "Well, you seem awfully chipper for five o'clock in the morning."

Just then, Patricia walked through the door, returning home from her short holiday. Stella ran to give her an unsolicited hug. Patricia's eyes widened in alarm, and she immediately looked to Ben for some sort of explanation.

"Thank you for never actually attempting to kill me, Patricia," Stella said in her ear.

"What is she talking about?" Patricia panicked.

"I think she's found a new appreciation for you," Ben reasoned, stifling a chuckle.

Patricia backed away from her, setting her purse down on the armchair. "Oh, so you've talked sense into her, then?"

"Patricia, could you put Stella's things in my room," Ben told her, beaming into his wife's sky eyes.

"I beg your pardon?"

"I believe Mrs. Caverly will be staying here indefinitely, Patricia," Anne answered, as she beheld this new development in her son's marriage, with a very pleased expression. With a knowing twinkle in her eye, she added, "One day, you two will have to tell me more about this adventure of yours."

"Yes," Stella shrugged. "Maybe one day."

# 38

## THE DEVIL'S DEN

The two men waited impatiently. Deep in the realm too dark to mention, they stood in front of a large door. It was a strange door. On one side, it held minimal appeal, as it was very dull and wooden, with a small lock but no doorknob. On the other side, it kept the most sinister and calamitous of immortal forces in careful restriction.

Korbl's prison could not be breached from the inside, and it could not be entered from the outside, save it be by a very particular mortal who bore the key to the inaccessible entrance. The bearer of the cursed key sauntered her way in between the expectant men. Spyros rolled his eyes in annoyance.

"What took you so long?" he whined.

Ava held her hands up to display her appearance more elegantly. "I had to dress for the occasion."

She wore a fitting black gown embossed with intricate gold patterns across her chest and torso that snaked down her legs. Her heels clicked with deadly precision as she walked; she knew how her master liked her, and she worked to gain advantage over others, somewhat effortlessly.

Bastien cleared his throat, trying not to stare. "Shall we, then?" he waved to the door.

Ava smirked and pulled the chain around her neck from out of the top of her dress to reveal the aged key, scuffed and tarnished but without a trace of rust. Smoothly, she unlocked the door and winked at the other two. As soon as she stepped back, the large door opened, beckoning them inside.

This was no ordinary prison. Furnished with luxuries and various comforts, the most inconvenient aspect of Korbl's imprisonment was his stifled magic. He sat lounging lazily on an armchair, his booted feet propped up on a short table. His dark clothes were well-pressed and sleek, while his expression was deep yet relaxed.

This was a different Korbl than previously seen in battle. Here, he had no threats, provided he remained within the enchanted walls. It was a safe place, albeit restricting, where he could regularly convene with his mistress and occasionally his generals. It served as both private quarters as well as a conference room. Chairs were arranged around his comfortable throne but could be dismissed just as quickly as the unwanted generals, should it tickle his fancy.

Korbl's pensive demeanor intimidated most, but Ava crossed the room with lazy determination. Looking up from his distracted stare, he grinned as she approached. Ava ran her fingers through his black hair before perching herself on his lap.

"Master," Spyros spoke warily. "What are we to do now?"

"The loss of one realm is hardly worth weeping over," his master groaned, lazily snaking his arm around Ava's petite waist. "Everything is already in motion. Myk's little champion may have conquered his first world, but there are many more he'll need to defend. The job wears down a mortal man so easily it's almost unfair."

Ava giggled.

"But this Keeper...this Aerest Keeper," Spyros protested. "He and his Companion are more of a threat than we've ever seen before, Master."

"Yes, so you keep telling me," Korbl growled. "We've been waiting for the Aerest. Their power should hardly intimidate you. You yourself have magic as well, if you recall."

"The Keeper has brains," the mistress contributed leisurely.

Korbl kissed her neck and considered this, but only for a moment. "So do I. And while the majority of you lovely people are somewhat lacking, there are a treasured few who found no trouble outwitting Keepers in the past." He winked at Ava, who winked at Bastien, who merely rolled his eyes.

"But the Creator, master. If she is the Aerest Companion....?" Bastien posed.

"Ben and Stella Caverly may be of some concern, but they should not be your concern," Korbl aimed to Spyros. "All that should concern you is your next assignment."

"And what is it that concerns you?" the vixen challenged. She was the only one with the audacity to make such an address. "The rat isn't wrong. If Stella is the Creator, she could be even more of an obstacle...."

Korbl looked at her scarred eyes, admiring his work, and replied softly to Ava alone. "Let us just say that the Aerest is not my primary fear. They are not Myk's last champions, are they? We only need to bide some time. Killing this Keeper right away would move things along too quickly. As for the Creator....I believe I've fairly abated the threat. For now, at least. I'll play around with them for a while. Until I'm ready for the next threat."

"So it's only just begun, then, Master," Spyros contributed.

"Oh no, you lout," Korbl crooned. "It's already near the end. And Yonas the Fool thinks he's ready for it."

But Yonas was much wiser than Korbl anticipated. He sensed the unrest of the Scada and anticipated his wayward son's every movement. Not one of Korbl's efforts could throw off the intended course of events. While individuals in this saga may harness control of their own destinies, the outcome of this war was resolutely written in prophecy. It's just the journey that changes.

The Aerest Keeper and his fearless Companion were an unbreakable, a force with which to be reckoned. And there are always good people. No book is so bad that there is not something good in it. No realm is an easy conquest. Korbl would cleverly make his moves, but with every dose of evil, there is a Keeper and his people to stand against it.

Both sides felt what was to come, but not all knew how it would end. Plato wrote, "*Only the dead have seen the end of war.*" For once, I don't know if I'm inclined to believe him. In this war, at least, even the dead remain restless.

Not all stories have to end, and this one is just beginning.

# Epilogue

## 24 Years Later

The weather can be awfully revealing. In fact, Shakespeare himself used it to express a particular tone or atmosphere for various scenes he constructed. I am sure the great Bram Stoker utilized such methods in his own work. However, I highly doubt he anticipated a fierce rainstorm in his realm setting the stage for arguably the most significant assignment in the Aerest's entire reign.

They waited along the side of the great hill which hosted one of the most legendary castles in literature. The rain pounded, but the heroes stood firm. Ben was not alone, of course. Beside him was the invincible force of his lovely Stella, aged only mildly from their two decades of travel together. Loyally following his lead were a Regent pair they happened to recruit while passing through the pages of *The Hunchback of Notre Dame*.

Gunari and Eden Lasko were of strong gypsy blood, a sturdy and tough breed. Middle-age had little effect on their stamina. Gunari happened to be a skilled swordsman, and his wife Eden was unparalleled with a slingshot.

"I have a feeling we were expected," Stella muttered. Ben had them keep cover behind the trees, awaiting further instruction. Stella's shoes were soaked, and the bottom of her trousers had collected enough dampness to weigh her down.

"Should we wait 'em out?" Lasko suggested. He was a stout man of practical and abrupt manners, but Ben had quickly grown an affinity for him.

"No!" Stella and Eden replied in hushed unison. Their maternal instincts drove their passion for this particular assignment.

"We can't afford to wait," Stella argued.

"No, we can't," Ben agreed.

He sized up the castle and those who kept it fortified. Four Scada soldiers stood guard at the castle's door. That was all of the enemy's reinforcements, but that was all that was needed. Dracula was more than capable of protecting his keep. Two of his vampire mistresses stalked the ramparts along the top of the castle. The third must have been inside guarding the target, where Dracula presumably stationed himself as well.

"Then what is our plan, Caverly?" asked Lasko.

"Let's give him a moment, Gun," his wife scolded him.

In any good pairing where one is abrupt and impatient, the other must be the epitome of grace. While Eden was more admonishing than graceful, she saw where patience was needed when her husband did not.

Stella chuckled. "He needs less than that." Of all the Regents they'd recruited over the years, the Laskos were her favorite.

Ben smiled at her confidence in him. While he weighed their options, the most basic of strategies kept presenting itself in his mind. Simple distraction. The enemy had the gate guarded, while the more powerful units watched from above. Anyone and anything could distract the average Scada soldier. It was the vampire mistresses who required special consideration. There was one thing that could inevitably entice a thirsty vampiress: fresh meat.

"Okay, now I have a plan," he declared.

"Told you," Stella nudged Eden.

Adapting obediently to Ben's carefully constructed scheme, the crew separated. Eden assumed her new role, approaching the castle gate from the front, appearing alone and unarmed. The four Scada scoffed at this attempt to breach their defense. Laughing to themselves, they each raised their weapons half-heartedly.

Instead of attacking, Eden quietly stood there, staring. The Scada were confused. They each took a step closer to her, physically threatening her efforts. But, the Regent Companion was unmoved. She tucked a loose strand of black hair behind her ear and sighed as if waiting for something.

While Eden bewildered their foes from the front, her Regent Keeper and the Aerest crept along the sides. The two of them scaled the opposing walls of the castle, careful to move with speed and agility. As expected, however, they managed also to catch the attention of the fanged mistresses, hungry for prey.

In perfect synchrony with the distractions at every angle, Stella moved swiftly through the back of the castle, scaling the wall and climbing her way to the room most likely containing their desired treasure. As soon as she settled herself into an empty corridor, catching her breath, she heard precisely what she had hoped.

A woman screamed.

And then there was a high-pitched shriek from outside.

Stella heard the smooth movement of Dracula hastening to his mistresses' aid against the attacking Keepers. The Keeper and his Regents had successfully focused the enemy's attention to one central point. With the threat of the vampire king temporarily alleviated, Stella slowly crept further down the hall toward the screams.

The screaming of a woman can mean a great many things. It could suggest absolute horror, raging fury, impending doom, or the heralding of a grand arrival. Behind the door at the end of the corridor, Stella listened for the explanation.

At the conclusion of the screaming, she heard tiny, precious cries.

Her heart leapt.

This was their assignment.

This was what she must have been promised.

In the rush of her excitement, Stella hurried to the door, took a deep breath, and flung the door open.

"Intruder!" a shriek came from down the hall.

Dracula's third mistress slid into the door frame to prevent Stella from entering. Upon seeing the bleeding mortal mother, the mistress—Narcisa, as she was named—froze. She exposed her fangs, ready to sink them into anything to satisfy her craving, her blood-lust overwhelming her.

The human midwife quivered in fear, holding the newborn infant in her arms. The vampires had been ordered to remain outside during the birth of the child, but nothing was to stop them from feeding on the midwife afterward, and the poor portly woman knew this.

Only mother and child were to be protected.

Lucky for her, Narcisa's thirst was distracted by Stella's interference.

The Arch Companion moved in front of Narcisa's view of the child and mother, looking directly in her bloodthirsty eyes. This did not deter the vampiress, however. Instead, she widened her eyes and zeroed in on the vein in Stella's neck, which slightly throbbed from the excursion of climbing the castle wall.

"I've never tasted an Arch before," she drooled.

Aiming her fangs, Narcisa went in for the kill, but Stella dodged, elbowing her in the face as she slid away. Angered, the vampiress hissed, reassessing her attack.

This time, she saw the infant as a more satisfying bite— ignoring all orders. Stella did not come unarmed, however. In her hand, she held an unnaturally sharp, long silver dagger, gripped and aimed to inflict damage. At the first sign of the vampiress flinching toward the infant, Stella smoothly waved a calculated blow with her blade, slicing through Narcisa's neck, decapitating the beast.

An intense struggle made its way to the corridor outside. The Keepers and Eden had killed the four Scada, and now only the surviving vampires stood between our heroes.

Stella spoke no words, taking a page from Ben's book of permitting actions to speak louder. She took the baby from the terrified midwife's arms and grimaced at the recovering mother. The nurturing part of her heart encouraged Stella to worry only about the poor child and leave the mother to fend for herself.

Before she could decide on the value of the mother's life, Ben breached the vampire line of defense and burst into the room. Dracula and his horrible visage soon followed, storming after his attackers. The Keeper suddenly became painfully aware of two other unfortunately familiar faces as they appeared—the one who claimed ownership of the child and his mistress.

Korbl's destructive presence threatened the success of the birth of the baby, but now that the task was complete, there was nothing to stop him from thwarting the Keeper's rescue mission.

As quickly as Ben had burst into the room, Stella rushed to him, clutching the baby in her arms. She reached for Ben's jacket, and the moment she laid a hand upon it, she and the child were transported safely to the Arkis, leaving Eden and the Keepers to stand against the devil.

"You won't keep it, Caverly," Korbl snarled. With one hand gesture, he stopped Dracula and the undead mistresses from taking another step toward the Keeper.

Gunari stood behind Ben with his finger on the trigger of his pistol, ready to fire at Ben's command. The loyal goof was still too inexperienced to understand his folly. If a gun had no effect on a vampire lord, it would surely have no effect on a Dark Galdere. But I suppose his heart was in the right place. Eden shifted her weight closer to him, away from the hungry eyes of the bloodthirsty vampire king.

"I think you'll find that we will, actually," Ben stated clearly. His gumption had undeniably grown in his years with Stella.

"You've taken what doesn't belong to you," Ava spoke with piercing venom.

"Perhaps next time you'll learn: you can't win by tainting what Myk has sworn to protect." Ben's venomous tone now matched hers. He took a step toward her, raising Caliburn threateningly. Before Ava could move, Korbl lifted her by the waist and vanished, carrying Ava safely away from the threat.

With the Dark One's absence, and facing the loss of one of his mistresses, Dracula spat hatred to the Keeper and followed suit, transporting himself and his surviving mistresses out of the realm and surrendering his castle to the Aerest. The Arkis summoned him and his Regents back to see the result of their assignment in the flesh.

Stella held the precious infant they rescued in her arms for the returning heroes to see. They stood around her, in the center of the common room with the mystical blue flame flickering behind them in the fireplace. Eden, being a devoted mother of three, swarmed the child with instinctual doting, while the two Keepers looked on with pleasant but exhausted smiles.

The child was safe.

When Myk entered the room to greet them, Stella beamed. "Myk, we—"

He held up a hand to cut her off. His expression was not nearly as enthusiastic as her own. Though faintly smiling, Myk's eyes were preparing Stella for words that would steal her beam. "Hand the child to Mrs. Lasko, Stella."

Stella's mouth tightened as she looked from Ben then back to Myk. "Myk....you promised me...."

"Sir, I don't know if—" Eden began, in Stella's defense.

"Please, Eden," Myk stopped her. Treading lightly, Myk stepped closer to Stella, softening her with his gaze until tears began to fall down her cheeks.

"But I thought..." she breathed.

"I know, Stella. I know," he whispered gently. "I need you to trust me. For your sake and the child's."

Ben, hesitant to intercede, moved in to wrap his arm comfortingly around his wife. "It's all right, my love."

Clinging momentarily to the infant, Stella's sky eyes stung. After all that had been taken from her, all she had been promised—and now she was being asked to give up even more. Feeling Ben's warmth against her and hearing his encouragement for obedience, despite the shakiness in his voice, gave her strength. Slowly she looked up from the infant's little green eyes to meet Myk's expectant gaze.

"You promised me....this is the one I wanted...." she uttered.

Myk smiled softly. "And this is the one you shall have—when the time is right. Do you trust me, Stella?"

Swallowing hard, Stella handed the child to Eden's uncertain arms and inhaled sharply. "Yes, I do. So you better not let me down." She forced the smallest teasing grin, causing Myk to chuckle.

"You know I won't," he told her.

He sighed and looked at Ben, silently confirming his promises. Ben understood well enough. He realized what the child meant and what was most likely to come.

The job was done, the victor was recognized, the losers retreated, and the assignment fulfilled. But that was not all. No, not even close. It's never really the end of anything, is it? On the contrary, it's always the beginning of something much greater. In all twenty-four years of this new era, not one development had been such a turning point as this. The Keeper had now crossed previously unthinkable territory—and the stakes had now become perilously higher than ever before.

For devils cannot be expected to remain in hell after it all breaks loose.

## END OF VOLUME I

# Volume I
# Appendix

Pronunciation Guide

The History of the Keepers

# Pronunciation Guide

ARKIS                    are-kiss

CAVERLY                  ca-ver-lee

YONAS                    yoh-nus

KORBL                    core-bull

MYK                      mick

SCADA                    scah-duh

ALDEN                    all-din

FAEGRIAN                 fay-gree-un

NIMUE                    nim-oo-ay

# The History of the Keepers

The War of the Galdere was waged in a realm separate from time. The chosen battlefields were gathered by Yonas from a variety of bookstores across time and space within Middangeard. Arkis scribes have compiled accurate accounts, to be sure, but for this cursory record, there have been details redacted according to the reader's necessity.

Please be advised that, while the following events are recorded chronologically, there is no specific bearing on numerical time frames, as time passes differently from realm to realm.

# First Era

ASA -

- The war begins and Galderean souls are sent to mingle in the newly made realms, their memories wiped while in their newly crafted mortal shells.
- Keepers are established, once sought out by Myk, by the use of conduit leather.
- Lydia, Asa's wife and Arch Companion, dies in childbirth.
- After only three assignments, Asa is killed by Cromer in battle.

KOL –

- Cromer rescues the beast Fenrir from imprisonment inflicted upon him by the Norse Gods and becomes his alpha.
- The first Creator, **Ingrid**, is born in her mortal shell. She embarks on territorial wars against a Keeper, until an alliance and strategic marriage are agreed upon, marking the first union between Creator and Keeper.
- Circe and Medusa become the first of The Lady's Queens, later named the Queens of Avalon.
- Kol is poisoned by one of the Fallen, Dreda. Ingrid, the Creator, sets off on a quest to find the next Arch Keeper.

CLAEC –

- Amazonian queen, Penthesilea, is saved on the battlefield by Korbl. She vows allegiance and becomes the first Nidling.

- The Nidlings are ordered to combat the ever-growing Queens of Avalon.
- Ingrid partners with Claec for the first portion of his Keepership.
- Sage, a Nidling, betrays Penthesilea and joins the Keeper, becoming an Arch Companion.

RHYS –

- Circe sustains wounds from battle. Medusa is charged with taking her to the nearest witch in the realm for healing.
- Baba Yaga joins The Lady's Queens.

SILAS –

- Ingrid, still grieving the loss of her Keeper, begins to self-destruct, endangering a realm. She baits Silas, the Arch Keeper, into killing her to spare the realm.

# SECOND ERA

EWAN –

- After sustaining a head wound during a hostile takeover of his village, Spyros is discovered by Korbl. Korbl mends his wound and questionably enforces the Scada oath.

## BASIL –

- The Arch Keeper, Basil, institutes The Keeper's Guild—the longest-standing organization of Keepers in the entirety of the war.

## CORMAC –

- The second Creator, **Cressida**, is born into her mortal form.
- Cressida and Cormac double the size of The Keeper's Guild.

# THIRD ERA

## NICHOLAUS –

- Medea, from Euripides' *Medea*, is recruited as a Nidling, and quickly gains rank.

## GREGORY –

- Lucan, of the Fallen, battles The Lady and her sister Alysia. He leaves the battle with doubts his ability, and even his allegiance. Offering relief from confusion, Korbl tricks Lucan into surrendering his soul.
- Lucan is stripped of his soul, losing both memory and magic, and is believed to have fled in confusion. The first piece of Fallen regalia is created.

- Alysia is relocated to a remote, currently untouched realm in a protective form.

## MILO –

- The third Creator, **Lyra**, is born into her mortal form. Her childhood best friend, Milo, becomes her Arch Keeper.

# FOURTH ERA

## ALEXANDER –

- Penthesilea is captured by The Keeper's Guild, after being betrayed by Medea. The Nidlings are without a leader and temporarily scattered.

## HENRY –

- Penthesilea is recovered and reunites the Nidlings, alongside a seemingly repentant Medea.
- Henry joins forces with an abandoned Companion whose Keeper was corrupted by Scada, taking her child with him.

## FULCO –

- Avalon, the first realm given life at the start of the war, is re-entered by Galdere and established to be the chosen battleground for the final battle.

- Fulco assists a king in testing the worthiness of his kingdom.
- Dreda, of the Fallen, enters *Le Morte D'Arthur* and proclaims herself a Lady of Avalon. She creates Scanlon, the cursed sword.
- Merlin is recruited by The Keeper's Guild and attempts to recruit his own apprentices.

FARRIS –

- The fourth Creator, **Mersi**, is born into her mortal form.
- A scrounger named Farris steals the conduit leather jacket off of the deceased body of Fulco, the Arch Keeper. While initially posing as the Keeper to avoid penalty of theft, Farris is ultimately chosen by the conduit leather and appointed by Myk as the final Arch Keeper of the fourth era.
- Scanlon is taken by Scada out of the realm.

# FIFTH ERA

MORYS –

- Lady Macbeth, of *Macbeth*, is recruited by Scada.
- With the help of the Queen Creator's Soter Stones, Myk and The Lady bear triplets: William, Stephen, and Helena.

- Helena Liffrea settles in Middangeard and marries John Dunaway, with whom she has several children. She is hunted by Scada after Korbl suspects her of being the fifth Creator.
- William trains as a Regent Keeper under Morys' guidance, along with The Keeper's Guild.
- Stephen is seduced by Hecate, a Nidling sorceress charged by Penthesilea with bearing a Galderean child. Stephen sires Timo Liffrea.
- Realizing he had been fooled, Stephen abandons Hecate and her infant son. He hides in shame in the realm of *The Frog Prince*. He meets and marries a storyfolk woman who had been cursed by a witch to not bear children. Despite the curse, Stephen and his new wife conceived and bore Riddock the dwarf.
- Hecate, brokenhearted, destroys a realm in her grief, leaving a parentless Timo to be raised by the remaining Nidlings.

GEOFFREY –

- Thorne becomes the second of the Four Fallen to be tricked by Korbl into surrendering his soul. He's stripped of his memory and magic, therefore creating the second piece of the Fallen regalia.
- The Keeper's Guild lose a battle in *Le Morte D'Arthur*, reducing their numbers dramatically. Geoffrey, an Arch Keeper without a Companion, keeps his remaining Regents as close as possible, limiting the reach of Regent assignments.

- A disillusioned William Liffrea finds his Companion, Maya, in *Arabian Nights*. He steps away from what was left of The Keeper's Guild to relocate his Companion. He changes his name to William Rolfe and starts his family in a neutral realm.
- Once completely abandoned by the now disbanded Keeper's Guild, Geoffrey meets the fifth Creator, **Kalia**, in *Arabian Nights*, finally gaining a Companion.
- Geoffrey and Kalia defeat Scada in nearly a dozen realms on their own.
- **Kalia** gives birth to twin sons before Geoffrey is assassinated by Nidlings. She continues fulfilling her duties with her sons, as she closes the era alone.
- Fighting alongside the Creator, The Lady faces Korbl directly. She is stripped of her soul, losing memory and magic. Her regalia, however, is quickly retrieved from Korbl's hands by Myk. Her now amnesiac form, however, is lost, wandering an unknown realm.

# SIXTH ERA:
## (OTHERWISE CALLED THE FAIRYTALE CRUSADE)

MYK –

- To recover and reunite with The Lady, Myk begins his mortal Keepership. While searching for her whereabouts, he comes upon his surviving children and grandchildren.

- Stephen is found by Myk, dying. He confesses the abandonment of his first child and begs his father to keep his posterity safe.
- Ava Dreher is targeted in her mortal realm of *Cinderella*. Korbl promises to restore her sight after her stepsister's birds pecked her eyes out. With further promises of power and fulfillment, Korbl successfully recruits her.
- Korbl realigns his focus with fresh paranoia that Myk's most dangerous operatives are being hidden in the form of children.
- The Lady is found traveling realms, believing herself to be a fairy. The trace amounts of Creator magic still in her physiology from childbirth have allowed her to blend in with the fairies of the realm of *Beauty and the Beast*.
- The Lady's soul is returned to her, in the form of a single crawling star earring.
- While regaining The Lady's trust, Myk rescues the infant stolen by Rumpelstiltskin. Clancy is taken to the Arkis to be raised as a scribe. Rumpelstiltskin is recruited by Scada.
- During her visit to *Le Morte D'Arthur*, The Lady is reunited with her Queens of Avalon and begins regaining memory.
- Myk speaks The Lady's true name and, using the Soter Stones, restores the fulness of her Galderean form.
- Zuberi is discovered in his young adulthood and included among The Lady's ranks.

- Dreda is coerced by Korbl and stripped of her soul, becoming the third of the Four Fallen to lose memory and magic. Korbl then collects the third piece of regalia. She's left wandering the realm.
- Allora the Fairy and the sorceresses Nimue and Morgan Le Fay all become a Queens of Avalon.
- Frank
- Myk takes on the Curse of the Beast to spare James Dunbar's prospective Companion, Elsie. Korbl then slaughters Myk in his mortal form.
- Myk returns in his full Galderean form and imprisons Korbl's own Galderean form in an immortal prison, in a realm with no name.

## JAMES DUNBAR —

- The Nidlings failed to thoroughly brainwash the part-Galderean child left in their care, and so abandoned Timo Liffrea shortly before he approached pubescence.
- Sparked by deep envy over Cromer's attentions to Ava, Penthesilea breaks her oath to Korbl and attempts to kill her romantic rival. Penthesilea is then horrifically killed at Korbl's hand.
- Medea is named the new Nidling leader, maintaining Penthesilea's original oath.
- Allora the Fairy returns to her home realm of *Pinocchio* and is faced with her first altercation with Ava.

- Timo and his longtime friend Bram sell invisible clothing to an emperor. The success of this exploit marks the birth of Timo's Company.
- Ava and Cromer enter the realm of *Goldilocks and The Three Bears*, with the intent of capturing the child and the bears for their respective goals. Goldilocks is believed to be burned to death in the bears' home, but is in fact recovered by Timo and his Company.
- Conall O'Leary is reared as a Regent under the tutelage of the widowed James Dunbar.
- Charles Dodgson is accidentally pulled into the world of *The Snow Queen*, where he meets a talking flower named Alice.
- Alice takes the form of a human child when she comes into contact with Vivienne Rolfe, the eldest child of William and Maya Rolfe. This identifies **Vivienne** as the sixth Creator.
- James Dunbar is killed by Ava, in a similar fashion as his late Companion, Elsie.
- Conall O'Leary becomes the Arch Keeper; the Creator becomes the Arch Companion.

CONALL O'LEARY –

- As they establish a family, Conall and **Vivienne** begin also gathering a new generation of Regents, affectionately but unofficially referred to as O'Leary's Boys.

- Ava makes a final attempt to capture and recruit children. She succeeds in capturing Hansel and Gretel, but unintentionally kills Gretel during the oath-giving process. It is learned that children cannot be administered the oath because, aside from Myk's protection over them, their bodies cannot handle the strain of the Dark magic used.
- Conall recruits Hansel as a Regent Keeper. Hansel develops chronic pain and traumatic nightmares as a result of the botched oath-giving.
- After failing with Hansel and Gretel, Ava appears to struggle with the loss and comes to the O'Leary's for penitence. She helps **Vivienne** and her youngest son, Declan, escape Scada so they can seek refuge in the Arkis.
- Ava targets a Regent named Bastien Autry and convinces him that Conall is preventing him from becoming an Arch Keeper. Bastien's corruption marks the beginning of the systematic Regent Purge.
- Neil O'Leary, the eldest son, makes a faulty decision while on assignment with his brother Lanzo and Hansel. He alters his father's orders, and as a result, Conall puts him on probation.
- Conall is told to deviate from focusing on Ava's new objectives and instead redirect to the growing threat of Cromer.
- Ava is relatively unseen by Conall and his Regents for the remaining years of his Keepership. Her assignment is unknown to even her closest colleagues.

- In Middangeard, Thomas Hastings fights in the Irish Revolution alongside a soldier named Ryder, who becomes officially labeled MIA toward the end of the revolution.
- Neil attempts to gain Rapunzel as a Companion, but fails when she seems to prefer James, the second son, who was generally uninterested.
- Thomas Hastings is recruited by Conall as a promising new Regent.
- Hastings notably and singlehandedly defeats a corrupt dragon while on assignment with Neil and James O'Leary.
- Despite Hastings' efforts to console his new comrade, Hansel takes his own life when his pain and nightmares from the failed oath become too unbearable.
- Lanzo O'Leary is turned into an owl as punishment for straying while on assignment. He and his ladylove, Marnie, join Timo's Company.
- Cromer infiltrates the realm of *Little Red Riding Hood* and intercepts product sold by Timo. In utilizing the unknowingly cursed wolfskins, O'Leary's Boys, as well as the Alden assisting them in the operation to protect the village, were driven into animalistic madness. While some recovered from this travesty, **Vivienne O'Leary** was found among the dead.
- A Regent was identified as the guilty party who killed the Creator. Thomas Hastings was immediately ostracized and separated from the surviving Regents.

- Neil rebels and exiles himself from his remaining family. He wanders into the London setting of *Peter Pan*. And has an affair with Mary Darling, resulting in the birth of his illegitimate son.

## ALBERT TOWSON –

- World War II begins in Middangeard. Gabriel Towson is reported MIA on the battlefield, motivating his elder brother, Albert, to enlist and search for him.
- The king and queen of Faegrian, in the realm of *Briar-Rose*, seek out an enchantment that will allow them to have a child. They come upon The Lady, who then helps them conceive a daughter named Rose. At the age of sixteen, Rose faces the threat of Korbl's direct attack. She is then placed into a comatose state by The Lady as a form of protection. While asleep, Rose is mentally attacked by Korbl's influence on her realm.
- Myk finds Albert as he chooses to go AWOL in the war in his own realm. Albert is recruited with the promise that he will gain answers regarding his lost brother's whereabouts.
- Albert enters the realm of *Briar-Rose* in order to prematurely awaken the princess before her 100-year sleep ends. Albert and Rose defeat Korbl's forces and marry, becoming the new king and queen of Faegrian.
- Stella Towson is born. At the age of two, Faegrian is once again under attack, resulting in the death of

Princess Rose and the relocation of the surviving Towson family.

- The Regent Purge, causing the death or corruption of active Regents, continues. Griffin Rolfe and James and Declan O'Leary were all who remain following the attack on Faegrian.
- Cromer is believed to be killed by Albert in vengeance for Rose's death. As he is left in his weakened state, Cromer's soul is stripped by Ava, providing Korbl with the final piece of regalia of the Four Fallen.
- Seraphina joins the Queens of Avalon.
- Albert decides to defy orders and travel through *The Wizard of Oz*. Within the realm, Albert makes enemies of some notable witches—one of whom he defensively entraps in a tower in the realm of *Le Morte D'Arthur*.
- Glinda the Witch of the North is recovered from her prison tower and recruited as the final Queen of Avalon.
- James O'Leary gains a Companion—Lenora, the fairy who saved Beauty. Not long after, Lenora is tragically captured and killed by Scada. James then becomes dangerously reckless without her.
- Griffin Rolfe is killed by Spyros.
- Albert befriends a fellow student at Oxford and attempts to recruit Walter and Anne Caverly as Regents. They accompany him on one assignment and then resign to neutrality in their home realm.
- *The Little Mermaid*, Marin, is promised a soul by Ava, in exchange for her allegiance. While attempting to

rescue her, James O'Leary is killed by Ava, while his younger brother, Declan, is captured—this marks the end of the Regent Purge.

- Albert spends the remaining decades of the era gaining redemption and embarking on assignments on his own, only occasionally accompanied by Myk himself.

# SEVENTH ERA

BENJAMIN CAVERLY –

- The mortal half of the realm of *Le Morte D'Arthur* is prepared by the Aerest Keeper and Companion.
- A new Round Table is established for the purpose of the final battle, and the migration that ensues after the Aerest leaves.

# About The Author

Renée Tamsin was raised in various parts of the Southern and Midwestern U.S. The one constant in her ever-changing environment was her stories. When not writing tales of adventure and intrigue, she's busy reading them. Things As They Were is Tamsin's debut novel, aiming to pull emerging adults back to the classics. She's currently working on continuing the saga of The Arkis Tales.

Like what you've read? Support Renée by leaving reviews and sharing her stories with friends and family.